CITY OF THE LOST

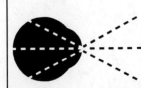

CITY OF THE LOST

KELLEY ARMSTRONG

WHEELER PUBLISHING
A part of Gale, Cengage Learning

GALE
CENGAGE Learning·

Farmington Hills, Mich • San Francisco • New York • Waterville, Maine
Meriden, Conn • Mason, Ohio • Chicago

Lg Print
Armstrong

GALE
CENGAGE Learning·

Wheeler Publishing Large Print Hardcover.
The text of this Large Print edition is unabridged.
Other aspects of the book may vary from the original edition.
Set in 16 pt. Plantin.

LIBRARY OF CONGRESS CATALOGING-IN-PUBLICATION DATA

Names: Armstrong, Kelley, author.
Title: City of the lost / by Kelley Armstrong.
Description: Large print edition. | Waterville, Maine : Wheeler Publishing, 2016. |
  Series: Wheeler Publishing large print hardcover
Identifiers: LCCN 2016015369 | ISBN 9781410491893 (hardcover) | ISBN 1410491897
  (hardcover)
Subjects: LCSH: Women detectives—Fiction. | Abused wives—Fiction. |
  Murder—Investigation—Fiction. | Large type books. | GSAFD: Mystery fiction. |
  Suspense fiction.
Classification: LCC PS3551.R4678 C58 2016b | DDC 813/.54—dc23
LC record available at https://lccn.loc.gov/2016015369

Published in 2016 by arrangement with St. Martin's Press, LLC

Printed in Mexico
1 2 3 4 5 6 7 20 19 18 17 16

For Jeff

ONE

"I killed a man," I say to my new therapist.

I've barely settled onto the couch . . . which isn't a couch at all, but a chaise lounge that looked inviting and proved horribly uncomfortable. Like therapy itself.

I've caught her off guard with that opening line, but I've been through this before with other therapists. Five, to be exact. Each time, the gap between "hello" and "I'm a murderer" decreases. By this point, she should be glad I'm still bothering with a greeting. Therapists do charge by the hour.

"You . . . ," she says, "killed a man?"

The apprehensive look. I know it well — that moment when they're certain they've misheard. Or that I mean it in a metaphorical way. *I broke a man's heart.* Which is technically true. A bullet does break a heart. Irrevocably, it seems.

When I only nod, she asks, "When did this happen?"

"Twelve years ago."

Expression number two. Relief. At least I haven't *just* killed a man. That would be so much more troublesome.

Then comes the third look, as she searches my face with dawning realization.

"You must have been young," she says. "A teenager?"

"Eighteen."

"Ah." She settles back in her chair, the relief stronger now, mingling with satisfaction that she's solved the puzzle. "An accident of some kind?"

She's blunt. Others have led me in circles around the conclusion they've drawn. *You didn't really murder a man. It was a car accident or other youthful mishap, and now you torture yourself with guilt.*

"No, I did it on purpose. That is, pulling the trigger was intentional. I didn't go there planning to kill him. Manslaughter, not homicide. A good lawyer could argue for imperfect self-defense and get the sentence down to about twelve years."

She pulls back. "You've researched this. The crime. The sentence."

"It's my job."

"Because you feel guilty."

"No, it's my *job.* I'm a cop."

Her mouth forms an O of surprise, and her fingernails tap my file folder as she makes mental excuses for not reading it more thoroughly. Then her mouth opens again. The barest flicker of a smile follows.

"You're a police officer," she says. "You shot someone in the line — No, you were too young. A cadet?"

"Yes, but it wasn't a training accident." I settle on the chaise. "How about I just tell you the story?"

An obvious solution, but therapists never suggest it. Some, like this one, actually hesitate when I offer. She fears I'm guilty and doesn't want me to be. Give her a few more clues, and she'll find a way to absolve me.

Except I don't want absolution. I just want to tell my story. Because this is what I do. I play Russian roulette with Fate, knowing someday a therapist will break confidentiality and turn me in. It's like when I was a child, weighed down by guilt over some wrongdoing but fearing the punishment too much to confess outright. I'd drop clues, reasoning that if I was meant to be caught, those hints would chamber the round. Magical, childish thinking, but it's what I do.

"Can I begin?" I ask.

She nods with some reluctance and settles in.

"I'd gone to a bar that night with my boyfriend," I say. "It was supposed to be a date, but he spent the evening doing business in the back corner. That's what he called it. Doing business. Which sounds like he was dealing coke in some dive bar. We were actually in the university pub, him selling vitamin R and bennies to kids who wanted to make it through exam week. . . ."

TWO

Blaine and I sat at a back table, side by side, waiting for customers. His fingers stroked the inside of my thigh. "Almost done. And then . . ." He grinned over at me. "Pizza? Your place?"

"Only if we get enough for Diana."

He made a face. "It's Friday night, Casey. Shouldn't your roommate have a date or something?"

"Mmm, no. Sorry."

Actually, she was out with college friends. I just wasn't telling Blaine that. We hadn't had sex yet. I'd held him off by saying I was a virgin. That was a lie. I was just picky.

Blaine was my walk on the wild side. I was a police recruit playing bad girl. Which was as lame as his attempt to play drug lord. On a scale of bad boys, Blaine ranked about a two. Oh, sure, he claimed he was connected — his grandfather being some Montreal mobster whose name I couldn't even find with an Internet search. More likely the old guy played bookie at his seniors' home. Blaine's father certainly wasn't mobbed up — he was a pharmacist, which was how Blaine stole his stuff. Blaine himself was pre-med. He didn't even sample his merchandise. That night, he nursed one beer for two hours. Me? I drank Coke. *Diet* Coke. Yep, we were hard-core.

A last customer sidled over, a kid barely old enough to be in university. Blaine sold him the last of his stash. Then he gulped his beer, put his arm around my shoulders, and led me from the pub. I could roll my eyes at his swagger, but I found it oddly charming. While I might not have been ready to jump into bed with Blaine, I did like him. He was a messed-up rich kid; I could relate to that.

"Any chance of getting Diana out of your apartment?" he asked.

"Even if there is, the answer is no."

He only shrugged, with a smile that was half "I'll change your mind soon" and half genuine acceptance. Another reason why I wasn't ready to write him off as a failed dating experiment — he never pushed too hard, accepted my refusals with good-natured equanimity.

We started walking. I wasn't familiar with the campus area. I was attending the provincial police college outside the city and spending weekends with Diana, a high school friend who went to the local community college. Neither of us was from here. So when Blaine insisted that a dark alley was a shortcut to the pizza place, I didn't question it . . . mostly because I was fine with what he had planned — a make-out pit stop designed to change my mind about getting Diana out of our apartment.

We were going at it hard and heavy when I heard the click of a gun. I gasped and pushed Blaine back. He looked up and jumped away, leaving me with a 9 mm pointed at my cheek.

"I only have fifty bucks," Blaine lied — the rest was stuffed in his sock. "She has some jewelry. Take that and the fifty —"

"Do we look like muggers, Saratori?"

As the gun lowered, I saw the guy holding it. Early twenties. Dark blond hair. Leather jacket. No obvious gang markings, but that's what this looked like: four young guys, one with a gun, three with knives.

I couldn't fight them — I didn't have a weapon, and martial arts doesn't work well against four armed attackers. Instead, I committed their faces to memory and noted distinguishing features for the police report.

"Does the old man know you're dealing?" the lead guy asked.

"I don't know what —" Blaine began.

"What I'm talking about? That you're Leo Saratori's grandkid? Or that you were dealing on our turf?"

Blaine bleated denials. One of the guys

pinned him against the wall, while another patted him down. They took a small plastic bag with a few leftover pills from one sock and a wad of cash from the other.

"Okay," Blaine said. "So we're done now?"

"You think we want your money?" The leader bore down on him. "You're dealing on our turf, college boy. Considering who you are, I'm going to take this as a declaration of war."

"N-No. My grandfather doesn't —"

A clatter from the far end of the alley. Just a cat, leaping from a garbage bin, but it was enough to startle the guy with the gun. I lunged, caught him by the wrist and twisted, hearing the gun thump to the ground as I said, "Grab it!" and —

Blaine wasn't there to grab it. He was tearing down the alley. One of the other thugs was already scooping up the gun, and I was wrenching their leader's arm into a hold, but I knew it wouldn't do any good. The guy with the gun jabbed the barrel against my forehead and roared, "Stop!"

I didn't even have time to do that before the other two slammed me into the wall. The leader took back his gun and advanced on me.

"Seems we know who's got the balls in your relationship," he said. "The pretty little China doll. Your boyfriend's gone, sweetie. Left you to take his punishment." He looked me up and down. "A little too college-girl for my tastes, but I'm flexible."

I thought he was joking. Or bluffing. I knew my statistics. I faced more danger of sexual assault from an acquaintance or a boyfriend.

"Look," I said. "Whatever beef you have with Blaine, it has nothing to do with me. I've got twenty dollars in my wallet, and my necklace is gold. You can take —"

"We'll take whatever we want, sweetie."

I tugged my bag off my shoulder. "Okay, here's my purse. There's a cell phone —"

He stepped closer. "We'll take *whatever* we want."

His voice had hardened, but I still didn't think, *I'm in danger.* I knew how muggings worked. *Just stay calm and hand over my belongings.*

I held out my purse. He grabbed it by the strap and tossed it aside. Then he grabbed *me,* one hand going to my throat, the other to my breast, shoving me against the wall. There was a split second of shock as I hit the bricks hard. Then . . .

I don't know what happened then. To this day, I cannot remember the thoughts that went through my brain. I don't think there were any. I felt his hands on my throat and on my breast, and I reacted.

My knee connected with his groin. I twisted toward the guy standing beside us. My fingers wrapped around his wrist. I grabbed his switchblade as it fell. I twisted again, my arm swinging down, and I stabbed the leader in the upper thigh as he was still falling back, moaning from the knee to his groin.

Afterward, I would piece it together and understand how it happened. How a response that seemed almost surreal was, in fact, very predictable. When the leader grabbed me with both hands, I knew he was no longer armed. So I reacted, if not with forethought, at least with foreknowledge.

Yet it was the lack of forethought that was my undoing. I had stabbed the leader . . . and there were three other guys right there. One hit me in the gut. Another plowed his fist into my jaw. A third wrenched my arm so hard I screamed as my shoulder dislocated. He got the knife away from me easily after that. Someone kicked me in the back of the knees, and I went down. As soon as I did, boots slammed me from all sides, punctuated by grunts and curses of rage. I heard the leader say, "You think you're a tough little bitch? I'll show you tough." And then the beating began in earnest.

I awoke in a hospital four days later as my mother and the doctor discussed the possibility of pulling the plug. I'd like to believe that somewhere in that dark world of my battered brain, I heard them and came back, like a prizefighter rising as the ref counts down.

But it was probably just coincidence.

I'd been found in that alley, left for dead, and rushed to the hospital, where I underwent emergency surgery to stop the internal bleeding. I had a dislocated shoulder. Five fractured ribs. Over a hundred stitches for various lacerations. A severe concussion and an intracranial hematoma. Compound fracture of the left radius. Severe fracture of the right tibia and fibula with permanent nerve damage. Also, possible rape.

I have recited that list to enough therapists that it has lost all emotional impact. Even the last part.

Possible rape. It sounds ludicrous. Either I was or I wasn't, right? Yet if it happened, I was unconscious. When I was found, my jeans were still on — or had been put *back* on. They did a rape kit, but it vanished before it could be processed.

Today, having spent two years as a detective in a big-city Special Victims Unit, I know you can make an educated guess without the kit. But I think when it disappeared, someone decided an answer wasn't necessary. If my attackers were found, they'd be charged with aggravated assault and attempted murder. Good enough. For them, at least.

As for my injuries, physically, I made a full recovery. It took eighteen months. I had to drop out of police college and give up the job waiting for me. As the victim of a serious

17

crime, I was deemed no longer fit to serve and protect. I didn't accept that. I got a bachelor's degree in criminology, a black belt in aikido, and a flyweight championship in boxing. I aced the psych tests and, five years after the attack, I was hired and on the fast track to detective.

My parents had not been pleased. That was nothing new. When I'd first declared I wanted to be a police detective, their reaction had been pure horror. "You're better than that," they said. Smarter, they meant. Not geniuses, like them. While they considered my IQ of 135 perfectly adequate, it might require extra effort to become a cardiologist like my dad or chief of pediatric surgery like my mom or a neuroscientist like my sister. Still, they expected that I'd try. I wanted none of it. Never had.

After I had to leave police college, they'd been certain I'd give up this nonsense and devote myself to a meaningful career, preferably with a string of letters after my name. We argued. A lot. They died in a small plane crash four years ago, and we'd never truly mended that fence.

But back to the hospital. I spent six weeks there, learning to walk again, talk again, be Casey Duncan again. Except I never really was. Not the Casey Duncan I'd been. There are two halves of my life: before and after.

Four days in a coma. Six weeks in the

hospital. Blaine never came to see me. Never even sent a card. I'd have ripped it to shreds, but at least it would have acknowledged what happened. He knew, of course. Diana had made sure of that, contacting him while I was in emergency. He hadn't asked how bad I was. Just mumbled something and hung up.

When I'd seen him run away in the alley, my outrage had been tempered by the certainty that he would get help. Even as the blows had started to fall, I'd clung to that. He must have called the police. He must have.

The last thing that passed through my mind before I lost consciousness was that I just had to hold on a little longer. Help was on the way. Only it wasn't. A homeless guy cutting through the alley stumbled across me, hours later. A stranger — a *drunk* stranger — had run to get help for me. My boyfriend had just run.

Blaine did need to speak to the police after I woke up and had told them what happened. But in Blaine's version, *he'd* created the distraction. I'd been escaping with him, and we'd parted at the street. The muggers must have caught up and dragged me back into that alley. If Blaine had known, he'd have done something. To suggest otherwise, well . . . I'd suffered head trauma, hadn't I? Temporary brain damage? Loss of memory? Clearly, I'd misremembered.

I didn't call him when I got out of the hospital. That conversation had to happen in person. It took a week for me to get around to it, because there was something I needed to do first. Buy a gun.

Blaine's routine hadn't changed. He still went jogging before dawn. Or that was what he'd say if he was trying to impress a girl: *I run in the park every morning at five.* It wasn't completely untrue. He did go out before dawn. He did run in the park. Except he only did it on Fridays, and just to the place where he stashed his drugs. Then he'd run back to campus, where he could usually find a few buyers — kids who'd been out too late partying, heading back to the dorms before dawn, in need of a little something to get them through Friday classes.

I knew the perfect place for a confrontation. By the bridge along the riverbank, where he'd pass on his way home. The spot was always empty at that time of day, and the noise of rushing water would cover our discussion.

Cover a gunshot, too?

No, the gun was only a prop. To let him know this was going to be a serious conversation.

I stood by the foot of the bridge. He came by right on schedule. Walking. He only jogged where people could see him.

I waited until I could hear the buzz and crash from his music. Then I stepped out into his path.

"Casey?" He blinked and tugged at the earbuds, letting them fall, dangling, as he stared at me. "You look . . ."

"Like I got the shit beat out of me?"

"It's not that bad."

"True. The bruises have healed. There are only ten stitches on my face. Oh, and this spot, where they had to shave my head to cut into my skull and relieve the bleeding." I turned to show him. "Plus a few teeth that will need to be replaced after my jaw's fully healed. My nose isn't straight, but they tell me plastic surgery will fix that. They also say I might walk without the limp if I work really, really hard at it."

He listened, nodding, an overly concerned expression on his face, as if I were an elderly aunt detailing my medical woes.

When I finished, he said, "You'll heal, then. That's good."

"Good?" I stepped toward him. "I almost *died,* Blaine. I had to drop out of police college. I'm told I'll never be a cop. That I'll never move fast enough. I might never *think* fast enough."

Another long pause. Then, "I'm sorry this happened to you, Casey. I gave you a chance to run."

"No, I let *you* run. You did, and you never

even called for help."

"That's not how I remember it." He pulled himself up straight, ducking my gaze.

"No?" I said. "Does this refresh your memory?"

I took the gun from my pocket.

I'd envisioned this encounter so many ways. All those nights, lying in a hospital bed, fantasizing about it, I'd realized I didn't want him to break down and beg forgiveness too quickly. I wanted to have to pull the gun. I wanted to see his expression. I wanted him to feel what I'd felt in that alley.

Now I pointed the gun at him, and he blinked. That was it. A blink. Then his lips twitched, as if he was going to laugh. I think if he had, I'd have pulled that trigger. But he rubbed his mouth instead and said, "You're not going to shoot me with your training weapon, Casey. You're smarter than that."

"Did I mention I had to drop out? This *isn't* my training weapon. Now, I want you to think hard, Blaine. Think back to that night, and tell me again that you let me run."

"Oh, I get it." He eased back. "You want me to confess on some hidden tape so you can —"

I yanked off my jacket. It wasn't easy. My left arm was still in a cast, and my shoulder blazed with the simple act of tugging off clothing. But I got it off, and I threw it at him.

"Check for a recorder. Pat me down if you want. I'm not taping this. It's for me. I want to hear you tell the truth, and I want to hear you apologize."

"Well, then you're going to have to pull that trigger, because I don't have anything to apologize for. We ran, and you must have doubled back."

"For what?" I roared. "What in *fuck* would I double back for?"

"Then they must have caught you. You were too slow —"

"I did not run! You know I didn't. I grabbed him, and you were supposed to pick up the gun he dropped, but you ran. Like a fucking coward, you ran, and you didn't look back, and I nearly died, and you never even called the goddamned hospital to see if I was okay."

"You *are* okay. Look at you. Up and about, waving a gun in my face. Well, actually, I'm not sure I'd call that okay. I think you need help. I always did. You're messed up, Casey. I bet a shrink would say you have a death wish."

I went still. "What?"

He shifted forward, as if he'd just remembered the missing answer in a final exam. "You have a death wish, Casey. What normal girl wants to be a cop? Does that martial arts shit? We get mugged in an alley, and I'm trying to play it cool, and what do you do? Grab the guy. Hell, thank God I *did* run, or I'd have had the shit beat out of me, too."

I hit him. Hauled off and whaled the gun at the side of his head. He staggered back. I hit him again. Blood gushed. His hands went to the spot, eyes widening.

"Fuck! You fucking crazy bitch!"

"We were not *mugged,*" I said, advancing on him as he backed up, still holding his head. "You were selling dope on some other guy's turf. Apparently, you knew that. You just didn't give a shit. I grabbed that guy to save your ass, and you ran. You left me there to die!"

"I didn't think they'd —"

"You left me there."

"I just thought —"

"Thought what? They'd only rape me? A distraction while you escaped?"

He didn't answer, but I saw it in his face, that sudden flush right before his eyes went hard.

"It was your own fault if they did rape you," Blaine said. "You couldn't leave well enough alone. Now give me that —"

He lunged for the gun. I shot him. No thought entered my head as I pulled the trigger. It was like being back in that alley.

I saw Blaine coming at me. I was already pointing the gun at his chest. So I pulled the trigger.

The end.

THREE

"And he died?" the therapist says.

I swing my legs over the side of the couch and sit up. Her expression is rapt, as if she's overhearing a drunken confession in a bar.

"And he died?" she prompts again.

"I called 911 on his burner phone. By the time I got through, he was gone." *No, not gone. Dead. Use the proper terminology, Casey. Don't sugarcoat it.*

"What did you tell the operator?"

"Dispatcher," I say, correcting her automatically. "I said I heard a shot, and I raced over to see two men fleeing the scene. One had a gun. I gave descriptions roughly matching two of the guys who beat me. I said I was going to follow them to get a closer look. She told me not to, of course, but I was already hanging up."

"You'd thought it through."

Her tone should be at least vaguely accusatory. Instead, it's almost admiring. She's been abused in some way. Bullied. Harassed.

Maybe even assaulted. She's fantasized about doing exactly what I did to whoever hurt her.

I can't even take credit for "thinking it through." A situation presented itself, and I reacted. One therapist explained it as an extreme response to the primal fight-or-flight instinct. Mine apparently lacks the flight portion.

"What did you do with the gun?" she asks.

"I wiped it down and threw it in the river. It was never found."

"Have you ever pulled the file? As a cop?"

She doesn't even bother to say "police officer" now. All formality gone.

"No, that could flag an alert," I say. "It didn't happen here anyway."

"Was the boy's family really connected? Like capital *F* family?"

She says it as if this is an episode of *The Sopranos.*

"I guess so," I say, which is a lie. I know so. The Saratoris aren't major players, but Blaine's grandfather Leo is definitely part of the Montreal organized crime scene.

"Don't you worry they'll find out and come for revenge?"

Every day of my life, I think, but all I grant her is a shrug.

"Biggest therapist fail ever." I down a shot of tequila two days later, my first chance to have a drink after work with Diana. "I might as well have confided in that chick over there." I point at a vacant-eyed girl in the corner. Hooker. Crack addict. If she's old enough to be in a bar, I'll turn in my badge.

"Remind me again why you put yourself through that," Diana says. "Oh, right. You're a sadist."

"Masochist," I say. "Also, possibly, a sadist, but in this situation, it's masochism."

She rolls her eyes and shifts on her stool. She's already sitting on the edge, as if placing her ass — even fully clothed — on the surface might result in lethal contamination. At least she's stopped cleaning her glass with an antiseptic wipe before drinking from it.

Another shift has her sliding off the stool, and she does a little stutter-jump to get back on, tugging down her miniskirt as she does. One of the guys across the bar is checking her out. Or he's checking out her hair, blond with bright pink tips. He squints, as if suspecting he's had too much to drink. They don't see a lot of pink hair in here.

"So how was work?" I ask. Diana is in accounting. Her exact title seems to change by the month, as she flits about, not climbing the corporate ladder, but jumping from rung to rung, testing them all for size.

"We're not going to talk about your therapy session?"

"We just did."

I down my second shot of tequila. The

bartender glances over and jerks his thumb at the soda fountain. It's not a hint. Kurt knows I have a two-shot limit. I nod, and he starts filling a glass.

"So work . . . ?" I prod Diana.

Her lips purse, and that tells me that's not a good question. Not today. I just hope it doesn't mean she's been demoted again. Lately, Diana's career hops seem to all be downward . . . and not by choice.

"Is work . . . okay?" I venture.

"Work is work." She gulps her drink, and there's an uncharacteristic note of bitterness in her voice.

I try to assess her mood. We haven't always been best friends. In high school, it'd been on and off, the ebb and flow that marked many teen friendships. It was the attack that brought us closer. She'd stood by me when all my old friends shied away, no one knowing what to say. After I shot Blaine, she'd found me frantically changing out of my blood-splattered clothing, and I'd told her everything, and that cemented our friendship. Forged in fire, as they say. Fire and secrets.

"Let's talk about something else," I say. "Did you bump into that guy at the coffee shop? The musician, right?"

She shrugs and runs a hot-pink fingernail around the rim of her martini glass . . . which is actually a regular whiskey glass, but it's currently holding a lemon-drop martini. I know she has something to say. Something about therapy, I presume, but I pretend not to notice, as Kurt brings my Diet Coke.

"You staying till closing?" he asks me.

"Maybe."

A smile lights his eyes. When I stay until closing, I usually end up in the apartment over the bar. His apartment.

"You should," he says. "Looks like you could use a break."

I'm sure he's about to make some smutty suggestion about ways to relieve my stress. Then his gaze slides to Diana, and instead he heads off to wait on another customer. He thinks he's being discreet, but Diana knows about us, and she's just as horrified as he suspects she'd be. Diana does not approve of casual sex, especially not with an ex-con bartender who works at the docks by day. She has no idea what she's missing.

Normally, she'd make a smart comment as Kurt walked away. But tonight she's lost in the mysteries of her lemon drop.

"You okay?" I ask.

"It's . . . Graham."

"Fuck," I mutter, and sit back on my stool.

Graham Berry is Diana's ex-husband. Respected lawyer. Community pillar. Also one of the most goddamn brilliant psychos I've ever met. He knows exactly how to stalk and torment her while keeping his ass out of prison. Restraining orders? Sure, we can get them. But any cop who's spent time in SVU knows they're as useful as cardboard armor in a gunfight.

She downs her martini and signals Kurt for a refill. Diana rarely has more than one, and when he comes over to deliver it, he gives me an *Is everything okay?* look.

"Rough day," I say.

When he says, "Maybe tomorrow will be better," I know he isn't talking about Diana.

"It will be," I say.

"Graham's in town," she blurts out when Kurt leaves. "He claims he's here on business."

"And he wants to see you, because he loves you and he's changed."

I look her in the eyes as I say this, steeling myself for the guilty flash that says she's considering meeting with him. Like many abusive relationships, theirs is a complicated one. He'd beat the shit out of her, and then he'd be so very sorry, and she'd go back to him, and the cycle would start again.

It's been two years since she left him and convinced me to move to a new city with her. I'd resisted, not because I was reluctant to help but, honestly, because I expected I'd relocate my life for Diana and then find myself alone in that new city when she went back to Graham. But I'd decided to give her one last chance . . . and she'd finally decided he'd had enough chances. She's been free and clear of him ever since, and now I don't detect any guilt in her eyes, any sign that she wants to see him.

"Okay, step one," I say. "You'll stay at my place tonight and work from there tomorrow. Call in sick."

I brace for her to suggest she stay longer. When her lease came due, she hinted — strongly — about moving into my place instead. She'd gotten very little in the divorce, having signed a prenup, and had long since run through it. The demotions haven't helped her ever-worsening financial situation. I'd pointed out that my single-bedroom place wasn't big enough, but still I feel like a selfish bitch. I help by footing the bills when we go out and "loaning" her bill money that I never expect to see again.

She doesn't suggest a longer-term stay, though, and I feel like a bitch for *that,* for even thinking it at a time like this, as if she'd manufacture a story about Graham to move in with me.

"With any luck," I continue, "it'll take him a while to track your home or work address, and if he really is on business, he won't be here long . . ." I catch her expression. "He's already found you."

"He — he stopped by the office. The usual crap. He just wants to have coffee, talk, work things out."

"And then?" I say, because I know there is an *and then.* In public, Graham plays the besotted ex-husband. But as soon as no one is around . . .

"He waylaid me in the parking garage."

I reach for her wrist, and she flinches. I push up the sleeve to see a bracelet of bruises.

"Goddamn it, Di!"

She gives me a whipped-puppy look.

"Graham showed up at your office, and you didn't call me? You walked into the goddamn parking garage —"

"Don't, Casey. I feel stupid enough."

Her eyes fill with tears, and that's when I really feel like a bitch. Blame the victim. I hate it so much. But Diana never seems to learn, and I'm terrified that one day I'll get a call that she's in the morgue because she gave Graham another chance and I wasn't there to stop her.

"He's going to do it one of these days," she says, wrapping her hands around her glass. "You know he is."

I don't want to follow this line of thought, because when I do, I think of Blaine and how easy it was to kill him. I fear that one day I'll decide there's only one way to protect Diana. No, really I'm afraid she'll ask me to do it. I don't know what I'd say if she did. I owe her for keeping my secret about Blaine. But I don't owe her enough to repeat the mistake with someone else. Not even Graham.

32

"I've been researching how to disappear," she says.

"What?" I look up sharply.

"We could disappear. You and me."

I don't ask why she includes me. When she'd asked me to relocate and I'd resisted, she'd pointed out the ugly truth — that I'd had no reason to stay. That hasn't changed. I have a furnished apartment I've never added a picture to. I have a lover whose last name I've never asked. I have a sister I speak to three times a year. I have one friend, who is sitting in front of me. I do have a job I love. But that's all I care about. My job and Diana. The job is replaceable. Diana is not.

"Let's just focus on keeping you safe for now," I say. "Graham will give up and go home, and then we can discuss how to handle this long-term."

I put money on the table and catch Kurt's eye as he deals with a drunk. He mouths, "This weekend?" meaning he can see something's up and tomorrow probably isn't going to be better. I nod, try for a smile, and then turn to Diana and say, "Drink up, and let's go."

FOUR

I'm at work the next day, trying not to worry about Diana. Of course, I do. I've felt responsible for her since we met. She'd just moved to my district, and I spotted her in the cafeteria with her tray, looking like a rabbit about to dine among wolves. I'd waved her over to join me and my friends, and I've been there for her ever since.

I keep thinking about Graham being in town. About the other times he's tracked her down and what he did. Got her fired. Trashed her apartment. Beat the shit out of her. And the last time, tried to run her down with his car.

"Detective Duncan?"

I look up from my desk. It's Ricci, a new detective from Special Victims.

"Are you, uh, busy?" he asks.

I resist the urge to glance at the piles of paperwork on my desk and say instead, "What's up?"

"Got a, uh, victim in hospital and she's . . .

She won't talk to me. My partner's off with the flu, and she said I could ask you."

What he means is that he has a rape survivor refusing to speak to a male detective. Our division is small enough that the lines aren't drawn in permanent ink.

When I hesitate, my partner, Timmons, leans over. "Boy's giving you the chance to escape paperwork for a few hours, and you're arguing? Go. I've got this."

Ricci fills me in on the ride. The young woman kicked out her addict boyfriend a week ago. He came back for his things . . . and took what *didn't* belong to him, raping and strangling her. Or that's the story given by her roommate, who spotted the ex fleeing the scene. The victim herself insists it was a random home invasion.

As I listen to the story, I try not to think of Diana. I still send her a text, reminding her that she's supposed to order takeout for lunch and not leave my apartment.

I know the rules, Casey, she replies, and I mentally hear her add, *I'm not a child.* As an apology, I tap back a note that I'll grab her a chai latte on my way home.

We arrive at the hospital and take the stairs to the room, which is being guarded by an officer I don't recognize. He whispers to Ricci, "You aren't supposed to take anyone else in there. Doctor's orders."

"Constable Wiley, this is Detective Duncan," Ricci says.

I shake his hand. He stares a little too long and then covers it with a laugh that's a little too loud as he says, "Guess the force doesn't have height restrictions anymore, huh?"

"They haven't in years," Ricci says. "That would be discrimination against gender and race."

He slides me a look, as if expecting a pat on the head. He's referring to the fact that I'm also half Asian — my mother was Chinese and Filipino.

"Is Ms. Lang . . . ?" I wave toward the room.

"Uh, right," Ricci says, and grabs the door for me. As we walk through, he whispers, "Thank you for doing this. I really appreciate it. Maybe we can grab a drink after shift?"

I really hope you're not hitting on me in the hospital room of a rape survivor, I think, but only murmur something noncommittal. Then I tug back the curtain around the bed and —

It looks like Diana.

It isn't, of course, but that's the first thing I think. I see a blond woman wearing pink barrettes that, for a moment, look like pink-tipped hair. Her face is purple and yellow and swollen. A ring of bruises circles her throat. She wears a cast on one arm, has one leg raised, not unlike me twelve years ago.

I imagine Diana here, in a hospital bed, like me and like this girl, beaten and left for

36

dead, and I realize I can't keep ignoring Graham. I owe it to Diana to make sure she never ends up like this.

Then I push that aside, and I see this girl. Only this girl. Our eyes meet, and there are traces of defiance in hers, but only traces, and she clings to that, as if refusing to turn in her ex is her choice. As if he doesn't have her so terrified she can't see any other option.

I move to her bedside, lean over, and whisper, "Let's make sure he never does this again," and she starts to cry.

I bang on Graham's hotel room door.

"Casey," Graham says as he opens it, grinning like I've brought his favorite takeout. "I was hoping you'd find me. Come on in."

As I enter, I put my back to him. That's my way of saying he doesn't scare me. Only once I sit on the couch do I face him. Graham Berry. Forty years old. Looks like he should be the spokesmodel for some high-end law firm, all white teeth and perfect hair and chiseled jaw. I can still hear Diana's excited whisper. "Oh my God, Case. You have to meet him. He's gorgeous, and he's brilliant, and he's charming, and he asked me out. Can you believe it?"

I wanted to, because Diana deserved some good in her life, having gone through a string of abusive losers since high school. Except she was right — it was hard to believe a guy as outwardly perfect as Graham Berry was madly in love with Diana. That's cruel, isn't it? But there's a dating hierarchy, and though you can move up or down a notch or two, when you're attracting the attention of someone a half dozen rungs up? You need to ask yourself why.

In Diana's case, the answer was that Graham saw the same thing her loser exes had — her deep vulnerability and eagerness to please. Like my parents, Diana's set a higher standard of expectation than she could reach. Unlike mine, hers vented their displeasure in more than words, and she'd spent her childhood convinced she deserved every beating she got. That made her the perfect target for Graham's particular brand of sadism.

"You look good, Case," he says, those white teeth glimmering.

"Knock it off. We both know I'm not your type."

"Mmm, not so sure about that." He walks over and sits on the coffee table, right in front of me, so close our knees brush. "How about a deal? You give me a night, and I'll go home happy. I'll let you bring the handcuffs. We can arm-wrestle for who wears them."

"If I ever got you in handcuffs, Graham, I don't think you'd like where it ended up. I want you to leave Diana alone."

"Oh, I know, but Diana doesn't really *want*

me to leave her alone. It's a game we play. You've never understood that."

"If you hurt her —"

"I never hurt her. Not against her will, anyway. You've got me all wrong, Casey. You always have. I love Diana, and if our relationship is a little unconventional, well, that isn't a crime."

He smiles. I know exactly what that smile means — that if I'm wired and trying to entrap him, I'll catch nothing. He's so damned careful.

"I want you out of town," I say.

"Mmm, you make a very sexy sheriff, Casey. Shall we set a time, then? High noon or pistols at twenty paces?"

"It's well past noon. Let's say six. Or . . ." I open my bag, take out a file folder, and drop it beside him on the coffee table.

He opens it. And he stops smiling.

"Britnee Spencer. Sister of a boy you coached in basketball two years ago. You went over to give him some private lessons and ended up giving *her* some, too. In a whole different kind of sport."

"Who told you — ?"

"I'm a detective, remember? She was fifteen. That makes it stat rape, and I have what I need to see charges pressed. The evidence is in there. Keep it. I have copies."

"This is bullshit," he says. "She told me she was eighteen."

"You can explain that to the police. Six o'clock, Graham. Better pack fast."

As I drive, I grip the steering wheel to stop my hands from shaking. I haven't threatened Graham with that file before because it's 50 percent bullshit. When Diana left Graham, one of the reasons was that she suspected he'd fooled around with Britnee. I'd contacted Britnee . . . who'd told me to go to hell. If I did take the case to the police, she'd deny everything.

When my phone rings, I look down to see *Private Caller,* and I'm sure it's Graham calling my bluff. I steel myself and hit Answer on my Bluetooth.

"Detective Duncan? It's Stefan." A pause. "Stefan Ricci?" His voice rises, as if he's uncertain of his own name.

"Yes?"

"I want to talk more about the, uh, victim interview. You brought her right around, and I . . ." A strained chuckle. "I have no idea how to do that. I mentioned drinks earlier, and I didn't get a chance to ask again, so I'm asking now. I just finished my shift. Can I take you out? To talk about, uh, your interview techniques."

I stifle a sigh. *You seem like a sweet kid, Ricci. Really you do. And I'd be more than happy to discuss interview techniques with you.*

But that's not what you're asking, is it?

"I need to meet a friend for dinner," I say, which is technically true.

"Oh, okay. Maybe after? Or —"

"How about coffee tomorrow? At the Grounds."

It's the shop right beside the station, which means this will be business only, and his voice drops as he says, "Uh, I guess so?"

"Totally up to you. If you want to, just pop by my desk."

I sign off and turn on CBC, hoping to distract myself. It's midway through a story about one woman's hike across Alaska, and as I listen, I imagine myself doing that, and I'm swept away by a feeling that is so normal for others and so rare for me — that little thing called daydreaming.

I pull into the station's underground lot and park my Honda. It's the first car I bought, almost a decade ago, and it was well used when I got it. The guys in the department prod me to buy something newer, safer, with air bags and ABS brakes. It's not like I can't afford it. My parents left me with a seven-figure bank account. But the car runs. When it doesn't, I'll replace it.

I've gone about five steps when I realize someone's watching me from the shadows. I don't see him. Don't even hear him. I just know he's there.

I stop midstride and take a long, slow

survey of my surroundings. On the return sweep, I spot an arm poking from behind a van. Then, slowly, the arm withdraws, the figure vanishing entirely.

I walk toward the van until I can see him through the window. The image is blurry, but I can tell it's a guy. Late twenties. Short, curly dark hair. Looks Italian. Also looks familiar.

"Ricci?" I say.

He drops from sight as if ducking.

"Hey!" I say. "If that's you, Ricci, this really isn't the way to get my —"

I hear a scuffle and realize, three seconds too late, that he didn't just duck — he bolted. I jog after him, but when I get to the exit, there's no sign of anyone. I shake my head and continue up to the station.

FIVE

At seven, I call Graham's hotel, and I'm told he checked out early. That's a good sign, but I still don't dare spend the night with Kurt. I really need a break, though, and Diana's going stir-crazy enough in my apartment that she agrees to a drink at Kurt's bar.

Kurt doesn't seem happy to see me. The looks he keeps shooting me suggest he has something to say, and I realize what's coming. The point of having a regular hook-up is the "regular" part. I've been too busy to hold up my end, and as nice a guy as he is, he's decided it's time to move on.

"Just a sec," I say to Diana, who's on her second lemon drop. "I'm going to talk to Kurt."

She drains her glass and wordlessly hands it to me. I take it to Kurt.

"Everything okay?" I whisper as I slide onto a bar stool.

He shrugs and makes the lemon drop. Then he says, "If I'd known you were coming by,

I'd have told you not to."

I force myself to say, "Okay," as casually as I can. "So would you like me to stop coming by, then?"

"Huh?" He searches my face, frowning, and then says, "You think that's a kiss-off? Hell, no." He leans forward, his forearms on the bar, his face coming down to mine. "I'd like to think I'd do that with a little more class."

"Sorry." I made a face. "Rough week. I'm braced for the worst."

"Well, this isn't it." His fingers hook mine, a discreet bit of physical contact. "When I said I'd have told you not to come by, it's because I got a couple calls earlier. A guy phoned the bar and asked for me by a name I don't use anymore."

From the old days, he meant. Kurt had grown up in the kind of neighborhood where making a name for yourself almost certainly entailed jail time. He'd dropped out of high school and worked as an enforcer for a local "businessman." After his second stint in prison, he cleaned up his act before a third strike could steal his last chance.

"Someone trying to pull you back in?" I ask.

"Dunno. Can't imagine why. I've been out too long, but maybe someone got my name, figured I might be tired of the straight life, looking to make some fast money. I said I don't know anyone who goes by that name anymore. Hour later, I get the same call to my cell. I delivered the same message. That's why I was going to suggest you stay away for a few days. Give me time to sort this. I don't want you getting involved."

"I'm a cop. I can handle it."

"Right. You're a cop . . . which is why we've been keeping this on the down-low." He casts a meaningful glance over at a table of detectives in the corner. "You don't need the bullshit of dating an ex-con. I get that."

"Umm, no," I say. "If I'm discreet, it's because I'm *always* discreet. I save my energy for *private* displays of affection."

His grin sparks then. "Which I totally appreciate."

"Glad to hear it. However, if you want, I could make an exception right now."

I reach and wrap my hand in his shirt. He grins but shakes his head and jerks his chin toward the back hall. I lead him into the single-occupancy ladies' room and show him how much I've missed him. It doesn't go beyond kissing, though. A quickie in the bathroom isn't our style. Given that he might not want me coming by for a while, though, I consider making an exception. When I tell him this, he chuckles.

"If you're okay dealing with my shit, you can come by any time you like."

He leans into me. I'm sitting on the counter, my legs around him, and he presses closer, murmuring, "No pressure, but . . . what are my chances for tomorrow?"

"About fifty-fifty. Diana —"

He cuts me off with a kiss, a deep one that makes me temporarily forget what we were talking about.

"Your friend's having trouble," he says. "She comes first. But if you *can* get away tomorrow, I promise I'll take your mind off that . . . and everything else that's bugging you. I'd like your phone number, though. Again, not pushing, but I should have it in case there's a problem."

I'm about to ask if he lost my number . . . and then realize I never gave it. We've been seeing each other for six months, and I never got around to that. Shit. I pull out my phone. "Give me yours."

"Um, pretty sure I did already. Twice."

The first night I came by, with some guys from work, Kurt left his number on my napkin. I hadn't kept it. I returned a week later, though, and he gave it to me again after I spent the night. At the time, I still hadn't been prepared to save it, and then . . . well . . .

When I'm slow to answer, he shakes his head and rattles it off. I text him my cell number, work number, and home address. His phone buzzes in his back pocket. When he reads the message, he grins like I've handed him the keys to my apartment, my car, and my safe-deposit box.

I see that grin, and I feel a prickle of guilt. I tell myself we keep things casual by mutual agreement. We both have busy, complicated lives. If he doesn't get annoyed when I don't make contact for a week, that only proves he feels the same way I do.

Or that he's a sweetheart of a guy who's taking what he can get. What I can give.

"About Diana," I say as I slide off the counter. "It's an ex who hasn't accepted that he's an ex. He's been quiet for months, but he made contact again yesterday. That's why I had to take off last night. She told me while we were here."

"This guy have a name?" Kurt doesn't actually flex his biceps — he'd never be so trite — but he shifts, muscles bunching, telling me exactly what he has in mind.

"Tempting . . . ," I murmur.

"Just give me a name. He doesn't understand it's over? I can drive home the message."

"I bet you could. And after dealing with this asshole for years, I'd almost pay to watch."

"Oh, you wouldn't have to pay." A devilish grin. "Not in cash, anyway."

"You have no idea how much I'd like that. The problem is that it would only piss him off, and he'd take it out on her. I'm working on another resolution."

"All right. But if you need muscle for the

47

job, you now have my number. Day or night, I'll be there."

I'm back at the table. I expect Diana to comment, but she barely seems to have noticed I left. When I deposit her third lemon drop, she reaches for it as if it's been there all along. After a sip, she says, "Graham called this afternoon. He said he had to fly back early and wouldn't be able to do dinner. Not that I'd agreed to dinner . . ."

She stares across the room, her eyes unfocused.

"That's good, right?" I say tentatively. "That he left?"

She blinks hard before forcing a humorless laugh. "Yes, sorry. Did that sound like regret? Absolutely not. I was just thinking . . ." She turns to me. "Is it ever going to end, Casey? He only has to call, and I'm in lockdown again. Do you know what I did today? Checked my life insurance. I wanted to be sure it was paid up so you wouldn't be on the hook if anything happened. Can you believe I even thought that? Me? Miss Happy-Go-Lucky?" Her fingers tighten on the glass. "Not so happy these days. Definitely not so lucky."

"How about a vacation?" I ask. "God knows I've got a shitload of time banked."

She nods, absently, and I struggle to think of "fun" things to do, but it's like asking a pastry chef to fix a broken carburetor. My idea of a holiday is the guy behind the bar.

"I keep thinking about this place," she blurts out. "And don't laugh, okay? Because I know it sounds crazy, and maybe it just proves how desperate I am. But in my therapy group, there's this woman I have coffee with, and we talk about our escape plans, what we'd do if things got too bad. She has a place she'd go."

"A cabin or something?"

"No, a town. For people who need to disappear. A place where no one can find them."

"Like an underground railway for abuse victims?"

"For anyone in trouble. It's an entire town of people who've disappeared."

I shake my head. "I'm sorry, Di, but that sounds like a classic urban legend. Think about it. An invisible town? In today's world, you're never really off the grid. How would a place like that work? The economy, the security. . . ."

"I'm not saying I believe in it. The point is that it proves how far I've fallen, Case. I can't stop thinking about it. Obsessing over it. Telling myself maybe, just maybe, it could be real."

"It isn't," I say. "Now, if you want to talk real strategies and escape plans, we can do that. But no fantasy bullshit. It's a real problem; it needs a real solution."

Six

Everything goes fine the next day. Ricci stops by and takes me up on that offer of coffee, and he's all business. I don't mention the parking garage. If it was him, he must have just been trying to work up the nerve to ask for a drink again and changed his mind.

As for Graham, all is silent. I insist on Diana spending another night at my place, but I don't see the need to stay with her.

When I walk into the bar that night, Kurt's washing glasses. He squints against the dim lighting to be sure it's me. Then he smiles, puts down the glass, and has a shot of tequila poured before I reach the bar.

He doesn't say anything. I down the shot and let him pour another. Someone hails him from across the room, and he slings the dish towel over his shoulder and walks off, leaving me to take my second shot, slower now, as the burn takes hold.

We barely exchange a dozen words over the next hour. Usually, if I'm here without Diana, we talk. How's work? How's life? Did you see the forecast calls for rain all week? Yep, deep conversation. That's no reflection on Kurt. He's joked that we only have one thing in common: I arrest people, and he's been arrested.

Tonight he can tell I'm not in the mood for chatter, and he takes no offense at that, letting me sip my tequila in silence.

The bar should close at two. Kurt shuts it down at one. The only remaining patrons are too drunk to check their watches. I doubt any of them even own one. He scoots them out the door with a cardboard cup of coffee and a good night. He doesn't bother telling them not to drive. There's little danger of them owning vehicles, either.

By the time he comes back, I have the tables cleared and I'm washing glasses. He nods his thanks and finishes cashing out. He's supposed to make the deposit tonight. He'll get it later. No one's going to break into his apartment for a few hundred bucks. Not when the last guy who jumped him spent a week recuperating in hospital.

He's done first and takes the dishrag from me to finish up. I wait. He tosses the rag in the sink, and I follow him into the back, where stairs lead up to his apartment.

It's a tiny place, half the size of mine. Kurt has two jobs and an ex-girlfriend with a five-year-old son. His son. His responsibility. Not

51

that he plays any role in his child's life. He's just the ATM. His ex has decided her new husband is "Daddy." Kurt still insists on paying child support, even if it means working two shitty jobs. He's also saving money. Saving it for what? *No fucking idea,* he said when I asked. I guess we have that in common, too.

He's locking the door as I walk into the living room. I hear him follow me, but he doesn't say a word, just stands behind me as I stare out the window.

"Casey?"

I turn. He doesn't move. He's trying to gauge my mood, whether I've changed my mind about staying. I unbutton my shirt, and he smiles, staying where he is, watching. I left my bra off when I changed to come over, and as my shirt falls open, he sucks in breath. I start toward him.

"You are fucking gorgeous, you know that?" he says.

"Considering what I'm here for, I do believe you're obligated to say that."

"Nope. You're gorgeous, Detective Duncan. Also? Shit at taking compliments."

I laugh, and he crosses the floor to scoop me up in a kiss.

We're in his bed, entwined in the sheets — or what remains of them, most pushed onto the floor.

He leans over to kiss me. "Any chance

you're staying the night?"

"Planning to."

"Good." He squeezes my hip as he slides from bed. "I need to make that bank deposit. You know the drill." As an ex-con, he doesn't dare keep it in his apartment overnight. "But I'll be quick. You want me to stop at the diner?"

I smile up at him, and he says, "Dumb question. Burger and rings and a Diet Coke. Though I don't quite get the point of the diet pop."

"Balance."

He laughs, kisses me again, and heads for the other room, where we left our clothes. I watch him go. It's a helluva view. Broad, tattooed shoulders. Muscled arms. Great ass. He notices and turns, his gaze moving slowly over me.

"You keep looking at me like that," he says, "I'm not going to make it to the bank."

I pull my knees up in invitation. He starts toward me. I shut my legs and tug the sheet over them.

"Tease," he growls.

"Drop off the money. Bring me onion rings. I'll show my sincere appreciation."

"*Sincere* appreciation? I like the sound of that."

He dresses and then leaves. When the door closes, I'm on my phone, zipping through work-related messages before I check in on

Diana. I go to hit Speed Dial. Then my gaze shoots to the door.

Phone. Kurt.

Shit, I never asked if he'd had any more weird calls. And now he's taken off on a 2:30 A.M. bank run.

I'm still doing up my shirt as I fly down the stairs. I know I'm overreacting. But it's my way of admitting he's important to me, that I'm not going to get distracted with my own problems when he has his own.

I'm on the street now. Even in the daytime, it's not one of the city's safest neighborhoods. At this hour, it's unnaturally quiet, as if a predator lurks around every corner, waiting for some foolish prey to break the silence. It's a wet September night, rainwater still dripping from eaves, that plinking the only sound I hear until I catch the slow thump of Kurt's footsteps. Unhurried, deliberate footsteps, ones that tell the world he's here and doesn't give a shit if they know it.

I tear around the corner. He glances over his shoulder, still unhurried, even the pound of footfalls not enough to concern him. He's twenty feet away, under a flickering streetlight, and he frowns as he sees me.

"Everything okay?" he calls, his voice echoing in the darkness.

I slow to a walk. "I just decided I want a milk shake instead of the burger and Coke."

"You did keep my number, right?"

"I needed the exercise."

He chuckles. "I planned to give you that after I got back."

I laugh. He's waiting under the light, and I'm walking over, the gap closing. Ten feet, nine. . . .

Movement flickers in the shadows. I don't wait to see what it is. I charge, yelling, "Kurt!"

He turns, it seems in slow motion. A gun rises. I shout. I hit Kurt in the side, and a gun fires, and he goes down, and I don't know which comes first — the shot or the fall. Then he's hitting the ground, and I'm twisting, and there's a guy there. The same one I saw in the parking garage. Not Ricci. A dark-haired stranger. Holding a gun on us.

"Present from Mr. Saratori," he says.

He lifts the gun. I don't think. I don't need to. I'm already in motion, grabbing his wrist and wrenching, the gun clattering onto the pavement. A hiss of surprise. The thug turns, his fist swinging. Then the gun appears, seeming to rise from the sidewalk on its own.

No, not on its own. Kurt's pointing the gun at the thug. His face is ashen. There's blood on his shirt. The guy twists, pulling me into the line of fire. And I'm thinking I'm dead. Kurt will pull the trigger before he sees I'm in the way. Except Kurt isn't me. He doesn't react like me. He just points the gun, and the guy breaks free and runs. Kurt shoots, but it's deliberately wide. A warning. *Keep run-*

ning, asshole.

I reach for the gun to go after the thug. Then I see Kurt. See his white face. See the blood on his shirt. The hole ripped through it, blood gushing. He slaps a hand to the hole, as if that will stop the blood.

He hands me the gun. "Get out of here."

His voice is weak, his eyelids flickering. He's going into shock. I push him gently down onto the sidewalk.

"You need to go —" he begins.

"He's gone."

"You can still —"

"No."

I grab my phone.

"Don't." He wobbles to his feet. "Whatever this is, you don't want to get involved."

"This isn't about you. That was for me."

He hesitates, but then shakes his head. "I don't care. I don't want you getting in trouble. I know a guy. Comes by the bar. A doctor. He lost his license, but —"

"Hell, no," I say. "I'm getting you proper medical —"

He teeters, his eyes starting to roll up. I break his fall as he topples. Then I dial 911.

Seven

I'm at the hospital, beside Kurt's bed. I paid to upgrade him to a private room, and he's sleeping now. He's been in and out of consciousness since the ambulance came, first from shock and blood loss, now from painkillers and exhaustion.

Leo Saratori has found me. My game of Russian roulette with therapists is over. The bullet has slid into the chamber.

Four days ago, I confessed to a new therapist; today, Saratori catches up with me. That's no coincidence. That therapist looked up the details and found my story. She told someone. Maybe she found a way to contact Saratori. Maybe she just called the police and someone figured they could get a windfall from Saratori if they told him first.

However it happened, I made a mistake. *Many* mistakes.

I'd mentioned Kurt to the therapist — no name, just that I was seeing a bartender. Saratori's thug had been stalking me and followed me to the bar. He got his boss to run Kurt's name and learned of his gang affiliations. Then he called to make sure he was talking to the right guy.

I've misjudged Leo Saratori. He knows that perfect revenge is not dumping my body in the river — it's making me live, knowing I'm responsible for my lover's death.

But Kurt is alive. Thank God, Kurt is alive.

The doctor has assured us Kurt will be fine. The bullet went through, did some muscle damage, missed everything critical. Forty-eight-hours-in-a-hospital serious, not permanent-injury-or-death serious.

While Kurt is sleeping, I make some calls. First to Diana to tell her to take a cab to work in the morning. She doesn't pick up. Not surprising, given it's 4 A.M. Then I phone my work and Kurt's to say we won't be in today. I'm hanging up from the last when his eyelids move. After a few flutters of indecision, his eyes open.

"Hey," he says.

"Hey."

He clears his throat. I hand him water, and he sips it, then says, "Those are some damn fine drugs. You'll need to refresh my memory: did I piss someone off or did you?"

"Me. All me. I saw the same guy tailing me the day before last, but I mistook him for another detective. It was a stupid, careless mistake." Nearly a fatal one.

He takes my hand and tugs me over, shifting on the bed to make room for me. When I resist, he says, "If I have to tackle you, I'll be stuck in this bed even longer."

I sit. He keeps hold of my hand and my gaze.

"I'm okay," he says.

"No, you're not. You were shot, and that's my fault."

"Bullshit. It's the fault of the asshole who shot me."

"That's not —"

His hand goes to my mouth. "Stop. Shit happens. Doesn't matter what side of the law you're on."

"It's not related to my job. It's from . . . before that."

"Something to do with all this?" His fingers touch a pucker on my forearm. Where bone once jutted through my skin.

He's seen the scars. The damage is impossible to cover without hiding under the sheets, and I don't hide. The first time we slept together, he didn't seem to notice the marks until afterward. He just touched one of the knife scars and said, "You okay?" and that was an invitation to explain, but when I only said I was fine, he dropped it.

I nod. "I got myself into some trouble back in college."

He tilts his head, and I know he's thinking my marks aren't like his own physical reminders of a youth lived hard and wild: the scars, the tats, the old needle tracks. Mine suggest a single incident. A single attack.

"You paid someone back?" he says. "For doing that to you?"

I try not to look surprised that he's hit so close to the bull's-eye. "Something like that."

"And it was the kind of person who remembers, the kind who won't let you walk away and consider the score even."

"Something like that."

"I'm not looking for an answer, Casey. Not unless you've got one to give. I'm just figuring stuff out. Someone is on your ass. Someone dangerous enough to hire thugs. We're gonna need to do some serious thinking on how to fix this."

"I'll handle it."

"*We'll* handle it. I'm not in any shape to go after anyone right now, but I will be soon. If that's not enough, I know guys. Guys who owe me. We'll fix this. Until then, I know you don't like carrying your service weapon, but you need to. At all times."

He continues on, planning, working out how to keep me safe, and I can only stare at him. This man just took a bullet for me. He's lying in a hospital bed because I brought my crap to his doorstep. And all he's thinking about is how he can help me fix this. What he can do for me.

"You're really something else," I say as he finishes.

"A good something or a bad something?"

I lean over, my lips brushing his. "An amazing something."

"Nah, I'm just building up credits."

"No, you're amazing," I say. "Also? Shit at taking compliments."

He laughs, puts his hand on the back of my head, and pulls me down into a kiss.

As I walk up to my apartment, I'm thinking about the last few hours. A night of hell. A night of surprises, too, chief among them the shock of realizing I can still feel. And what I'm feeling right now? Pain and regret.

As soon as Kurt's back on his feet, I need to cut him loose. Even the thought makes me gasp for breath. It hurts. Physically hurts. I want to be selfish and jump at his offer to help and tell myself it'll all be fine and I can have this, I can have him.

Tough shit, Duncan. You dug your grave twelve years ago, and if you give a damn about Kurt, you're not going to let him fall into that grave with you.

This is what I'm thinking when I unlock my apartment door. It's not until it swings open that I realize Diana hasn't secured the interior deadbolt. I swear under my breath. I hate treating her like a child, but sometimes . . .

The security panel flashes green. Unarmed.

I dash in to see a lamp toppled to the floor, the shade three feet away, the bulb smashed across the carpet.

There's blood on the floor.

Blood on the floor.

Oh, God. Oh, *fucking* God. First Kurt. Now Diana.

I never called to warn her. No, worse — I called, and when she didn't answer, I thought, *Huh, guess she's sleeping.*

The blood turns to drips in the hallway. Those drops lead into the bathroom, and there's Diana lying on the floor, bloody water everywhere, a red-streaked towel clutched in her hand. I drop beside her, my fingers going to the side of her neck.

She's breathing.

I carefully turn her onto her back. The blood is from her nose. Broken. Again. Her lip is split; more blood there. A black eye. Torn and bloodied blouse. I quickly check for holes — bullet or blade. She moans when I touch her chest, and I rip open her shirt to see bruises rising on her torso. She's breathing fine, though. No broken ribs. No lung damage.

I take out my phone to call 911. Her eye opens. One eye, the other swollen shut. One bloodshot eye that looks up at me as she whispers, "No."

EIGHT

Diana won't let me call 911. I help her into the living room, set her on the couch, and try to argue, but she's crying, verging on sobs, shaking her head so vehemently that blood and tears fleck the sofa.

"You need a hospital," I say.

"I'm fine," she says, and shudders as she gets her crying under control.

"You were passed out on the goddamn —"

Her flinch asks me not to swear.

"You passed out on the floor, Di."

"No, my head was hurting, so I lay down. I didn't fall."

"And that makes a difference? A blow to the head means a concussion —"

"Which we have some experience treating, don't we?" She tries for a smile, and her face crumples instead. "I can't do it, Casey. I know you want me to be stronger, but I'm just so tired of this. The police won't believe me, and I can't keep defending myself. Nothing good comes of it."

"Whatever your attacker said, don't listen. It's not about Graham this time. It's my problem. I'll fix it."

Her face screws up. "You?"

"Leo Saratori found me," I said. "It was that therapist. That goddamn therapist."

Diana continues to stare in confusion. "Therapist?"

"She must have looked up my story and told someone and somehow it got back to Saratori. But it's definitely him, so no matter what your attacker said —"

"Casey, it was Graham."

"He said it was Graham?"

"No, this." She waved at herself. "It was Graham. He did this."

Is it possible to screw up more than I have in the last few days? First I tell a stranger my deepest secret and expect client–therapist privilege to cover it. Next I'm stalked in the parking garage and dismiss it. Then I go to my lover's and lead my stalker to him. And, finally, I believe my best friend is safe because her psycho ex checked out of his hotel.

I screwed up. People suffered. People I care about.

Diana tells me that Graham came by around midnight. He must have figured out she was there and, not seeing my car in the garage, hoped I wasn't.

"I did open the door," she says. "But I was

64

holding it. I only wanted to get rid of him. I had my phone out to call you if he wouldn't leave, and the next thing I knew, he was inside and he had my phone."

"We're calling the police. There's video this time. The lobby has surveillance. It'll show Graham coming and going, and there's going to be blood on him when he leaves. We've got him, Di. We've finally got him."

The superintendent knows I'm a cop, which is damned inconvenient most times — I'm the tenant she calls when she has a question about anything from eviction to parking enforcement. But I've been patient and polite, and it pays off now.

The security tapes show Graham arriving at 11:48 P.M. Twenty minutes later, he's walking out. Both times, he's wearing a jacket.

"He took it off," Diana says. "When I answered the door, he had it over his arm."

Of course he did. Easier to punch without a jacket restricting your swing. Also easy to put it on afterward and hide the blood.

Graham looks at the camera. He smiles. He mouths, "Hi, Casey," winks, and continues on.

"He said something," Diana whispers. "Right to the camera. Did you see that?"

I nod.

"Can you make out what he said?"

I shake my head. What would I say? *I did*

this. I'm sorry, Di. I was trying to fix the problem. Desperately trying to fix it, and I made a mistake. All he had to do was switch hotels and lie low for a day, and I sauntered off to spend the night with Kurt, convinced I'd scared Graham off.

I hadn't scared him off. I'd *pissed* him off.

I watch the video three more times, searching for even a smear of blood, but the quality is too poor, and he's too careful. He's done it again, and I've failed her. Again.

It's dawn when Diana begs me to let her look into her impossible town. *For both of us. Just let me ask my contact. You don't have to do a thing. I won't tell anyone your real story. We'll make something up. I'd never put you in danger, Casey. Never. I know it's a risk, but . . . Graham. And now Leo Saratori. I need to be safe, Casey. I need you to be safe, too.*

I know this town isn't real. But the only way she'll accept that is to find out for herself.

I say yes.

NINE

By the next day, Diana has a phone number to contact these people. That seems too easy — shouldn't we need to provide details, prove ourselves first? — so I insist on making contact, and she doesn't argue.

I find a pay phone and place the call. A woman picks up with "J & L Moving Services. How may I help you?" and I almost hang up. Then I process the business name. Moving services. Okay . . .

"I was given this number —"

"To discuss engaging our services to assist in your move," she says. "Yes?"

"Yes, but —"

"That's all we need to discuss at this moment. We run a very confidential service, to protect the privacy of our clients." In other words, *Stop talking. Stop talking now.* "I am unable to answer any questions you might have until we agree to proceed with serious consideration of you as a client. We are very selective. Do you have access to a fax machine?"

"Uh . . . yes?"

"Please fax us a copy of your passport and driver's license along with a number where we may reach you. That is all we will require at this time. Thank you for your interest in —"

"There are two of us," I say.

A pause. "I'm sorry. You have been misinformed. We provide services for single individuals only. We cannot assist in the moving plans of spouses, partners, children —"

"She's a friend, and we both need to move."

Another pause. "All right, then. Send both sets of identification. Thank you for your interest in our services and good-bye."

I fax the identification and provide the number from a prepaid cell I buy for communication. It's less than twelve hours before I get a call requesting our "reason for moving" — that is, prove why we need to go into hiding.

"Fax us a written note explaining the situation, along with all supporting documentation. We will require that documentation — proof of your claim."

"Anything else?" I ask. "Details on us personally."

The matter-of-fact tone takes on a slight edge of amusement. "We have your identification. That is enough for us to retrieve what we need, Detective."

Okay, they've already started doing their homework.

"There is also the matter of our fee," she says. "Five thousand each to cover the costs of the transfer and integrating you into your new home. I trust that's satisfactory?"

We'd already been warned of this, and I've agreed to pay Diana's fee as well as my own. I say that's fine and sign off.

I scan and send supporting documentation from Diana's hospital visits and official complaints against Graham, along with newspaper articles on my attack and a copy of the police report on Kurt's shooting.

Her story is the truth. Mine is that those who attacked me in the alley years ago had mistaken me for someone else, and they continued to stalk me, culminating in the attack on Kurt. Do I expect them to believe that? Not really. If there's any chance this town is legit, I'm hoping if these people call bullshit on me, they'll still grant Diana admission. She'll be safe, and that's what counts. Then I'll transfer to a new city to protect Kurt, and then . . . well, whatever. The point is that they'll both be safe.

Again, it's less than twelve hours before the next call. I'm told we've passed the documentation check and are proceeding to the next step: the in-person interview. She rattles off a time and an address.

"That's local?" I say.

"We come to you."

"And I'll meet what, a selection committee?"

"You will meet Valerie, our firm's representative and client liaison."

"She'll answer my questions, to verify the legitimacy of your firm?"

Silence.

I say, "What I mean is —"

"Yes, I understand your meaning. You wish to make sure we are what we say we are; we can do what we say we can. Most clients don't bother." A soft sound that may even be a chuckle. "But of course Valerie will do her best to satisfy your doubt, Detective. She cannot get into details — she must put our existing clientele first. But she should be able to satisfy your concerns."

Three days after Graham beat Diana, she and I are set to meet the people who say they can take us to this magical town where the lost can stay lost. I can't believe how fast it's happening, and that's not a pleasantly surprised disbelief — it's a growing certainty that we're walking into a trap. Twelve years of waiting for the worst means I don't just look a gift horse in the mouth — I want DNA samples and X-rays, and even with those, I'll convince myself there's a bomb hidden in its Trojan gut.

We meet Valerie at 10 P.M. in a random office building. Yes, an office building. She even looks at home there: middle management, late forties, graying hair cut in no discernible style, decade-old suit.

There's no small talk, no offer of coffee or tea. She ushers us straight into a meeting room that's as stark and impersonal as my apartment. Rent-an-office? Never knew there was such a thing. It does come with an interesting feature, though: one-way glass. I walk to the mirror and pretend to fuss with my hair. Then I wave into the mirror and take a seat.

Valerie is pulling a folder from her satchel when the door opens. A guy stands there. He's around my age with dark blond hair cut short, and a beard somewhere between shadow and scruff. Six feet or so. Rugged build. Tanned face. Steel-gray eyes with a slight squint, crow's feet already forming at the corners. A guy who spends a lot of time outdoors and doesn't wear sunglasses or sunscreen as often as he should.

"You," he says, those gray eyes fixing on me. He jerks his chin to the door.

"We've just started —" Valerie begins.

"Separate interviews."

"That's not —"

He turns that gaze on her, and she freezes like a new hire caught on an extra coffee break. He doesn't say another word. Nor does she. I follow him out.

71

He takes me into the room behind the one-way glass and points to a chair.

"Local law enforcement, I presume?" I say.

He just keeps pointing. Now *I* fidget under his stare, like I'm the misbehaving new hire.

"You're not getting in," he says.

"To your town, you mean. Because I don't take direction well?"

"No, because of Blaine Saratori."

I sit down. I don't even realize I'm doing it until it's too late. He takes the opposite chair.

"Did you really think I wouldn't figure it out?" he says. "You and Saratori get attacked, and he runs, leaving you to get the shit kicked out of you. Then, apparently, the guys who beat you up come back and shoot him . . . two months after your attack. Which is also a week after you get out of the hospital. And the person who called in the shooting? A young woman. I got hold of the police report. They questioned you but, considering your condition, ruled you out. Which means they were fucking lousy detectives."

No, I was just a fucking good actor. The broken eighteen-year-old girl who could barely walk, couldn't even think straight yet, certainly couldn't plan and get away with murder.

I could deny it. He can't have proof. But I'm tired of denying it. I just say, "I understand."

I don't really. There's a little part of me

that wants to say, *Why?* For the first time ever, I actually want to defend myself — to point out what those thugs did to me because of Blaine, to say I didn't intend to kill him, to say I've punished myself more than Leo Saratori ever could. Instead I only say, "I understand."

"Good," he says. "Saves me from a bullshit interview. Now we'll sit here for twenty minutes."

I manage two. Then I glance through the one-way glass. Diana is talking to Valerie.

"Will she get in?" I ask.

"No."

I look at him, startled. "But she needs it. Her ex —"

"I don't like her story. Not enough supporting evidence. You're the detective. Would you believe her?"

"Given that I'm the one who's had to mop up her blood? Yes, I would."

"You expect me to take your word for that?" He shakes his head before I can answer. "Doesn't matter. We don't run a charity camp. Usefulness is as important as need. We don't have any use for someone in — what is it — accounting?"

"Then she'll learn a trade. She can sew — she makes most of her own clothes. You must need that."

When he doesn't answer, I think about what he's just said. Two things — that he doesn't want me in this town, and that they favor those with relevant skills. Now I understand why they rushed to grant us this interview.

"Your town needs a detective," I say. "And something tells me it's not because you're low on your visible-minority quota."

He frowns, pure incomprehension.

I continue, "Someone who outranks you wants a detective, and you don't appreciate the insinuation that you — or your force — need help."

I thought his gaze was steel before. I was wrong. It was stone. Now I get steel, sharp and cold.

"No," he says, enunciating. "I am the one who requested a detective. I just don't want you."

"Wrong gender?"

Again, that look of incomprehension. It's not feigned, either, as if he genuinely doesn't know why that would be an issue.

"My age, then. I'm too young."

"You're two months older than me, and I'm the sheriff. So, no, it's not age. This isn't open for debate. I need a detective, but I don't want you. End of discussion."

"Is it? Someone made you go through with this meeting, meaning it's not entirely your decision to make, Sheriff." I look at the one-way glass again. "How about a deal? Take Diana. She won't go without me, so tell her I'm coming. Tell her that I need training and debriefing before I arrive. After she's there, I'll change my mind."

"Bullshit."

"Not bullshit. I don't want to go; I just want her to."

He looks at me as if I'm on a dissection table and he's peeling back layer after layer. At least a minute passes, and he still doesn't answer.

"One more thing," I say.

He snorts, as if to say, *I knew it.*

"I don't believe in Santa Claus," I say. "Never did. Not in Santa, not the Easter Bunny, not four-leaf clovers. Which is the long way of saying I don't believe in your town. Give me proof, and you can have Diana."

"*Have* her? I don't want —"

"But you don't want *me* even more. So this is the deal, Sheriff. . . . I ask questions, and if I'm convinced your town is plausible, I'll proceed with my application. You'll throw your support behind us getting in. Once Diana is safely there, I'll change my mind. Fair enough?"

He studies me again. Then he gives a grunt that I interpret to mean I can proceed.

I ask for the population and basic stats. Just over two hundred people. Seventy-five percent male. Average age thirty-five. No one under twenty-five. No one over sixty.

"No children, then," I say.

He pauses, just a split second, but it's enough to make me wonder why. Then he says, "No children. It's not the environment for them, and it would raise too many issues, education and whatever."

"How does the town run?" I ask. "Economically."

"Seventy percent self-sustaining. Game and fish for meat. Some livestock. Lots of greenhouses. Staples like flour are flown in."

"Flown in? It's remote, then."

"No, it's in the middle of southern Ontario." His look calls me an idiot, but I've already figured out that if a place like this *could* exist, it'd be up north. I'm just testing him.

"And how do you stay off the radar?"

He eyes me before answering carefully. "The location handles most of that. No one wanders by out there. Structural camouflage hides the town from the rare bush plane passing overhead. Tech covers the rest."

"Fuel? Electricity?"

"Wood for heat and cooking. Oil lamps. Generators, but only for central food production. Fuel is strictly regulated. ATVs for my department only and, mostly, we use horses. Otherwise, it's foot power."

"Which keeps people from leaving."

He says nothing. That's another question answered. They don't live in a walled com-

76

munity — it's just too far from civilization to escape on foot.

"No Internet, obviously," he says without prompting. "No cell service. No TVs or radios. Folks work hard. For entertainment, they socialize. Don't like that? Got a big library."

"Alcohol?"

It takes him a moment to say yes, and his tone suggests that if he had his way, it'd be dry. I don't blame him. I've met cops from northern towns, where entertainment is limited. Booze rules, and booze causes trouble.

"Police force?"

"One deputy. He's former military police. Militia of ten — strictly patrolling and minor enforcement."

"Crime rates?"

"Most of what we deal with is disturbances. Drunk and disorderly. Keeping the peace."

"Assault? Sexual assault?"

"Yes." His expression says that's all I'm getting.

"Murder?"

"Yes."

"In a town of two hundred?" I say. "When's the last time you had a — ?"

"You aren't coming to my town, Detective. You don't need this information."

But I want it. His town is in need of a detective, and there may not be much in life

I get excited about, but a new case is one of those things. A potentially unique case is enough to practically set me drooling as my mind whirs through the implications. What kind of crime would he be having trouble with, how would it be different investigating in such a distinctive setting, what would it be like, what could I learn, how would I tackle it? He's right, though. I'm not going to his town and so I can't afford to be curious, or I might regret that I'm staying behind.

So I say, "I'm asking because it shows me what I'd be sending Diana into."

"Assault is higher than it should be. So is sexual assault. So is murder. None of which I'm proud of. I've been sheriff for five years. It's a work in progress, which is why I have requested a detective."

"Five years? You're at the end of your tenure, then? We were told it's a minimum of two years in town and a maximum of five."

"Doesn't apply to me."

"Back to the crime rates. I'm suspecting they're higher than normal, given the circumstances. People feeling hemmed in, lacking options, drinking too much."

"Which is no excuse."

"No," I say. "But it'd be tricky to handle. It's worse because you must have a mix of criminals and victims, those escaping their pasts."

"We don't allow stone killers in our town,

Detective. Anyone who has committed a violent offense, it has to have extenuating circumstances, like in your case, where the council feels confident you won't reoffend. No one running from a violent crime is . . ." He chews over his words. "Those running from violent crimes are prohibited from entering," he says finally, and that chill has settled again, as if he's reciting from the rule book. "But it's the victims who concern me. They come to escape that."

Being in the same room as this guy feels like standing on a shock pad. I'm on edge, waiting for the next zap, unable to settle even when those zaps stop. But he's saying the right things, even if he doesn't mean to.

"Last question," I say. "Finances. I know Diana pays five grand to get in. In return, she gets lodging and earns credits for working, which means she isn't expected to bring expense money. There's obviously some level of communal living, but that won't cover everything. Running a secret town has got to be expensive. Who's paying?"

"Not everyone there's a saint. We have white-collar criminals whose entrance fee is not five thousand dollars."

In other words, people who made a fortune stealing from others now paid for the victims. Fittingly.

"All right," I say. "I'm satisfied. So do we have a deal?"

He makes a motion. I won't call it a nod. But it's assent of some sort, however grudging. Then he escorts me out, and as I leave, I realize I never even got his name. Not that it matters. I have what I want. So does he.

TEN

The next morning, I get a call from Val. Me, not Diana. We're in, and they need to meet us to discuss the next steps. By "they," I mean Valerie and the sheriff. I don't realize that until we show up in a local park at noon and he's there. He doesn't say a word, just points at me and then at a trail into the forest.

"Is it just me," Diana whispers as he walks away, "or is he seriously creepy?"

He turns and fixes Diana with a look, and she gives a little squeak.

I tell her to go with Valerie, and I jog after the sheriff. Even when I catch up, he doesn't acknowledge I'm there.

"Thank you," I say, because I mean it. I really do.

Only once we're past the forest's edge does he slow. His shoulders unknot just a little, and he says, "You're a goddamn train wreck, Detective Duncan."

I stutter-step to a halt. "Excuse me?"

"That's why I don't want you in my town.

Not because of what you did. I ask for a detective, and they give me one who's hell-bent on her own destruction. I don't need that shit. I really don't."

I should be outraged. This asshole presumes to know me after a background check and a twenty-minute chat?

Except I'm not outraged. I feel like I've found something here. Something I didn't get in all those damned therapy sessions, pouring my guts on the floor for the professionals to pick through, like augurs. *Ah, here's your problem, Casey Duncan.*

"Runaway train," I say.

"What?"

"A train wreck implies I've already crashed. If I'm hell-bent on my own destruction, I'm still heading for that crash. Which is probably worse, because the crash is still coming."

His eyes narrow as if I'm mocking him. I push my shades onto my head so he can see I'm not. He only snorts, his all-purpose response.

"Are you warning me off in case I try to renege on the deal? I won't. I made it; I'll stick to it, and I genuinely thank you for anything you did to get Diana in."

"Six months."

He resumes walking. Before I can speak, he leaves the path and heads into the forest. It doesn't seem to be a conscious change of direction. He just walks that way as if the path veered.

"She can only stay six months?" I say. "Okay, that's —"

"You. They insist on it. If you don't show up, they'll kick her out."

"Who's they? The selection committee?"

"Council."

I nod. "The town council. Mayor and so forth. Guess you can't escape politicians even in a town like that."

I give him a wry half smile, but he doesn't notice, just mutters under his breath. Then he stops short as the shade of the forest creeps over us, and he stares as if the trees have risen in our path.

An abrupt turn and he heads back to the path. "The council will say it's a two-year stay, but you get six months. That's between us. I'll work out an exit strategy."

When I go silent, he says, "And this is one reason I don't want you there. I'm offering you escape, and you don't give a shit."

"No, I —"

"You don't think you deserve escape. You killed a man, and you should pay the price."

I tell myself there's nobility in that, honor and justice. But in his voice, all I hear is disgust, like I'm a penitent flagellating herself.

"I'll go," I say and as I do, I realize I'm not all that upset at the prospect. There's a case up there. An experience up there. A new and unique experience. I'm chomping at the bit to ask for more — is it a string of robberies, assaults, a murder? — but I know it's not the time. Not just yet.

I continue, "You might not want me there, Sheriff, but you won't regret it. There's one thing I'm good at, and that's my job. I might be able to help with your problems."

He shakes his head. "I've seen your record, Detective. Fucking impressive. But that's here. And where we're going? It's not here."

ELEVEN

I have ninety-six hours to prepare for my disappearance. Diana has twenty-four. I expect my extra three days come courtesy of the sheriff. As a cop, he knows I shouldn't walk away from my job.

I'm about to disappear. I'm not going to fake my death. I'm not even going to vanish into the night. The art of disappearing, it seems, is not to disappear at all. You just leave . . . after extensive and open preparation. Cancel all appointments. Pay your bills. Give notice at your job. Tell your friends and family. Make up a story. Lie about where you're going, but make it clear they shouldn't expect to hear from you for a few years. If possible, give those messages at the last moment, when it's too late for them to argue.

The core concept is simple: give no one any cause to come after you. We're even supposed to overpay our taxes, as painful at that might be.

There is some misdirection involved as well,

because no matter how careful you are, a friend or family member might try to file a missing person's report. So you leave hints about where you've gone. Calgary, Valerie recommended for us. Don't say that outright, but run computer searches on apartment rentals and jobs in Calgary. Leave an "accidental" trail in case someone decides to hunt us down.

I tell my sister I'm going. It's a brief conversation. We exchange duty calls at Christmas and birthdays, and that's it. She expresses no surprise that I'm moving with Diana again. It's what she expects from her feckless little sister.

I set up my departure at work by talking to my partner about Kurt's shooting and mention bad memories resurfacing from my own assault. I tell him about the attack on Diana and vent my frustration with the system. I'll quit at the last moment, with an e-mail to my sergeant, cc'ing my union rep. I spend most of those four days at the station, getting my cases in order, so they'll know, looking back, that I'd been preparing for this.

It's the day before I'm due to leave. Kurt was released this morning, and he's ignored the doctor's orders to go straight to bed. "Had enough of that shit," he said. We're in the bar, early afternoon, the place still closed. He's not due back at work for two days, but he's prowling about, bitching like Martha Stewart come home to find her mansion in disarray.

"Fucking Larry," he says, yanking near-empty bottles from the bar. "Doesn't replace anything until the last drop's gone, no matter how many times I tell him. You let a bottle run dry, someone's gonna ask for a shot so they can stick their hand in the till while you're in the back getting the replacement. And look at the bar. Idiot hasn't wiped it down since I've been gone." He reaches for a dishrag, then wrinkles his nose. "Is this the same one I left?"

I take it from him, toss it into the laundry bin under the sink, grab a fresh rag, and tell him to restock the bottles.

I clean up, though I suspect no one other than Kurt will even notice. The bar has more rings than a Beverly Hills housewife. It's a piece of shit, but when Kurt's here, it's a spotless piece of shit.

He passes me on his way to the back and catches me around the waist, pulling me into a long, hungry kiss. I haven't told him I'm taking off, but he senses something's up.

He's replacing the last bottle when I say, "I need to leave."

He stands there, back to me, hand still on the bottle. "And by leave, you mean . . ."

"Going away. Someplace safe. Someplace" — I inhale — "permanent."

His hand tightens on the bottle. Still he keeps his back to me, his voice level. "Can I talk you out of it?"

"No."

He turns then, eyes meeting mine. "What if I —"

"No." I walk to him, and I put my hands around his neck, and I kiss him, and I pour everything I'm feeling into that kiss, everything I can't say. How amazing I think he is. How sorry I am to get him mixed up in this.

For six months, Kurt has been my hook-up. The guy I go to for a little companion-ship, but mostly for sex. He's been safe. No one I'd ever fall for. But in this last week . . .

Could we have had something? I don't know. I won't think about it. I can't.

When I pull back, he puts his hand under my chin and searches my gaze.

"You'll be safe?" he says.

I nod.

A pause. A long one. "And there's nothing I can say or do —"

"No. Please, no."

"When're you going?"

"Tomorrow."

He swears and pulls back, looking around. Then he says, "Can I have tonight?"

"You can, though I know you're probably not up to —"

He kisses me, even hungrier now, hands on my ass, pulling me against him. Then he takes my hand and slides it to his crotch.

"Am I up to it?" he asks.

I manage a laugh. "Yes, but that's not what I meant. The doctor said —"

"That I should stay in bed. Which is exactly what I'm going to do. All night. I'm gonna take you someplace nice, too. Not my shitty apartment."

"You don't need to —"

"Too bad. I'm gonna." He waves to the door. "Go on, then. Do what you gotta do. Come by at seven. Okay?"

I agree, and I leave him there, cleaning up his bar.

Kurt takes me "someplace nice" — a touristy inn outside the city. He's rented the best room, with a Jacuzzi tub, king-size bed, chocolate-covered strawberries, and cheap champagne. Diana would roll her eyes if I told her, so I won't. This is ours — our last night together — and it's damn near perfect.

We finally start to drift off to sleep around four. I'm curled up against him, and I feel him reach for something on the bed stand. He nudges me, and when I open my eyes, he's holding out a gold chain with a tiny martini glass on the end, an emerald chip for an olive.

"Couldn't find a shot glass," he says.

I smile, and he fastens it around my neck.

"Just something to remember me by," he says.

"I'm not going to forget."

"Good."

He kisses me, then presses something else into my hand. I look down. It's a key to his apartment. He catches my gaze and doesn't say a word, just nods when he knows he's said what he needs to say, that his door's always open. Tears prickle my eyes. I drop my gaze. He pulls me over to him, my head against his chest, and we fall asleep.

I don't sleep for long. I can't. I have to leave at six for my flight. So I catnap just enough to let Kurt fall into a deep, exhausted slumber. Then I slip from his grasp and tiptoe to the bathroom, where I stashed my clothing.

Before I go, I leave something for him. A letter. Saying everything I can't.

In that note, I tell him he's an amazing guy. That I'll never forget him. That I'm so glad I met him. I don't say I'm sorry for what happened — he knows that, and this is about him, not me. I tell him it's time to stop stashing away his money. Time to quit his job at the docks and go back to college for business, to get a job running a real bar and then someday open his own. That's his dream, and the only thing holding him back is self-doubt.

Even if six years have passed since he went straight, Kurt still feels like a two-bit convict. He's not. Never was. He screwed up as a kid

— we all do. It's time to get past that and make a real life, for him and his son. Yes, his son. It's time for that, too. To fight for visitation rights. To stop listening to his ex tell him how wonderful her husband is, how much better a father he makes, how much better a role model. *Kurt* is the boy's father. He's supported his child since birth, and he deserves this, too. Time to take what he's owed, as hard as that might be. He'll be better for it. His son will be better for it. I have absolutely no doubt of that.

I put the letter on my pillow, resist the urge to risk waking him with a good-bye kiss, and then I leave.

TWELVE

My journey starts with a rental car in the park where we'd last met, keys under the floor mat with instructions for me to drive not to my local airport but to one six hours away. Then I'm to catch a plane to Vancouver. When I land, I get the confirmation code for my second flight up to Whitehorse. That's Whitehorse in the Yukon Territory.

Flying out of Vancouver, I see nothing but city and mountain and sea. When we descend from the clouds? Green. At first, it looks like fields. Then we dip low enough for me to realize it's trees. No fields in sight. No towns, either. Just trees in every direction.

I see mountain ranges, too. I only hope the snow on top of them is glacial ice and not a hint to expect winter already.

One thing I don't see? Signs of people, not until we're closer to the airport, where a few roads cut through the forest. They're beige zigzags wandering through the hills, as if going nowhere in particular. There are lakes too, including one with bright green water, almost neon.

I'm so busy gawking that I barely notice we're landing until we're down. It's a small airport with only a couple of baggage carousels. The sheriff meets me at one. He doesn't ask how my flight went. His greeting is "Got a six-hour drive ahead of us. Get your bags and then we'll hit a drive-thru for dinner."

"I ate earlier. I'll just grab something at our destination."

"Nothing will be open when we get there. You want to eat on the way? Your options are pop, chips, and whatever else you can buy at a gas station."

"Okay, we'll hit a drive-thru." My bag arrives. I grab it and then ask, "How's Diana?"

"Fine."

That's all I get. As we're heading out, I say, "Do you have a name?"

"Most people do."

We cross the road to the parking lot.

"I could just call you Sheriff for six months."

"Works for me." He pops the back on a little SUV. "Dalton," he says at last. "Eric Dalton."

Then he gets into the car. It's going to be a long six hours.

We pick up dinner and head out. The city fades in a blink, giving way to forest and mountain. When something black shambles onto the road, I jolt forward in my seat, saying, "Is that a . . . bear?"

"Yeah."

Dalton stops the SUV and drums his fingers on the wheel as the bear ambles across, taking its sweet time. When it's halfway over, it turns and snarls.

"Yeah, yeah," Dalton mutters.

"Is it safe to be this close?"

He gives me a look like I'm asking if it's safe to be this close to a dog crossing the street. "It's a black, not a brown."

"Okay . . ."

"Black bear," he says. "Browns are twice the size. Better known as grizzlies."

"There are grizzlies here?"

"About seven thousand of them. They usually stick to the mountains."

"And the town isn't near a mountain?"

"No. It's near two."

Great . . . I'm quiet for a moment, seeing if there's anything pressing he needs to discuss. When he stays silent, I see the chance I've been waiting for.

"You have a case for me," I say.

"What?"

"Something's going on up there. Something that urgently requires a major crimes detective."

"I never said that."

"You said you needed —"

"I admitted that I'm not qualified to investigate serious crimes," he says. "My father is in law enforcement, so I grew up with it, but I don't have any formal police training. Definitely no detective training. The town needs more than a thirty-year-old sheriff. I'm making sure it gets everything it needs."

"But there must be a case. A current one. Otherwise, you guys wouldn't have jumped at the chance to bring me in."

He looks at me. "How many detectives you think apply to come up here? I figured, if we were lucky, we might get some old drunk who hasn't been off a desk in twenty years. A young homicide detective with a record that impressed even me? Of course I jumped. Same as we'd jump at someone with medical experience, even if we have a damn fine doctor and no urgent need of more. We get too many like your friend, practically useless in a town like ours."

"So you have absolutely no outstanding major cases?"

He shrugs. "Got a guy went missing a week ago. Took off into the woods."

"I'm a detective, not a bloodhound."

"Well, then, guess you'll have to wait for a real case. In the meantime, there's lots of regular policing to keep you occupied."

I want to call bullshit. They were too eager to bring me in, even at the cost of my "practically useless" friend tagging along. Something's going on. But Dalton's not telling me about it. Not yet.

"All right, then," I say. "Can you tell me about the regular policing? What are my duties?"

"Take everything a small town cop would do . . . and double the workload."

He spends the next half hour giving just a taste of what I'll be doing in the town — Rockton, as he calls it. That half hour is his limit for conversation, though I suspect we only scratched the surface. After that, it's a silent drive on an empty road. We enter an area where periodic signs mark past fires with dates, and I can still see the damage, twenty years later. I catch a glimpse of what looks like a huge deer at the roadside.

Dalton grunts, "Elk," and that's it for the next thirty minutes, until I start seeing brown rodents darting across the road and popping up along the side to watch us pass.

"Are those prairie dogs?" I ask.

"You see prairie?" Before I can answer, he says, "Arctic ground squirrels." I think that's all I'm getting, but after a few more kilometers he says, "Won't see them much longer. They'll hibernate soon, sleep for seven months." Another pause, maybe a kilometer in length, then he says, "Body temperature goes down to below freezing."

"How's that possible?"

He shrugs. "Bigger question is how their

brains survive on stored energy for that long. I've read some articles. It's interesting. Potential applications for human brain degeneration."

I try to prod him on that. Or I do after I recover from the shock of it, because he does not strike me as a guy who sits around reading scientific journals for fun. He ignores the prods, and I wonder if it's because of my pause — if he offered something that could start an intelligent conversation, and I was obviously floored by the prospect, so to hell with me.

We've been on the road for about three hours when he stops for gas. When he'd said that would be the limit of my dining options, I'd thought he was exaggerating. We *have* passed two restaurants. One was closed. The other was not the sort of place I'd trust with my digestive health.

The "towns" we've passed though were no more than hamlets. When I remark on this to the store cashier, she laughs and says there are more moose than people in the Yukon. I think she's joking, but when I ask Dalton the territorial population, he says it's thirty-five thousand, three-quarters of whom live in Whitehorse.

"How large is the territory?"

He climbs into the car. "You could put Germany, Belgium, and the Netherlands in it and have room to spare."

I remember dismissing the idea that you could hide a town in this day and age. I have only to look out the window to imagine how one could lose a town of two hundred in the wilds beyond this lonely highway.

When we finally reach Dawson City, Dalton says it's too late to fly out to Rockton. We'll stay the night and leave early.

Outside the town, I see endless piles of gravel covering the landscape — as ugly as scars after hours of forest and hills and lakes.

"Did something happen here?" I ask.

"Gold."

"I know. The Klondike Gold Rush. Over a hundred years ago."

"Nope, gold's still there. Those are dredge-tailing piles, from mining the river. Stopped in the sixties and restarted a few years back. Floating excavators spit up this shit on the ground and leave it because, hell, it's only empty land. Doesn't matter if you dump a damned riverbed all over it."

"They don't have to clean it up?"

"It's not environmentally harmful, and up here no one gives a shit about the rest. Lots of other places to look if you want scenery."

He might brush it off, but I can tell the blight on the landscape offends him.

As we continue into town, I feel as if I've time-warped back to those Klondike days. Old-fashioned wooden buildings. Dirt roads. Board sidewalks. When we stop at an inn,

Dalton tells me to remove my shoes inside.

"Is that a custom here?"

"When the roads are made of dirt, it's common sense."

"Is there a reason for the dirt roads? Construction issues? Materials? The climate?"

"Tourism."

As I leave my sneakers in a "shoe room," Dalton checks in. He's clearly been here before, but he doesn't say much to the proprietor, just tells her we'll be having breakfast and then gives me my key and says we're heading out at eight.

I'd been a little surprised that eight was Dalton's idea of an early departure, but when I rise at seven, it's still dark out. We're far enough north that the days are getting short fast.

I go down for breakfast and Dalton's there, staring out the front window at the empty street. It's an equally empty room, and I wonder if he'll want to enjoy his meal in peace, but he waves me over.

I chat with the owner, who's from Switzerland and brings a plate of cold cuts, cheese, yogurt, and amazing freshly baked bread. Dalton continues staring silently out the window at the dark morning. Then, as I'm polishing off another slice of bread, he plunks my cell phone between us.

"You said you don't have ties. Just a sister,

and you aren't close." He gestures at the phone. "You forgot your boyfriend."

"I said —"

"You told us the guy who got shot is someone you were hooking up with. That" — he gestures at the phone — "is not a hook-up."

Following instructions, I'd shut my phone off as soon as I left home and removed the SIM card shortly after. Once here, I turned it over to Dalton for safe disposal.

I turn on the phone. There's a message that must have come in just before I took out the card, and I'd been too distracted to check.

Got your note. It means a lot. Means a fucking lot, Casey. You're right, and I'm going to stop pissing around and step up. But I want you to do the same. Wherever you go, start over and do it right. Get a life, as the saying goes. Even if you don't think you want one. You deserve it. I know you said I won't see you again, but if I do, I want to see you happy.

I sit there, holding the phone, staring at that message.

"I need to send —" I begin.

"No."

"But —"

"No." Dalton leans forward. "Is this a problem, Detective?"

My hands shake a little. I clench the phone to stop them, but he plucks it from my hands.

He's right. I've missed my chance to reply, and that's my fault for not checking. Any message I send now could be traced to Dawson City.

"I'll — I'll get my things," I say.

I push back my chair and hurry off.

THIRTEEN

When I realize we're heading to the local airport — not a private runway — I ask Dalton how we're going to leave without giving a flight plan. At first, he only says it's been taken care of. Then he relents and says that flying from a private strip would be more suspicious, and it's better to stick close to the law as much as they can. As far as the airport authorities know, he works for a group of miners, flying people and supplies in and out of the bush. Given their occupation, they're a little cagey about where exactly they're working, so his flight plan is approximate.

It might also help that this is the smallest commercial airport I've ever seen. The terminal is one room with a ticket counter and a few chairs. There's a hatch in the wall labeled baggage. Apparently, that's the luggage carousel.

I presumed the car was a rental, but the terminal doesn't have a rental agency. When I ask, Dalton says that someone will pick it up. There are no rentals in Dawson City. At all.

Inside, he takes a bottle of water from his bag along with a tiny pill envelope. "From the doc. She's on the selection committee, so she sees the files, real names redacted. Given your background, she thought you might need those."

I look at him, uncomprehending.

"They're for flight anxiety or whatever."

I keep staring, and he says, "Your parents?"

My cheeks flame as I realize he means because I'm about to get into a small plane, not unlike the one my parents died in. I didn't even think of that. I suppose that's because it happened so quickly. Another couple — fellow doctors — owned the plane, and the four of them had been heading to Arizona for a golf weekend. I hadn't even known they were going.

I don't need the pills. Even as I think now of how my parents died, I don't fear the same will happen to me. Should I? Is that proper empathy? Proper grief?

I pocket the pills with thanks, say I should be fine, and follow him out.

We spend the next ninety minutes in a bush plane so noisy both of us wear earplugs and neither says a word. Below, trees stretch as far as I can see. It's as beautiful and majestic as it is haunting and terrifying.

I've often heard people talk of feeling small

and lost in a city. I've never experienced that, having always lived in one. Out here, looking at those endless trees, I feel it, but it's not a bad small or even a bad lost.

During the first pass over Rockton, I notice a clearing that looks like a lumber camp. The buildings . . . It's hard to explain, but I don't see most of the buildings, just a big clearing with a few wooden structures. Structural camouflage, like Dalton said. He also mentioned yesterday that there's a blocking system that keeps passing planes from picking up the town's footprint.

When we make a lower pass, I see Rockton, and it really is what Dawson City tries to be — a Wild West town. Dirt roads. Simple wooden buildings. A clearly defined town core. Houses a fraction the size of those found in a modern city. Chicken coops and a small goat pasture. I even spot a stable with horses out for their morning feed.

When Dalton brings the plane in, there's no one around. No ground crew. No welcoming committee. Am I disappointed by that? Yes. I expect to see Diana here, eagerly awaiting my arrival. But if she's not, that must mean she's settling in, not anxiously waiting for me. Which is good.

Dalton leaves me to unload our luggage while he drives an ATV out of the hangar. A cloud of dust brings another ATV zooming our way. I start to smile, certain it's Diana. It isn't. Not unless she's turned into a black guy with bulging biceps and a US Army tattoo. The deputy, I'm guessing from the tat.

I peg him at early thirties. Seriously good-looking. When he grins, I update that to "jaw-dropping." Yet as much as I'm appreciating the view, it's a neutral appraisal, like admiring a sunset. I won't mind gazing at this guy across my desk every day. That's all.

He's off the ATV and walking over, hand extended. "Welcome to Rockton, Detective."

"It's Casey," I say, and before I can add a *please,* Dalton says, "Butler." That's my new surname.

"Casey, then. I'm Will Anders."

I detect a slight accent that reminds me of a guy from Philly I once dated.

"You'll call me Will," he continues. "Just like you'll call him Eric, no matter what he says."

A snort from Dalton, who takes my bag and heaves it onto the ATV.

"And as much as I'd like to pretend I came roaring out to greet the new hire, it's business." He turns to Dalton. "We found Powys by the streams. Looks like . . ." Anders glances my way. "Natural causes."

Well, I guess that's my welcome, then — a dead body the moment I arrive.

"Heart failure?" I guess.

"Environmental. When I say natural . . ."

"You mean nature. Okay. Let's go take a look."

Dalton slaps a hand on the ATV's backseat, blocking me. "Will? Get on. Butler? Take that one."

I glance at the other vehicle. "I can't drive —"

"Station's two minutes that way." Dalton points.

"That's not where the body is."

"But that's where you're going, Detective. This isn't a homicide."

"Which is up to me to determine, sir. That's my job."

He doesn't remove his hand from the seat.

"All right, then," I say. "I guess I'm walking."

I don't get more than five steps before Dalton is off his ATV and in my path, so close I nearly ram into him. When I back up, he advances, uncomfortably close.

"Eric . . . ," Anders says, his voice low.

"Did I give you an order, Detective?"

"Yes, but —"

"No buts. Either I gave you an order or I didn't, and I don't know how it works down south, but out here, you disobey an order, and you'll find yourself in the cell until morning."

Anders steps between us. He shoulders Dalton back, keeping an eye on him, much the way one might ease off a snarling dog.

106

"He's kidding," Anders says. "He'd only keep you in there until dinner hour." A wry smile, and I'd like to think *he's* kidding, but I get the feeling he's not.

"I know you'll want to come along," Anders continues, "but you just got here. What we have out there is death by misadventure. Not homicide. Normally, that'd still be your gig. But let's just hold off. We'll bring the body back, and you can take it from there. Reasonable?"

I nod.

He looks at Dalton. "See how that's done?" Then a mock whisper for me. "*Reasonable* isn't really in Eric's vocabulary. You'll get used to it."

The grin he shoots Dalton holds a note of exasperated affection, as if for a sometimes-difficult younger brother. Dalton only snorts and points at the back of the ATV.

"I thought I'd drive today, boss," Anders says. "You hop on back."

Dalton gets on the ATV and revs the engine.

"That means get on or I'm walking," the deputy says to me. "Eric drives. Always."

I nod. It's not a tip about transportation. Employee relationships might be a little casual here, but Eric Dalton is in charge, and I'd best not forget it. Which is fine. That's one reason I like being a cop. My brain understands paramilitary relationships, often better than normal ones.

Anders gives me directions to the station and then says, "Go directly there. Park out back and head in the rear door. Anyone flags you down? Pretend you didn't see him. Anyone comes into the office? Tell him to come back when we return. Wait for us to make the proper introductions." He glances at Dalton. "Well, wait for *me* to do it. Poke around the station, and we'll grab lunch when we get back."

"Is Diana — ?"

"Later," Dalton says. "You're on the clock, Detective."

"Diana is fine," Anders says. "A bunch of us went out for drinks last night. She's doing great. As much as I'm sure you want to see her, wandering around town isn't wise. Not until you've settled in."

He waves me to the ATV, gives me a ten-second lesson on how to drive it, and takes off with the sheriff.

Fourteen

As Anders said, getting to the station is easy. The fact that I made two wrong turns may have more to do with the ATV ride itself. Dare I say it was fun?

My first boyfriend had a dirt bike. He'd lend me his sister's so we could ride into a nearby gravel pit. I encouraged those gravel-pit trips, which gave his ego a much-needed boost. I just never admitted it was more for the ride than the make-out sessions that followed.

When my parents found out, they grounded me for three months. Not because I was sneaking off with a boy. I was fifteen, and they trusted I was smart enough not to jeopardize my future by getting pregnant. It was the dirt bike that disappointed them; I'd showed a distinct lack of judgment. My mother gave me medical files from horrific motorcycle accidents and then quizzed me afterward to be sure I'd read them. The world is a dangerous place. You don't add to it by doing crazy things like riding dirt bikes. Or fighting back against gangbangers in an alley.

Sometimes, though, taking risks is the only way to feel alive, and that's what I feel as I whip along those wooded trails, purposely missing my turns. I want to keep going, to ride into the forest and see what's out there, lose myself in that emptiness. But that's where embracing risk becomes irresponsible, one lesson my parents did manage to drive into my brain like an iron spike. Never be irresponsible. People are counting on you.

The scenery — like that on the drive up — is breathtaking. As Dalton said, the town is in a valley between two mountains, but they're distant enough that they don't cast shade. One is partly bare on this side, and when I see it, I think, *I wonder if I could climb that?* And I laugh to myself, imagining what my parents would say.

The police station is on the edge of town. Like all the other buildings I can see, it's a basic wooden box raised off the ground. There's a rear deck with a single Muskoka chair and a tin can full of beer caps. The can is rusted, as are the caps below a layer or two. Someone bringing the occasional beer onto the deck, not someone regularly getting loaded on the job. Good to know.

Inside, it's dark and cool and smells of men: spicy deodorant laced with a thread of sweat. The main room is the size of my apartment bedroom. There's one desk, a couple of extra chairs, a fireplace with a hanging kettle, and filing cabinets. That's it. Two doors lead to other rooms. I open one, expecting to see the sheriff's office. It's the bathroom. The other reveals a tiny holding cell.

I look around. One desk for three cops? This should be interesting.

The filing cabinets are all locked, and not flimsy jobs that can be pried open with a butter knife. So much for advance case study.

I look at the desk. The top is clear, without so much as a paper clip to play with. And the drawers? Yep, locked.

Anders told me to poke around. That's taken exactly five minutes. I scan the room again and see one thing I missed: a bookshelf. It's mostly empty, the space being used for office supplies instead. I count five books. The first one I pull out is a history of the Mongol tribes. I flip through, expecting to find it contains hidden information. Nope, it's actually a history of Mongol tribes. I walk to the desk, plunk myself in the chair, and start to read.

About twenty minutes pass before the front door opens. A thirty-something guy rolls in on a wave of sawdust. He's muscular in a top-heavy way. Longish hair that looks like it's been raked back with a hand covered in wheel-grease, leaving a streak of it on his cheek. Shirtsleeves pushed up to show off overdeveloped arms.

My first thought is uncomfortably like my thought on seeing someone in a prison — I wonder what he's in for. That's not fair, of course. Not here, where most are like Diana, running from a problem that isn't their fault. And Dalton has already warned that I'm not entitled to a resident's backstory unless he deems it pertinent to a case.

"Hey, there," the man says. "You must be the new girl."

"Detective Butler," I say. "Casey. If you're looking for the sheriff or Deputy Anders, they'll be back in an hour or so."

"Left you all alone on your first day? Typical Eric. Well, I'm Kenny, and I'm with the local militia, so I'll take over as the welcoming committee. We can grab lunch, and I'll show you around a bit."

A hand reaches from nowhere and lands on his shoulder. "Down, boy."

A woman steps around him. She's probably in her early forties. Wearing a business-smart dress that shows off an admirable figure. Dark eyes. Dark hair laced with silver. A very attractive woman, even without makeup, which is one of those "nonessential" items we have to skip up here.

"I saw you boys hanging around out front," she says to Kenny. "Finally figured out she slipped in the back, did you? How much did you pay the others to let you come in first?

Or was it a coin toss?"

Kenny grumbles. Her hand tightens on his shoulder and turns him toward the door.

"Head thataway, Kenny boy. If Eric catches you horndogging on his new detective, he'll dunk you in the horse trough again. At least it's not winter this time."

She pushes him toward the door. After he trudges out, she looks at me for the first time. It's a thorough once-over, as if she's sizing me up for a bikini.

"Oh, my," she says. "Good thing you *didn't* come in the front door, sugar. Kenny would have needed to put his buddies down before they'd let him get the first hello. Your friend is cute, but you . . . Did Eric bring a body-guard to keep you company? Because otherwise, that boy is in for some trouble."

"I'll be fine."

"He did mention the male-female ratio in this town, didn't he?" she says.

"I'm accustomed to working in a male-dominated environment."

She throws back her head and laughs. "Ah, sugar. You have no idea what you've walked into. But we'll discuss that another time. Right now, I need local law enforcement at my establishment, and it seems you're it. Ever break up a bar fight?"

I check my watch. "Not before noon."

"Welcome to Rockton."

As we walk, the woman introduces herself. Isabel Radcliffe, owner of the Roc.

"Used to be called the Rockton Arms," she explains, "until we lost most of the sign in an ice storm. Did Will tell you about the Roc? I'm not going to ask if Eric did. Our local sheriff is a lot better at communicating with his fists. Luckily for us."

I glance over to see if she's being sarcastic. She catches my look. "Again, welcome to Rockton, sugar. Whatever you think you know about keeping the peace? It doesn't apply here. This place does something to folks. You just met Kenny. Any idea what he did down south? His occupation?"

"Construction worker? Carpenter?"

"Try high school math teacher. When he arrived eighteen months ago, he'd never have worked up the courage to talk to you. People come here, and it's a clean slate. A chance to be whoever they want for a while. Fantasy land for grown-ups. Which leads to a whole lotta trouble for the local constabulary, because nothing folks do up here will follow them home."

As we walk down the main street, I can't shake the feeling I'm being tailed by acrobats and a marching band. People spill out of doors to get a look at the new girl. Every half dozen steps, a guy saunters our way. Isabel raises a hand. She doesn't say a word. That hand goes up, and it's like casting an invisible force field. They turn back. When one whines, "I'm just being friendly, Iz," she says, "You want to set foot in the Roc this month? Turn your ass around." He does.

She waves me to a building that looks as nondescript as the police station. From the end of the second-story balcony hangs a sign announcing it as THE ROC. A wooden sign under that depicts a bird that is probably supposed to be a roc, but the artist has confused the mythical creature with a rook.

I don't hear any trouble within. Is the fight over? Or is this some kind of local welcoming ritual? I decide to play dumb and follow Isabel inside.

The main floor is twice the size of the police station. There's a bar along one end. Tables fill the rest. It's not nearly as run-down as Kurt's place, but there's still that sense of basic utility, the one that says you're here to drink and nothing more.

The bartender is a few years younger than me. A burly, dark-haired guy, he looks quite capable of handling any fight, but he's currently reading a novel, as is a pencil-necked guy in the corner. Another man is drinking a beer and so engrossed in his thoughts that he doesn't even look over when we walk in. The last two patrons are a couple in their late thirties, sharing a half pint of wine. Both are nicely dressed. Average-looking. They could be any long-married couple out for a lunchtime tipple.

"I'm not seeing the fight," I say.

"Oh, it's coming. Wait right there, Detective. You might want to pull out your firearm. Just don't shoot straight up. There's a customer sleeping it off right above your head." She nods toward the bartender. "That's Mick. Former city cop. Former local cop, too. He'll help out if you need it, but I'd just as soon keep him behind the bar."

Because he's extremely busy reading that novel. He gives me a nod, though, friendly enough.

Isabel walks to the couple. She stops beside the woman and stands there at least twenty seconds. The guy keeps glancing up, but the woman is making a concerted effort to pretend she doesn't see Isabel.

"You aren't welcome in here, Jen," Isabel says finally.

"It's a public place, bitch."

The insult — and the venom behind it — startle me. The woman looks like she should be teaching third-graders.

"No," Isabel says, more respectfully than I'd have managed. "My establishment is not communal property. I pay for that privilege. Now, go home, get clean, and then we'll discuss you coming back."

Get clean? I could say Isabel meant "sober up," but I get the feeling this lady is careful with her word choices. I walk closer and size up Jen. I notice her pallor, despite the fact summer has just ended. Her pupils are slightly constricted. Her clothing hangs as if she was two sizes larger when she got it. It's not proof positive of drug addiction. This is a restricted community. They may choose not to prohibit alcohol, but they sure as hell should be able to control drugs.

"What are you looking at, asshole?" Jen says. I think she's talking to me. Then I see she's addressing the guy sitting with her, who's staring at me like I'm covered in chocolate and sprinkles. His eyes are glazed over, and my gut tells me it's not from a half glass of Cabernet. Jen looks up at me, and her eyes narrow. "Fuck, don't tell me you're the new cop."

"She is," Isabel says. "And she's here to escort you out."

Jen snorts. "That itty-bitty girl? Fuck, no. And, you, asshole, stop gaping at her or — Hey, I'm talking to you!"

She lunges at the guy. Literally dives across the table, grabbing him by the shirtfront, screeching like a banshee. As I go after her, Isabel murmurs, "Well, that's not how I expected it to go down, but the end result is the same. I'm going to have blood to clean up."

I grab Jen. She takes a swing. I wrench her arm behind her back, and she howls. She keeps struggling, though, and I keep wrenching, until I'm about a quarter inch from breaking the bone. When she still doesn't stop, I slam her against the wall. That's when her companion decides some chivalry might be in order. He's on his feet, telling me to let her go.

"As soon as she stops trying to hit me," I say.

"Back off, Ted," says Mick, who is walking our way, possibly having hit a chapter break.

"Sit and enjoy the show, Ted," says the beefy guy with the beer.

Ted grabs for my arm. I see it coming, and a roundhouse kick puts him down without me needing to release Jen. The guy with the beer shows his appreciation by cheering while Ted dives for my leg and tries to bite it. Yes, bite. Another kick sends him flying and then Beer Guy is on his feet tackling Ted, and two other guys have come from God knows where, and they're getting into it, and someone outside shouts, "Bar brawl!"

I don't know exactly what happens after that. Not because I'm caught up in the chaos, but because I'm ignoring it. I have my job, and that job is getting Jen out of the bar.

I'm strong-arming her toward the door when the pencil-necked guy with the book decides to make a break for it. He elbows past us . . . and catches a right hook from a shape filling the doorway. I'm about to use Jen to power past the newcomer when I see his face. It's Dalton. He ignores me and barrels down on Book Guy, who's sprawled on the floor.

"He's not part of it," I shout over the chaos.

"The hell he's not," Dalton says, still bearing down on the poor guy.

"No, really, he —"

Someone tries to take Jen from me. I go to yank her back and then see it's Anders.

"Ignore him," he says, waving at Dalton. "Jen? Sheriff's here, and you know how he feels about rydex. You got five seconds to —"

Jen's already running.

"Good choice," Anders says. "Now, let's clear this mess. You know how to do it?"

"Stomp the bullies first."

He grins at me. "You got it. Let's have ourselves some fun."

FIFTEEN

We're back at the station. With the pencil-necked guy. Dalton marched him, in cuffs, all the way from the Roc. Now he's got him pinned to the cell wall, lifted clear off his feet and gasping for breath.

Some older cops bristle at the term *police brutality.* "Intimidation," they call it. Or, as others would say, "speaking the only language assholes understand." But they only mean physical dominance. Shove the guy around. Grab him by the hair. Dig your fingers into his kidneys *accidentally.*

That isn't what's happening here. I'm watching my new boss choke a guy half his size. A guy who wasn't part of the brawl. Who hasn't raised his voice or a finger in his own defense.

Every time I rock forward, Anders shakes his head. Telling me to keep it cool. Promising me answers. But I don't know Anders. I don't know either of them. All I know is that I'm witnessing something that makes me very uncomfortable.

"Butler?" Dalton says. "Empty his pockets."

I do. There's a wallet, keys, and the worn paperback he was reading in the bar. That's it.

"Now take his clothes." When I hesitate, Dalton turns that gaze on me. "Did I give you an order, Detective?"

I manage to get the man's shirt and trousers off. Dalton has me seal them in an evidence bag that Anders holds out.

"I warned you the last time, Hastings," Dalton says. "I'm going over your clothes with a goddamn magnifying glass, and if I find even a speck of powder —"

"There's always powder," Hastings says. "I'm a chemist."

"No, here you're a lab assistant. Which means if I find powder, you'd better hope to hell the doc confirms it's from this morning's work."

"I don't wash my clothes every day, you moron. We aren't allowed —"

"Don't care." Dalton hauls the smaller man up to eye level. "You're the only fucking chemist in town, Hastings. Which means you're the one making rydex. And as soon as I can prove it, I'm kicking your ass out."

"You can't. I've only been here a year, and I was promised a two-year —"

"When I say kick you out, I mean put your ass on the back of my ATV and dump you in the forest. You know what's out there, Hastings?"

The man glowers at him.

"No," Dalton says. "I don't think you do. But it's your lucky day, because I have visuals. We found Harry."

"What?" Hastings takes it down a notch. "Is he okay?"

"For a smart man, you ask some dumb questions. He spent a week in the forest. From the looks of it, he didn't last past the first nightfall. But don't take my word for it. I'm going to escort you to the clinic, where you can see exactly what'll happen if I find out you have anything to do with the rydex. Fair warning, though? I really hope you haven't had lunch yet. Because you're about to lose it."

Dalton hauls Hastings out the front door, still dressed in his boxers. We watch them go. Then Anders turns to me. "So, speaking of lunch, are you hungry?"

I do not want lunch. What I want at this moment is to grab Diana and get the hell out of here. But I squelch that and tell Anders I want to see the victim.

"Sure, I'll take you over." Then, "And Eric's right. Better skip lunch until afterward."

As we walk, I resist the urge to ask Anders about the body. Better for me to see it and form my own impressions. I do ask about the

122

drugs, though.

"Rydex," he says. "That's the local name for it. Opiate based. Highly addictive. And one of the most serious problems we're dealing with right now."

"One?"

"Yep," he says. He doesn't elaborate, just goes on to explain that rydex is a homegrown drug that's been circulating for a few years, which means it predates Hastings's arrival, but it was only *after* Hastings got to Rockton that it became a serious problem, meaning Dalton suspects Hastings tinkered with the formula to make it more addictive.

"Where's he getting the ingredients from?" I ask. "Presumably, if he's working at the clinic, he's using prescription drugs, but it's easy enough to monitor that. And only Dalton has access to the outside world, right?"

He catches my look. "Hell, no. Don't even go there, Detective. Eric might not have made the best impression so far, but he's the last person who'd smuggle in dope. There are other shipments. Drop-offs. The ingredients must be getting in that way. We just haven't figured out how."

"Okay, but . . . ?" I say. "Not to sound critical, but this is a town of two hundred people."

"Why can't we contain it? Therein lies the real problem of Rockton, Casey. We can't control anything they don't want controlled.

And by 'they,' I don't mean . . ." He waves at a few people on the street.

"You mean the town council."

He gives a humorless chuckle. "Around here, we just call them the council. Can't be a town one if they aren't actually in town."

"What? The sheriff said . . ." No, I'd called them a town council — he just hadn't argued. "So the selection committee is an off-site board, and the town politicians are a different local governing body."

"There is no local governing body. There are long-term residents who have clout — Eric, Isabel, the doc. But the people in charge live down south. They're the investors. They sure as hell don't live here. They have Val here to act as their mouthpiece. That's all."

"But what are they *investing* in? They can't possibly make money . . . Wait. Sheriff Dalton mentioned white-collar criminals who pay more to get in. Not all that money goes to running the town, does it?"

"Nope."

"So Rockton is run by a bunch of investors who sit in an office tower and make decisions for a town they visit every year or so."

He snorts a laugh. "I don't think most of them have ever set foot in Rockton. This town is an unholy mess, Casey, and the first thing you need to know is who gives a damn and who doesn't. Those who do? *Really* do? I can count them on one hand. Top of the list? The guy you're working for."

I must look doubtful, because he says, "We won't debate his methods. I could, but I think you're best to just watch and draw your own conclusions. In his defense, I'll only say that *no one* cares as much about Rockton. Eric isn't like everyone else here. First off, he's native."

I consider this for a few steps. I'm not wondering whether our blond-haired, gray-eyed sheriff could have First Nations blood — my sister can pass for white, while I can't. What I'm wondering is what his heritage has to do with his commitment to the town.

"So Dal— Eric is . . . a Native Canadian," I say.

Anders looks over and then laughs. "No, not like that. He acts like it, with all the time he spends in that forest or sitting on the damn porch staring at it. Though I suppose that'd be a stereotype, wouldn't it? No, I meant he's from here."

"The North?"

"Here." Anders waves around us. "Born and bred, never going to leave."

"You mean he's actually *from* Rockton. I didn't think anyone — Well, obviously some would be. You can't fill every position with people looking to escape, and you can't have them all leave again after five years."

"True. Some folks are in this for the long haul, like me. But up here, 'long haul' usually

125

means ten years tops. Eric is the only exception. His parents came here together. His dad was the former sheriff, and Eric was born here."

That's why Dalton had hesitated when I mentioned kids. Rockton used to have one: him.

Anders continues. "When his folks retired down south, Eric took over as sheriff. He's not going anywhere. Which means he's the one person you can count on to have Rockton's best interests in mind. Not necessarily the best interests of every individual person, but the town as a whole, as a concept, if you know what I mean."

"A sanctuary for those who need it."

He nods. "Exactly. And for Eric, that sure as hell doesn't mean bringing in healthy people and sending back addicts. I was an MP in the army. I know what isolation can do to people's heads. I know what being away from home and feeling unaccountable can do, too. Add drugs to that mix, and it's ugly, Casey. Just plain ugly. This town has enough problems without that."

SIXTEEN

On our walk across town, I ask about the raised buildings. Anders explains that's to keep them off the permafrost, so you don't have icy floors or tilting houses.

Every building also has lots of windows, and I ask Anders about that too, because there's obviously no place nearby to make glass. He says it's flown in, which isn't easy or cheap, especially since they're all triple-paned for the weather. But they splurge on windows to let in as much natural light as possible and keep the houses from feeling too much like prison cells in the long and dark winters. And they all have shutters to help keep out those winter blasts.

There are plenty of decks and balconies, too, and people are making use of them, sitting outside as they work. I notice Anders isn't the only one in short sleeves, enjoying what must be a warm fall day to them. It's only September, and sunny, but I'm wearing a jacket, and when that sun drops, I suspect

I'll be unpacking my gloves.

We arrive at the clinic, which looks like every other building. And, like every other one, it seems to be only as big as it needs to be. I'm guessing that's the heating issue and possibly conservation of overall space and materials.

As we open the door, we hear Hastings.

"— how long you'd last as a real cop, you knuckle-dragging psycho? Real cops don't get away with this shit, which is why you hide up here, where you can act like the fucking sheriff in a fucking Wild West show."

I glance at Anders. He's paused in the reception area, making a hurry-up gesture in Hastings's direction, waiting for the tirade to end. Just another day in Rockton.

Hastings is still going strong. "You think you can intimidate me, asshole? I've been dealing with bullies like you all my life. You might be bigger and stronger, but I'm a helluva lot smarter, and you're going to regret you ever laid a finger on me."

Silence. Then Dalton with, "You done?"

"No, I'm not. I'm speaking to the council, and I'm going to make sure you're disciplined, Dalton."

"Disciplined?" Dalton says the word slowly, as if testing it out, and I can't suppress a small smile. "Sure, if that's how you want to handle this. I thought you said you were going to make me regret it, though."

"Oh, I'll make you regret it. Using my brains. Not my fists."

"By tattling to the council on me? Shit. I was hoping you were going to get creative."

Anders chuckles and then walks to the doorway.

"Hey, boss," he says. "Doc ready to talk to us yet?"

"I am," says a woman's voice from deeper in the building. "Jerry? Take the afternoon off and cool down. Will? Come on back."

Hastings storms past me without a sidelong glance. He strides out the door, apparently having forgotten he's still in his boxers.

I follow Anders into what looks like an examination room. It's no bigger than the reception area — which held two chairs and the requisite table stacked with old magazines. We follow Dalton into a slightly bigger room, with another exam table and instrument trays. I resist the urge to look at the covered body and turn my attention to the doctor herself.

She's in her late thirties. Chestnut-brown hair pulled back in a ponytail. Dressed in jeans and a T-shirt, she's pulling on a lab coat as we walk in.

"I don't know whether I'm hoping you're right about Jerry or not, Eric," she says. "If he's making rydex, I can fire his whiny ass. But it also means I lose my lab assistant. How sure are you?"

"Ninety percent."

She swears under her breath. Then she sees me. "Ah, yes, sorry. First thing we lose out here? Basic manners." She extends a hand. "Beth Lowry. Harvard med school class of '01. Charged with malpractice in 2010. Guilty."

"Charged with . . . ?" I say, certain I didn't hear correctly.

"I'm getting it out of the way." She flashes a humorless smile. "People come up here and meet the local doctor, the first thing they think is, 'I hope she's not fleeing a malpractice suit.' So I clear the air with an affirmative. I'd been working double shifts for a month after two surgical residents quit. Living on amphetamines. I could point out they were supplied by the chief of staff, but that would suggest I was a wimp who didn't have the guts to refuse." She purses her lips. "Not entirely untrue. Point is, a patient died in my care, due to a stupid mistake that was one hundred percent my fault. But two other patients had died that month, under mysterious circumstances, and the administration fudged the records to make it look as if I'd played a greater role in their treatment. I was willing to take the blame for the mistake I made, but not the ones I didn't. When it started looking like a criminal case on top of the malpractice, I came to Rockton."

"Okay," I murmur, because I have no idea

what else to say.

"The good doctor believes in laying her cards on the table," Anders says.

"You'll find that a lot up here," Lowry says. "People who just say 'screw it' and either embrace total honesty or fabricate their lives from whole cloth."

"You done confessing?" Dalton asks.

She shoots him a look. "It's not —"

"Sure as hell is, Doc. Now tell us what we've got here."

"A dead man."

Now that look comes from Dalton. Lowry smiles and turns to me. "I'm guessing you know all about the case, Detective Butler?"

"It's Casey. And I haven't been . . . fully briefed yet."

"Really, boys? Here's a hint. If you hire a detective, you want her to detect. That requires talking to her about the cases."

"She's smart," Dalton said. "She'll pick it up."

"Oh, I know she's smart. IQ of one thirty-five. University GPA four-point-oh."

She rattles off my stats like they're tattooed on my forehead, which is a little disconcerting. And a little weird.

"I'm on the admittance committee," she explains. "Plus, I have a photographic memory. Your mom was a chief of pediatric surgery. Dad was a cardiologist, well enough known that I recognized his name. Medical-field background and a near-genius IQ. So I have to ask, Detective, what the hell are you doing in law enforcement?"

I say only, "It's what I like."

"Good answer. Bet you got used to saying it to your parents."

I don't reply and try to conceal my discomfort with the rather blunt observation.

"Want to know what my parents were?" she says. "Law enforcement. Never could understand why I'd want to go around cutting people up. Especially when my own IQ is barely above a hundred." The grin returns. "The photographic memory is what got me through med school."

Anders leans over and mock-whispers, "Don't mind Beth. She's a little odd. Everyone here is. Except me, of course."

"Are we cutting this guy up today, doc?" Dalton says. "Or is tomorrow better for you?"

"I'm making conversation. It's not often we get new bodies in town." She looked at the covered corpse. "Dead ones, though? A dime a dozen."

"She's kidding," Anders says.

"Have you told her the homicide stats?" Lowry says. "I interned in Detroit. Rockton's rate is ten times that."

"There are extenuating circumstances," Anders says.

She shakes her head and disappears through a door in the back.

He continues, "And ten times the rate only means we had one homicide in the past year."

"Better make that two," she calls back.

Anders looks down at the covered body. "Shit."

As Dr. Lowry scrubs up, she calls for Anders to fill me in.

"First," he says, "we weren't trying to make things tough for you. At least, I wasn't." A meaningful glance at Dalton. "It's just that everything up here is a hundred layers of complicated. Ideally, you'd have come in, and things would have been quiet, and I could have spent a few days showing you the ropes and gradually explaining —"

"No time," Dalton says.

"Right, so the point is —"

"The point is there's no time for a gradual explanation," Dalton says. "Including right now. It's not going to take Beth a week to scrub in." He points to the corpse. "Harry Powys. Former doctor. He was caught doing illegal organ transplants, using illegal immigrants who weren't always dead before he started. And you can wipe that look off your face, Detective. We sure as hell didn't approve a son of a bitch like that. We approved a pharmacist who'd been blackmailed by a prescription drug ring."

"That was my fault," Lowry says as she walks in. "I sympathized with the blackmailing, and I wanted someone with pharmacy training."

"Stop confessing. We all approved him. Including me. And before you think we're all fucking morons, Detective, I'll point out that the paper trail was solid."

"You mean they're fabricating records," I say. "Those in charge. The council."

Dalton stops, mouth still open. I seem to have accomplished the impossible: I've surprised him.

I continue. "Drugs are being smuggled in, presumably in the drop-offs handled by the council. You have Hastings, a chemist who can manufacture designer drugs. Now you have this guy. It's possible he faked his background records, but more likely the council did. They're letting in hardened criminals. Including murderers who'd woo immigrants hoping for a better life and carve them for a profit."

"It's not the whole council," Lowry says.

Dalton gives her a look, as if to say, *And that makes it better?* Then he says to me, "Good work, Detective. You've earned your rep. Yeah, we believe they green-light criminals who will pay a shitload for the privilege. Unlike with the white-collar guys, none of that extra goes to running the town. The council members pocket it all."

I stare at him.

"Back to work," Dalton says, as if we've

just discussed a rather dull town bylaw. He waves at Lowry. She hesitates and glances at me, knowing I want more. I nod for her to go on. I'll deal with this later, after I've processed it.

Lowry peels back the sheet. I see the body of Harry Powys, and my stomach churns. I'll partially blame what I've just learned — about the town and about him. But the body . . .

I've witnessed autopsies. I was always fine with taking that chore from my partners. My parents inured me to gore — via surgery videos — from an early age. That's because they wanted me to have a strong stomach for a career in medicine, but they inadvertently prepared me to be a cop, too.

One thing you don't see on a city beat? Predation — the point at which a victim turns into meat. That's what I'm looking at here. A side of half-devoured meat wearing a human head and the tattered remains of clothing.

I don't throw up. I'm not even tempted. But I do decide I'll skip lunch today. Anders looks green, though he stands his ground. And Dalton? He's right in there, as if this is a biology dissection sample. He's circling the body, leaning down for a better look, poking at the spots where both legs have been removed. He even grabs a blunt probe from the tray and prods aside some of the mangled flesh.

Lowry watches while he examines the ribs. Then he looks at her. She nods.

"Fuck," he says.

He shakes his head and drops the probe back on the tray with a clatter.

"You said homicide?" I begin.

She nods. "Looks like massive blood loss."

"We didn't see that at the scene," Anders says.

"Because the body was moved."

"By predators?" There's a note of hope in his voice. *Please, please tell me this was a grizzly.*

"Possibly," she says. "There are signs of animal predation."

I look at her and hope my disbelief isn't too obvious. *Signs* of animal predation? The body is hamburger. *Half* a hamburger. You don't need a medical degree to know something has eaten Harry Powys.

"So, massive blood loss," I say. "Could be a bullet in the femoral artery, but we don't have the legs to check that. It's not the neck." The head is the one part relatively untouched, except for the eyes, which have been pecked out. "Stabbing?"

"Cutting."

"Cut . . ." I look toward the missing legs. "You mean he was . . ."

"Alive, most likely."

"A saw?" I manage to ask.

"Hatchet."

"At the hip?" I say. It's not an easy cut, and I'm struggling to imagine holding a man down for that.

"The upper cut appears to be postmortem. I'm guessing there was a lower one. Likely the knee."

"I've seen dismembering once. But that was chopping up a corpse for disposal. Why kill him by hacking off his lower legs and *then* remove the thighs?"

I walk to the tray and take the blunt probe Dalton used. I push aside flesh from the ribs. As I do, I mentally process the condition of the flesh. It isn't tattered. Not the way I'd expect from a beast with teeth and claws. I'm looking for evidence of those teeth and claws on the ribs. Instead, I see knife marks.

Harry Powys hasn't just been murdered. He's been butchered. By humans.

SEVENTEEN

When I tell the others what I think happened, Anders stares at me. Then he looks at Lowry and Dalton. After a moment, Dalton says, "Yeah." Anders looks at the body again. Then he's in the next room, puking in the sink. It only takes a minute, then he's storming back into the autopsy room, wiping his face on his sleeve.

"You knew about this," he says to Dalton.

The sheriff grunts.

"Cannibals?" Anders stalks over and plants himself in front of Dalton. "You've got fucking cannibals in the forest, and you didn't see fit to tell me?"

"Did you read the files?"

"What?"

"The files I gave you. The town's background. What we have out there."

"I went through them."

"*Flipped* through them. Didn't actually read them. Or you'd have known that we've found evidence of cannibalism before. Been a few years and, yeah, it's questionable. But the possibility has always been there, in the files. Not my fault you did a half-assed job reading them."

"Cannibals, Eric? Fucking cannibals, and you can't be bothered —"

"Telling people everything that might be out there? Yeah, I'm just lazy that way."

"I don't mean —"

"Folks don't argue when we insist on escorted hikes and hunts, because they know ninety percent of the danger out there. The other ten? That's the fine line between scaring people and shoving them into outright panic." He waves at the corpse. "This would be panic. So it's need-to-know, and if you didn't read the goddamn files, then I guess you don't need to know too badly."

"Um . . . ," I say. "Cannibals? Can we talk about —"

"Read the files." Dalton heads for the door. "Then we'll talk."

"Where the hell are you going?" Anders says.

"To think. You stay for the autopsy. Beth? The report goes to Detective Butler."

Anders mutters under his breath. Dalton gets as far as the next room. Then, "Butler?" Curt. Impatient. As if I should know I'm supposed to follow him. I take one last look at Powys, and then I leave.

■ ■ ■ ■

We get three steps out of the clinic, and Dalton says, "Beer?"

I jog to catch up. "What?"

"You drink beer?"

"Uh, no. There are a few things we need to talk about, Sheriff, and beer definitely isn't on the —"

He wordlessly turns into the Roc. There are more people there, and the bar has been cleaned up since the fight. Isabel's at a table, talking to a patron. She says, "Sheriff," when Dalton walks in. He strides behind the bar.

"What do you drink?" he asks me.

"Tequila, but I don't need —"

He pulls out two bottles. "Which one?"

I hesitate before pointing to the cheap brand. He snorts, puts that one away, and takes the other to the door.

Isabel blocks his exit. "Help yourself, Sheriff."

"I did."

"From your pissier-than-usual mood, I'm guessing that you didn't find anything on Jerry. Can I bar him from my establishment now?"

"No."

"I'd like —"

"Too bad. I want him to keep coming here," Dalton says. "It's the place he's most likely

140

to screw up."

"And what do I get in return?"

"My grudging tolerance of your establishment."

"You can't shut me down, Eric."

"Not officially, but I can sure as hell find a way to make you decide to shut your doors." He moves her aside. It's not a shove, but it's not a gentle nudge, either.

As we pass, she calls after him, "You know what, Eric? I bet you'd be a lot happier if you did more than *grudgingly tolerate* my establishment. I don't believe I've ever met a man more in need of —"

He turns on her so fast she jumps.

"I was teasing you, Eric," she says, her voice softening.

"You want to make me happier? Stop complaining about Hastings and help me pin something on him, so we can get these drugs out of our town."

"I know," she says. "I'm sorry."

He grunts.

She moves closer. "About Powys . . . I know you don't like answering questions on open cases, Eric, but I heard . . . it was bad."

"He'd been in the forest for a week. Course it's going to be bad."

She studies him. "And if anyone asks, that's what I tell them. Until you're ready to say more."

"Yeah."

She nods and he starts walking.

She calls after him, "Keep the bottle, okay?"

"I planned to."

"Asshole," she says, but there's no venom in it.

Dalton walks half a block and then lifts the bottle of tequila. "One shot."

"I don't really need —"

"One shot on the job. Off the job? Three max."

"I don't drink more than two shots. Ever."

He glances over. "You got a problem?"

"You mean, am I an alcoholic? No. It's a personal choice."

He studies me, in that way that makes me struggle not to squirm. Then he grunts and turns away.

"Stick to it," he says. "I catch you drunk? Twenty-four hours in the cell. I catch you high? I'll march you down to Beth for testing, and if it comes back positive, you're on maintenance duty for the rest of your stay."

"All right."

He stops, eyes narrowing. Then he notices we're being watched by a half dozen locals, and he marches silently on to the station. As soon as we get inside, he closes the door and says, "I'm serious, Detective. I don't make idle threats."

"The last time I was drunk, I wasn't even legal drinking age. The last time I got high was on pot at eighteen, and it made me throw up. I don't drink, and I don't do drugs, and I'm not going to start because the job's rough or I get bored. But if somehow I do, then you can throw me in your cell or fire me. I wouldn't say 'all right' if it wasn't, and I don't appreciate being growled at for agreeing with you."

I expect a snapped reply, but instead he seems to contemplate this. Then he walks to the bookcase, takes a mug, and pours a rough shot of tequila in it. I consider telling him — again — that I don't want it, but after what I saw and heard at the clinic, I wouldn't mind that shot. I'm just wondering if he's testing me. After he pours my shot, though, he takes a beer from the icebox. So I down the shot before he can uncap his beer. His brows lift. I put the mug on the table.

"Can I see those files?" I ask.

"That's what we're here for. I thought you could use a drink while you read them."

"It's tequila. You don't sip it."

He grunts and, beer still in hand, unlocks a file cabinet and flips through, pulling files. Then he passes the stack to me. I look around at my choice of chairs, but before I can pick one, he says, "Weather's good," and motions me to the back deck.

I start toward it. He says, "Grab a chair."

"I'm fine."

We go outside. He takes the Muskoka chair. I lower myself to the deck. He looks at me.

"Get a chair, Butler."

"I'm fine."

His lips move in a "fuck," and he shakes his head. I feel like there's some expectation here, and I keep falling short, and I'm not quite sure why. I've been in town only a few hours, and I've already held my own in a bar fight. I didn't complain when he roughed up a local. I didn't puke over a grisly corpse. I figured out that the council is taking kick-backs for letting in criminals, *and* I determined what happened to that corpse. Yet what *does* make an impression — the wrong one — is when I decide I don't need a chair. There's a code here, and I can't decipher it yet, so I just settle in with the files.

Two hours pass like that. I'm reading the files, and Dalton is thinking. Or I presume that's what he's doing. For two entire hours he sits, sips his beer, and stares — just like Anders said — into "that damned forest." At first I think he's there to answer my questions, but several times I look over expectantly, even clear my throat. He ignores me.

I read the files. I do some thinking of my own. Then I go inside and get my notebook, and I come back out and make notes, and Dalton never even glances my way. Finally, when I'm done, I say, "Can we talk? About this?"

He doesn't even look over, just says, "Tomorrow. It's getting late."

While it's barely past six, the sun is dropping fast. I walk to the front railing and sit
on it, not directly in front of him but no
longer behind him, either.

"I'd like to meet the council," I say. "I know
they don't live here — I mean meet them by
satellite phone or however Val stays in touch.
I don't want to question them or confront
them — I just think it'll help me get a better
handle on things."

He shifts, as if it takes genuine effort to
turn and look at me. "They won't talk to you.
They barely talk to me. You have to speak
through Val, who's just their hired spokesperson. I'd suggest you ignore her. I do."

"Is she involved in . . . ?"

"Green-lighting criminals?" He shrugs.
"Doubtful. Does she know about it? Maybe.
But if she does, I bet she figures they've committed crimes a whole lot lighter than murder. I can't see her hanging around if she
thought there were hardened killers in our
midst."

"Exactly how many murderers do you
suspect are here? After everything Diana's
been through, I sure as hell didn't expect her
to be trapped in a town with —"

"What about you?"

"If you're pointing out that her best friend
is *also* a murderer —"

"Would you tell me you're different?"

"No, I would not."

That should be the right answer. But his jaw sets, as if this isn't the response he wants.

"Your friend is safer here than she is down south," he says. "Our murderers aren't psychopaths or serial killers. Powys is the closest thing I've found, and in his case it was all about profit; there's no illegal organ trade up here. The last two murders we had were alcohol and frustration and a basic lack of self-control . . . by people who came to Rockton legitimately. That doesn't mean I want these other sons of bitches here. Anything I can do to kick their asses out, I will."

I'm processing that when he rises and says, "Time to show you your quarters. Best to get an early night." As we walk inside, he says, "I'm going to insist on that early night. Once you're in, you're in. Someone will have dropped off basic supplies and dinner. I'll come by at eight tomorrow to collect you."

"I'm under house arrest? What have I done to deserve that?"

"You arrived in a town full of bored people looking for novelty. And you arrived on a day one of our residents was found murdered."

"I'm accustomed to dealing with the press and nosy neighbors, Sheriff. I've worked on high-profile cases."

He looks at me as we walk to the front door. "Do you want to go out?"

"I'd like to see Diana, obviously."

"She's free to come to you. Otherwise, do you *want* to go out?"

When I don't answer, annoyance crosses his face. "So you're just arguing for the sake of challenging my authority?"

"I —"

"This isn't how you're used to working or living," he says. "I get that. But you forfeited your civil liberties when you came up here. That was made very clear. You want to get on my bad side? Whine about your rights, like Hastings this afternoon. This isn't a democracy. It's a police state, and you're the police, so start acting like it. If you want to go out tonight, then I'll arrange something. But don't argue for the sake of arguing. We'll find plenty of real issues to fight over up here."

He doesn't give me time to agree, just locks the front door and leaves out the back, expecting me, as usual, to follow.

EIGHTEEN

The forest starts about fifty feet from the rear of the buildings. That gap has been left not so much for yard space, I suspect, as security, making it tough for large animals to wander up unseen.

We cut through those "backyards" from the station to the north edge of town. From what I saw in the air, houses near the core are tightly packed; the configuration loosens at the edges. All the boundary houses are identical — one-and-a-half-story buildings with steeply pitched roofs. A rear deck and upper-level balcony add extra living space to homes that would have less than a thousand square feet inside.

Dalton walks onto one rear deck and opens the door. We go in and it reminds me of a cottage. A nice cottage, that is, with polished wood floors and tongue-and-groove walls.

The back door opens into the kitchen. He points out the amenities. No electricity — generators and solar power are only for food service buildings. They can't afford the fuel to give everyone a generator, and covering the town with solar paneled roofs would turn it into a big, shining beacon for planes passing overhead.

As for water, an indoor tank is filled weekly from one of the two nearby springs. The tank is elevated, allowing pressure, and there's a hand pump if needed. The stove takes wood. There's an icebox, which contains actual ice, harvested in winter and stored for warmer weather. The icebox itself is under the floor, to keep it low and cool.

Dalton walks into the living room. I follow. There are two chairs and a sofa. All are rustic but sturdy, with wooden frames and thick cushions.

I look around. "I'm staying here?"

His gaze moves to my bag, which someone has left across the room. That answers my question, saving him from speaking.

I gingerly lower myself onto the sofa. It's big and soft and wonderfully comfortable.

"There's a fireplace," I say, and I can't fight a small smile. I've never had a fireplace. My parents turned ours into a significantly safer media cabinet.

"Two fireplaces and a woodstove," Dalton says. "You'll need to learn how to chop wood."

"Okay."

He looks at me as if I'm being sarcastic.

When he sees that I'm not, he nods. The front door opens, and he starts for the hall.

"Casey?" Diana calls.

I smile and rise from the sofa. "In here."

She barrels past Dalton and throws herself at me in a hug. "Finally! I kept asking when you'd come in, and no one would give me a proper time, and then all of a sudden, I hear that you got in this *morning.*"

"She was busy," Dalton says.

"I asked to be notified —"

"And I vetoed that. She's here to work. I had work for her."

He's already heading for the kitchen. Leaving out the back, I presume.

"Ignore him," I murmur. "How's everything going?"

She grins then, a huge blazing grin, the sort I haven't seen since the day Graham asked her to marry him.

"It is *amazing,*" she says. She runs her hand through her hair, droplets of water flying. "I just got back from a quick dip. It's freezing, but it feels so good."

"There's a pool?"

She laughs. "The pond. There's a lake, too, but you need an escort to go there."

"Um, you do know there's no filtration system in a pond, right? Or a lake?"

Her grin widens. "Yes, we went swimming in a dirty pond."

"We?"

From the way her face glows, I know the other half of that "we" isn't a woman. I try not to stare at her. I probably do. Thrown into a new situation, Diana usually just lies low and observes, like a rabbit in its hole. I was certain she'd be hiding in her lodgings, waiting for me to come and take her around. Obviously not, and I'm thrilled to see it.

"So are you boarding here?" she asks.

"I guess so."

"Hopefully it won't be for long. I had to board the first night because my place wasn't ready. I have an apartment now. If you'd like, you can bunk with me until they find you a permanent place."

"I'm sure this will be fine. But thanks."

We walk into the kitchen and find Dalton poking through boxes on the table.

"There's dinner in there," he says, pointing at one. "Enough for your friend if she stays. Basic supplies in the rest."

"When do I get to meet my landlord?"

He frowns at me.

"The people I'm boarding with."

"There's no one else, Detective. This is your place."

Diana blinks. "This is Casey's *house*? But . . . I get . . . I have an apartment. It's less than half the size of this, with no yard and —"

"Essential services. If you provide one, you get better lodgings than those who don't."

"How's that fair?"

He turns those steel-gray eyes on her. "Casey will be working her ass off, twelve-hour shifts, six days a week, to keep this town safe. You work five hours a day sewing patches on jeans and new buttons on shirts. You want better? Work harder or train for a new position. *That's* fair." He heads for the door, calling back, "Eight A.M., Butler. Be ready."

Diana joins me for dinner but has to leave at nine.

"I have a date," she says, that glow returning.

I smile as we settle onto the sofa. "With your swimming partner?"

"Nope, someone else."

Her grin turns wicked, like she's sixteen and announcing that she kissed two different boys in the same weekend.

When I don't react, she jostles me. "Haven't you always said I need to date more? You should be happy for me."

"I am happy," I say. "This is my happy face, remember?"

She laughs. "Okay, okay. I'll admit, the male-to-female ratio in this town helps my popularity, but it's more than that, Case. It's the whole . . ." She waves her hands. "Atmosphere. It's like band camp. Which you never went to, and it's not like you needed that anyway. You never have a problem meeting guys. So I've been taking advantage of the opportunities before you arrive and they all forget my name."

"That's not —"

"When we walk into a bar, guys only glance my way if you shoot them down."

I protest. This topic of conversation comes up far too regularly for my taste. I'm no femme fatale, and Diana is no wallflower. I joke that she's welcome to all the guys in town and then say, "Work will keep me plenty busy. And I'm . . . not exactly looking." I absently finger the martini glass necklace.

"How's Kurt?"

"Doing okay."

"Good." A moment of awkward silence. Then, "Speaking of guys, how about that deputy, huh? He's just your type. Brawny. Gorgeous. Not likely to win a Mensa membership anytime soon."

"Hey," I say, with genuine annoyance.

"Oh, I'm sure Will is bright enough. Just not on your level. No one's on your level."

I try to keep my voice even. "Plenty of people are *above* my level."

"I'm not."

Goddamn it, Di. Five minutes ago you were glowing with confidence. And now this shit?

She makes a face. "Sorry. I'm a little scattered. It's great here, but . . . after Graham . . . I guess I'm a little on edge, waiting for the other shoe to drop."

"It won't." *I'll make sure of it.*

She twists her rings. "Maybe I should cancel my date. I agreed yesterday, when I didn't know you were getting in today."

"We have another hour. Then you're walking out that door and going on your date."

She struggles for a smile. "Is that an order?"

"It is."

After Diana leaves, I clear my head by exploring my house. The upstairs is a loft bedroom, with a balcony overlooking the forest. Standing on it, I wonder where I can get a chair so I can sit out here with my morning coffee and watch the sunrise. When I realize it might not be that easy to procure a chair up here, there's a split second of near panic. And I have to laugh, because I have never bought a piece of furniture in my life. Nor have I ever had the urge to sit out and watch the sunrise. My new balcony doesn't even face east.

But I have a house. And it's kind of awesome.

Without a book to read, I'm in bed by ten. But once I'm there, all I can think about is those files Dalton gave me. I also realize how quiet it is. My back window is cracked open, and I hear nothing. For a city girl, that's unnerving. When I strain, I do pick up sounds: a distant laugh, the crackle of undergrowth, the hoot of an owl. But there's no steady roar of street traffic or even the hum of a ventilation system. When I hear a howl, I practically fall out of bed.

There aren't any dogs in Rockton. No pets allowed. And I know what a coyote sounds like; this isn't it. That can mean only one thing: I'm hearing wolves.

I push open the balcony doors and step out to listen. The sound is distant, meaning there's no danger that a pack of wild canines will charge from the forest. It's not that kind of sound anyway. Not a warning cry, but a beautiful and haunting song. I go back inside to grab my blanket, and I lower myself to the balcony floor, my back against the wall as I stare into the forest and listen to the wolves.

There's more out there than wolves. More than bears and wild cats. That's what I read in those files. What is beyond the town borders and how it got there.

Rockton was founded in the fifties by Americans escaping political persecution during the McCarthy years. Some had returned to the US when they felt it was safe. Others remained and opened Rockton to people seeking refuge for other reasons. When the town struggled in the late sixties, a few wealthy former residents took over managing it and organized regular supply drops. That's when the town began evolving from a commune of lost souls into a police state secretly sheltering hardened criminals.

Some residents became dissatisfied with the

changes, wanting a more natural and communal lifestyle. They left Rockton in small groups and "went native," as the saying goes, giving up even the primitive comforts of the town to live off the land. Rockton calls these people — and their descendants — settlers.

But there are others out there, too. Those who aren't just living like a modern-day Grizzly Adams. Those who lost something when they left Rockton — lost their humanity and ultimately reverted to something animalistic. The hostiles.

That's why residents can't wander around in the forest without armed escorts. Sure, wolves and bears are a concern, but the bigger threat is the people who live in the forest. Step on their territory, and they'll treat you like a trespassing predator and kill you on sight.

Like the wolves, though, the hostiles aren't exactly on our doorstep. They're a bigger danger to the settlers, because both live deep within this seemingly endless forest, while the average Rockton citizen doesn't go more than a half mile in, and only on escorted trips during daylight hours. The deaths occur mostly with hunting parties and the deep-woods patrols that keep an eye out for hunters, loggers, and other potential intruders.

As for cannibalism, like Dalton suggested, the evidence is far from conclusive. It's just a matter-of-fact possibility. In his notes, I saw the man who'd talked about the medical implications of ground squirrel hibernation. It was like reading an article in a sociology journal, the language precise, the vocabulary wide, the text thoughtful and analytical at the same time. He doesn't think there are mad savages in the woods intent on devouring the flesh of their enemies. Rather, if there is cannibalism, it will be a matter of survival, the need for food during harsh times.

It's not winter now, though, meaning there was no such reason for butchering Powys. Either we were seeing signs of a more ritualistic cannibalism or Powys had been deliberately cut up as a message — a warning from those in the forest.

Like Dalton, I'm a realist. I'm not shocked by accounts of man-eating bears and tigers. If you're on their turf, you're a threat and potentially dinner. Fair enough. As for humans doing the same, obviously I'd like to think we're above that, but if we've lost what it means to be human, would we not see people as these animals do?

What does bother me, thinking of those hostiles, is an anxiety I can't quite nail down, so I sit on my balcony, with the wolves howling and the breeze bringing tendrils of fireplace smoke, and when I close my eyes to drink it all in, that's the last thing I remember thinking. That I like it here. In spite of everything, I like it.

NINETEEN

"Butler?" The voice cuts into dreams of whipping along a forest path on an ATV.

"Butler?" Then, "Goddamn it," and a brusque hand lands on my shoulder.

I bolt awake, blanket falling free. Dalton is on my balcony, looming over me.

"Huh? Wha— ?" I shake off the confusion and start to rise, then realize I'm dressed only in my panties. I pull the blanket to my neck as I get to my feet.

"What are you doing out here?" he says.

"I . . ." I blink hard and look out at the still-dark forest, my brain refusing to find traction. "I couldn't sleep. And wolves. There were . . ." I trail off, realizing how silly that sounds, but he nods, as if this requires no further comment.

"You'd better have your service revolver under that blanket," he says.

I blink harder. Then I realize Dalton is standing on the balcony. *My* balcony. In the middle of the night.

"Wait," I say. "Did you break into my —"

"I have a key. You weren't answering the door."

I yank the blanket higher and peer into the dark night. "Tell me it's not eight A.M. already."

"It's not. We have a problem. First, though, if you're out here at night, you'd damned well better have your gun."

"Why?" I wave over the side of the balcony. "Do we have flying monkeys in the forest, too?"

"Keep your gun at your bedside. Always. That's an order, Detective."

I shake my head. "I'm not being difficult, Sheriff. Therapists call it a hypersensitive survival instinct. If I have a gun and I see a threat, I could use it to defend myself before I fully process the extent of that threat."

He snorts.

"And no, that's not my excuse for what I did down south. But if I'd had my gun out here, there's a good chance I would have shot you."

He shakes his head and walks back inside, saying, "Get dressed. Come down. Hastings is missing. Someone saw him heading into the woods two hours ago. We need to find him before he gets himself killed."

We step outside, and Dalton hands me a lantern. A blast of bitter wind hits me, and I pull my jacket tighter.

"You want to grab something warmer?" Dalton asks.

"I'm fine."

"Let me rephrase that: Get the hell back inside and put on something warmer, Butler."

I obey. I'm grabbing a sweater when I remember seeing a bag of what had looked like outerwear with my supply boxes. I dump it and find gloves, a hat, and boots, all much thicker than the outerwear I brought. I scoop up the hat and gloves and hurry outside.

Anders has joined Dalton on my front porch. My first thought is, *I have a front porch?* Followed by, *My front porch has a chair — I could haul that up to the balcony.* I shake off the whim and yank on my gloves as I greet Anders. Dalton is already on the move, disappearing into the dark.

"Rule number one for working with Eric: keep up," Anders whispers as we jog after the sheriff. "Two years later, I'm still trying."

Dalton has headed around the rear of my house. He's moving fast along that strip of yard, as if this is his secret road past the traffic-jammed streets of Rockton.

When we reach him, I say, "Can I make an observation?"

He snorts. "Well, that's a fucking stupid question. I hired a detective, not a mime."

"It's an observation that might question

what we're about to do."

"Still a fucking stupid question. If I wanted someone to blindly obey everything I say, I'd have hired another army boy."

"Thank you, Eric," Anders says.

"Though, on second thought, Will, blind obedience might be a step up, considering you never read those files."

"Not going to drop that, are you?" Anders said.

"Nope. Butler? Talk. And if you ever have an idea about an investigation and you *don't* tell me about it . . ."

When he doesn't finish, I say, "Trying to figure out how you could enforce that without mind-reading skills?"

Anders chuckles. Dalton looks over, sees my smile, and nods.

"Yeah, it's unenforceable," he says. "So I won't threaten. But you get the point. I hired a detective because I expect ideas. I'm tired of doing all the thinking in this department."

"Ouch," Anders says.

"That's not an insult." A few more steps. "Not really. I *could* use more thinking from you, Will. You're smart enough, so there's no excuse other than that you're accustomed to following a commanding officer. You're a good soldier. I need that. I also need more."

"You know what neither of us really needs at two A.M., Eric? Brutal honesty."

Dalton stops short. I think he's going to

comment on that, but he's scanning the darkness.

"You got the militia up and out?" he asks Anders.

"I'm a good soldier, remember?"

Dalton ignores the sarcasm. We're right on the edge of the woods. He's still stopped. I start to speak, but an abrupt raised hand stops me.

"He's listening," Anders whispers. "The wind speaks to him."

The deputy gets a look for that. Then Dalton starts walking again and says, "Butler? Talk."

"Right. Okay, so you said Hastings took off into the woods, but I'm questioning the logic of that, given what he saw on that autopsy table. Even if he doesn't realize it might have been cannibalism, the sight of someone presumably ripped apart by wild animals is not going to send him running *into* the woods, is it?"

"Your suggestion?"

"That he's still in town. He's a petty little man who is not above sending you on a wilderness goose chase at two A.M."

"Good," he grunts. Then he keeps walking into the forest.

"Good but wrong?" I say.

"Good call on character. Hastings is a weasel. Fifty percent chance he's done exactly what you said. Which is why I have the militia searching town."

"Oh. So you're a step ahead of me."

"I'd be a lousy sheriff otherwise."

"But you still think he could be in the woods. May I ask why?"

He motions for us to stay back while he hunkers down at the forest edge to examine something.

"Because the locals don't always believe us about the woods," Anders answers for him. "It's like saying the moat is filled with man-eating sharks and killer electric eels. Some think we're lying about the danger to keep them inside."

"But Hastings saw the corpse."

"And might be telling himself *we* did that to the body."

"What? That you or Dalton butchered Powys postmortem? Why?"

"To keep folks out of the woods. As a scare tactic, it'd be senselessly extreme and stupid, not to mention revolting and barbaric, but you heard Hastings — to him Eric is a savage with a badge."

Dalton's on the move again. We're following.

"I know there aren't any pets in town," I say. "But wouldn't it be good to have a dog for tracking?"

"Don't need it," Anders says. "We've got Eric."

Dalton shoots him the finger and keeps

walking along the forest's edge. He stops abruptly and crouches again, and now I realize what he's doing — searching for signs of where someone might have entered the woods.

When I say as much, Anders nods. "There are only two maintained paths heading in, but there are smaller walking trails if you know where to find them. Running pell-mell into the forest is crazy. Following one of those maintained paths is also crazy, unless you're looking to get caught fast."

We look over to see that Dalton has disappeared.

Anders sighs and calls. "Yo, boss! We missed the nonexistent signal. Follow or wait?"

No answer. Anders glances at me. "That means follow. You eventually learn to read the code. It'd be easier if we just equipped him with signal lights. Red for stop. Green for follow. Yellow for 'take a guess and get your head bitten off if you're wrong.' Except it'd probably be stuck on yellow most of the time."

"I heard that," Dalton calls back.

"Good. And yes, we're following."

I don't see the path until we're on it. I've hiked before. But my idea of a path is a groomed trail wide enough to ride a bike on. This is barely a slice through the trees; branches catch me on both sides. Even the worn dirt underfoot vanishes as the trees close in and the ground becomes a carpet of dirt and needles.

"Patrol check?" Dalton calls back.

"He's asking about the daily militia patrols," Anders explains. "They report in to me. One thing they look for is signs that someone went into the woods."

"Patrol check?" Dalton repeats, with an added snap.

"I'm using a teaching moment. It's the only way Casey will learn anything. And the patrols haven't found evidence of a wanderer in three days." He glances at me. "That tells Eric whether the signs he's picking up could be from another day. It's not impossible that someone wandered off without us knowing it, but we've got a good catch ratio. High penalties for wandering — combined with regular escorted trips. Means there's no excuse for breaching the perimeter."

"Why not erect a fence?"

"There was one, years ago. First a wooden fence. Then a barbed-wire one. Followed by some high-tech generator-powered boundary-marking system. The last just plain failed — it took too much power, and it broke down easily. What Rockton learned from erecting fences, though, is that they don't make people feel safe; they make them feel like captives. Folks breached that fence far more often than they breach our marked perimeter. They prefer us to treat them like responsible adults and say, 'Look, we don't want you wandering in the woods for your own good.' With ninety percent of them, that's enough. It's the other ten that give us grief."

"You done talking?" Dalton asks.

"I don't know. Are you going to *start* talking?"

"Sure, I'll talk. We want Hastings to hear us, right? So he can find us and spend the rest of the night tied to a goddamn tree."

"Okay, you can stop talking now, boss. We need to be quiet and listen."

Another flashed finger.

I whisper, "Is he serious?"

Anders nods. "Punishment for running? Spend a night out here tied to a tree. Course, we keep an eye on them, but they don't know that."

I should be horrified. But it is a fitting punishment, one that'll teach them why they don't want to be out here, as I'm sure every whistle of the wind becomes the howl of rabid canines.

I wouldn't mind spending the night out here. Preferably not tied to a tree. I'm remarkably at peace in these woods. Maybe that's because I'm a city girl — I don't fully comprehend the threats I'd face. I think I do, though. I've never romanticized wild places. There's danger at every footfall here, walking through dense, pitch-black forest, our lanterns kept purposely dim so our prey won't see them.

Our prey. Interesting way of putting it.

I'll just say that I don't feel what I expected to in these woods. I don't feel fear. I don't feel loss of control. I felt an odd exhilaration, as sharp and biting as the wind, but as refreshing, too, like whipping along on that ATV, knowing a single missed branch or rut could send me flying, but enjoying the challenge and, yes, the danger.

Even the smells surprise me. Conifers and soil and rainwater and greenery and the occasional whiff of musk, like we're downwind of invisible woodland creatures. I hear them, too, scampering and calling and rustling and bolting. Dalton knows exactly what each sound is and whether the creature making it is big enough to be Hastings, and he stops for those but ignores the others.

I'm fascinated watching him track. I remember Anders saying Dalton has lived here all his life, and I can see that now, his comfort in these woods, the way he moves as surefooted as I would down a city street.

Eventually, though, Dalton loses the trail. He backs up and double-checks, and I ask if there's anything I can do to help. He doesn't answer, and Anders shakes his head, nicely telling me not to interfere.

Five minutes pass of Dalton pacing and examining and even squinting into the treetops. Then, "Fuck."

After a few seconds of silence, Anders says, "Can we buy a few more syllables, boss?"

"Trail ends there," Dalton says, pointing.

I walk to the spot and peer around.

"I, uh, don't think he swung through the trees," Anders whispers when he sees me squinting into the dark treetops.

"No," I say. "But I noticed Sheriff Dalton —"

"Call him Eric," Anders says. "Please. Otherwise, you set a bad precedent."

"Okay, well . . . *Eric* looked up, and I realize what he was checking. The tree cover is unusually dense here. That explains why the ground cover is unusually *sparse*. Which means there aren't any signs to show which way Hastings went."

"Just say that, then," Dalton says.

"Teaching moment," Anders says. "Which I appreciate. Okay, so the solution is to split up. I know you hate that, Eric, but we're all armed, and this patch isn't more than a few hundred square feet. No one's going to wander off and get lost. Right, Casey?"

"Right."

Dalton grumbles, but it is the efficient next step, and he assigns us directions. Then he says to me, "We're looking for prints, crushed moss, broken twigs. If you see any, call me over to make sure it's not just an animal."

We get to work. The toughest part? Checking for signs of passage without leaving them yourself. *Wait! I see a footprint! It's a boot, about size six . . . er, never mind.*

I move slowly and methodically. I want to impress Dalton. I won't deny that. I'm a woman, and I'm a visible minority, which means when I made detective and zoomed up to major crimes, people blamed affirmative action. I'm accustomed to proving that I got my position because I deserve it.

I find prints, but they're all animal. As for broken twigs or crushed undergrowth, my section is the barest — not by accident, I suspect. Dalton can be an ass, but he's an ass in *support* of the job, not *against* it. In other words, he isn't going to hand me a challenging segment to check so I can screw up and let Hastings escape.

Without vegetation to examine, I cover my strip quicker than the others, despite moving slowly. I'm near the edge when I find a spot with bent twigs, as if something large passed not long ago. I'm looking for prints when the wind flutters through the trees, and out of the corner of my eye I catch sight of something white. Too white to be natural in this forest.

TWENTY

My hand drops to my holstered gun. As I step to the left, squinting into the darkness, I can see a pale oval against a tree. A face? It's the right size.

I glance back for the others. No sign of them. I'm within shouting distance, but I'm sure as hell not going to shout. Nor am I going to walk away and give my target time to escape.

I creep forward. I've turned off my lantern. I'm dressed all in dark colors. I pull my hat down farther and hunker low as I move. I can see the white oval now, on the other side of what looks like a clearing.

I have to inch through the trees to get a better look. I move at a snail's pace, and the whole time I'm hoping Dalton or Anders realizes I'm out of sight. But no one comes, and I can't leave my target, so I continue easing forward. Sliding my feet keeps me from crunching small twigs. It does not keep me from rustling when my foot slides straight into a pile of dead leaves. The crackle sounds as loud as a twenty-one-gun salute, and I freeze, my gaze fixed on that pale shape, hand on my gun.

The oval doesn't move. I pick up my pace, certain I'm going to realize I'm seeing moonlight reflecting off a tree or something equally innocuous, and then I'll be really glad Dalton didn't come running —

I stop. I see black patches on that oval where the eyes and mouth should be. The height is about right to be a person, though. It's as I'm measuring that height that my gaze drops and I see . . .

Beneath the oval is a tree trunk, maybe two feet wide. I don't see shoulders or arms — just the narrow straight line of the trunk.

I push past the last tree, and I move too fast, stumbling into the clearing. Hand still on my gun, I catch my balance and look up and —

I let out a curse. I don't mean to. But I see what's on that trunk, and I can't stifle an oath of surprise. At least I don't scream.

I yank my gaze away to do a slow sweep of the clearing, making sure I haven't stumbled into a trap. There's no one else here.

I look at that pale oval. It's a human skull nailed to a tree. The remains of a pair of jeans are nailed up below it. Boots sit below the cuffs.

The jeans legs are in two pieces, bottom

and top, the middle shredded and completely dark with blood. The top half of the jeans is flat against the tree. The bottom is not. I grab a stick and move closer and prod at one of the lower legs, and the fabric falls, propped up rather than nailed. I'm looking at a mangled and bloodied lower leg, hacked away at the kneecap.

As I back up, brush crunches underfoot. I spin, hand on my gun, as Dalton strides into the clearing. His eyes are blazing, and it takes everything I can muster not to step backward.

"Did I tell you not to take off?" he says.

"I saw something. I thought it was a person."

"I don't give a damn what —"

I point at the skull. He stops. Then he mutters, "Aw, fuck." That's it. Like I'm pointing out signs of illegal campfire activity.

"You've seen this before, I take it?" I'm struggling to keep my voice steady.

"Yeah," he says. "It's a territorial marker for one group of hostiles. Never this close to the town, though."

His gaze drops to the boots. And that severed leg. That's when he stares. And when he says "fuck" this time, it's in a whole different tone.

"That's not normal, I'm guessing."

"Hell, no. Like I said, the skull is a territorial marker. Primitive tribes used shit like that to scare off others. We had one of the skulls removed and tested, and it was fifty years old. Something they'd dug up and put in the sun to bleach."

"Not an actual enemy's head, then."

"No, no. They don't do anything like . . ." He trails off, and his gaze returns to those amputated legs. "Fuck."

I take a closer look with my lantern. "They don't appear fresh enough to be Hastings. Powys, I'm guessing."

"Yeah. I recognize the boots."

"So we keep looking for Hastings?"

He shakes his head. "Trail's lost. We'll do a wider search in the morning. ATVs. Horses. Full militia." He turns and calls. "Will? I need you over here."

And thus ends our hunt. With the three of us staring at a pair of amputated human legs, staged in jeans and boots, before Anders marks the tree with bright yellow tape and we return to town.

We're back in Rockton. I'm shivering. I don't think the guys notice — everyone's lost in their thoughts — but before we separate for the night, Dalton says, "You know how to build a fire?"

"I'll be fine."

"Fuck," he mutters. Wrong answer, apparently.

Anders cuts in before Dalton can continue. "I know you don't want to impose, Casey.

Especially at four in the morning. Up here, though, no one's going to give you brownie points for toughing it out, and some of us" — a pointed look at Dalton — "will get pissy if you try."

"It's a waste of time," Dalton says.

"Right. Inefficient, to put it a nicer way. If you don't know how to build a fire, admit it. If we were both too tired to come and get one going tonight, we wouldn't offer. I'd tell you where to find extra blankets. Eric would say, 'Then you'd better learn.' Either way, no one's going to —"

"Speaking of wasting time . . ." Dalton says.

"Go home, Eric. I'll get Casey's fireplace going."

"No."

"It'll take me five minutes —"

Dalton cuts him off with a snort.

"What's that supposed to mean?" Anders's words turn brittle.

"Five minutes? You go over there, you won't leave again before dawn."

Anders narrows his eyes. He murmurs for me to "hold on a sec" and then leads Dalton aside. They walk about ten paces, not far enough for me to avoid overhearing in the stillness of the night.

"You want to yank my chain?" Anders says. "Go ahead, but there's a line between needling me and insulting me, and that crossed it."

"How?"

"She just arrived today. Traveled all yesterday. Was trapped in a car, then a bush plane with you for hours. Lands to find we have a body she can't investigate. Then discovers we have cannibals in our woods and spends her night tramping around those woods, only to find a skull and severed legs. Do you really think I'd invite myself back to her place in hopes of getting laid? *Seriously?*"

"No, I think you'll go back to her place and keep talking until the sun comes up. And then neither of you will be in any shape to search tomorrow."

"Oh."

"Yeah, *oh.*" Dalton shakes his head and walks back to me. "I'll get that fireplace going. Come on."

Dalton gives no outward sign he's unsettled by what we found in the forest, but I can tell he's off his game by the simple fact that he forgets he's supposed to be an asshole. He gets my fire going and shows me how to do it. He explains where to buy wood but advises that I learn to chop instead to save credits — downed trees are hauled into the woodlot, where they're free to anyone who'll chop them. Anders might be more comfortable explaining things, but Dalton is a damned fine teacher when he's in the mood.

Once the fire's going, I discover he's somehow transported that bottle of tequila to my house. We go into the kitchen, and it's there, and he's pouring me a shot without asking if I want it.

He pours one for himself, too. Then he sniffs it with some suspicion, and I try not to laugh.

"Never had tequila?" I ask.

"Nope."

"It's not going to taste good," I say.

"Then what's the point?"

I shake my head and down my shot. It burns all the way, that delicious heat that muffles my brain on contact.

He eyes me and then takes his shot. He only gets about two-thirds in before sputtering and coughing. He squeezes his eyes shut, hands resting on the table. A moment's pause. He opens his eyes. "Not my way, but I get it." He finishes the shot, slower now.

"Long day, huh?" I say.

"Yeah." He pauses, glass in hand, before carefully setting it on the table and looking over, meeting my gaze as if preparing some earthshaking pronouncement.

"It's not usually like this," he says. "In Rockton."

I laugh. I can't help it. I burst out laughing, and he looks at me, as startled as if I'd broken into song. He watches me, that look on his face, the one I've come to think of as his dissection look. Like I'm an alien life-form he's trying to understand.

After a moment, he says, "Yeah, I guess that's obvious. At least, you'd hope so." He smiles, and when he does, all I can think is, *Goddamn, Sheriff, you should do that more often.* It's the tequila, of course, and the long night and the long day and feeling like I've been walking through a minefield on tiptoes. When he smiles, it is — in an odd way — reassuring, like the ground finally steadies under my feet. *Things aren't so foreign here. Even Sheriff Dalton can smile.*

It only lasts a moment. He doesn't wipe it away, as if remembering he's supposed to be a jerk. It simply fades, and I realize that the "jerk" mode isn't an act. We all have our different aspects. That's one of his. So is the quiet, reflective guy who sat on the back deck with me and stared into the forest for two hours. There's a lot going on in that head, little of it simple or uncomplicated, and most of it weighed down by the responsibility of keeping the lid on this powder keg of a town. Which doesn't mean Eric Dalton is a nice guy. I don't think he can be. Not here. This is as nice as he gets, and I appreciate this glimpse, the way I appreciate the smile, and I also appreciate that he doesn't backtrack to cover it up, to be the asshole again.

I fill our shot glasses halfway. He takes his. We drink them. Not a word exchanged for at least two minutes afterward, until he says,

"I'll come by at ten. Yeah, not a lot of time to sleep . . ."

"But we have a manhunt to launch. I know."

He nods and leaves without another word. I lock the door behind him, settle on the couch in front of the blazing fire, and soon fall asleep.

TWENTY-ONE

I only get a few hours' sleep after our manhunt, and I'm awake by the time the sun's up. I make breakfast before I head out. It's simple fare: toast and a hard-boiled egg. Well, actually, the toast is just bread with peanut butter after I burned two slices trying to brown them on the woodstove. I planned to have a fried egg, but that seemed to be pushing my luck. Figuring out the French press coffee maker had been tough enough, so I just used the leftover water for boiling my egg.

Fortunately, between what Anders has said and what Dalton explained on the drive, my poor camp-cook skills won't be a serious drawback in Rockton. There are three restaurants, plus a place that does takeout only. That's not so much a matter of convenience as conservation of resources — you'll waste less buying a precooked meal for one than cooking for one. The chefs are also more flexible and more skilled at making the substitutions necessary under these conditions.

Anders says the restaurant food is reasonably priced. Just don't expect the menu to be vast. Or to find the same thing on it from one day to the next. Again, it's a matter of availability and conservation. Right now, blueberries are just ending their local season, so I have a box on my counter, but in another week, the only way I'll be able to get them is in jam, which the local cooks are madly bottling as the picking expeditions clear all nearby patches.

I finish my breakfast, and I'm at the office before nine. I figure Dalton will put some time in before he picks me up at ten, and I'm like the little girl who chases after her big brothers to prove she can do anything they can. I spent my youth refusing to live up to the standards set by my parents and my sister, and ironically, I spend my adult life chasing my colleagues. At least here I have a chance, so I pursue my goals with a childhood of repressed ambition fueling my fire.

I'm making coffee when Dalton walks in just past nine. I get a "fuck" for my efforts.

"I was awake," I say, "and I figured you'd stop by here and get some work done before you picked me up."

"When'd you arrive?"

"Ten minutes ago."

He grunts at that, and maybe he just doesn't want me overdoing it . . . or maybe

I'm not the only one with a competitive streak. Either way, he carries his coffee out onto the back deck. I pour the rest of the pot into a thermos — there's no hot plate here to keep it warm. Then I take my mug and follow.

"Can I talk to you?" I ask as he settles into his chair.

"What's stopping you?"

"When you come out here, you seem to want quiet."

He shrugs. "You can talk. If I don't want to listen, I'll tell you to go away."

My lips twitch. "Some people might take offense at that."

"Then let's hope you aren't one of them, or you're going to spend most of your time here being offended."

I give him a full smile for that, and he tilts his head, as if trying to figure out exactly what prompted it.

"If you're going to talk, talk," he says. "Once this mug's empty, we hit the trails. It'll be a full day of searching."

I walk to the railing. I don't sit in front of him — I have a feeling that'd be a little too close for both of us. But I perch on the corner of the railing, and he looks over, assessing again. I feel as if he processes data like a computer, detecting and analyzing every nuance. *She's smiling. She's sitting on the railing instead of the deck. Is that good?*

182

It is. It means I'm relaxing and settling in. Yet there's a wary look in Dalton's eyes, as if he accepts nothing at face value, always searching for deeper meaning, potentially negative.

"I took a quick look through the case files this morning —" I begin.

"I thought you just got in."

"At ten to nine. I started the water and then flipped through the files to check on something. I was looking at the cases of other attacks. Specifically, how close they were to the town and the level of violence involved. The other bodies were found deep in the forest. Powys was barely a kilometer from town, and the level of violence was a huge escalation."

"Yep." That's all he says. Then he drinks more coffee.

"Have there been problems with the, uh, hostiles lately? Could this be a response to a provocation?"

I'm expecting him to snap back that no provocation would justify cutting a man off at the knees — literally. But he says no and continues drinking.

"Is it possible the death was staged?" I ask. "That someone in town did it and is trying to blame these hostiles?"

"Yes." The answer comes without hesitation.

"You've already considered this," I say. "Were you going to discuss your thoughts with your new detective?"

"Sure. If you didn't bring it up. Gonna give you a chance to prove you aren't an idiot first."

"Thanks."

He nods, accepting the gratitude without seeming to catch the sarcasm. He's draining his coffee, and I'm struggling to pick through my thoughts and choose the best question before my window evaporates, but before I can, he says, "The thing you need to understand about the hostiles is that they're animalistic."

"Brutally violent, you mean."

He swings his gaze my way, a laser beam that slices through me like I've misstepped in a high-tech heist.

"Do you know anything about animals, Detective? Predators?"

I think fast. "Yes, they . . . Oh, okay. When you said *animalistic,* I took that colloquially. You mean literally. That they're like predators. They kill for survival. For food, trespass, threat, and such."

A grudging nod, and I feel as if the laser has stopped just short of cutting a major artery, but it hasn't backed up yet.

I continue. "You mean that the hostiles are predatory. Which is what you implied in your notes on the possible cannibalism. To them, it would be about survival. They won't die from starvation because of a cultural taboo.

While they'd certainly kill Hastings if he posed a threat — and might even kill him if they were experiencing a severe food shortage — the actual level of violence inflicted was unnecessary. It's sadistic. Which is human. Primate, at least. Some apes have been shown to demonstrate . . . Well, that's not important."

He hesitates, as if he's about to say, *No, explain.* New data for that curious mind. But then he nods abruptly, acknowledging this isn't the time for digressions, and I put the subject in my back pocket, as something I might be able to pull out later, to engage him in conversation.

"That's what you meant, right?" I say.

"Yes."

"Okay." I sip my coffee, which is cooling quickly in the brisk morning air. "Can I ask you about —"

"Coffee's done." He gets to his feet. "Time to head out."

"Okay, but can we talk about the hostiles as we walk? It'll help if I better understand —"

"I'm getting Will. Meet me at the stables."

"Stables?" I say as we walk through the station.

"Your background check said you can ride."

"From summer camp, when I was twelve." *How thorough was my background check?*

"Stables. Twenty minutes. Saddle up." He opens the front door. "Don't take my horse."

The door is closing. I catch it and call after him. "Which one's yours?"

"You're a detective," he calls back. "Figure it out."

I grab the coffee thermos, lock up the files, and set out. The stables are on the edge of town. The pasture is encircled by a solid eight-foot barrier to keep predators from thinking the horses look yummy. Dalton mentioned there's a permanent stable hand living over the barn, but she's nowhere to be seen. The horses are up and in the pasture, though, and the stalls are mucked out.

I'd hoped Dalton was being sarcastic about figuring out which horse was his — that I'd find his name over its stall. No such luck.

The obvious choice is the black stallion. The biggest, baddest horse for the local hard-ass. But stallions are notoriously temperamental, and Dalton wouldn't have the patience for that. Nor would he give a damn about riding the most impressive steed.

I assess the options: five horses to choose from. I saddle up three. I'm leading out a big gray gelding when Dalton and Anders come ambling along.

"That's not my horse," Dalton says.

"I should hope not," I say. "Because I've put Will's saddle on her." I pass the reins over. "Correct?"

Anders smiles. "Correct, Detective. And

good morning to you, Casey."

"Good morning. The coffee thermos is inside the barn. I figured the boss might not give you time to make any."

His smile grows to a grin. "Excellent deduction. I owe you."

Dalton follows me inside. His saddle is on a roan gelding, a hand or so smaller than Anders's horse. Nothing fancy, but a good sound steed. He grunts and looks over at my choice — a young black mare. He shakes his head. "Take the gray mare. That one's not fully broke."

"The gray mare's too old. I'm better with spirited than plodding."

He mutters something that sounds like "suit yourself," and continues out.

TWENTY-TWO

I do fine with the horse, whose name is Cricket. I hadn't been trying to show off. I recalled from my riding days that one of the reasons I quit was that my trainer kept putting me on the most docile steeds they had. I was too restless, she said. Too high-strung myself. I needed a patient horse.

I could see her logic, but it was flawed. I did better on the younger horses because my restlessness wasn't the race-around-the-barn type, but a quieter energy that played well off a horse's spirits, as it does today with the black mare.

We spend the morning searching. At noon we return for lunch and to speak to the militia, who are searching on foot. Then it's back into the woods to painstakingly work through quadrants, divided but never out of sight. That's the rule. I swear if I so much as passed beside a large bush, Dalton would snarl, "Butler!" as if I'd made for the hills.

Back to town for dinner. People ask how

the search is going. A few mention they've heard about Powys, but the most we get there is "helluva thing." I'm sure they're curious. I'm sure rumors are winding through town. But no one expects answers from Dalton.

We're back on the horses until past dark. I'm supposed to go out with Diana and her new friends this evening. At both the lunch and dinner breaks, I tried to track her down. When I couldn't, there was a weird moment of panic as I realized there was no easy way to leave her a message. I've never considered myself a technophile, but I grew up in a world of e-mail and texts and voice messages, and to have all that stripped away is unsettling.

At the day's end, Dalton and I head back to the station. Anders has an errand and arrives a few minutes later, saying, "I ran into Diana. She said you were going out for drinks with her and some others tonight?"

"No," Dalton says. "You've got work." He continues past me, heading for the back door.

I follow. "Um, no. My shift ended an hour ago."

"I mean you have to work tomorrow. Early."

Anders prods me out onto the deck with Dalton. "She's not actually asking permission, Eric. Casey just arrived. Socializing is —"

"A fucking bad idea for a cop."

"Um, I do it."

"Like I said . . ."

They exchange a glower.

"Socializing affects how people see you," Dalton says. "How they relate to you. You don't see me doing that, do you?"

"Because you're the bad cop here. I'm the one they *can* relate to. The one they come to with their problems. I thought you appreciated that."

"I do. For you. As my deputy. Butler is my detective."

I cut in. "I'm only having a drink or two with Diana and her friends. I don't intend to join the local party scene. I just want to meet people."

"Fine. I'll introduce you. To better people."

Anders winces. "Eric . . ."

"You want to help your friend?" Dalton says. "Find her a higher class of drinking buddies."

"They're fine," Anders says. "I hang out with them sometimes."

"You mean you screw around with them sometimes. There's a difference."

Anders grimaces in embarrassment. "Christ, Eric."

Dalton flips the cap off his beer. "It's true. They've got nothing going on upstairs. Which doesn't mean they're stupid. Just that they don't bother thinking because it interferes with the drinking and the partying and the screwing."

Anders turns to Dalton. "Casey and I are

going out for drinks with Diana and her friends tonight."

Dalton grunts as if to say, *Fine.*

I get the feeling I'm being chaperoned, but I know Anders is only trying to smooth things over. I agree, and he says he'll meet us later — he needs to cover the evening shift at the station.

I freshen up at my house. Then I head to Diana's place. It's the upper apartment of a big house. After a day on horseback, climbing the outside steps is tougher than it should be. Hell, walking is tougher than it should be. I head along the balcony to the second apartment and knock, and I don't think I'm very loud, but the next door opens and it's Jen, the chick from the bar fight. She's stark naked. Behind her, an unseen guy whines, "Shut the damned door. It's freezing."

She ignores him and says, "What the hell do you want?" to me.

"Sorry," I say. "I was looking for Diana. Have you seen —"

"No. Now, get the fuck off my balcony."

I knock on Diana's door again. Jen lunges and grabs my arm. Two seconds later she's flying through her door, hitting the floor hard enough to make the balcony quiver, and her guest is standing there, as naked as she is, his gaze sliding up and down me.

"Well, hello, neighbor."

"That bitch isn't —" Jen begins.

"You want to party?" the guy says. "Jen says you like to party."

"No, thanks, but I'm —"

"Got everything we need. Dope, booze . . ." He grins at me. "And credits. I pay well. Just ask Jen. You come party with us, and I'll show you a good time. A *profitable* good time."

"I'm the new detective."

His grin grows. "Offer stands, babe. A party with all the fixings, and you walk out a hundred credits richer."

"A hundred?" Jen squawks. "You're giving me twenty."

" 'Cause you're worth twenty. She's worth a hundred. I'll make yours thirty, though, if you play nice. Have some fun with your new neighbor."

"You son of a —" Jen howls, and launches herself at him. I pull the door shut and walk away.

I'm passing the Roc when a voice calls, "Hey, girl," and I turn to see Isabel relighting a lantern outside her bar.

"What are you doing out and about at this hour?" she asks.

"It's not even ten."

"Let me rephrase: what are you doing out and about *alone* at this hour?"

"I'm fine." I pull back my jacket so she can see my gun.

"Mmm, that's not going to help, sugar. No

one's going to drag you into an alley for your wallet. Or for anything else. They're just going to pester you, and I'd strongly suggest you don't shoot them for that, as annoying as they might be."

"I'm fine. No one's bothered —"

"No one stopped you on your way here?"

A couple of guys had tried, but I say, "Not really." Then, "Have you seen Diana? I'm supposed to have drinks with her tonight."

"I wouldn't count on her remembering. That girl has an active social life." She steps closer and lowers her voice. "You might want to have a talk with her. I'm all for partying — *clean* partying. Not much else to do up here. But sometimes the freedom is a little too much. Your friend likes the booze, and she likes the boys. That isn't a safe combination."

I'm about to say no, Isabel is misunderstanding the situation, but I know protesting won't help, so I just nod. "I'll talk to her. Thanks for the heads-up."

I start to say good night, but she says, "You're not walking home alone, Miss Casey. Yes, you don't appreciate being treated like a girl in hoopskirts, and believe me, I'd be the last person to say a lady can't take care of herself. But slow down. Let people get used to you. Until then, save yourself the hassle." She leans into the Roc and shouts, "Mick!" and the bartender appears. She puts one hand on his burly biceps and says, "You're going to walk Ms. Butler home."

"It's Casey, please," I say. "And I don't need —"

"You will escort Casey home. If she argues, walk two paces behind her. Unless she tries to shoot you." She looks at me. "Please don't shoot him."

I smile. "I won't."

"And don't worry about him, either. He's perfectly safe. I keep him plenty occupied." She winks at me and then smacks Mick's ass and sends us on our way.

Mick isn't a conversationalist. We don't exchange a word until we reach my porch and I say, "Thanks," and he says, "Anytime," then adds, "About your friend, Diana. She's . . ." He shifts, looking uncomfortable. "She's getting into some trouble."

"So I heard. I'll talk to her."

"Isabel's . . . Well, Isabel's worried. She worries about all the new women in town, but in Diana's case, it's moving fast into 'pissed off.' The best thing your friend can do is talk to her, if this is what she wants. It'd be safer that way."

"Safer?"

"Just tell her to talk to Iz. Okay?"

I nod and say good night and go inside.

I barely make it into my place when there's a tap-tap-tap at the door. It's Diana, bouncing like a kid.

"Ready to go?"

I check my watch. "Doesn't the bar close in an hour?"

"Sure," she says, grinning. "That's when we go have some real fun."

I remember Isabel's warning and say, carefully, "There's a curfew for a reason. Everyone needs to be at work the next day. It's not like home, where if we call in with a hangover, someone can cover for us."

"God, you've been hanging around that sheriff too long already. I haven't missed an hour of work yet. Now, come on and let's go get a drink."

TWENTY-THREE

We go to the other bar: the Red Lion. Apparently someone envisioned it as a quaint British pub, but that vision doesn't extend beyond the name. The place looks like a set piece for a Western saloon. Wooden building. Wooden bar. Wooden chairs and tables.

At first, Diana's friends seem to be exactly what Dalton said they were. They remind me of the kids Diana so desperately wanted to hang out with in high school.

In eleventh grade, the popular girls had invited Diana to eat lunch with them . . . an invitation that did not extend to me. I barely saw her for two weeks afterward. Then she showed up at my house crying, because it turned out all they wanted was to meet her cousin, who was an actor in a new TV show, and when she admitted she hadn't seen him since a family reunion ten years earlier, they dumped her.

I'm barely in my seat before a guy says, "So, Powys. Rumor says it was murder. Can you confirm, Detective Butler?" He holds out his beer glass like a microphone, as if I'm at a press conference, with this smirk on his face that makes me think he really was a journalist in a former life. Or at least a blogger who thought he was one. A woman grabs the glass from him and says, "Don't be a dick, Dick," and the table erupts in snickers. She turns to me and extends a hand. "Petra. That's Richard. He prefers Rich, but feel free to call him Dick if he acts like one." Rich shoots her the finger, but it's good-natured enough as he eases into his chair, saying, "We're just curious. People have a right to know."

"Sure," Petra says. "You're free to ask. Just don't sneak behind Eric's back and try weaseling answers out of his new detective. You have questions? Go straight to the man himself. Stand up to him and tell him all about your right to know."

That gets a round of genuine laughter as people start ribbing Rich, daring him to do exactly that and then laying bets on exactly how many profanities the response will contain and how inventive the punishment for "bothering the sheriff" will be.

"He calls it 'interfering with law enforcement,' " Petra says with a grin. "But really, it's just pissing him off."

Nods and smiles follow, and not a single grumble. I have to stare, certain I'm misunderstanding. I can understand Dalton needs to keep a tight lid on Rockton and, yes, may trump up charges against anyone who interferes with his job, but I cannot believe people don't complain about that.

Petra catches my incredulous look and shrugs. "We know the drill. He can be a jerk, but he does his job. It's not like we can afford a police public relations liaison to deal with questions. But if you ever want one, I'm your gal."

The man beside her nods. "Dalton's an asshole but a fair asshole. He'll tell us what he can when he's ready. He always does."

"You mean he tells Will," Petra says. "Who then tells everyone else."

Another round of smiles and nods.

"Well," I say, "for now I can say we haven't made an official decision on Harold Powys. We're focused on finding Jerome Hastings. The longer he's out there, the less chance we have of a positive outcome."

Rich raises his glass. "And we can all agree on that. Let me buy your first drink then, Detective, as an apology for living up to my name."

Despite my misgivings, I enjoy the next half hour. Conversation is lively, if not exactly deep. And they have a sense of fun that's infectious. They're stuck in Rockton for a few years, and they aren't providing essential services, so they can just cut loose and party, beholden to no one and nothing.

It's just past ten thirty, and I'm talking to Petra. Turns out, she's a comic-book artist, which she jokes makes her all but useless in Rockton. We're deep in conversation about our favorite graphic novels when Diana perks up beside me. She straightens her shirt and tucks her hair back, and I think, *Huh, who's the guy?*

I look up to see Anders coming our way. He's grinning, and Diana is practically vibrating in her seat. And I smile, because now I know she wasn't pushing me in his direction — she was testing whether my gaze had already turned that way. When he catches her smile and returns it, I'm glad. I slide out, motion for him to take my place, and then sit in the empty seat on Petra's other side. Anders pulls up a chair and plunks it down next to me.

"Got a story for you," he whispers as he sits. "Rockton policing life at its finest."

There's a moment of silence, and I realize everyone at the table noticed the interplay with Diana.

"You've met Diana, right?" I say, and as the words leave my mouth, I want to kick myself.

Diana looks as if she wants to drop through the floor. Anders just smiles at her and says, "Sure, we've met." There's a snicker from someone farther down the table, and as genuine as Anders's smile seems, I detect a bit of distance in his eyes. That's when I realize it's no secret Diana has her eye on Anders. She's let him — and everyone else — know . . . and he's made it clear he isn't interested.

Shit.

"Hey, Di," I say, leaning forward, "you want to go for a walk?" I lift my shot glass. "I've hit my limit, and I could use the air."

Yes, it's an awkward excuse, but I'm desperate to fix this. She only gives me a cool look and says, "I just started my drink."

Anders takes a long gulp of his beer. "Give me a minute, and I'll walk with you."

"No!" I say, a little too sharply, and Petra gives a sympathetic chuckle.

"We should both turn in soon," Anders says. "Eric will give me proper shit if you so much as yawn tomorrow. I'll walk you home and tell you that story."

Diana glowers as if I'd asked Anders to play escort. I want to take her outside and set her straight. But that won't change the fact that she's hurt, and the more I try to fix it, the more humiliated she'll be. So I go back to talking to Petra, who picks up where we left off. Anders joins us as he finishes his beer, and then we leave.

"You doing okay?" Anders asks when we're outside.

"Sure."

He glances over as we head into the street.

"You seemed to be having a good time when I got there. Did I . . ." He clears his throat. "I mean, I realized afterward that I probably shouldn't have just waltzed in and pulled up a chair and started talking like you'd been waiting for me."

"You didn't."

He walks a few feet in silence, before checking my expression and nodding. "Okay. I just . . . It got a little awkward."

"No, nothing like that. So what was the story you wanted to tell me?"

"Story?" It takes him a second, then he shakes his head. "Yeah, idiot, the *reason* you waltzed in there and barged into the conversation. Before I get talking — because God knows, once I start, I don't stop — do you want to go straight home? Or walk a bit, so I can add to the grand welcoming tour the boss took you on yesterday."

"Uh . . ."

"What? You didn't get the tour? I did." He points down the moonlit street. "Police station, general store, restaurants, lumberyard, and bar. No, wait, it was more like: *Bar's over there, and if I fucking catch you ever staggering out of there, dead-ass drunk, you'll be drying out in the cell all night.*"

I give a soft laugh, and he smiles over.

"Proper tour, then?" he says. He motions at the moon. "We've got enough light for it."

201

"I would love a tour, but do I still get the story?"

"Of course. Can't forget the story, since it was so damned important."

We start walking and he says, "You missed your first chance at a grizzly sighting tonight. Right on the edge of town."

"What?" I look at him. "Dalton said they don't —"

"*Usually* come this close. Always note the *usually,* Casey. So someone reported seeing a bear rubbing against a tree, scratching its back and grunting. I grab the rifle and every militia guy I pass on my run across town. I'm creeping up on the spot with Kenny and a couple of the others at my back. And there's the beast. It looks a little small — maybe six foot. Wide enough for a bear, though. Definitely rubbing up against that tree with plenty of grunting. Then I see it's got four legs, four arms, and is wearing clothing. Well, some clothing."

"Ah, the elusive beast with two backs."

"Not nearly so elusive around here. Yep, so that was our bear. A couple who tried to sneak twenty feet into the woods for a little privacy . . . and found themselves with an audience who'll be spreading the story for days. They'll also be slapped with chopping duty for being outside the boundary."

"Chopping duty?"

He glances over. "Man, Eric really didn't

tell you anything, did he? It's the main form of punishment here. We can't keep anyone in the cell for long, and we can't impose harsh fines or they won't be able to buy food. So we do what they did in Dawson City during the gold rush: sentence folks to chopping wood for the municipal buildings."

"Smart."

"Especially in winter, when we need a lotta wood. Now, if you look to your left, you'll see the lumber shed and chopping circle just past those buildings, which are . . ."

We continue down the street and he carries on with the tour.

The next morning: more searching for Hastings. At noon, Dalton decides it's time to scale back. The militia will stay on it, led by Anders. The sheriff will return to dealing with the local law enforcement issues that have piled up in the last forty-eight hours. I'll get to work on the Powys case.

First, I talk to the doctor — Beth, as she insists — and get her full autopsy report. The next step would be to reinterview those connected to his disappearance — who saw him the night he took off, who might have played some role. But I have a different idea I want to pursue first.

I spend most of the afternoon reading through other homicides and disappearances. There aren't many . . . if I don't remind myself exactly how small this town is. When I do, that small stack makes Rockton the Bermuda Triangle of the North. Most of it, though, can be chalked up to the situation. We come here because we've either done bad shit or we've got serious baggage. The fact that almost everyone survives the stay and goes home again is actually remarkable. But that means every year one or two won't be going back. Some wander off into the woods, either dying alone or making a home there. Others die by homicide or misadventure. Or they commit suicide.

That's what Irene Prosser's death is filed under. I read it three times to make sure I'm not missing anything. Then I wait for Sheriff Dalton to return. At five, he walks straight through, coffee already in hand. I follow him onto the deck.

"Busy," he grunts.

"Irene Prosser." I slap the file on the railing. "Suicide? She was found in a water cistern. With both wrists cut to the bone."

"We don't have bathtubs."

"Excuse me?"

He speaks slower. "Most people who cut their wrists do it in a tub because it's less painful, apparently."

"Less painful? Her hands were practically cut off."

"She left a note in her handwriting."

"Presumably written *before* she nearly

amputated her own hands?"

He shrugs and stares into the forest. I walk into his line of sight.

"You're not stupid, Sheriff, and I don't think you're corrupt, so what the hell is going on here?"

"I ruled the death a murder."

I ease back. "Okay."

"Beth thinks the killer intended to hack off Irene's hands, but the blade wasn't sharp enough. The killer then realized it *could* look like a suicide and faked Irene's handwriting. Any idiot can see it's not suicide. The council disagreed. So I am not allowed to officially investigate."

"*Officially.* Meaning you have investigated."

"If I had, it would be on my own time and any notes would be kept in my home, because if the council found out, they'd give me their usual threat — to stick my ass on a plane down south. One way."

I want to ask why that's such a big deal. Then I remember what Anders said — that Dalton was born here and doesn't intend to leave. I'm guessing that's how the council keeps him in line. Threatens to kick him out, because he has no right to stay.

"Irene was Harry Powys's ex-girlfriend," I say. "She died two weeks before he went missing."

Dalton takes a gulp of his coffee.

I continue. "You didn't randomly decide

you'd like a detective on staff. Like I said in the car on the way up here, you *already* needed one. This is why I'm here, and you just stood back and let me figure it out for myself."

"No," he says. "I had one woman dead, presumably homicide. Another woman went missing seven weeks ago. Then Powys disappeared. I've wanted a detective for a while. Your file just hit our desk at the right time."

"Missing woman?"

"Abbygail Kemp."

I choke back a growl of frustration. "Were you going to tell me about her? Or just wait until I figured it out? If you want to test my detection skills, amuse yourself by making me figure out which horse is yours."

He turns cold gray eyes on me. "What you and I are doing right now, Butler? It's not about proving you're a detective. It's about proving I can trust you. Because you came along at a helluva convenient time."

I pause. "You think I'm, what, a plant? Spying on you?"

"Wouldn't be the first time. What's the adage? It's not paranoia if they really are out to get you?" He puts down his coffee. "The council expects one thing from me, Detective: blind obedience. I don't provide it, so they want me gone. The problem? There are still people around who financed this town in the early days. Permanent stakeholders. They want me here, and unless the council can prove I'm incompetent, I stay. So, yeah, I'm suspicious."

"I'd like the file on Abbygail Kemp."

"Inside. Second cabinet. Second drawer."

"I also want your notes on everyone you think the council smuggled in."

He looks up at me. "I don't keep —"

"Bullshit. If you don't want to show me, okay. We'll just discuss them."

"It won't help."

"Of course it —"

He gets to his feet. "Abbygail's file is inside. For the rest? Start from scratch." He heads for the door.

"I'm not asking for a hand up. I'm asking for the opinion of the person who knows this town better than —"

The door closes behind him, and I'm left alone on the porch.

TWENTY-FOUR

An hour later, Dalton's on the deck again, having done . . . Honestly, I have no goddamn idea what he was doing.

He settles into his chair, and I walk out there, Abbygail's file in hand.

"Read it?" he grunted.

"Nope." I dump the file on his lap. "I will, but first you're going to tell me about the case."

He snorts.

"Oh, sorry," I say. "Am I interrupting your whatever the hell you're doing out here? The answer is *nothing,* Sheriff. You're doing nothing. You're sitting on your ass and ordering me to read files when the best person to discuss this town is you. Tell me about Abbygail Kemp. Then I'll read the file."

He goes inside, and I think he's refusing. I start to follow, only to see he's switching his coffee for a beer. He comes back, sits, and takes a long drink from the bottle. Then he sets it down and says, "Abbygail Kemp is my fucking biggest failure as sheriff, Detective."

I think I've misheard. Or this is some sarcastic faux confession. One look in his eyes says it's not.

"She came here at nineteen. Youngest resident we've ever had, and I fought tooth and nail to keep her out. Didn't want that kind of responsibility. Like taking a teenage girl and dropping her off in the middle of Las Vegas at midnight. I said hell no. I'm not a babysitter. It was Beth who talked me down. Said *she'd* take responsibility. And the girl's story . . ." He shook his head. "I wasn't arguing that she didn't need help. I just didn't think she needed Rockton."

"Her story?"

"Ran away at sixteen. Drugs. Prostitution. The family situation . . . ?" He shifted in his seat. "I won't pretend to understand the family situation, Detective. I know my limitations, living up here, and so I read up on stuff like that. I still don't understand because, to me, it's black and white. If your kid runs away and sells her body for money, you must be shitty parents."

"Not necessarily," I say. "If she was into drugs before she left, that would explain a lot."

"I guess so. Anyway, leaving didn't mean she hated her parents. She got herself into trouble on the streets, though. Big trouble. She ran home. The trouble followed. Some

209

gang guys set her house on fire. Her parents didn't get out in time."

"Damn."

"Yeah. She was a fucking mess when she got here. Strung out and hating herself and hating anyone who tried to help, including Beth. But Beth wouldn't give up on her. No one did, Detective, and that's what you need to understand about this town. People here pull shit they never would down south. What's that saying? What happens in Vegas stays in Vegas? Same in Rockton. Except here, you can't be an asshole and fly home the next day. You need to live here. So, as fucked up as it is, when things go really wrong, most people will pitch in to make it right. Someone like Abbygail shows up, and folks do their best. Eventually, she understood we weren't putting her on a flight home, no matter how much shit she pulled. And she understood I wasn't going to let her pull that shit. She spent nights in the cell. She spent days on logging duty. A year later, she was working for Beth, training as a nurse, making plans to go to college when she got out of here. And then . . ."

He trails off and takes a long draw on his beer, finishing it. "Mick saw her heading into the forest one night and gave her shit for it, and she turned around . . . but only long enough to make him walk away. Beth woke the next morning to find she'd never come home."

"Why would she go into the woods?"

"She liked the peace and quiet of it. Her parents used to take her to the mountains every summer, and I guess those were good memories. I did everything I could — Fuck, no. That's an excuse. If I'd really done everything to keep her out of those woods, she would never have gone in. I tried to manage the situation. Let her join the militia, come on patrols, gave her time in the forest under supervision."

He looks at me. "You think I'm an asshole, Detective. I am. I'm going to ride you and everyone in this town every chance I get, and I'm going to be very clear who's in charge. This is why. Because just when I think maybe I'm too hard on people, something like this happens, and I realize I can't be hard enough."

I don't tell him this wasn't his fault. That no matter how harsh he is, people will find a way around the rules, and with a young woman barely out of her teens, that goes double. He knows that. He doesn't want absolution.

He continues. "It was the biggest search this town has ever seen. Round-the-clock manhunts for the first week. I don't think Will or Mick slept the whole time."

Not Dalton, either, I bet.

211

"Daytime searches for another week," he says. "By that time . . . by that time we knew we weren't looking for a survivor. We kept at it, though. No one was happy when I finally called it quits. Had to, though. Time to accept that we'd failed."

"You said this was two months ago?" I say.

"Seven weeks."

He still counted it in weeks, probably only recently stopped counting it in days. That's what you do with the cases that haunt you.

"So about four weeks before Irene was murdered," I said. "Five or so weeks before Powys disappeared."

"Yep."

"You think there's a connection," I say. "That Abbygail didn't just wander into the forest. No more than Irene Prosser nearly cut off her own hands."

He reaches for his beer. Remembers it's empty and makes a face.

"Could Abbygail have been murdered?" he says. "I am not the person to make that determination. Not me. Not Will or Beth or Mick or anyone else who feels responsible for what happened."

I take the file. Before I go in, I murmur, "Thank you. For explaining." If he hears, he gives no sign of it. He's already staring into the forest again.

Night falls. I'm packing up to leave, and

Anders comes in.

"Want to grab a drink?" he asks.

I don't. I'm in a funk, thinking about Irene and Abbygail, and all I want to do is go home and curl up and maybe have a shot of tequila on my own. But I get the feeling that drinking alone out here is the first step toward darkness. What I really want to do is see Diana. But she's avoiding me.

I tell myself it's temporary. Low self-confidence causes her to stay with guys like Graham, and it also means sometimes she decides she's stuck in my shadow and needs to escape for a while. She'll back off until her confidence returns.

Tonight, though, the loss of Diana just seems one more weight on the load already dragging me down. I'm in this godforsaken town with cannibals outside and a killer inside, and now the friend I've come here to help has abandoned me.

So no, I don't want to go for a drink. But there isn't any reason to take out my mood on Anders, so I say, "Okay," then, "I need to drop a few of these files at my place. I'll meet you —"

"Those files stay in that cabinet," Dalton cuts in from across the room.

"All right," I say, as evenly as I can. "I'll drop off my notes —"

"Your notes stay here, too."

I turn on him. "Excuse me?"

He's sitting at the desk, doing paperwork. He doesn't even lift his head. "It's nine o'clock at night. You're going for a drink. Work will wait."

"All right. I'll finish a couple of things and lock them in the file cabinet. Are we going to the Roc or the Red Lion?"

Silence. I look over at Anders.

"The, uh, Roc . . . ?" He turns to Dalton. "You explained, right? About the Roc?" When Dalton keeps working, Anders curses under his breath. "Of course not. Stupid question." He looks at me. "The, uh, Roc is for . . . Well, the women there . . . It's not really a bar as much as . . . ."

"It's a brothel," Dalton says.

I turn to him. "What?"

"You heard me."

"No, I'm pretty sure I didn't, because there's no way in hell you'd allow a house of *prostitution* —"

"Not my call."

"It sure as hell is your call, Sheriff. You've told me this town has a problem with the lack of women. I went to see Diana last night and got hassled by three men on the way there. Then I'm knocking on her door, and the next thing you know, a guy is offering me a hundred credits for sex."

"What?" Anders says.

I look at him. "You're shocked? Really?"

"Hell, yes. No one should —"

214

"You live in a town where women *do,* apparently, sell sex, and you're honestly shocked that a woman would need to deal with being offered money for sex? It's called the setting of expectation and precedent. Sure, I'm not a whore, but no harm in asking, right? You just gotta find the right price. And if you can't? Well, from the looks of your sexual assault file, I think we know what they do when they can't find the right price."

I don't wait for a reply. I scoop up my notes and the case files, and I walk out.

Twenty-Five

I'm in the office at ten to eight the next morning. I don't put on the kettle for coffee, and not because I'm being pissy, but simply because I don't think to do it. With everything that's going on, I didn't exactly get a good night's sleep, and I'm distracted. I walk in, start the fire in the woodstove, and sit at the desk to work on my notes.

Dalton shows up at the stroke of eight. He takes a bound journal from his coat pocket.

"My notes," he says. "On residents."

When I look up, he shoves it back into his pocket. I struggle to keep my expression neutral. I rise and walk to the water dispenser to fill the kettle.

"I don't *allow* a brothel in my town," he says. "That should have been clear when you heard me arguing with Isabel. If I had a choice in the matter, I'd shut her down."

"Okay." I put the kettle on the stove.

"You think I'm full of shit," he says.

"I think if you wanted it shut down, it'd be

shut down."

"Then you overestimate my influence here, Detective."

I return to my seat. He's standing there, looming over me, waiting for some accusation he can deny. I resume my note taking.

"The council argues that the brothel reduces the problems we have," he says. "Before it opened, women were already selling sex. It's a market economy. The problem was that if they sold it once, men kept expecting it, and when they said no, things got ugly. Isabel's argument is that by having the brothel, she can keep the women safe and be sure it's what they really want to do."

"Okay."

Silence. He shifts his weight, making a noise not unlike a growl. He wants to debate this, to defend it or deny his culpability in it, and I'm not letting him do that.

Finally, I lift my gaze to his. "The problem is the environment it creates for other women. I spent a year in vice, working with prostitutes, and I'd be the first person to argue for legalizing the sex trade. It isn't going away. It's better to regulate it and keep the workers safe. But that's in a large city, where the overall effect is minimal. Having a brothel in a town with such a small female population creates the kind of environment where women are going to have to deal with an expectation they should never have to deal with. Do you even understand that?"

He says nothing for about five seconds. Then he shifts his weight, backing out of looming mode. "No, I did not understand that, Detective. I do now. No one's ever complained about being propositioned before."

"Well, you can sure as hell bet I'm not the first. They're being asked, and they're dealing with it on their own. It's embarrassing and humiliating to have a guy presume he can buy sex from you."

The kettle sings. He goes to make the coffee, and I think the conversation's at an end, so I pull out another file. A few minutes later, he's looming again.

"I want to know who offered you money," he says. "If you don't have a name, a description will do. I'll make an example of him and —"

"And he'll tell everyone I overreacted. That the new girl is a stuck-up prude who can't take a joke. Or that he was drunk and made a silly mistake. No matter how it's handled, I'll be a bitch, and he'll be the misunderstood guy who was just trying to tell me he thinks I'm cute."

"I would like the chance to handle this, Detective."

"If it happens again — or if I hear about other women being hassled — I'll take my lumps and be the bitch. But having you fix it for me only says I can't."

He stands there. Then he sets his journal on the desk. I look up to see he's left a mug of coffee there, fixed with creamer, exactly as I take it.

I watch him head out onto the back deck.

I don't understand you, Sheriff. Not one bit.

Anders checks in at eleven. The last few days have been all hands on deck because of Hastings's disappearance, but we're back to regular shifts, which still aren't all that regular — we come in when Dalton tells us to and work ten hours, give or take.

When Anders arrives, he makes a beeline for my desk. Well, *the* desk. Dalton is out back. He's come and gone a few times in the last few hours, but he always ends up out on the deck, not a word to me on the way.

"Hey," Anders says. "About last night —"

"Good, you're here." Dalton appears from nowhere to intercept Anders. "I need you out at the airstrip. Got a delivery coming in."

"Sure, but there's no sign of the plane yet, and I wanted to talk to —"

Dalton backs him up clear out the door and closes it behind them. I can't hear their conversation, but I can pick up enough to know it's about the Roc. Anders wants to talk to me about it, and Dalton is telling him to drop it.

Anders leaves. Dalton comes in. When I

219

look up, he's standing there. He gestures at the journal.

"Better now?" he says. "Or worse?"

"I understand your point," I say carefully.

"So I wasn't just being an asshole?" He snorts and shakes his head. Then he heads for the back door. I'm figuring that's the end of the conversation, but he gestures, as if to say, *Well, come on.* I scrape back my chair and follow him out.

We settle in on the deck. The temperature is dropping, and I zip my hoodie. There's no official uniform, because it's not as if anyone here doesn't know we're the local PD. Dalton wears a T-shirt and doesn't seem to notice the chill. I've noticed that's common here, as people adapt to the climate.

I take my place on the railing, and he says, "So do you think I'm a paranoid son of a bitch?"

"I think you have a reason to be. It's like . . ." I rub the back of my neck. "As a city cop, you don't kid yourself about people. You walk into the suburbs, look at those nice houses, and wonder who really lives there. Addicts, abusers, pedophiles, rapists, even murderers. So when you told me criminals get smuggled in, as disconcerting as that was, I told myself it was the same thing."

"And it's not?"

I shake my head. "In my old job, it was a hypothetical. You see fifty houses and know a killer could lurk within one. But you realize part of that is a cop's misanthropy, and there's a good chance there isn't an actual killer. Here? It's a guarantee. And not just one, either."

I take the journal from my pocket and finger it. Powys is in there. So is Hastings, though only as speculation — Dalton thinks Hastings may be a man accused of murdering his mother for his inheritance.

Dalton has positively identified ten people who are here under false pretenses. There are twenty more he is actively researching. That's 15 percent of the population. I'm struggling with that. I really am.

"Thank you for letting me read it," I say finally. "I'm not sorry I did. I just . . ."

I trail off, and he says, "Yep," and we fade to silence.

We don't stay quiet for long. Dalton asks if I have any questions. It's an honest offer, and we discuss his methods of research. He keeps a list of things he wants to look up when he flies out, but it's not exactly a weekly trip. Dawson City does have places where he can access the Internet — the tourism office and two cafés. The problem is that he sure as hell doesn't dare snoop using the laptop the council has given him.

"You could buy a tablet," I say.

"Tablet?"

"You know, like an iPad, except I'd suggest generic to save money, since all you want is the browser, not Angry Birds and Netflix."

His look isn't confusion. It's caution, that tightening of his face that says he realizes he should know what I'm talking about. Like being asked to run when you're trying to hide a limp.

I try to think of a way to phrase an explanation that won't sound condescending. There isn't one, so I just say, "A tablet is like an oversized cell phone that doesn't make phone calls. The bigger screen means it's a lot easier to browse the Internet. And not being a phone, it's usually cheaper than one."

"I've seen people on the plane with them. Wondered what the hell they were. I don't . . ." He shrugs. "Don't take commercial flights that often."

"Makes sense." I manage a smile. "Believe me, you're not missing anything —"

"Stop." His voice is low, the word barely more than a grunt.

"I'm just —"

"Will told you about me. I get it. Now drop it. I don't appreciate being made to feel like a freak, Detective."

"I would never —"

"But you're curious. Everyone's curious. What's it like to grow up someplace like this? To never leave? Don't you want to leave? Do you know how to drive a car? Have you ever been to a movie theater? No, really, tell me, what's it like?" He meets my gaze. "I'm not an anthropological study, Detective, and I can't tell you what it's like because I have nothing to compare it to."

"I get that, and I won't pretend I don't think it's interesting, but I wouldn't pry. The only thing your background means to me is that you're the best source of information on this town. Right?"

A pause, like he's itching to argue. Then, "Yeah."

"About the tablet, then. I think that would help. I brought cash — yes, I know, that's not allowed, but I still did. Either I can tell you what to get or you can take me on the next trip. Which is me offering to help, not angling for a day pass. Either way, a tablet would be easy to smuggle and would let you do research whenever you have access to an open wireless router."

He agrees that makes sense, and we move back to the subject of the murders.

I say, "The near amputation of Irene's hands and the amputation of Powys's legs suggests the same killer. The question is whether their romantic connection is significant."

"Powys dated about a dozen women here."

"So, not overly significant. What about drugs? Powys had a medical background, and Hastings was a chemist. Did you suspect both of being involved with rydex?"

"I considered it, but they didn't move in the same circles. Also, one of the reasons I knew Powys's backstory was a lie was that Beth says he knew shit about pharmaceuticals."

"Maybe Irene and Hastings, then? Her tox screen showed she was high when she died."

"Yeah, but there were no signs of long-term use. My theory is that she was doped before she was killed. That's not in the file because I've put nothing in it that could get my ass kicked out of Rockton."

He rubs a hand over his beard shadow, the *skritch* of it filling the silence. "I've made it pretty damn clear I don't like to talk about my background, about me being *from* here, but I'm going to say this once, and only because you need to understand the stakes. The council knows I don't want to leave Rockton. Wouldn't know what to do with myself down south. I don't have a proper education. I don't have proper ID. I don't *exist* outside Rockton, and I don't know *how* to exist outside Rockton. If I wanted to, I could figure it out. But I don't want to."

"This is your home."

"It is, and I hate that they can hold it over my head, but I'm a fucking lousy actor. I've tried. A year before Will got here, I started saying maybe I *wanted* to try living down south. They got me solid ID and began interviewing local replacements."

"They called your bluff."

"Yeah, and I folded. So that's where we stand."

"How will that affect my investigation? Are they dead set on covering up the murders?"

"No, it's not . . ." He makes a face and leans back. "The council ruled Irene a suicide because she left a note. It's not so much covering it up as turning a blind eye. But they also let me bring you in. I've told them how Powys died, and they aren't trying to rule it a death by misadventure. If you make the connection to Irene?" He shrugged. "Well, you're a detective. You figured it out. I'm just the hick sheriff who didn't."

TWENTY-SIX

I'm on the trail of Abbygail Kemp. That isn't easy. Dalton's not the only one who feels as if he failed her. Beth can barely talk about it. We're in the clinic, and she's trying to distract herself by cleaning up while I ask questions, but the memories rattle her so badly, she slices her finger on a scalpel.

She winces as she dabs it. "Sorry. It's just . . ." She tries hard for a smile. "Not a subject I ought to discuss while handling sharp objects."

"I understand. The sheriff says you still have her things. Do you mind if I take a look?"

She silently leads me next door, to her home. It's nearly identical to mine, except there's a futon in the living room.

"That's where she stayed," Beth says. "During the drug withdrawal, she couldn't live on her own. Later, we gave her an apartment, but . . ." She tugs her gaze away from the futon and says, a little gruffly, "She'd gotten used to it here. We'd gotten used to each other." A few moments' pause. "I have an appointment at the clinic in a few minutes, so I need to run. Her things are under there." She points at the futon. "If it helps to take the bag, go ahead. I don't . . . I don't know what to do with it. Standard procedure is to throw out belongings. I can't do that. So . . ."

"I'll take it back to the station," I say. "Her things are potential evidence. We can't dispose of them."

"You think she was . . ." She pushes her hands into her lab coat pockets, wincing as she brushes her cut finger. "Of course you do. I just can't quite wrap my head around the idea that anyone in town would hurt her. But she was young and she was pretty, and I guess, maybe, sometimes that's enough, isn't it?"

"Sometimes."

"Eric blames himself. He thinks he didn't try hard enough to keep her out of the forest. He's wrong, though. The fact she disappeared into it is — for me — the best proof she was murdered. She wouldn't have worried him like that. Eric was . . . Eric was special. To Abbygail. The handsome young sheriff who rescued her."

"She had a crush on him."

She smiles then, her eyes brightening. "A *huge* crush. Not a serious interest, though. Yes, she was twenty-one, but she knew he would never see her that way. So it was a schoolgirl infatuation. The kind she should have had *in* school, but for Abbygail, that wasn't an option. She got to have it here, instead, with her white knight. She would argue with him and pretend to rebel against his rules, but it was like a twelve-year-old girl teasing the boy she likes." She looks at me. "If he said stay out of the woods, she'd never have gone in without good reason. Never."

Abbygail's belongings. Almost everything seems to have been acquired post-arrival. There are books — romance novels and nursing texts. Clothing and toiletries, all generic. An equally generic stuffed animal, the kind you get at the fair in those everyone's-a-winner games — a creature that could be a dog, a cat, or a bear. It's tattered enough to suggest it was one thing she *did* bring from home. There's a necklace around the animal's neck. A tin heart with a makeshift inscription. *JP & AK 4ever.* It looks like the sort of thing a preteen boy would give a girl, and I wonder if it's the same one who gave her the bear — a first love, long gone, relics of another life.

I think that's all there is. Then paper crinkles in the lining of her old suitcase. I tug it out, hoping to see some secret clue to start me on my path.

It's a photo. The old-style Polaroid kind.

But it was taken here. There are decorations in the background, as if for a party. The girl in it must be Abbygail Kemp. Dark hair. Tan skin. Mixed-race background, and I won't speculate what it is — I hate it when anyone does that with me. Her thin face is lit up in a grin as she mugs for the camera. She looks happy. That's my first thought — *she's so happy* — and I think that's why she kept the photo and hid it, because she wanted to remember Rockton after she left.

Then I see the whole picture. There's someone beside her. It's Dalton. He's not posing for the photo. Doesn't even seem to know it's being snapped, because he's looking off to the side, in the middle of saying something to someone. Abbygail is making a face behind his back, fingers raised to give him bunny ears. This is why she kept it. *He's* why she kept it. Squirrelled away in the lining of her bag. I see that photo, and my heart breaks a little for a girl I never knew. A girl who was happy here in Rockton. A girl with a cheap stuffed toy and tin necklace and a picture of a man she'd never have, but that'd been okay, because she just liked the feeling of having a crush. Of being a normal girl.

Abbygail wouldn't want Dalton to see that photo. Wouldn't want him to know she'd held on to it. I tuck it back under the lining. I'll keep her secret for her.

■ ■ ■ ■

I have interviews scheduled for that afternoon. Well, they're on *my* schedule. That's all that counts in Rockton, because I have complete freedom to interview anyone I want, whenever I want, wherever I want.

Dalton tags along for the first few, making sure everyone's playing nice with the new detective. They are. Then he's called off on a problem — something to do with resource management, which doesn't exactly seem like law enforcement, but I get the feeling Dalton's job description extends well beyond throwing drunks in the cell.

I'm interviewing a guy named Pierre Lang. Two days before Abbygail disappeared, he'd hassled her at the clinic when she refused to refill a prescription without Beth's say-so. It turned out the refill was legit, but Abbygail had no way of knowing that — the script existed only in Beth's perfect file cabinet of a brain. So Abbygail had been right to refuse, and the delay was only an hour or two, but Pierre had gone off on her loudly enough for Kenny and a couple of the other militia boys to hear from the street and come running to her rescue.

Now Lang — a tall, fussily tidy man with a goatee — sits in the living room of his apartment, telling me how everyone overreacted.

"Including you?" I ask.

"No, Ms. Butler, I did not."

"It's Detective Butler."

He bristles. I get a vibe that says he doesn't like women very much. Or maybe it's not a vibe as much as an extrapolation, given what I read that morning.

Lang is in Dalton's journal. He's one of the confirmed cases. And having read what he did, I cannot forget it, as hard as I'm trying to remain neutral.

"I did not overreact, Detective Butler. I need that medication."

"Fluvoxamine," I say.

"How — ?" He pulls himself taut with indignation. "My medical history is my private business."

"Yep," I say. "It was before you got here and, presumably, it will be when you leave. Did you read that waiver before you handed over your money, Mr. Lang? Or were you in too big a hurry to get up here?"

He glares at me. "Yes, I read it, but yes, I was in a hurry. If you've read my medical file, then I'm sure you've read the rest, too. If you want to mock me for it, go ahead and get it out of your system, *Detective.*"

"Because you came here fleeing an abusive relationship? Why would I mock that?"

His mouth tightens. He means that he expects mockery because he's a *man* fleeing abuse. Which makes no difference to me. Or

231

it wouldn't, if that were what he was really here for.

"Do you really need the Fluvoxamine up here?" I say. "I'd think Rockton would be the perfect solution to your problem. No little girls anywhere."

"What?" he squeaks, indignation surging. "My *problem* is anxiety and depression."

"Fluvoxamine is an SSRI. A selective serotonin reuptake inhibitor. Used to treat pedophiles by inhibiting sexual desire and fantasy."

He loses it then. Rants and rages at me. It's true that the drug is most commonly used for depression. But according to what Dalton found, my reason for the prescription is the right one.

Pierre Lang has a long history of minor convictions, pleading guilty to misdemeanors and getting wrist slaps. Then he kidnapped and raped a girl on the cusp of adolescence. While awaiting trial, he disappeared, apparently having bought his way into Rockton.

"I could be wrong," I muse. "I'll check with the doctor. I was pretty sure, though —"

"You *are* wrong. And I'm going to report you for . . . for slander."

"Slander only counts in a public statement. In private, I can say what I like. Being a detective, it's my job to speculate. Speaking purely as speculation, I can understand why they might allow a pedophile in, if he paid well enough. Like I said, there's no temptation here. Well, not unless there's a girl who looks young for her age, and that pedophile is desperate . . ."

"I'd like you to leave now," Lang says.

"I'm sure you would," says a voice behind me. Dalton walks in and plunks himself down on the sofa as Lang squawks.

"Door was unlocked," Dalton says.

"Does it matter?"

"Guess not. I have the key."

"That isn't what I meant." Lang settles for glaring and pulls himself in, like a bird hunkering down, wings wrapped around itself. He tries to shoot a glare at Dalton, but his gaze doesn't rise above the sheriff's collar.

"So . . ." Dalton sprawls on the sofa, legs out, arms stretched across the back. Establishing territory, taking as much as he can while Lang draws himself ever tighter. "You were saying, Detective Butler?"

I glance over. Dalton meets my gaze, expressionless, but I still catch the message. He overheard my accusation. He's not stopping me, but he's here to make sure I don't give away anything more.

I ask Lang about Abbygail. When's the last time he saw her? And the first time? And he balks at that one — how would he remember? But he does. I can see that in his eyes. I keep circling, prodding, poking. After about twenty minutes, I close the interview and we leave.

"How much did you hear?" I ask when

we're away from the house.

"Starting at the part about the meds."

"I overstepped there, didn't I?"

"Yep."

As we walk, three people wave at Dalton. Two more call greetings. They don't seem to even notice that he doesn't wave or call back.

"I'm not sure how to put aside what I read," I say. "Am I supposed to?"

Dalton scratches his chin. He walks another three steps. Then he says, "Depends on you, I guess. How you deal with it. How you compartmentalize."

A woman greets him, and this time he replies, and that makes me look up and see one of the local chefs. In his book, she's suspected of escaping charges related to befriending girls for a forced-prostitution ring.

I understand what he's saying. That if I read his journal, I have to compartmentalize. Look at this woman who cooks my meals and forget what she's been accused of, unless, like Lang, it plays into an investigation.

"Lang did notice Abbygail," Dalton says as we continue walking. "There was a . . ." He tilts his head, searching for a word. "Frustration there. Not really an interest. A frustration."

"Because she was the closest thing here to what he likes. Yet she was an adult woman, which he does *not* seem to like."

He nods. "I saw it. Monitored it. Warned Abbygail as best I could. Maybe not enough . . ." He drifts off for a moment, then comes back with, "She seemed to understand."

"She would have," I say. "Being from the streets, she'd have been able to sniff a predator and steer clear."

"He's still a suspect," Dalton says. "I've been watching him since she disappeared."

"Nothing?"

"Yeah."

He slows, and when I look up, we're behind the station, at the shed where they store the ATVs.

"Border run?" I say, trying not to betray a spark of excitement. My day could really use this.

"Nah, taking you out for a visit. Time to talk to a guy in a cave."

TWENTY-SEVEN

I figure the "guy in a cave" thing is a local joke, like saying you need to speak to a man about a dog. Dalton certainly doesn't elaborate. We go into the drive shed, and I get a much more in-depth ATV lesson than I did when I arrived.

Dalton may grumble that he doesn't like explaining things, but he's a natural teacher. He's patient and . . . I won't say enthusiastic, which implies a level of emotion I don't think our sheriff is capable of, but it's like when we discussed the hostiles in the forest, and I mentioned primates and there was a spark of genuine interest there. A hound catching a scent. Except, for Dalton, that intriguing scent isn't prey — it's knowledge.

When he finishes the safety lesson, he starts to explain how the throttle works, and then checks himself, as if realizing this is more than I need to drive it. But it's not more than I *want,* and when I ask questions, he pairs the driving lesson with one on basic mechanics, so I can understand how an ATV operates.

Dalton's not the only hound who likes to pursue a trail of knowledge. When we're riding and he slows to give me directions or point out an obstacle, I always have a question — *what's that animal that scurried across the path?* or *what are those trees with the berries?* At first he suspects I'm sucking up, and his eyes narrow as he carefully responds. But I genuinely want to know, and he must see that in my face, because soon he's giving the answers freely.

When we stop and get off the ATV, I don't ask why. I get the feeling that's *not* the kind of question Dalton likes to answer. Instead, as we walk into a clearing off the path, I notice what looks like a campfire ring.

I point to it. "One of yours? Someone from the town, I mean?"

He hunkers down beside the ring. "We have our bonfires in the town square. If we light one out here, it's usually on hunting trips, when you're a lot farther from town than this. We'll also build them at the logging area or the fishing ponds, when it gets cold. This is from settlers."

"People who live outside the town but aren't actually hostile."

"Not *actively* hostile. If you stumble on them and point your gun, yeah, expect trouble. What you have here looks like a hunting party. Maybe trapping. You can tell it's settlers because they use stones for the fire pit. The fire's also a little too large. Hostiles are more careful. They're also a little less . . ." He purses his lips, considering his word choice. "Structured."

"They aren't going to fuss with hauling in fire pit stones and a log to sit on."

"Yeah."

"And you can tell it's a hunting or trapping party because . . . ?"

He points. "Decaying offal pile over there. Scavengers dragged away the better parts. There's a broken arrow here, which suggests hunting, but trapping is still a possibility."

Even when he points, I can't see what he's indicating until I go over and have to crouch to make out the signs he picked up in a casual sweep.

"If you're out on patrol, you need to write anything like this in the logs," he says. "Your notes will tell me how fast I need to get out here to assess."

"Is there a guide for what things mean?"

He gives me a look like I'm asking for an app for my phone. Then he taps the side of his head.

"It's all up there," I say. "It would be more helpful if you wrote it down."

"Tried. No one read it. Either they don't give a shit or they don't have an eye for reading signs." He pushes aside a branch. "Mostly the latter. Like Will. Fucking worst tracker ever. Once reported grizzly tracks that turned out to be boot prints. *His* boot prints."

I laugh.

"People learn in different ways," Dalton continues as he walks back to the path. "Will's a smart guy. College educated. Pre-med before he joined the army. But reading doesn't do it for him. Hearing it, doing it, that's how he learns. So not much point in me writing shit down."

We continue right past the ATVs. Soon I see why, as the path becomes so narrow that we can't even walk side by side. When I notice a sandy patch alongside the trail, I crouch for a better look.

"Speaking of prints," I say, "what are these?"

He barely gives them a glance. "Cat."

"Bobcat? They seem small."

He snorts. "No bobcats here. Lynx mostly. And one cougar."

"One?"

"We're a little out of their range, which runs in a swath from Whitehorse to Dawson City. There is one, though. Her prints are nearly as big as a grizzly's. You can't miss them. And stay out of her way, same as you would a grizzly. She's no friendly kitty. Killed a guy on a hunting trip couple years back."

"I didn't see that in the files."

"No investigation needed. She jumped from a tree. Landed on his back. Snapped his neck and dragged him off to her kittens." He rubs his chin. "Who may also have hung around, now that they're full grown."

I peer up into the treetops.

"Too dense for her here," he says. "And she's not likely to strike when you have company. Predators are smart. They don't bite off more than they can chew . . . or haul away."

"Lovely . . ."

"The guy who got killed had wandered off from the party. We only knew what happened because he screamed and someone spotted the cat dragging his body away. I suspect she only went after him because of the kittens. Spring's when you need to be particularly careful."

"I won't need to worry about it, since my six months are up by then."

He grunts in acknowledgment. And yes, that stings, because I want him to be impressed enough already to change his mind, even if I haven't made up my own.

"Lynx, then?" I say, pointing at the tracks again.

"Too small. Lynx aren't big cats, but like cougars, they have oversized paws. Adaptation to walking on snow. Those prints are *Felis catus.* Domestic cat."

"Isn't that *Felis domestica,* Sheriff?"

"Nope. That would be a common but incorrect taxonomic name, Detective. It can also be *Felis silvestris catus,* which combines woodland and domestic cat. And in this case, that might be more accurate."

"So they're former house cats?"

He motions for me to resume walking as he says, "Escaped from town when they allowed them."

"You have feral cats in the forest?"

"And dogs. Rabbits, chickens, few hogs. All descended from escapees. Dogs were for security. Cats for mousing. The others for food. Back when there were fifty, sixty people in Rockton, raising livestock made sense. Now? Too much land needed to raise more than a few dozen chickens for eggs and goats for milk."

"Why did they get rid of the cats and dogs?"

"No idea. They weren't documenting things back then. I do, for the day-to-day stuff — what kind of problem we faced and how we resolved it. For the dogs and cats, I've heard rabies outbreak. They put them down and didn't want to risk bringing in more. I also heard it was something as stupid as allergies — one of Val's predecessors was allergic, so he made a no-animal law, and no one's changed it."

"Have *you* considered changing it?"

He looks surprised by the question. "Course. You can't just say that we should keep doing a thing just because it's always been done. Cats eat their fill of mice, so upkeep is minimal. Dogs can eat the parts of game we throw out. Fresh water is plentiful. I've been considering it. Getting new animals — not taming the ones out here. You don't do that shit. Once they're wild, they stay wild."

"Are the feral dogs dangerous?"

"Fuck, yeah. More than wolves. They're bigger and meaner. Lot less scared of humans, too. It's just wrong to go from being wild to tame or vice versa. If you see a dog, I'm not saying to shoot it on sight. But if it makes any aggressive moves? Yeah, you have to put it down."

We step out of the woods into an open area near some foothills. I admire the scenery for a moment before coming back with, "But the cats are fine?"

"Unless they're rabid. Or just crazy. It happens. Fucking with nature is a problem, like I said. Worst, though, are the hogs. More dangerous than the black bears."

"Tell me the wild chickens aren't dangerous."

"Unless they fly out in front of your horse, which they do sometimes. Unseated a guy years back. Broke his neck. The rabbits, though? The rabbits haven't killed anyone." He pauses. "So far."

Twenty-Eight

As we continue along the foothills, I drink in the scenery. Most of the trees are evergreens, but there are enough deciduous trees changing color to remind me of home. It's a perfect autumn day, crisp and clear.

"Given the many, many dangers of the forest, I'm presuming you guys don't do a lot of activities out here."

He shrugs. "Nah, we do. Some of us, anyway."

"Any rock climbing?" I say, gesturing at the craggy face of the mountain.

He nods. "Anders is into it. We go out sometimes with a few of the others. Caving, too. Former resident was into that. Mapped out caves. Taught me. We go sometimes — Anders, me, few others. Only those who can handle themselves out here."

"So that's a no, then?"

He frowns back at me.

"You're subtly telling me not to ask to join you."

He snorts. "If you think I'm capable of being subtle, you aren't very perceptive, Detective." He peers over. "You want to come out with us?"

"I might." I shrug.

I'm trying for nonchalance. I don't want to sound like I'm brown-nosing. Nor do I want to jump in like an eager kid. But his thoughtful look vanishes, he turns away and grunts something I don't catch, and I've made a misstep.

Before I can try again, he points and says, "Gonna have to do a bit of rock climbing now. We need to get there."

I follow his finger to see what looks like a crack high in the rock face.

"What's up there?" I ask.

"Cave. Like I said."

"I expected something bigger."

"If the opening was bigger, there'd be something bigger in it. Like a bear. And it *is* bigger on the inside."

"Like the Tardis?" As I say it, I mentally kick myself — pop culture references make him uncomfortable — but he makes a noise suspiciously like a chuckle and says, "Yeah, except no time traveling."

He catches my expression, shakes his head, and says, "Ever heard of those amazing devices called DVDs?"

"Sure, but what do you play them on up here?"

"Tree stumps. If you carve them out just right and get ground squirrels to run around them really fast, you can project moving pictures on a wall."

"Yeah, yeah."

"We have a DVD player," he says as he starts up the slope. "We hook it up to a screen and generator for movie nights. As sheriff, I have a laptop and access to the generator for charging. I also have an income that I can spend down south on shit like DVDs. You want to watch something? Ask me. My collection is limited, though. Right now I've got *Doctor Who*, *The Walking Dead*, and *Game of Thrones*."

By now I know enough not to even wonder if he's joking.

"Also have *Deadwood*," he says. "That makes more sense to me than most of your so-called dramas. Otherwise, I stick to the fantasy stuff."

My foot slides on a particularly steep part. Dalton only glances back to make sure I don't tumble to my doom.

"I might borrow *The Walking Dead*," I say. "I haven't seen that."

"Good show. Also reminds you that no matter what kind of shit we have in these woods, at least it's not zombies."

"*Yet*. And you do have cannibals."

He sighs. "I never said we definitely have them. I said the evidence suggests it's possible. Even if we do, they're not charging out of the woods like a zombie horde."

"Yet."

We reach the cave. The opening is a gash in the rock, maybe three feet wide by eighteen inches high. When I catch the smell of a wood fire, I go still and scan the area. Dalton hunkers down to the opening and yells, "Brent! You home?"

"Depends on who's asking," a voice replies.

"Your ex-wife sent me. Something about you owing her money."

"You're gonna have to be more specific than that."

"I'm coming in, and I'm bringing company." Dalton hands me his backpack. "Pass this through to me." Before I can reply, he's on his stomach and crawling through the space. Then his hands appear. I give him the bag. After another thirty seconds, gray eyes peer out.

"You need an invitation, Detective? Sure as hell hope you don't need instructions, because you should have been watching."

I get down on my stomach. The gap turns out to be wider than I think. I slide through easily . . . and nearly fall onto my head.

Dalton catches me and helps me get upright, and I see we're in an open area that's more like I expect from a cave. Dalton walks, hunched over, to a slope heading down into darkness.

"You gonna turn on the porch light?" Dalton yells.

The hiss of a lantern. Then a wavering light that does little to illuminate what I'm presumably about to climb into.

Dalton grabs a rope on the side and lowers himself down the slope. This time, I pay careful attention. Then I follow. At the bottom, the light is disappearing as a man carries it along a passage. Even I need to crouch to get through this one. Then the man pushes at what looks like a door. It swings open. Flickering light and the smell of wood smoke pours out and I see a fire, the smoke rising into a hole in the top of what I'm guessing is called a cavern. It looks like one of those bomb shelters from the fifties, though. There's a bed, a table and chairs, and shelves — lots of shelves, with goods from books to canned food. Dried meat hangs from the ceiling along with dried roots and other flora that I presume is edible.

There's a man, too. And he also fits the scene perfectly, looking like a guy who retreated to his bomb shelter fifty years ago and just popped his head out now. He's about seventy, with gray hair in a ponytail, pale, wrinkled skin, and eyes that peer against the light. Right now, they're peering at me.

"Now *that's* a deputy," he says. "Much prettier than your last one."

"Ms. Butler is a detective."

"Really?" Brent's wire-brush brows shoot up. "Women do that nowadays?"

"Women do everything nowadays," I say.

He grins. "Except piss standing up."

"Oh, they can do that, too. It's just messy."

He laughs like this is the funniest thing he's heard in years. Then he ushers me to a chair — sorry, *the* chair — and pours me a glass of water from a collapsible pouch.

"Are you a police detective?" he asks. "Or a private eye?"

"Police," I say.

"I was in law enforcement, too."

"Brent was a bail bondsman," Dalton says.

"Bounty hunter, please. It sounds sexier." Brent turns to me. "Shitty job. Paid well, but do you know the problem with people who jump bail?"

"They don't want to be caught?"

He cackles a laugh. "Right you are. And they are highly motivated. Got shot three times and stabbed five, and I have the scars to prove it. Here, let me show you."

"Another time," Dalton says.

"Hey, I bet I've got the best damned body she's ever seen on a man my age. Living up here? Climbing in and out of this place? Take a look at —" He starts pulling up his shirt.

Dalton stops him with "save it for a special occasion." He looks at me. "Brent chased a guy up here. Fellow ambushed him with sulfuric acid. He will *not* show you the scars to prove that, but it made him decide to give up chasing bad guys and just stay."

"In Rockton?" I ask.

"Fuck no," Brent says. "Pardon my French. Do you know what that place really is?"

"Brent is a conspiracy theorist," Dalton says. "He's got a dozen of them for Rockton. Next time we come out, ask him to tell you the one where it's a test facility for biological warfare. That's his best."

"You think so?" Brent says. "I like the alien ones better."

"The alien ones are shit." Dalton hefts the knapsack he brought. "Got some stuff for you, presuming you have goods and intel to trade."

"Both for you, Eric. Always. Did you bring me that Canadiens jersey?"

"Couldn't find it. Picked up a Maple Leafs one instead. That's okay, right?"

Brent spends the next minute telling Dalton why it is *not* okay in a diatribe only a true hockey fan could appreciate.

Dalton only shrugs. "Stupid fucking game anyway."

He gets another minute of fan ranting for that. Then he pulls out a Canadiens jersey and tosses it to Brent, who takes it and mutters, "Asshole." Then he turns to me. "I played for the Habs, you know."

"One season," Dalton says. "He warmed the bench."

"Asshole," Brent mutters.

"Keeping you honest." Dalton lowers himself to the floor in front of the fire and makes himself comfortable. "What do you have for me, Brent?"

Brent gives him a rundown on everything he's seen in the past week or so. The camp we'd spotted below was trappers — two men and a woman who are apparently part of a tiny community of former Rockton residents now living about ten kilometers east. Dalton knows them and grumbles because they were supposed to "check in" when they were in the area, so his militia didn't mistake them for bears.

Speaking of bears, Brent spotted two grizzlies, a "sow" and a young "boar" — I make a mental note of the terms. Dalton knows the female and wonders if the male is her son from a few springs back, and they debate that, rather like trying to figure out the parentage of a local kid based on whom he resembles.

Brent also spotted a feral dog that has been giving them both trouble. He shot at it with his bow. "Lost the goddamn arrow," he says. He saw signs of a hostile, too, but that was way out, when he was on an overnight hike. It was a woman, who only watched him. Dalton suggests she might have thought he looked like good husband material and razzes

him about that, but otherwise seems unconcerned.

I listen, saying nothing, fascinated by what
I'm hearing. It is all so far outside my realm
of experience. And yet it isn't. Take out the
details, and it sounds exactly like me dealing
with a confidential informant. Brent lets
Dalton know what is going on in the area, in
return for goods like clothing and coffee and
other items impossible to come by for a guy
living in a cave.

When Brent finishes with the basic report,
Dalton asks specific questions about Powys
and Hastings. Brent never saw the former,
hasn't seen the latter. He's a little annoyed
by the question, too.

"If I spotted one of your people out here
alone, you don't think I'd tell you?"

"Depends. Last time we had a runner, you
admitted you saw him and never told me."

"I would have as soon as I saw you again."

"Could come by the town."

"I wasn't in a sociable mood."

"If you see anyone, will you come by?"
Dalton pauses for at least ten seconds before
adding, "Please." Brent sobers at that, as if
the *please* tells him how serious this is.

"Everything okay, Eric?" he asks.

"That first guy I mentioned turned up dead
with his legs cut off. There were signs he'd
been butchered."

"Jesus." Brent pales. "You're serious?" He

doesn't even wait for an answer before saying, "Course you are. Sorry. I just . . ." He looks like he wants to sit, and I rise, but he waves me back down. "Butchered? You're sure?"

"Am I sure someone cut off parts and ate them? No. Am I sure someone wanted it to look that way? Yeah."

Brent exhales. "Okay. Right. I just . . . The cannibalism thing . . . I've had some damned hard winters, but no matter how bad it gets, even if I stumbled over someone who was already dead . . ." He shudders. "No way. No fucking way." He glances sheepishly at me. "Sorry."

"Like I said, women do everything now. Even swear."

The smile grows, just a little, and they continue talking. Then they barter goods, and I'm not sure how much use Dalton has for the fur and cured meat, but he bargains hard, as if he does.

Before we leave, Brent says, "Hold on a sec. Got something for the little cutie-pie here."

"Her name's Casey," Dalton says.

Brent grins. "Please tell me you had a dog named Finnegan."

"Sure did," I say. "When I was five. He was a brown dog, just like the one on the show. He only existed in my mind, but he was the best imaginary pet ever."

Brent lets out a whoop of laughter, and I

say to Dalton, "It was a kids' show. *Mr. Dressup.* There was a puppet named Casey —"

"Who had a dog named Finnegan." He offers a brief smile and a nod. "Got it."

"Well, that tells me what present to pick for you, then." Brent disappears into a dark corner of the room and hunkers down by an opening into what must be like a closet for him. He rattles around inside it and brings back a fist-sized woodcarving.

"Fox," he says. "I don't have a dog, but this is close."

"It's gorgeous," I say, and it is — so intricately carved that I can feel the fur under my fingers. "Did you do this?"

He nods with a gruff, "Lots of free time in the winters."

I thank him and ask if I can come back with Dalton sometime.

"Anytime," he says, and looks genuinely pleased.

We go to leave. I climb out first. When I'm nearly at the top, I hear Brent say, in a low voice to Dalton, "You seen Jacob?"

Dalton's reply comes quickly. "No. Why?"

"We were supposed to go hunting together three days ago. He never showed."

"What?"

"Nothing to worry about, Eric. It's not like he can call my cell phone if he has to cancel. I did see him the next day. Just caught a

253

glimpse of him as I was coming down the mountain. I tried to hail him, but he didn't seem to hear."

"But you definitely saw him."

"I did. Sorry. Didn't mean to spook you."

I continue out through the cave entrance, and their voices fade behind me. A few moments later, Dalton passes out the backpack.

All the way down the side of the hill, he says nothing. Then, at the bottom, he looks over to see me admiring the woodcarving, and I can feel that laser gaze drilling into me.

"You don't need to go back," he says.

"Is that your way of telling me I shouldn't?"

Frustration flashes in his eyes. "If I was telling you not to —"

"Then you'd tell me not to. Sorry. I'm still new at this, Sheriff."

He nods. Then we take a few steps before he says, "Brent has some problems. Beth says he might be mildly bipolar. You know what that is?"

"I'm a city cop. I need to know what that is."

"He's never been a threat, but he makes Will nervous. I'm not sure if it's the mood swings or just the idea of someone living like that. Which is the long way of saying that if you aren't comfortable going back . . ."

"Then I'd never have offered. He's interesting. His situation is interesting, too, living out there. Which isn't to say that I'm looking

254

at him like some kind of freak, either."

"All right, then."

After a few more steps, he glances over. I'm behind him and he looks out over his shoulder rather than directly back at me.

"You were kind to him." A moment's pause. "I appreciate that."

I nod, and we continue on to the ATVs.

TWENTY-NINE

When we get back to the station, I take off to find Diana and try to make dinner plans. She's getting ready for a date, though, so I return to the office until seven then go home and, well, work some more. Or I do until nine, when Anders spots my lantern glowing and pops in to say he's grabbing a beer with Dalton and asks if I want to join them. I do.

We take a table in the back corner of the Red Lion. Or I should say *Dalton* takes it, a jerk of his thumb making the couple who'd been there move without so much as a glower. Dalton waves me to the chair against the wall, and he and Anders pull up the other two across from me. Any guy who wants to get friendly with the new girl needs to pass both of them. No one tries.

I have a tequila shot followed by an iced tea. There's no chance of ordering a Diet Coke here. They fly in liquor, but otherwise it has to be something you can brew or mix with water.

We order nachos, too. The chips are cut and baked from homemade tortillas and the salsa is freshly made from greenhouse veggies. Both are delicious. There are a half dozen chefs in Rockton, and they're among the highest-paid residents, which means only the best get the job, and they do their damnedest to keep it.

Nearly two hours pass, eating and drinking and talking. The bar's full, but we aren't bothered for our table.

". . . we go into the forest," Anders is saying, "looking for this so-called wolf and —"

"Deputy!" a voice calls behind him. "I thought you were too busy to come out and play."

He turns, and I see Diana grinning in a way that I know means she's had too much to drink.

"You've been busy a lot, William," she continues. "And I'm trying not to take it personally, but —" She sees me and stops short. "Oh." Then with a sharp twist of sarcasm, "Well, that explains it."

"We were just grabbing after-shift drinks." I wave at Dalton, making it clear this isn't a tête-à-tête between me and Anders. "You're welcome to pull up a chair."

"Oh, am I? How generous." She walks to Dalton and leans over his shoulder to whisper loudly, "That means I get you. I always get the reject."

I freeze, certain I've misheard. Then I push to my feet. "Maybe we should step outside —"

"And settle this like men?" She lifts her fists as she sways. "Winner takes all? Or just one?" She leans to fake-whisper between the guys. "Casey doesn't do threesomes. She acts all liberal, and God knows she's not particular, but it's only one at a time, so don't get your hopes up."

I have her by the arm now. "All right, we're stepping out —"

She wrenches from my grasp and turns on Anders. "I figured this was the problem. I show up last week and you're all into me, but then less than twenty-four hours after you leave my bed, you seem to have forgotten my name. Because Casey arrived."

Anders is on his feet, sneaking glances at me as he lowers his voice to say, "We both had way too much to drink that night, Diana, and I feel like I took advantage. I said that afterward. I meant it."

"And I said you *didn't* take advantage, which means it's a bullshit excuse. I was fuckable when you were drunk. Why not just say that and —"

"Di, let's step out," I say.

"I asked if you had your eye on Will, and you brushed me off, when obviously —"

"When obviously I'm having a drink with

both my co-workers —"

"But you've only got your eye on one." She turns to Dalton. "Don't bother. Casey might have lousy taste, but one thing she doesn't go for? Weird."

"Di!" I say.

"What? He is. Everyone says so. He's got more screws loose than you, which is saying a lot. No, like I told Casey, Will, you're exactly her type. Hot guys with more muscles than brains."

My fingers are locked around her arm again as I hiss, "That's enough —"

"Did she tell you boys about the guy she left behind? Ex-con bartender who could barely spell his own name. The guy was so dumb he took a bullet for her, and when she tells him she's leaving, the chump still gives her that necklace she's wearing."

I've released her arm, and I'm shouldering my way through the crowded bar.

"Hey!" Diana calls. "Where are you going? Can't take the truth, Casey . . ."

She keeps talking. I walk out.

I'm in the gap between the bar and the next building, catching my breath, trembling with rage.

I'm not angry over what she said about me. An ex once said there was no use insulting me because nothing he could say was worse than what I already thought of myself. I think he was 50 percent full of shit — a frustrated psych major who couldn't get into grad school — but the other 50 percent . . . ? I don't know.

What I'm pissed off about is letting Diana insult two guys who sure as hell didn't deserve it. I should have wised up and realized she'd stop once her target was gone.

Footsteps sound behind me. I wait to be sure they're coming my way, and it's not just some random drinker who decided he needed an outdoor piss. The footfalls keep coming.

"I'm sorry," I say. "That put you in a bad spot, and . . ." I turn, expecting Will, and see Dalton. "Oh."

"Will's walking her home," he says. "I asked him to."

"Thank you. I'm really sorry. She's drunk and —"

"She's a bitch."

I don't stiffen. I don't leap to her defense. I feel as if I should, because I always do, and she's my friend, and she's drunk. But I just say, "What she said about you was totally uncalled for —"

"Don't give a shit about that. You think I haven't heard it?" He puts one hand on the wall and leans against it. "I know what I am, Casey. Hearing it from someone like that sure as hell doesn't bother me. She's a vindictive, jealous brat, and the fact that you've actually been friends with her for half your life proves you had a martyr complex even before that Saratori business."

"Wow. Thanks. Really. Because what I need right now —"

"What you need right now is to stop feeling responsible for Diana. Maybe I'm exaggerating about the martyr thing, but if you tell me that you didn't initially befriend her because you felt sorry for her? I'm calling bullshit."

I say nothing.

"You felt sorry for her, and she's been clinging to you ever since. You give, and she takes, and then she has the gall to resent you for every imagined —"

"Can we not talk about this?"

"You know I'm right."

"I also know you like to tell me what's wrong with me, and I know I don't much like to hear it."

"Seemed you were okay when she was doing it."

I zip my jacket. "I'm sorry she ruined our evening. It was a good one. Thank you for that, and I'll see you tomorrow."

He follows me out and down the road. When I'm sure that's not just because he happens to be heading the same way, I say without turning, "If you're escorting me home, walk with me, please. Otherwise I feel like I'm being stalked."

He catches up with a few strides. We don't talk. We reach my porch, and I unlock my door and turn and say, "Thanks."

Then I pause. He can rub me the wrong way, and I sure as hell don't appreciate being psychoanalyzed, but otherwise it's been a good day for us. I don't want to end it being rude, so I say, "You're welcome to come in for a coffee, but after what Diana said . . ."

"Diana's a —" He cuts himself off, though it looks as painful as if he actually bit his tongue. "I don't give a shit what anyone thinks, Butler, in case that isn't perfectly clear by now. Whatever a guy down south might expect of being asked into a woman's place, I'm not from down south. I figure you're offering me coffee because I walked you home and it's cold out and you'd feel rude turning me away at the door. To which I'd say that you worry too fucking much about being nice, especially to those who aren't particularly nice in return, but apparently you don't like me pointing out your faults."

"Shocking, really, because most people *love* that."

I find a smile for him, and he nods, giving me a ghost of one in return, and then says, "Well, the polite thing for me to do now would be to say no, I don't want a coffee. But I do, so you're going to have to make me one."

Dalton starts the fire, and I put the full kettle on the hook. We wait in silence for it to boil.

262

I'm making the French-press coffee when someone raps at the door. Dalton grunts, "Got it." A moment later, I hear Anders say, "Oh, hey," and then, "Everything okay?"

"Yep."

"I got Diana home fine, but I wanted to talk to Casey —"

"About Diana?"

"Well, yes. About what she said and —"

"She doesn't want to talk about Diana."

"Right. Okay. I get that. Does she, um . . ." Anders's voice lowers. "Does she not want to talk to me?"

"She never said that."

"Did she, uh, say anything? About what Diana said? Me and her, and . . ."

Anders trails off, and Dalton seems to wait for more, then says, "Nope. Nothing. Talk to her in the morning."

I could go out and say no, that's fine, and invite Anders in. But I really *don't* want to discuss Diana. So I pretend not to hear them and take mugs from the cupboard.

"Right," Anders says after a moment. "Okay. So . . . see you tomorrow, I guess."

Dalton says good-bye and shuts the door.

THIRTY

We're in my living room, and damn, I'm content. Even bordering on happy. I shouldn't be. Since I arrived in Rockton, I've felt like I'm on one of those playground rides that spins as fast as the other kids can run, and at first it's exhilarating, but then you just want to get the hell off, and no one will let you, and when it finally stops, you're left lurching around, trying not to puke in the sandbox. Then, just as the ground seemed to be leveling today, I was sucker-punched by my best friend — the whole damn reason I stepped on the ride in the first place.

Maybe it's just a question of balance and juxtaposition. Compared with that merry-go-round hell, being curled up on the sofa in my own house, in front of a roaring fire, with a hot coffee in hand and a warm blanket pulled over me, I almost want to cry from relief. The world has stopped spinning, if only for a few moments.

Dalton is still here. I can't see him — I'm

staring at the fire, and he's in the chair to my left, out of sight. But I can hear his measured breathing, and it only adds to the calm, like a steady heartbeat. Maybe that helps, too, that I'm not alone. That someone is here who expects, at least for the moment, nothing from me. Not even conversation.

After a while, Dalton shifts, his jeans scratching against the fabric of the chair. We've hit the limit of silence, and something must be said before it turns awkward.

I look over at him first, and he's gazing into the fire, not noticing that I've turned, so I watch him, the light flickering over his face. He's so deep in thought that I resist speaking until he stretches his legs, shifting again, the silence chafing.

"Can I ask you something about the case?" I say. "Or are you off duty?"

"I'm never off duty. Not a whole lot else to talk about. Weather maybe? It's getting cold. It'll keep getting colder. Then it'll snow."

"Good to know," I say with a smile.

"I could ask what you think of the Jays' chances at the Super Bowl."

I laugh softly. "The Jays play baseball. The Super Bowl is football — and it's American."

"Huh. There goes that idea. Better stick to work. Go ahead."

"If I asked you for your background notes on Irene Prosser — why she was here — could I get them?"

"No notes." He taps his head. "It's all up here. The council tells me people's stories as part of the vetting process. That's a bylaw. Doesn't mean I'm allowed to write them down. That would be a breach of confidentiality. Also, they presume I'm not bright enough to actually remember. Irene was here for the same reason Diana and almost half the women are."

"Fleeing an abusive situation."

"The women are mostly running from bad choices in men. The men are mostly running from bad choices in life."

He tells me Irene's story. Like Diana, she was escaping an abusive ex whose stalking turned to violence and death threats. From *I love you and can't live without you* to *If I can't have you, no one will.* Chilling in its predictability.

"Do you have any idea the sort of injuries she suffered?" I ask.

"She had what your friend didn't — a long medical record of obvious abuse, complete with X-rays of broken bones."

"Not every kind of abuse results in broken bones, Sheriff, and I don't appreciate the insinuation."

"I'm not saying your friend wasn't abused by her ex. Nor am I saying you padded her application. I'm just . . ." He trails off and then straightens. "Back to Irene."

"Thank you."

"There were broken bones. Maybe a half dozen hospital reports. I can't recall details, but it was a clearly documented case of physical abuse."

There are a few moments of silence after that, and it *is* awkward now. Finally, he rises and takes his empty mug into the kitchen. I follow a moment later to see him, not preparing to leave, but pouring another half cup. He takes it to the window and looks out.

I've had enough coffee, but I join him in gazing into the night, and the silence softens until he says, "You've got a fox."

I look toward the carving Brent gave me, where it sits on my table.

"No," he says. "A real one."

He motions me to the window and reaches back to extinguish the lantern. Moonlight streams in. He points, and it takes me a minute, but slowly I make out the shape of a canine the size of a spaniel, half emerged from a fallen log. Then it steps out.

"That'd be the den," he says. "It's a red fox."

I squint against the glass. "Doesn't look very red to me."

"It's a cross fox. Which is a variant of a red. The coloring is dark red, and you'll still see the white-tipped tail, but it has a black line down its back and one over its shoulders."

"Hence the name."

He nods. "They're rarer than the traditional coloring, but not as rare as the silver variant. We've got one of those in the area."

"If you spot it on a ride, can you point it out?"

"Course."

"Thanks. I'd like to see that. Or any wildlife, really. Are there books? When I popped into the library, it seemed mostly fiction."

"I have books."

"Any chance of borrowing one?"

He nods. It's a laconic nod, but the glitter in his eyes says he's pleased.

"Do I need to worry about the fox being there?" I ask, mostly to keep the conversation going.

"Nah. Only a rabid one is a threat. I'll tell you how to spot rabid animals, but they're extremely rare, and we have the antidote. As for the fox, just keep your garbage covered. That's a general rule, though. Raccoons and bears are the real troublemakers there. Occasionally, foxes will be bolder than other animals. It might let you get closer than you expect. Or it might sit and watch you, but that's only a problem if it approaches you or tries to attack."

"Because that suggests rabies."

"Yep. And don't feed it. It's a wild animal. Let it stay wild. You'll only do more harm than good otherwise, as much as you might think you're helping."

He's staring into the forest again, his expression tight. After a moment, he shakes it off and clears his throat. "Anyway, the fox shouldn't be a problem, so you can leave it be. The only thing I'll warn you about is that if it's a vixen — a female — and you're here in mating season, her call will probably scare the crap out of you. Every year I get some panicked new resident pounding on my door in the middle of the night, shouting about the woman being murdered in the forest."

"I'll consider myself warned."

He steps back from the window. Then he stops and peers up.

"Are those your blankets on the balcony?" he says. "Don't tell me you're still sleeping outside."

"Okay, I won't tell you."

He gives me a look.

I shrug. "It's a little weird, I know. Maybe it's the fresh air or the quiet, but I slept so well that first night that I kept doing it."

"Just don't expect me to help drag your bed out there."

"It's too big. I tried taking out the mattress, but that won't fit through the door, either."

He looks to see if I'm kidding, realizes I'm not, and shakes his head.

"It's safe, though, right?" I say. "We ruled out flying monkeys?"

"Yes, but we have another primate who can

climb out there."

"Oh." I step from the window. "Maybe it's not such a good idea, then."

"Nah, it's safe. The hostiles don't come this close, and even if they did, no one can see you up there. Just . . . I know you don't like sleeping with your gun, but I'm going to ask you to have it there. Put it out of reach nearby."

"I will."

He sets his empty mug in the sink and heads for the door. I follow to lock it behind him. In the front hall, he stops and says, "What we talked about. With Irene and . . . well, pretty much everything related to this case. That's between us."

"I know."

"I mean it. I'm not saying I trust you more than other people. I don't." He looks over at me. "I'm sure it's rude to say that outright, but you know it's the truth. Trust takes a helluva long time to build out here, and ours is situational."

"Because I'm the detective on the case, and you're not going to solve it by withholding information I need. I understand that."

"Good. And of the people I *do* trust in this town, Beth's near the top of the list. But we share case details with her on a need-to-know basis. For her own good and her own safety. That goes for Will, too."

"Will?"

"Yeah. He's the best damn deputy this town has ever had, and on that short list of people I trust, he's *at* the top. But Will likes to talk, as you may have noticed. He goes out and has a few drinks, and sometimes it's one too many, and then he does shit he regrets in the morning."

"I got that impression."

"With Diana? Yeah. Will likes to cut loose. Dealing with baggage and all that. He can be a little careless, and that's why I don't tell him anything that would get him in trouble. Or jeopardize an investigation."

"One of the things they warn you about at the academy is that you can't talk about cases to a friend, a lover, a spouse, anyone. For me, that comes naturally."

"Good. Keep it that way."

The evening ends so well. I'm relaxed and centered and settled. Then I remember what Diana did, and I'm in bed, half asleep, but all I can think about is her. In a surreal way, it's as if I'm back downstairs with Dalton, and I'm talking it through and I'm seeing his reaction and . . .

And I realize I'm angry. I'm so damned angry. I don't want to cut Diana any slack. I don't want to say she was drunk and didn't mean what she said. Of course she meant it. Alcohol doesn't transform us into different people — it just lowers inhibitions. *In vino veritas.* Pour enough alcohol down someone's throat, and they'll start sharing opinions and beliefs they never would otherwise.

Diana's tirade was nasty and downright cruel. She may have aimed some of that invective at Anders and Dalton, but they were collateral damage. The venom was for me. Insulting them was just a fast route to humiliating me.

I think of all the other times she's lashed out. When she ran off to join the cool girls in high school, I tried to warn her, and she accused me of being jealous, made it very clear she'd only befriended me because I was the one who stepped up. Afterward, she begged and cried and swore she hadn't meant any of it, and I'd let her back because I felt bad for her. Then, when I warned her about Graham, she said I was a jealous, selfish bitch who — post-attack — had lost most of my friends so I clung to her. When she ran back to me again, I let her, because I owed her for keeping the secret about Blaine. And from there? From there, it became like a long-running marriage. We'd fight. She'd needle and insult me, but by that point I just didn't give a shit. Like my ex said, there was nothing anyone could say about me that was worse than what I said about myself.

And now this. I came here for her, and she was acting like I was a puppy who'd followed her home. No, worse — like I was her nemesis, spoiling her fun and stealing her lovers.

Well, fuck that. Really. Fuck that.

I wasn't ready to cut her loose. I didn't have the headspace for that — I had murders to solve. But those murders would keep me properly busy, and so I would step back. Skip the ugly confrontation and hope that this was what Diana needed — what we both needed. A truly fresh start for both of us.

THIRTY-ONE

I start my day with more interviews. Dalton joins me again. He's calm today, his edges muffled, until an interviewee gives me grief and then all he needs to do is rock forward, his jaw setting, and she falls in line so fast it's like having a rottweiler at my side, dozing until he smells a threat and then rising with a growl and a lip curl to douse that threat in a heartbeat. Very handy.

My first interview is with the last person to see Powys alive. It's a woman, perhaps not surprisingly, given that he disappeared in the middle of the night. From her bed, apparently. She's convinced he was kidnapped on his way to the bathroom. According to Dalton, there was absolutely no evidence of a break-in, but she's not going to admit Powys screwed her and then snuck off in the night. Which means pretty much everything about her story is suspect. Including the part, I'm guessing, where they had sex four times that evening. Which was, as Dalton snorted, "irrelevant," though the fact she kept repeating it suggested this was highly relevant to her.

The second interview is Irene's co-worker, who was the last to see *her* alive. Irene worked in the greenhouses, having a background in horticulture. Her co-worker is also a gardener, and I remember her from Dalton's little brown book. She's in Rockton hiding from charges of poisoning her abusive husband and burying him in the flower bed. In researching her online, Dalton had uncovered a story about a very wealthy woman whose abusive husband had been found fertilizing her prize roses. She'd disappeared while out on bail. The article included her photo, which apparently matches the sixty-year-old woman now telling me what a sweet girl Irene had been. As for why she needed to buy her way into Rockton, that had less to do with her killing an abusive husband and more to do with the body found beside his — that of their twenty-three-year-old maid, pregnant with his child.

All that means I have a second witness I can't trust. Which I am beginning to suspect will be par for the course in Rockton. Even many who haven't bought their way in will have something to hide, like me. A town full of liars. Cases here will depend more on evidence than interviews.

Speaking of evidence, I want to talk to Beth, but she has clinic hours until noon.

Dalton says we'll go by after lunch.

He walks me to my last interview of the morning and then leaves. He has rounds to make, which is mostly about just being seen, reminding people he's there, to make them feel safer or to warn them . . . or a little of both.

This particular interview is all mine because he trusts the interviewee to cooperate, given that he's a former cop. I meet Mick in the Roc. It's closed for another hour, but he's there, cleaning up and waiting for me. There's no sign of Isabel, which is a relief.

When I walk in, Mick's polishing the bar, and that stops me in my tracks, my mind slipping back to another time, another bartender. I indulge the stab of grief and regret for two seconds before walking over and taking a seat at the bar.

Mick sets the rag aside and puts a steaming mug of coffee beside me, along with sugar and goat's milk from under the counter. He doesn't say a word, as if this is no grand gesture but just common hospitality.

I pour in the milk.

"So," he says. "Abbygail."

"I hear you two were involved."

He nods and begins folding the rag, meticulously.

"I'd ask if you want a lawyer present," I say. "I know cops realize that's wise for any interview. But I'm not sure where we'd find one."

He gives a short laugh at that. "Oh, there are plenty here. I think it's the most common former occupation." His lips quirk. "Surprisingly."

"Or not."

A shared smile, and he nods, his gaze slightly downcast. Not submissive, just quiet and contained, neither overly friendly nor unfriendly.

He sets the rag aside again. "I'm not blocking. Just working up to it. I'll tell you everything. It just . . . isn't easy." He takes a moment, then a deep breath, and says, "So . . . Abbygail. I would say what a good kid she was. Tough, strong, sweet, generous, all that. But everyone's going to tell you that. So I'll just say they're right."

"Good kid . . . ," I say.

"Yeah." He rubs his mouth. "That's not a slip of the tongue. When she arrived, she was nineteen. We started seeing each other a year later. I was twenty-five, and the youngest guy here. Which is why people thought we should give it a shot. Beth and a few others."

"Eric?"

A sharp laugh. "Uh, no. Definitely not Eric. He knew Abby wasn't ready. He didn't try to stop us, though, because she wanted to, and I . . . ." He rocks back on his heels. "This is going to sound shitty, but I gave it a try because she wanted to, so I thought I should. We were friends, and I wanted her to be happy."

Which doesn't sound shitty at all. It sounds sweet. But I understand what he means, that he feels bad about dating someone he wasn't romantically interested in.

He continues. "We went out for a couple of months. I can give you dates if that helps. It just . . . it didn't go anywhere."

"So you were lovers for two months."

"Uh, no. When I say it didn't go anywhere, that includes sex. With her background, I just couldn't . . . It felt wrong. Like I was taking advantage. It was dating. High school stuff, because that's what she was, Detective. Inside. I don't mean she wasn't smart or mature, just that she never had the chance to grow up in a real way. It was like she skipped her teen years, and in Rockton she got them back. Which is one reason it didn't work. There might have only been a five-year age difference, but I felt like a creepy old man."

"And the breakup?"

"Mutual."

"I hear you got together with Isabel about a month later."

"Yep."

"Was there any tension there? With Isabel and Abbygail?"

He gives me a real laugh for that. "Not at all. Abby knew I was checking out Isabel even before she and I got together. She'd tease me about it. When Abby and I broke up, she's the one who told me to go for it with Iz. She liked her. They liked each other. Iz . . ." He rubs his mouth again. "Isabel doesn't exactly wear her heart on her sleeve, but Abby's disappearance hurt her as much as anyone."

My nod must not look entirely convincing, because he says, "You're wondering how they could get along, right? The bordello madam and the former teen prostitute? I know what you think of Isabel, but she really believes she's doing the best thing for the women here. No, not believes. *Hopes.* She wants to do the right thing by the women here, and . . ." He studies my look. "And you really don't want to hear that. Anyway, Iz used to talk to Abby about her experiences, advice on how Isabel could run a safe establishment. But those talks? You know what Iz did before she came here, right?"

I shake my head.

"She was a psychologist. So she counseled Abby. Not officially. It was just talking. But it wasn't just talking, if you know what I mean. Iz wanted to help, and Abby needed help, so they talked, a lot." He picks up the rag and begins folding it again. "Which is the long-winded way of saying there wasn't tension between them."

"Was there tension with anyone? For Abby-gail?"

279

"A few of the guys. I can give you a list. But it's a short one."

"The sheriff says she didn't get bothered that way."

"Guys were mostly respectful. But a few came on to her. She'd never tell Eric, or he'd go after them and then she'd feel like she'd tattled and overreacted. You know."

I do know. It's exactly how I feel about telling Dalton who offered me credits for sex.

"She wanted Eric to think everything was fine," he says. "With Eric . . ." He clears his throat. "I don't like talking about her personal stuff . . ."

"She had a crush on him."

He exhales. "Yeah. I'd tease her about that; she'd tease me about Isabel. I think, when she encouraged me to give it a shot with Iz, she was hoping I'd say the same for her and Eric. I didn't. Wouldn't. She'd have gotten hurt, and I never wanted to see her hurt." He crumples the rag and puts it aside.

"Sheriff Dalton wouldn't have returned her attention."

"Hell, no. If I felt like the old guy with the teenager, it would have been even worse for Eric. Like dating your little sister." He shudders. "Just no. I think Abby understood that. Most times. Every now and then . . . well, she'd wonder, and I'd steer her away. For her own good. For his, too. If she came on to him . . . shit. That'd have been rough, knowing she saw him that way. He wanted to be her big brother, not her Prince Charming."

I must smile at that, because he laughs. "Yeah, no one's going to mistake Eric for Prince Charming. But he was *her* knight in shining armor, however much he'd hate to hear it. He's a good guy."

"I keep hearing that."

"Yeah, Eric's fans and friends are a little too quick to support him. Mainly because we know what a crappy first impression he leaves. And second. And third. How are you guys doing?"

"We had a rough start, but I'm starting to see the side that wins him fans."

The smile grows. "Good. You two seem to be spending a lot of time together."

"We're working a big case together."

"Still . . ." He catches my look. "Okay, I won't play matchmaker. You'll get plenty of that from others. So, back to Abbygail . . ."

"You were the last person to see her alive."

He flinches, as if I've poked a wound that hasn't healed.

"She was heading for the forest," he says. "I was over by the woodshed, hauling logs. It was after dark, and there was no way in hell she should have been that close to the forest. She said she'd heard an animal that sounded hurt. We scoured the area together, and I had no reason to think she wasn't telling the truth, which makes me feel like a complete idiot, but honestly? Eric said don't go into the forest, so Abby didn't go into the forest. She'd tease and poke, but she never disobeyed him. I really did think she'd heard an animal."

"But you didn't find anything."

He shakes his head. "So I walked her home. Beth's neighbors saw us — they can confirm that. Abby went inside, and everything seemed fine. Beth got home an hour later, after working late next door at the clinic, and when Abby wasn't there, she just figured we were out, and she went to bed. I think Abby grabbed a lantern and went back. She loved animals, and if she thought she heard a wounded one . . ."

"It's the only thing that would have drawn her into the forest."

"But not far. Yes, she might wander in farther than she meant to, chasing a noise, but I can't imagine she'd go in deep enough to get lost. Someone lured her in. I'm sure of it. Others might tell you different, and maybe they think I'm just covering my own ass because I didn't manage to stop her from going into that forest. Either way, it *doesn't* cover my ass, because I was still the last . . . the last to see her. I fucked up. And she disappeared."

He goes quiet, lost in that grief, until I break it by saying, "You mentioned a list? Guys who gave her trouble?"

He snaps from his reverie. "Right. Let me get a pen."

I pass him mine, and he writes it out and hands it to me. As I go to leave, he says, "Abby would have liked you."

I turn and look at him.

He shrugs, a little embarrassed. "I was just thinking that. She had a lot of women here playing mother and therapist. What she didn't have was a female friend." He fidgets. "It wasn't the same with me, and sometimes I think maybe if she'd had another girl she could have confided in, about anything . . ." He rubs the back of his neck. "I don't know. I'm probably being silly. We all keep wondering where we went wrong, thinking we missed something, failed to give her something, and if only this or that, then maybe it'd have been different. Anyway, all I mean is that she would have liked you. You're a survivor. Like her."

That gives me pause, but he only shrugs and says, "I was a cop, remember? I recognize the signs."

I nod and start to go. Then I say, "Everyone presumes she's dead. You knew her, as much as anyone. Maybe more. Is it possible she's . . ." I look toward the forest.

"Still out there?" His gaze drops. "I wish it was, Detective." He resumes polishing the bar, his voice rough with grief. "I really wish it was."

THIRTY-TWO

Mick's list is indeed short. Three names. One is Pierre Lang. Abbygail had mentioned getting a "weird vibe" around him. A few times in her last month, she'd had the feeling she was being followed. Not stalking, just someone following her for a short distance, watching her. A secret admirer who'd left a bowl of wild raspberries outside her door. Mick had suspected it was Lang, but he'd figured Lang was just a middle-aged guy with a crush on an inappropriately young woman, and it would end when she didn't reciprocate.

I'm walking to the station when Kenny catches up. He comes around once or twice a day. Just pops in to see what's going on, if anyone needs him for militia work. Today, he says he has a hot tip for me. Apparently, someone overheard Hastings bad-mouthing Dalton before he took off. Which is about as shocking as telling me the sun rose that morning.

I'm thanking Kenny when Isabel intercepts

us and shoos him with her fingers. "Stop bothering the new girl, Kenny. I know she's very pretty, but Eric didn't hire her for ornamental value."

"I had a tip."

"Yes, I'm sure you did. Now go."

When Kenny leaves, I continue walking and say to Isabel, "If you have a problem at the Roc, Sheriff Dalton just headed that way."

"Sheriff Dalton?" She laughs. "That's awfully formal. Are you and the boss not getting along, sugar?"

I look at her, and I think about my talk with Mick, and there's a part of me that wants to cut Isabel some slack. But I get the feeling if I do, she'll use it to her advantage and drag me into her battle with Dalton.

I climb the steps into the station. "Is there anything I can help you with, Ms. Radcliffe?"

"Ouch. All right. That cold front isn't for our good sheriff." She follows me in. "Do you want to talk about what I do?"

"I don't think there's anything to discuss. You've found a way to turn a profit in Rockton. And in return, the rest of the women have to put up with being treated like we'll all whore ourselves — it's just a matter of finding the right price."

"I think that's exaggerating —"

"I've been here four days, and I've still managed to be offered money for sex twice. That's not counting the guy who told me that if I ever need extra credits, he has some 'night work' for me. I'll just presume he wants me to come over after my shift and type his novel."

"You're young and attractive. It's an anomaly."

"And you know that how? Marketing research? Door-to-door surveys?" I shake my head and sit at the desk. "I can handle it. I'm sure every other woman in this town can, too, because it's not like most of them have had their self-esteem ground into the dirt by an abusive asshole." I look at her. "Right?"

Her reply is slow, careful. "I think that while you have a very valid point, if you could let me state my case, you'd see that we're damned if we do and we're damned if we don't. This is one solution to a very serious problem."

"That guys can't keep their pants zipped? That if you deprive them of women, they'll just take them? That's a hell of an insult to the men in this town."

She sighs. "I'd like the chance to explain, Casey. That's why I came by. To invite you to lunch."

"No, thank you."

I notice Anders has come in. He's standing in the doorway. He sees me look up, nods, and backs out with a motion that he'll be back in five.

"There are a limited number of professional

women in this town," Isabel says. "Most of us work in menial jobs, just like we did down south. Those in higher positions should stick together."

"I don't choose my friends by gender. Now, if you'll excuse me . . ."

She leaves without another word, and I return to my work.

Anders returns and sets a Tupperware box in front of me. Inside are cookies.

"I know," he says. "For cops it should be doughnuts, but we don't get those here."

"I prefer cookies anyway." I select one.

"Good, considering I probably need to score a few points after last night." He takes a cookie and the chair Isabel vacated.

"I'm sorry about Diana," I say. "I should have walked away sooner. You guys didn't deserve that."

He gives a half shrug. "I kinda did. Before you arrived, Diana and I were at the Lion, with others, lots of drinking, she seemed fun, and she's new in town and . . . And that really doesn't make me sound any better, does it?" He shifts in his seat. "Diana's having some . . . I'd say issues, but that sounds condescending. Cutting loose is fine, but with her, it seems a little . . ."

"Frenetic?"

"Yeah. Which I didn't realize at the time. So inadvertently I took advantage of the situation, and I feel bad."

"Deputy," Dalton says as he walks through the door, "did you come in today to talk or to work?"

Before Anders can answer, Dalton heads out the back.

"Good morning to you, too, boss!" Anders calls. Then he says, to me, "Sometimes I wonder why he doesn't just walk *around* the building."

"Not really an inside cat, is he."

He smiles. "No, he's definitely not. If he isn't prowling through town, he's sunning himself on the back porch."

"Sunning himself? Or watching for prey?"

"Much better analogy. An outside cat scouring the woods for predators and prey alike."

I finish my cookie and then say, "About Di, I know she was a bitch last night, and I'm not apologizing for her. That was unforgivable. She obviously likes you and wants to see more of you. I'm guessing you're not interested."

He exhales. "Shit. That sounds bad, doesn't it?"

Actually, no. Given how she's acting, I don't want to see him mixed up in that.

He continues. "In my defense, when we hooked up, I didn't say anything to suggest I wanted more than one night. But I still feel shitty."

"Don't. It was her mistake."

"Thanks for not thinking I'm a complete asshole."

"You aren't."

I smile, and he opens his mouth like he's going to say something. Then the door opens. It's Beth.

Anders gets up. "I'd better go do my rounds before Eric finds me still chatting. Hey, Doc." He lifts his hand to high-five her as they pass. The doctor makes a valiant, if awkward, effort to return it. Anders chuckles and keeps going.

"Hey, Beth," I say. "Thanks for coming by." I wave to the chair. She stays standing.

"I'm just popping in to see if you're free for lunch," she says.

"Oh." I push my folder aside. "I thought . . . Sorry, Eric knew I wanted to speak to you, so I thought he asked you to stop in."

"That's a no for lunch, then?" She smiles, but there's a wariness there, like she's screwed up the courage to make a friendly overture and it's being rejected.

"No, no. Lunch is good. Great, in fact." I check my watch. "I'm off in an hour. I'll come by then."

I pick up lunch, and we eat in the clinic back room that serves as Beth's office. My sandwich is peanut butter and Saskatoon berry jam. The PB is freshly ground, from nuts flown in. The jam is made from berries gathered every summer.

"Did Will ask you to invite me to lunch?" I ask as we eat.

She stops midbite and checks my expression. When she sees I'm smiling, she returns it and says, "Maybe."

"I figured that." Especially given that he left after hearing me turn down Isabel's invitation. "Helping me make friends."

"Both of us, I think. Will's always trying to get me to mingle more. It's just not my thing. In college, I was the girl with her nose stuck in her texts from freshman year to graduation."

"Well, don't let him make you feel like you have to be nice to the new girl."

"Oh, I'm fine with socializing. Just not the kind that ends with lampshades on your head, which seems to be the main form of entertainment around here."

"Except there aren't lamps. Which makes it even more awkward."

She smiles. "It does. You don't seem to be into that, but your friend . . ."

"Diana wasn't before she got here, either. But I'm glad she's enjoying herself while I'm busy with this case."

"Which segues nicely from the awkward talk of your friend onto safer ground."

I smile. "Maybe. I wanted to talk to you about Irene Prosser."

Beth wipes mustard from her lips. "You're not buying the story she nearly hacked off her own hands?"

"Not exactly."

"That suicide ruling isn't Eric's fault."

"I know. He's dealing with politics and angles and doing his best. I can see that."

"He is. As for Irene, yes, it wasn't suicide. Do you need my autopsy report?"

"I have it. I'm looking for observations that might not have gone into it. Specifically, proof of past injuries."

Her lips purse. "Past injuries?"

"Were there signs — in the autopsy or a previous medical examination — that she'd been the victim of abuse?"

"Ah. I see where you're heading. Let me check her file." She wipes off her hands and starts to stand.

"Eat first," I say.

"No, you've set me on a mystery. The sandwich can wait. Do you know how to read an X-ray?"

I follow her from the room. "You have X-rays?"

"I take all the equipment as they offer it. One thing I use the X-ray for is autopsies. Not exactly standard procedure, but it's here, so I put it to use."

She opens a locked drawer in the next room and takes out a file folder. An X-ray film goes into the viewer. There are five, covering

Irene's full skeleton. I see signs of a previously broken wrist, but nothing more.

"That's actually a childhood injury," Beth says. "I remember she hurt her wrist last winter, falling on the ice. She was concerned it broke again — once you've done it, it's very easy to do again."

I squint at the X-ray. "I'm not seeing any other signs of old breaks."

"Neither am I. Is that significant?"

"Just an angle I'm pursuing."

"In other words, mind my own business." She fends off my protest. "I'm sure Eric told you to keep me out of the loop for my own safety. He's very protective."

"Ah," I say as I remember Anders saying Beth often brought dinner for Dalton when he worked late.

She laughs. "If that means, 'Ah, so you two are an item,' the answer is a resounding no. Eric's a little young for me. And a little moody. A little difficult. A little demanding. A whole lot of other things, as you may have noticed." She hesitates before we sit. "You aren't interested in him, are you?"

"After that glowing recommendation?"

She smiles and shakes her head. "Eric's a good friend. As a romantic partner, though? I . . . really wouldn't go there, Casey."

"I'm not. Believe me."

She nods. "Good. Lots of women like the bad boys . . . then they realize Eric's not bad

— he's just cranky."

I laugh.

"He's a good-looking guy, so he gets more than his share of attention. Rumor has it that when he was young, he took full advantage. These days, though, he's a lot more discreet. Given his position, it's difficult to get close to anyone." She goes quiet, her expression thoughtful, a little sad. Then she gives her head a sharp shake. "If you're looking for company, I'd turn toward Rockton's most eligible bachelor: Deputy Anders. Looks, personality, and a sweet, sweet guy. Who has definitely taken notice of you."

"Thanks, but I'm not looking. I . . ." I finger my necklace from Kurt.

"Left someone behind?"

"Kind of. But as a friend, Will seems great."

"He is, and if you're happy with that, he'll be, too. That's the thing about nice guys. Now, back to lunch. If you're five minutes late, you'll hear it from the boss."

THIRTY-THREE

"We're going for a ride," Dalton says as I walk into the station.

"ATV?"

"Horse."

"I'd prefer ATV."

"Stables, Butler."

I salute. "Yes, sir."

We head out. He says nothing until we're halfway to the stables. Then, "You're happy today. Found what you wanted, I take it?"

"Maybe."

He nods. "You can tell me on the ride."

"Mmm, you said not to trust anyone."

"I think I like you better when you're not in a mood."

"This isn't *a mood.*"

"Yeah, it is. A good one. Normally, you don't have a mood at all. You're just there."

"I'll ignore that jab, since I'm in a good mood."

"It's not a jab; it's an observation. And you *are* going to tell me what you found, because

I'm your boss. That's why we're taking the horses, not the ATVs. So we can talk. Also, so we don't scare off the ravens."

"Ravens?"

"Hunting party spotted a flock of ravens." He pauses. "Which, technically, is an unkindness."

"What?"

"Murder of crows. Unkindness of ravens. And they can be pretty damned unkind if they're scavenging something, which they seemed to be doing."

"Shit."

"Yeah."

Our route takes us toward the mountain, and I ask him about a rodent that darts across the increasingly rocky path. He says it's a lagomorph not a rodent and this one is a pika, also known as a rock rabbit, coney, or whistling hare. He even stops, so I can hear the noise it's making — more of a loud *meep* than a whistle. Dalton says it's warning us off its territory. I ask about other animals, and that gets him talking as we ride, about wood rats and flying squirrels and marmots and more.

"We're in a good spot for wildlife here," he says. "Fly another hour north, and you're into the Arctic. And you'd better not have been taking an interest to distract me from asking what new information you got from Beth."

"I wasn't. I am interested."

"Good. Did you find any sign Irene's story wasn't legit?"

I move aside a branch. "What?"

"That's what you were looking for, right? Evidence that she'd been abused. Skeletal evidence, I'm guessing, since the soft-tissue damage would be long healed." When I hesitate, he says, "No, Beth didn't tell me what you talked about. It's a deduction."

"Remind me why you needed a detective?"

"Because I'm not the one who thought to check."

"Did you 'deduce' my theory, too?"

"Yeah, but that would be showing off."

"In other words, you didn't."

"Harry Powys was involved in selling illegal organs. Jerry Hastings may have murdered his mother for his inheritance. You were checking on the possibility Irene was also here under false pretenses."

"Okay, you *did* figure it out."

He lifts a hand, telling me to stop, and he scans the forest. Then he waves for us to take the left fork on the path.

"That is your theory, then," he says as we continue.

"It's a starting point. The problem is not knowing how many people were smuggled in. The fact that three of the four victims fit that profile might be no more significant than three having the same color hair. That's presuming there's a connection between the victims at all."

He's nodding. Then he stops and tilts his head, and I catch the croak of a bird.

He motions for me to dismount. We tie the horses to trees. His gelding — Blaze — starts pulling at grass, unperturbed. Cricket looks around, as if to say, *I don't want to stop.* I rub her neck and pull an apple from my pack, and she decides maybe a break isn't such a bad idea.

I spot a raven then. People from the east often look at big crows and think they're ravens, but seeing one now, I don't know how we make that mistake. The raven is the size of a hawk. It's black from its beak to its feet. That beak is thick and curved. Its neck is different, too — thick with shaggy feathers.

Dalton says, "Yukon raven." Then, "Technically, it's still a common raven, but they get bigger up here. Territorial bird."

"So steer clear."

He looks over as if confused, and then says, "Nah, I mean it's the Yukon Territory's symbolic bird."

"Duh, right. I knew that."

Dalton waves for me to fall in behind him. I unzip my jacket and push it back, exposing my holstered gun. He has his in his hand. He takes another step. Then his hand shoots up as a snarl reverberates through the forest.

I see what he does and . . . and I have no

idea what I'm looking at. It's like a small bear with stunted legs. The beast bares its fangs as it stands its ground, snarling and spitting.

"Do you see a kill?" he whispers.

I look across the clearing. "No." Then I spot something. "There's . . . I don't know what it is, but something's hanging from that tree. I think there's blood. But whatever it is, it's up high."

Dalton grunts. Then he shouts, loud enough that I jump. The creature waddles off, throwing snarls over its shoulder.

"What the hell was that?" I ask.

"Wolverine," he says. "Also known as a skunk bear, carcajou, quick-hatch . . ."

"Wolverine? Like the X-Men?"

He frowns at me.

"Sorry," I say. "Pop culture reference. So that's what they look like in real life. Not nearly as scary as the comic book version."

"They're scary enough if you interrupt them at a kill. Pound for pound, they're the nastiest bastards out here. They can take on a wolf and win, no contest, because a wolverine doesn't know when to give up. They keep fighting until someone's dead."

"Dangerous to humans, then."

"Not lethally." He puts his gun away. "Unless you were wounded and it was really hungry. Course, most times they're really hungry. Their Latin name is *Gulo gulo. Gulo* means 'glutton.' "

"Ah."

"You don't want to mess with them. Chances are, though, that's the only one you'll see while you're here."

Dalton peers into the clearing, and his gaze returns to that thing in the tree. He strides toward it.

As I scan the clearing, I see the sunlight glimmer in a way it shouldn't glimmer off anything in a forest. Dalton lifts his foot over a metal bear trap, and I lunge. An eyeblink later, he's on his back and I'm crouched over him.

He says nothing. Just lifts his head to look around, as if being randomly knocked to the ground is perfectly normal. Then he spots the trap and whispers, "Fuck." I ease off him and rise.

Dalton crouches beside the rusty bear trap. As he's examining it, I ask, "Would that be settlers? Or do other trappers come through here?"

"The odd hunter, trapper, miner," he says without looking up.

"Miner?"

"There's still gold. Mostly in the rivers. Our locals pan for fun during fishing trips."

He glances at me then, as if expecting a response, and I'm thinking it might be fun to pan for gold. But it seems a little silly, so instead I say, "Don't you worry about these outside miners or trappers stumbling on

Rockton?"

He grunts and turns back to the trap, and I think he's not going to answer, but then he says, "There are almost five hundred thousand square kilometers of wilderness in the Yukon. Rockton is less than one square kilometer. Our patrols sometimes get wind of people passing through, but trappers and miners are like bears. If they hear us, they steer clear. Even if they did find the town, we'd pass it off as a commune. People up here mind their own business." He gets to his feet. "This trap, though? It's ours."

"You put out unmarked —"

"Fuck, no. I mean it's an *old* one of ours. Stolen. Folks out here take our stuff when they find it."

"The hostiles?"

"Everyone out here."

The way he says it makes me scan the forest again, as if it's swarming with hermits and settlers and hostiles.

He sets off the trap with a stick. "Too bad it didn't catch that wolverine. Meat tastes like shit, but the fur repels frost. Good for lining a parka."

"You had your gun pointed at it."

"If it attacked, sure. Otherwise, shooting it wouldn't be fair. I don't *need* the pelt. Just would have been nice." He looks over at me. "I should say thanks, too. Excellent reflexes. I'll admit, when you told me that, I thought you were full of crap."

"Now you know why I don't carry my gun."

"I'll still argue my point, but I'll accept yours. For now. We'll work on it, retrain your brain to react in a way that doesn't involve firing a gun. And I need to work on paying more attention. I usually do, but . . ." His gaze returns to the tree.

"What the hell is that?" I ask.

"No idea."

It looks like a length of thick rope. It's been nailed to the trunk, maybe ten feet up. Claw gouges in the bark say that's what the wolverine was trying to reach, but it was too high. Presumably, it's what the ravens were after, too, but the position would have made it awkward to get at, though I see peck marks where they've tried.

I take another step. Then I stop as my stomach lurches.

"Intestines," I say.

"What?"

"It's —"

"Fuck. Yeah. I see now."

He moves closer, his gaze on the ground, watching every step until he's at the tree. I'm beside him, both of us looking up at about eighteen inches of intestine hanging from the trunk.

THIRTY-FOUR

"Could be from Powys," Dalton says as we stare at the intestine.

I shake my head. "We found Powys's body the day I got here. This hasn't started to rot, and it still looks pliant."

"Pliant," he repeats, and then nods as if deciding this is indeed the best word. The length of intestine isn't fresh, but it's not dried out, either, as it sways slightly in the breeze, the smell of it bringing those scavengers running.

"Hastings, then?" he says.

"I'll need to take it back to Beth to confirm it's even human. I'd guess it is, if they nailed it up here. But it's always possible it's . . ."

I trail off. Dalton is turning, with that look on his face that tells me he's caught some noise, and sure enough, I hear it two seconds later. I could say his hearing is sharper, but I think it's just better attuned to sorting out what belongs in a peaceful forest and what does not. This does not. I have no idea what

I'm actually hearing, only that it sends cold dread up my spine.

The sound comes from the edge of the clearing. We follow it, Dalton with his gun out, and . . .

And nothing. I still can hear the sound, a cross between a groan and a mewl, and it's right here. Exactly where we're standing. Except there's nothing in sight except trees.

The sound comes again. Dalton's gaze goes up.

"What the hell?" I say as I follow his lead.

It looks like a sack. It's attached to the trunk and to one tree limb and resting partially in the crook between two more branches. In other words, it's wedged up there as best it can be.

The noise comes again. And the side of the sack moves.

"There's, uh, something in it," I say.

"Yep."

"Something hurt."

"Yep."

"We should go back to town and get —"

"Nope."

Before I can say anything, Dalton is shimmying up the trunk. I used to be quite the climber in my tomboy youth, but scaling an evergreen is tough. He clearly has practice.

As I watch him, I see his point in not going back to town. What would we get? A ladder? A hydraulic lift? The animal in that bag is

303

hurt badly enough that it can't claw or bite its way out. I can tell now that the dark shadow on one side is actually blood. That's what brought the scavengers. Then, realizing they hadn't a hope in hell of getting to it, they'd tried for the nailed-up intestine.

Dalton is up there now, examining the sack. He reaches out and gives it a tentative push. Then, "Fuck."

"Heavy?"

"Yeah."

"We can switch places," I say. "I'll lower it for you to catch, but . . ."

"It's too heavy. Going to be tough enough for me to do it. You stay back. We have no idea what's inside."

"I don't think it's in any shape to attack. It isn't even reacting —"

"Doesn't matter. I lower. You stand clear. That's an order."

"Yes, sir."

He takes a few more minutes to evaluate. Then he pulls out a knife and cuts one rope. I can't quite see what he's doing up there, half hidden by branches, but he gets one rope wrapped around his hand before he severs the other one. He manages to lower the sack, but the rope isn't quite long enough and it stops about a foot from the ground, swinging as Dalton groans with exertion.

"Gotta drop it," he grunts.

"I can —"

"Orders, Detective. Stay the hell back."

He lets go before I can do anything except obey. The sack hits the ground, and the creature inside lets out a mewling cry of pain.

"Stay right there," he says. "And I'd appreciate you getting your gun out while I come down."

I train my weapon on the sack as Dalton shimmies down about halfway and then drops the rest of the way.

The sack is bigger than it looked in the air. Clearly, it's no fox or wolverine inside. I look at Dalton. He's heading for the sack with his knife out.

"Sheriff?" I say carefully.

"Yeah."

That's all he says — "yeah" — and I know it means that whatever I'm thinking, he's already come to the same conclusion. He bends beside the sack and moves it a little, as if putting it in a better position. The thing inside doesn't react. Dalton motions for me to keep my gun ready as he flicks his blade through the canvas. Then he rips the sack open, and we see what's inside.

Jerry Hastings.

He's bound hand and foot and barely conscious. He doesn't even seem to notice when Dalton opens the sack. His eyes are unfocused, his lips moving over and over as if he's saying something, but we don't hear a word.

His hands are bound in front of him. As Dalton cuts them free first, I clutch my gun. Then Dalton reaches down and gently pulls up the bloodied front of Hastings's shirt. There's more blood underneath, his skin painted in a wash of it. That doesn't disguise the thick blackened line, though. Where someone has crudely stitched him up and then cauterized the wound.

I turn away fast, and I come closer to throwing up at a crime scene than I ever have in my life. My stomach lurches, my hand reaching to grab something, anything. It finds a brace, not a tree or sapling, but warm fingers, clenching mine and holding me steady.

"Sorry," I say as I turn to Dalton. "I . . . It's . . ."

"Yeah, I know."

He rubs his chin with his free hand, and his fingers are trembling slightly. He exhales, breath rushing through his teeth in a long, slow hiss. I look back at Hastings, lying on the ground, that terrible black scar on his stomach. It's not the blood or the wound that sickens me. It's the thought of what's happened. Of what someone has done.

"We need to get him back to town," I say. "Fast."

Dalton already has his radio out. He calls Anders and tells him to get the big Gator out here now. And bring Beth.

I'm on my knees beside Hastings. He's in shock, his mouth working, making the same motions over and over, as if he's saying something, and it must be important, but when I lean in, it's just a meaningless garble, repeated as if his brain is stuck on it.

Whatever Hastings did down south, he didn't deserve this. Someone cut out part of his intestine and sewed him back up. That's not justifiable homicide; it's sadism.

We shuck our coats to cover him, trying to keep the shock from deepening, and I talk to him until Anders and Beth arrive. Once Beth gets past what's happened, she has to cut him open on the spot. He won't survive the bumpy trip back unless she gets a look at exactly what's happened. She sedates him and cuts and that's when the true horror hits, because whoever sliced out that length of intestine only cauterized the ends and shoved them back in. Septic shock has set in, and she does what she can, but Hastings is dead minutes after she makes that first cut.

Dusk has fallen by the time we get back with Hastings's body, but our day is far from over. First, a conference between Dalton, Anders, and me on how we'll inform people. Then over to the clinic for the autopsy. Back to the station to make notes. More talking. It's ten at night, and I'm on the station deck with Dalton as Anders does rounds, telling a few key people in town about the death. I hear a "hello?" inside the station, and I tense. Dalton does, too, his eyes narrowing as Diana walks in.

"I've got this," he says as he rises.

"No, I'll handle it."

Diana hovers just inside the station, one hand still on the door frame. There's this look on her face, exactly like when she had to crawl back after dumping me for the popular girls in high school.

"Can we talk?" she says.

"Casey's busy," Dalton says behind me. "We've had a —"

I cut him off by turning with a quiet but firm "I'll handle this."

Steel seeps into his gaze as it stays fixed on Diana. He looks about two seconds from throwing her back onto the street.

"I have it," I say, firmer.

He's still bristling, like a guard dog sensing trouble. But after a moment, he turns on his heel and stalks back onto the deck, muttering something I don't catch.

When he's gone, I turn to Diana. "We found Jerry Hastings, and it wasn't good. Dalton's right. I've had a long day."

"A drink? That'll help you —"

"No." I resist the urge to add an *I'm sorry.* I'm not doing it. "I'm going to turn in early. I'm sure I'll see you around."

"Can I at least apologize?"

"You don't need to." *Because I don't need to hear it.* "Go on. Have a good night. I'll go get some sleep."

I turn and walk out the back door before she can respond.

Thirty-Five

Dalton didn't even shut the inside door — just the screen.

"You *should* get a good night's rest," he says.

Not even going to pretend you weren't eaves-dropping, are you? I suspect he didn't mean to be rude — he was listening in case Diana gave me a hard time.

I nod. "I'm going to take off. I'll see you in the morning."

I start for the door again.

"Hold up," he says. "I'm turning in, too, and we're going the same way. It's quieter walking the back route. No one to pester us about the case."

I'm about to say I've never seen anyone even *ask* him about the case. I think they don't dare. But this is the second death, nearly on the heels of the others, and people *are* going to start asking questions. And demanding answers.

We set out, taking his personal highway

along the border. I ask how he's doing, given what we found earlier. He gives me a shrug and an honest "trying to forget it."

"Marginally successful?"

"Yeah," he says.

"Same here. I know Hastings wasn't a good person . . ."

"No one deserves to die like that."

I nod, and when I go quiet, he gives me that long, cool stare.

"Which doesn't mean some people don't deserve to die," he says. "Just not like that."

I squirm and veer a little to the side.

"Did you go there planning to shoot him?" he asks.

I realize he means Blaine. "Of course not," I say before I can stop myself. I take a deep breath. "I'd rather stick to —"

"Blaine Saratori *didn't* deserve to die. He deserved to be beaten within an inch of his life and spend weeks in hospital and months in rehab, and never really get over it, not physically, not psychologically. But that wasn't going to happen. You didn't plan to shoot him, but it's bullshit to pretend you killed an innocent man. And it's bullshit to even think about that in comparison to this."

"I don't believe I said I was thinking of it."

"You were. But I'll shut up about it. For now."

"How about for good?"

His snort says, *Not a chance.* Then he

points up. "That was a great horned owl."

I peer into the night sky.

"It's gone now," he says. "I'm changing the conversation. But as long as you're looking up, do you see that?"

I follow his finger to see a distant strip of swirling green through the clouds.

"Is that . . . ?" I begin. "The northern lights? I didn't think I'd be far enough up for them."

"You are. It's just coming into the right season, so you won't get a lot of good views yet."

"What causes it?"

As we continue walking, he explains that it's electrically charged protons and electrons from the sun entering the earth's atmosphere at the poles. I'm so engrossed in looking up that I nearly bash into a tree. He gets a chuckle out of that. When we reach my yard, he says, "There's your fox," and I see it slipping from the forest edge.

"It's not mine," I say, giving him a smile. "Because that would be wrong. A wild animal is not a pet."

He shrugs. "Can still be yours. Just don't try domesticating it."

We watch as the fox trots back to its den with something in its mouth.

"Grouse," he says.

"Which is a bird, right?"

He sighs.

"Hey, you promised me a book. I haven't seen it yet."

"Been a little preoccupied. And I'm making sure you actually want it and aren't just trying to be nice."

"I'm never nice."

"You're *always* nice, Casey. Or at least you try your damnedest to fake it, because you think that's what people want from you. Don't give me that look. If you walk into it, I'm allowed to analyze."

"Dare I invite you in for coffee?"

"Depends. Are you asking to be polite?"

"No."

"Then yeah, I'll take coffee. And don't ever ask to be polite, because then I'll say yes and you'll be stuck with me, and it'll just be . . ."

"Awkward?"

"For you. Nothing's awkward for me."

I smile. "Well, then, speaking of awkward, I'd be able to see those lights a lot better from my balcony, but that would mean inviting you up to my room."

"*Through* your room. It's not the same thing."

"True. Is that a yes?"

"It is."

We sit on my deck. Literally *on* my deck, because while I offer to bring up a chair, he refuses and grabs extra blankets from under my bed, which I didn't know were there. We sit on blankets with more wrapped around us. Or wrapped around me. He seems fine with just the coffee to keep him warm. We sit and we talk, and I watch the northern lights dance, and it doesn't matter how horrible my day became, this is as damned near perfect an ending as I can imagine. The wolves even start up, as if to prove to me that as good as things get, they can always be better.

Eventually the talking stops, and we just sit and watch and listen, and the next thing I know, I'm waking at dawn with the blankets pulled up to my neck and an extra one draped over me. The deck is empty except for my gun, now lying just out of reach. I smile, take it, and head inside to get ready for work.

There's an angry mob outside the station. Well, actually, three somewhat annoyed citizens, but Dalton still intercepts me and takes me in through the back.

"They want a statement, whatever that is," he says.

"It's where the police explain the situation, usually to the press."

"We don't have press."

"True, but you really should explain —"

"To three people?" He snorts. "I'll be doing it all day. Like one of those damned cuckoo clocks."

"We've had two murders in a week. The

more you ignore that, the more rumors are going to fly, and soon we really will have an angry —"

"I'm not ignoring them. I'm waiting until there are more so I don't have to keep explaining. The more times I say it, the more it'll sound like there's a serious problem."

"Um . . ."

His look darkens. "Fine, there *is* a serious problem. But they don't need to know that."

I open the door and call out, "We'll be giving a statement at nine. Please make sure everyone knows, because we're obviously very busy investigating this tragedy."

Dalton appears behind me. "She means that. You don't want to spread the word? Fine. But I'll tell everyone in town that you three know, and I might offer the opinion that it was awfully suspicious, you coming by, looking for information and not wanting to share it with others."

They're gone before he can close the door.

I sigh. "That's not how it's usually done."

"Welcome to Rockton, Detective."

Back inside the station, I ask Dalton whether Val should join us, and add, "But I understand if you'd rather she didn't interfere."

He makes a noise at that. It's like a snort, but it's also akin to a laugh. Then he shakes his head and walks to the fireplace.

"Is that a no?" I ask.

Another shake of his head, and I think that's my answer until he says, "I'm not the least bit worried that Val will interfere, because that would require her to actually show up. You want to walk over and invite her? Go ahead . . . if you need the exercise." He lights the fire and puts the kettle over it. "Exercise in futility, too. But go on. Coffee will be ready when you get back." He checks his watch. "Five minutes there, five minutes back. Ten seconds for her to tell you no."

Val lives on the edge of town opposite mine. As Dalton said, it's a five-minute fast walk from the station, and given how freaking cold it is these past few mornings, fast is the only way I move.

Her house is identical to mine. I climb the porch and knock, and here's where Dalton's schedule goes off track, because it takes me two full minutes of knocking — and then calling "Val?" — before she opens the door. I think I must have gotten her out of bed, but she's fully dressed, her hair brushed, a writing pad in hand.

"I know Eric updated you on the situation yesterday," I say. "We're making a public statement this morning."

There's a long moment of silence, and I begin to wonder if she even heard me. Then she says, "Is that necessary?"

"I believe it is, to keep people calm and informed."

"All right. If you think that's best, I trust your judgment."

"I'd like you to be there."

Her brows knit. "What for?"

"You're the spokesperson for the council. Your presence will reassure people."

"I don't think that's necessary, Detective Butler."

"I do."

"Unfortunately, that isn't your call to make."

She starts to close the door. I shove my foot in to stop her.

"If you don't want to say anything, that's fine," I say. "I'll do the talking. But the people of Rockton need all the reassurance they can get, and having you there will help."

Her lips curve in what can't quite be called a smile. "The people of Rockton don't give a damn whether I'm there. They rely on Sheriff Dalton for all their reassurances."

"Then just show up and stand beside him. Support him. He needs that right now."

"Sheriff Dalton doesn't need anything from anyone, Casey. The sooner you realize that, the easier your six months here will be."

I must have reacted at that, because she says, "You don't think I know about his little deal with you? As I said, Eric Dalton doesn't need anything from anyone. Let him run his little Wild West town, keep your head down, and get out of this hellhole as fast as you can.

There's your statement, Detective. Take it and go."

THIRTY-SIX

We give our statement at nine. Or I give it, with Dalton standing cross-armed beside me, his look daring anyone to speak when I ask if there are any questions.

I've always wondered why there isn't more dissent in police states. I'm accustomed to a world where people riot after a hockey game. Imagine what they'd do under a totalitarian authority. The answer, at least in Rockton, is not a hell of a lot.

I guess that isn't surprising. Rockton gives them sanctuary, and Dalton keeps them safe, and so whatever they might think of him, they don't seem to doubt his ability to continue doing so. They've given him a pass on Powys, trusting that he's doing his best. With Hastings, that's shifting, and I hear grumblings, the occasional whisper that maybe Dalton and I are a little young to be handling this. It doesn't go above whispering, though. Not yet.

The next five days pass with frustratingly

little progress on the case. I work my ass off, but I feel like I'm searching for the proverbial needle in the haystack . . . and I'm not even sure there is a needle. I have so little to go on. The autopsy report on Hastings didn't tell me anything new. There's no forensic evidence — Irene's crime scene is a month old, and both Hastings and Powys were found in the forest, which is a hell of a place to get evidence.

We scour the woods for footprints where we found Hastings, but it hasn't rained in over a week and the rocky ground is too hard to take an impression. We search for anything the killer might have dropped, spending two days combing an ever-widening circle. We even hunt for the kind of trace evidence — a snagged thread or clump of hair — that you only really find in TV shows. Beth scrapes under the nails of the victims. Hell, we dig up Irene to get samples from hers. No defensive wounds or signs of a struggle on any of them.

I interview everyone remotely connected to the four victims. That count includes Abbygail because, until proved otherwise, I include her as a victim. All that leads to exactly one clue.

In Hastings's case, Kenny had seen him head toward the forest and told the sheriff, which led to the manhunt. Powys, though, had simply disappeared. With the interviews,

I find out that someone had seen Powys walking into the forest. He hadn't come forward because, well, at the time he was sneaking from the house of his longtime girlfriend to the house of someone who was not his longtime girlfriend.

At just past midnight — which the witness knew, because he'd been waiting for his girlfriend to fall asleep — he'd been cutting through the yards and seen Powys, who had paused at the edge of the forest and looked around, making sure he wasn't seen. Which meant either both Hastings and Powys were lured out or both had randomly decided to take a walk in prohibited territory . . . and just happened to meet their killer there.

That isn't exactly a case-breaking revelation, and I still feel like I'm getting nowhere, but the guy who hadn't wanted me in this job is actually the one who keeps me going. As Dalton points out — with an impatient snap — I'm narrowing down my suspect list. For example, the killer had to be strong enough to get Hastings into that tree, which is no mean feat. Dalton and Anders rig up a pulley system out behind the station. We run some experiments. Anders can raise Hastings's weight. Dalton can, too, with serious effort. I only get the rock-filled sack two feet off the ground by pulling with everything I have. Then I lose my footing and go flying. Great amusement for the guys. Anders insists

I do it three more times — to be sure — and Dalton doesn't argue. We even add weights to my end, but I lack the upper-body strength to haul that bag into a tree.

What does this tell us? That our killer was male and at least as physically fit as Dalton. Which doesn't narrow it down as much as it would in an urban environment. Rockton is like prison in some ways, giving guys lots of free time and the chance to get those biceps and pecs they've always dreamed of. Plus there's the added motivation of getting in shape to impress the limited female population. That means a lot of guys like Kenny: former ninety-eight-pound weaklings who can now bench-press triple that much.

The impromptu surgery on Hastings suggests someone with medical knowledge, but the work had been crudely done. According to Beth, anyone with a basic knowledge of anatomy and butchering could do it. She's right — even with just what I learned from my parents, I could. Out here, people hunt, which gives them those skills. We also may have butchers, veterinarians, and nurses who've been smuggled in as something else.

That's the case, five days later. As for the rest of my life in Rockton, while I haven't quite adopted the "work hard, play hard" local mentality, I'm closer to it than I've ever been. I put in long hours yet rarely spend an evening alone at home. My companions vary.

I dine with Beth a few times — she even cooks for me. With Petra, I sit on my back deck, talking as she sketches the fox, sketches the northern lights, sketches me. I go to the Lion for drinks with Anders and Petra and sometimes a few others. I even manage to get Beth to come along, which Anders says is a feat.

Dalton joins us occasionally, but socializing isn't his thing. Still, I see as much of him outside work as I do anyone else, because I've taken an interest in the things that interest him. The night after we watched the northern lights, I came home to find a folding mattress and a stack of books in my front hall. When I thanked him for them the next day, he shrugged and said, "You wanted them. That's something."

"What's something?"

"You. Wanting anything."

I didn't ask him to explain that. I was pretty sure I didn't want to. The point is that I've developed an interest in my surroundings, which he shares, so he'll take me hiking, riding, ATV'ing. Sometimes Anders joins us, sometimes he doesn't.

As for Anders in general . . . in another life, that might have been something. Hell, in *this* life it might still be something. Just not right now. Right now, I want friendship, and that is as huge a step for me as Diana taking lovers.

Then there's Diana. That's been the most

difficult part of my five days. How horrible is it to admit that I find it easy to avoid her? Yes, I'm busy with the case, but I'm busy socially, too. She wants desperately to make amends . . . and I don't. We've been out together, as part of a group with Petra and Anders, and that's fine because I'm not ready to cut her loose. But there are no best-friend moments. I'm making new friends — Beth, Petra, Anders — and that's a big deal for me, and it makes it easier to shift away from Diana. I'm not exactly leaving her stranded — she's still as popular as the new girl in a one-room schoolhouse. New lives for both of us. Something we both needed.

On the fifth night, Anders and I stop by the Lion for a drink after work, and Diana's gang is there. She waves us over, but I pretend not to notice. Petra isn't with them, and that's my criterion for joining.

Anders and I take a table at the back, out of sight. We talk, drink, just relaxing after work. I use the toilet before we head out. Yes, I should be polite and call it a restroom, but that elevates it to a title it doesn't deserve. One more issue with living in the middle of nowhere? A lack of proper plumbing. It doesn't help that you hit permafrost a few feet down. Deep holes aren't possible. What we have instead are chemical toilets, like the kind you'd put in an RV. Which means they need to be emptied. As in most communities, the shit jobs — pun intended in this case — pay very well. Judging by the smell of the one in the Lion, that cleaning was a day or two overdue.

For that reason, I'm in and out as fast as I can be. As I leave, I nearly crash into Diana, right outside, trying to shake off a drunken guy.

"Hey," I cut in. "She's saying no."

He backs off fast, hands up, mumbling apologies. I nod to Diana and try to pass, but she grabs my arm and her hand is shaking.

"Thank you," she says.

"No problem. He just needed a firm no."

"From you. That doesn't work for . . ." She inhales. "I'm having a problem, Casey, and I hate to bother you with it, but . . ."

"Go on," I say.

"You . . . you know what Isabel does, right? I mean, the kind of place she runs."

I nod.

"She thinks . . ." Diana swallows. "God, this is so embarrassing. She thinks I'm free-lancing."

"What?"

"This guy gave me some credits." She lifts both hands. "Not like that. Not at all. It was the night before you got here. We went out on a date — dinner at the restaurant, drinks afterward at his place. He had wine, and I said I couldn't wait until my first pay so I could get myself a bottle. The next day, we went out for breakfast, and he gave me credits to buy the wine. He wasn't . . ." Her cheeks flare again. "It was like giving me a bottle of wine as a gift. I only took the credits because I planned to pay him back. A payroll advance. Only Isabel saw this guy giving me credits early in the morning, and she jumped to the wrong conclusion."

"I'll talk to her."

"She has Mick keeping an eye on me, and he makes me nervous. You know he used to be a cop here, right? And the sheriff fired him?"

I didn't know the last part, but I nod anyway. "I'll handle —"

"And I think they've told others. I've been offered . . . credits."

I look sharply toward the guy who'd been hassling her, now trying another woman at the bar.

"No, not him. At least, he hadn't gotten to it yet. I know you're still mad at me, Casey —"

"I'm not mad. Just very busy."

"Will you help me with this? Please?"

I tell her I will.

"Spelunking," Dalton says, leaning over my desk.

"It's an awesome word," I say.

"It is. And we're doing it tomorrow."

"We are?"

326

He heads for the back door. I've learned this isn't his way of avoiding a conversation — it's him moving it to another location.

He takes his seat. I take mine, perched on the railing as we watch a raven hop along the forest's edge.

"You gotta stop feeding her," he says.

"I don't know what you're talking about."

He snorts. After a minute, the raven hops up the steps and onto the railing beside me. She waits. I count off thirty seconds. Then I take a bread crust from my pocket. She waits until I hold it out, gingerly snags it from my hand, and flies off.

Dalton sighs. Deeply.

"It's your fault," I say. "You gave me the book that says ravens are smart. I'm testing that."

Another sigh.

"I am. She's learned to recognize me and know that she will get exactly one crust per day. It's a treat. Not a meal." I glance over at him, going serious. "If you really want me to stop, I will."

"Nah. Have your fun. But if I catch you giving her a name —"

"I won't. She's a wild animal. Not a pet."

He nods, satisfied that his student has learned her lessons well.

"What was this about us going caving?" I ask.

"A few of us are heading out tomorrow.

You've been working the case nonstop. A break will freshen your brain."

I say yes quickly. Another lesson assimilated. If I want something, admit it. None of this pissing around pretending I don't really care. He wants me to care — one way or the other.

"Petra's joined us before," Dalton says. "I think she liked it. Why don't you ask if she wants to come along?"

I smiled. "I will."

THIRTY-SEVEN

It's spelunking day. We're closing up the station at noon. Kenny and a couple of the militia guys will be in charge. I joke that we should make Val man the station, and we spend the morning trading quips about that. Or Anders and I do. Dalton just rolls his eyes and mutters.

I've given up on Val. She reminds me of a principal I had in elementary school. We swore she was a vampire who could only arrive before dawn and leave after dark, which explained why no one caught more than fleeting glimpses of her. We're sure Val is reporting on us via her satellite phone, but she comes out so rarely that we never have to worry about watching over our shoulder.

Val's only defender is Beth. "She's a deeply unhappy woman," she'll say.

"Then she should get off her ass, do some work, and be *less* unhappy," Dalton replies.

"That's not the solution for everyone, Eric. I think there's a story there."

"And I think you just want there to be one, to give her an excuse."

Anyway, that's Val. Dalton did tell her we were going caving. She didn't care.

The idea of taking off for the afternoon seems very carefree and spontaneous. Like skipping school on the first gorgeous day of spring. Except I never actually did that, and I suspect if Dalton had lived down south, he wouldn't have, either. So while we have every intention of cutting out at noon, the reality is a little different.

At ten, we get a call — which in Rockton means someone comes running through the station's front door. There was a break-in at the greenhouse last night. All three of us go to investigate. It seems like a simple case of someone deciding, presumably drunk or high, that he really needed a tomato. Or an entire vine of tomatoes. One is stripped clean, with a tomato crushed underfoot as the thief made his escape.

Yes, it's almost laughable. The Case of the Trampled Tomatoes. In Rockton, though, resource theft is a serious offense. It has to be.

We could abandon the investigation at noon. But it would send the wrong message to would-be thieves. Dalton sends Anders off to guide the other spelunkers and says we'll catch up.

At twelve thirty, we find the thief. It took

actual detective work — interviewing two witnesses, examining footprints left at the scene, and then banging on the door of the suspect, who was sound asleep, with squashed tomato on her shoe and three ripe ones on her counter.

Jen protests her innocence. She accuses me of having a vendetta against her. She attempts to hit me. I put her down. Dalton is amused. He even smiles. Then he lets me escort her, arm wrenched behind her back, to the cell, where she'll spend the afternoon, namely because we really do want to get off on our trip, and this is the easiest way to contain the howling woman.

I'm finishing a brief report on the incident when Diana swings into the station with a wide grin. For a second, I forget anything's happened between us, and I smile back.

"Hey," she says. "I heard you had some excitement this morning, and I'm betting you haven't eaten lunch."

"I —"

"So I'm taking you out. No tomatoes. I promise."

"Today's —"

"Your lucky day, my friend. Having solved the great tomato caper, even your asshole of a boss can't deny you an afternoon off." The door opens as my *asshole boss* steps in and stands behind Diana. I try to cut her short, but she's going full steam. "I have also wrangled an afternoon off, which means we are doing lunch and then going rafting. It's gotten too cold for pond dips, but it's still fine for raft lounging."

"She has plans," Dalton says.

Diana turns. "Work, you mean. I think Casey —"

"Has earned the afternoon off. Which she is getting. We're going caving today. You know that because I heard Petra telling you."

"I thought that was canceled due to tomato theft."

"Nope. Casey? Got your things?"

"Casey?" Diana says. "When did you pull the stick out of your ass and start calling her by name?"

"Diana," I say, sharply enough that I expect her to react. Maybe even apologize. She doesn't, and when Dalton motions for me to get ready, she says, "Yes, Casey. Hop to it. God forbid you keep the man waiting."

She's been drinking. That must be it. But I don't smell alcohol, and she's standing upright, no wobbles.

I open my mouth to ask her to leave, but she grabs my arm. "Come rafting with me, Case. You know you want to."

"No," Dalton says. "*You* want her to. Casey has been busy, and you don't like that. She's also been hanging out with Petra, and you don't like that, either. So you're . . ." He trails off, frowns at her, and says, "Look up."

"What?"

He motions for her to tilt her head up. He's not reaching out to touch her, but she bats his hand away as if he is. That's when I notice her pupils are constricted, despite the dim light.

"What'd you take?" Dalton asks.

"Take?"

"Any medications?"

"Aspirin for a headache. Is that a crime, Sheriff? Want to lock me up with Jen? Maybe you want to watch the catfight, too."

His look is complete incomprehension. She mutters something, but I know where the bizarre accusation came from. The same place as those pupils. Rydex's opiate base constricts pupils.

"Then you won't mind coming to Doc Lowry's," Dalton says. "Have her check you for that headache. Make sure it's only pain-killers you took."

"Are you accusing me of taking dex, ass-hole?"

"Diana," I say. "Don't."

She turns to me. "What? He can call me a druggie but I catch shit for calling him an ass?"

"Go home, Diana," Dalton says. "Or go rafting. I'm not going to call you on it this time, because if I do, Casey won't get to go caving. But the next time, you're taking the test."

"Asshole."

"Try a new insult. You're wearing that one thin."

She stomps out. I stare after her.

"She's fine," he says. "Pretty sure she took dex, but probably only to work up the nerve to talk to you."

I turn to him.

He shrugs. "I know you've been getting some distance from her since the bar thing. And I'd say it's about fucking time. Point is that she took dex to get up the nerve to waltz in here like nothing's happened, and all it did is unleash her ugly side again."

I say, "I think she's having other problems." I tell him what Diana said about the misunderstanding with Isabel.

"You talk to Isabel?" he asks.

"I spoke to Mick yesterday, who doesn't seem convinced it was a misunderstanding. He says that's not the only evidence of . . . an exchange of goods, so to speak."

"Credits?"

"No, no."

"So guys give her stuff after sex. But that's customary, right? Down south?"

I look up sharply and sputter a laugh. "Uh, no."

"Then what's that?" He points to my necklace.

I stiffen and my tone cools. "It's called a gift —"

"From a guy you were sleeping with. Obviously *not* payment for sex. That's my point. It's a cultural norm. Historically, guys pay for attention from a woman — dinner, a show, flowers, jewelry. . . . The problem is that up here, as you've pointed out, guys *do* pay for sex. So they could be giving Diana stuff in payment, and she's accepting them as gifts."

"Are you actually defending her?"

"I'm saying it might be an honest misunderstanding. However, I also think she's exaggerating the issue to get your attention. Same as coming in here high on dex. Maybe it wasn't just working up courage, like I thought. More attention seeking. She's high, I call her on it, she demands a drug test . . . and you spend the day taking care of her as you always do instead of going caving with Petra."

"That seems . . . extreme."

"For a normal person, yeah. Diana?" He shakes his head. Then he walks over to my jacket. "Enough of this. Her stunt failed to screw up your day. She's not going to screw it up by making us *fight* over her stunt. We're going caving."

The others have the ATVs. To be honest, as much as I love the thrill of those, the horses are winning me over. It's a quieter ride, one that makes me feel part of the forest rather than an intrusion on it. We can relay instruc-

335

tions more easily. I can gape about more easily. And I can pester Dalton more easily.

I'm also becoming rather attached to my horse. Yes, mine, because it's rare for anyone besides us and the militia to ride them, and the militia usually leave Cricket behind. I'm not quite the little girl who finally got a pony, but there is a little of that. Now, to completely compensate for my frustrated-animal-lover childhood . . .

"I want a dog," I call up to Dalton.

He shakes his head without turning.

"Hey, you're all about me wanting things. Maybe I'll just grab one of the ferals and tame it. Is that okay?"

He doesn't even dignify that with an answer.

"How about the dog we spotted on patrol a couple days ago? The one you and Brent have been trying to put down? Beth told me it took a chunk out of your leg last spring. Careless, Sheriff. Very careless."

I get a flashed finger for that.

"But I do admire its attitude," I say. "I think that's the one I want. I can muzzle it, if that makes you feel safer."

"Speaking of muzzles, you do know we're listening for trouble, right?"

"*You're* listening for trouble. *I'm* pestering you with stupid requests. Because I know how much you love that. I'd also like a hot tub."

He snorts a laugh. One of the locals had

336

started a petition for a hot tub. Dalton's reaction was a wondrously imaginative line containing six expletives and a single noun. I'd offered to write it up as an official response and pin it over the petition in the town square. Anders dared me to do it. I still might.

We continue in silence, and I'm considering asking about a bird I saw yesterday, when I catch a glimpse of something in the forest. There's a second when I think it's the dog, because that's the kind of place this is, where I'd tease Dalton about a feral dog . . . and it would promptly appear to bite his other leg.

I peer into the forest and see a man. He has pale skin, light hair worn shoulder length, and an old-style army jacket. That jacket is distinctive, and I'm certain I haven't seen it before.

"Eric?" I whisper. Yes, it's Eric now. As Diana pointed out, we've moved beyond surnames and titles. I ride up alongside him. "I saw someone. I think . . . I think we're being followed."

I describe our tracker. When I do, he relaxes and his lips twitch in a smile of relief.

"You know him?" I whisper.

"Yeah." He looks at me. "I'm going to ask you to stay right here. I won't go far, and I'll stay where I can see you, but I need to speak to him, and he's not good with strangers."

My gaze must flick toward his gun, because

he says, "Nah, nothing like that. He's uncomfortable with outsiders, but absolutely no danger."

He dismounts and passes me Blaze's reins. He gives the gelding the apple from his pocket and then strides into the forest. I slide off Cricket and pass her my apple as I make a concerted effort not to watch him go. I'm curious, of course, but I want to be respectful.

"Jacob?" Dalton calls.

I nod, understanding better now.

Dalton calls Jacob's name a few more times. He adds, "I'm alone. I'd like to talk to you." Finally, "Have it your way. Pain in the ass." He says the last with a mix of exasperation and affection. This isn't just someone he vaguely knows. There's a relationship here, and when he comes out, I say, carefully, "Jacob. That's the guy Brent was talking about."

"Yeah."

He climbs on Blaze, and I think the conversation is over, but as we start riding again, he says, "He's a good scout. Grew up out here. Few years younger than me. I've known him . . . well, I've known him a long time."

"And you're worried about him."

"Nah." He pauses. "I'd just like to tell him about Hastings and Powys. Pass on the news. Ask if he's seen anything. We missed our last meet-up, and I was a little worried. But you

338

saw him, so he's fine. Just being a pain in the ass. He heard us talking, and he was curious enough to see who the new voice is, but he's sure as hell not coming out to say hello." He rides a little farther and then says, "And I'm going to need to ask you to respect that, Casey. If you do catch a glimpse of him, please don't try to introduce yourself. He's not Brent."

"If you tell me he wouldn't want to meet me, I'd never try."

His voice dips with his chin, as if in apology. "I know. Thank you."

THIRTY-EIGHT

Exploring today's cave is not like walking hunched over through Brent's cavern. It's shimmying on my stomach through passages so narrow I'm sure I'll never get to the other side. It's shivering against a bitter and damp cold that gnaws at my bones. It's filthy, wet jeans that have burst at the knee, and I'm pretty sure I feel blood trickling down my leg. And the smell. God, the smell. Of cold, and of death. When I put my hand down and feel stones crackling under my fingers, I shine my headlamp on them to see they're actually bones from some tiny creature. There's another smell, too. Guano. Better known as bat shit.

It's cold and it's wet and it stinks and it's absolutely filthy. And I love it. Every time I squeeze through a tight passage, there's a moment of animal panic, when my shoulders or hips catch and I'm sure I'll be trapped in there forever. Then I make it through, and the relief . . . God, the relief. A shuddering, shivering relief that amuses the hell out of the others.

"Uh, you do understand the basic laws of mass, right?" Anders mock-whispers after I breathe that sigh of relief on surviving another chute. "If I go through first, there's no way in hell *you* can get stuck."

"Yeah, yeah."

He grins and then peers at me, tilting his headlamp down into my face. "Hold on. You've got bat shit on your face." He leans in and wipes his thumb across my cheek. "There."

"Gone?"

"No, I was just putting a matching streak on the other side."

I smack his arm. Beside us, Mick gives a soft chuckle before he moves on. Anders keeps grinning down at me, and I look up at him, and I think, *Maybe.*

Maybe I'm missing an opportunity here. I probably am. I look at him, and that grin, and it's not because he's gorgeous or sweet or funny or kind. It's this feeling that there's more to him. Something that resonates with me at gut level.

"Are we moving or freezing to death?" Dalton says.

Anders waves for him to lead the way. We squeeze through another tight passage. Then we gather in a cavern. As we start heading out, Anders catches my arm and says, "Hold on."

"More bat shit on my face?"

He smiles. "Lots. It's adorable." Then he calls to the others. "I'm taking Casey into the Dark Cavern. I want to show her something."

"Uh-huh," Petra says. "Given it's the *Dark* Cavern, I'm pretty sure she's not going to be able to see whatever it might be."

He shoots her the finger, and she laughs and says, "Go on, kids. Catch up with us in the Cathedral. There's something there that I want to show Casey. And don't worry, I'm sure it's not the same thing."

A round of chuckles for that. Dalton doesn't join in. He's peering down the dark passage that Anders is tugging me toward.

"We shouldn't split up," he says. "If you want to take Casey to the cavern, we should all —"

"It's too small. I've got this, boss. I can't track for shit, but my sense of direction is impeccable. We'll meet you in the Cathedral."

He motions me along before Dalton can argue. We crawl through two passages and end up in a small cavern.

"It's dark," I say.

He laughs. "Hence the name. The passages are switchbacks, so any illumination from out there doesn't get in here. Which is what I want to show you. Something you aren't likely to ever see outside a cave. Turn off your light."

I twist the headlamp on my helmet. He does the same, and when the lights go out . . .

"Wow. That's . . ." I begin.

"Dark?" He chuckles. "Absolute darkness. Not a single pinpoint of light. Now, if the others are far enough away, and I stop talking for once . . ."

He does, and the silence falls, as absolute as the darkness, and suddenly I'm alone. Absolutely alone in the dark. Every outside stimulus vanishes and there's nothing except me in the darkness and the silence.

I swear I can hear my thoughts. All my thoughts. And it's horribly uncomfortable, and I want to switch on the light and say something and shove that aside. But the feeling passes in a few panicked heartbeats, and then . . . and then it's indescribable.

This is what I've been looking for in all those therapy sessions. Not a chance to tell someone my story. A chance to be alone with it. Utterly alone with it, and maybe that makes no sense, but it's what I feel. Just me and that one defining moment in my past.

Grief and rage and pain and guilt and clarity. Yes, clarity.

After a few minutes, Anders's leg brushes mine, and he whispers, "You okay?"

I nod, only to realize that's pointless and say, "I am."

"I'll tell you a deep, dark secret," he says, and then chuckles. "In an appropriately deep, dark location. I come here sometimes. Alone. If Eric found out, he'd skin me. But . . . it's just . . ." He exhales, his breath hissing in the dark. "Sometimes I need a break from being good ol' cheerful Will Anders. This is where I find it."

I don't know what *to* say.

He continues. "I can be that guy. Most times I *am* that guy. But . . . not always. Shit, you know. The past. Mistakes. The stuff that doesn't let you really be what others expect you to be. What they need you to be."

"Yes." *I understand perfectly.*

He squeezes my knee. Nothing flirtatious. Just a squeeze that says, maybe, he knows that I do understand. I don't know why Anders is in Rockton. It's not something most people share, but I say, "The war?"

"Yeah."

"If you ever want to talk . . ."

Another squeeze. "Thanks. Maybe. Someday. For now, this works."

"All right." I understand that, too.

"If you ever want to come out here with me . . . ," he says.

"I'd like that."

"Good."

We sit in silence. Then I peel off my glove and find his hand, and it's the same as his squeeze on my knee. Comfort and reassurance and a wordless understanding that there is always darkness. In some part of us, there is absolute darkness, as much as we wish otherwise. As much as we pretend otherwise.

Anders shifts closer, his jeans whispering against the rock. He's still holding my hand, and I feel him there, beside me, hear his breathing, and I think . . .

I want to be like Diana and throw caution to the wind and embrace this new freedom. But I can't. I'm still me. Logical Casey. Rational Casey. Cautious Casey. A-little-bit-scared Casey. I cannot turn off my brain, close my eyes, and jump.

A scraping and thumping in the passage breaks the silence. Anders sighs and drops my hand.

"Hello, Eric. Were we gone five seconds longer than anticipated?"

"More like five minutes." Dalton's headlamp floods the cavern with light as we flick ours on.

"God forbid," Anders mutters.

"I got worried."

"That what? We'd been devoured by cave bears?"

"We need to get back before dark, and Petra still wants to show Casey something."

Another deep sigh, and Anders moves into the lead. As he passes Dalton, he murmurs, "Thanks, boss. I *was* worried. Those cave bears, you know. Dangerous and unpredict-able."

Dalton grunts and motions for me to fol-low Anders out.

What Petra wants to show me is a chute lead-ing off a huge cavern known as the Cathedral.

"It seems too tight for the guys, so they won't risk it," she says. "I fit, but you know Eric — either we stay within sight or we need a buddy."

"Cave bears," Anders says.

"Basic safety," Dalton says. He turns to me. "If you want to try the chute, go ahead. If Petra fits, you definitely will."

"Thanks," Petra says.

He ignores her. "But it's up to you. As always."

I stick my head into the chute. It's called that because it goes, well, down. Like a laundry chute. I can't even see what's at the bottom.

"It looks like a small cavern," Petra says. "With branching passages. We won't go far, but it would be nice to map a little more."

When I put my head in farther, my chest constricts, as if I can feel the walls pressing in. It looks impossible to fit through. But while Dalton may have been a little impolitic in pointing it out, Petra is bigger than me. Bigger bust. Bigger hips. If she can get through, I can.

"Let's do it," I say.

She lets out a whoop and taunts the guys. Then she goes through, headfirst. I wait until she calls, "In!" and then it's my turn. Mick crouches and gives me a few tips for the tighter passages. He's barely said a full sentence during the trip — he's not exactly a chatty guy — but he takes the time to be helpful, and I appreciate that.

The first section is easy. Then the chute angles slightly, and this is the "squeeze" — the part that keeps the guys out. I wriggle my head and shoulders through. Then my hips get stuck and my breathing picks up as I see that now-familiar image of me trapped forever in a chute. I can hear Mick's voice, as if he's whispering in my ear.

If Petra got through, so can you. Once your shoulders make it, the rest is fine. Relax and wriggle and be patient. Back out if you have to, but remember that'll be harder than going straight on.

I'm finally through. It may be a chute, but it has enough of an angle that I don't tumble out headfirst. When I see the end coming, I put out my arms, and it's like sliding into home base. Very, very slowly sliding . . . as I propel myself with my knees and feet and hips. Apparently this looks hilarious. Or so Petra's peals of laughter suggest as I finally touch down.

"You make it look so much tougher than it is, Casey," she says as I get up. "I really wish I had my sketch pad."

"Yeah, yeah." I brush off my knees. Which is a mistake, because I definitely have sliced one open, and I only rub dirt into the cut.

I look up to see I'm crouched in a small cavern.

"Check this out," Petra says, waving her headlamp at an alcove to the side. Inside, there are what I've come to know as soda straws — baby stalactites.

"Ten minutes," Dalton calls down the chute. "I'm timing it."

"I forgot my watch," I call back. "If we're late, just come down and get us."

Petra snickers. Dalton says something I don't catch. I won't give him grief. I check my watch — yes, I'm wearing it — and make a mental note of our deadline.

"Which way first?" I ask Petra.

There are three options. She bends to check the narrowest and declares it *too* narrow. I move to the biggest of the three. It's almost a straight drop, but wide enough to go feet first. When I shine my headlamp down, I can see the bottom, less than ten feet below, and the walls are rough and angled enough to climb back up.

"Can I go first?" I ask.

She grins. "Getting into the explorer spirit?"

"I am. Also, I'm the one with the gun

because, you know, cave bears."

"Of course. The chute is yours. Virgin territory awaits."

I slide down. The wider passage actually makes it a little tougher, because I can't just leap down the chute or I'd bang myself all to hell. I use my arms and legs as braces, find foot- and handholds, and slowly lower myself until I'm in the cavern. I smell something. Something that makes me drop the last few feet.

The cavern ceiling is only about three feet off the ground. Which means I have to wriggle down until I'm crouching. My helmet finally comes out of the chute and my light shines on . . .

An arm.

I'm staring at a decomposing human arm.

There's a moment when my brain says no. Just no. In the past two weeks, I've seen severed legs, a skull, and an intestine nailed to a tree. This just isn't possible. It's too much. I must be seeing a weirdly shaped stone or a bleached-out branch, and after so many damn body parts, I'm mistaking it for an arm.

But that's not the answer. I wish it was. God, I really fucking wish it was, because when I see that arm — the light-brown skin, the slim fingers, the nails with chipping purple polish . . . I know who it is: the girl who celebrated her twenty-first birthday two months ago. Who went missing a few days later.

Abbygail Kemp.

"Casey?" Petra calls.

"Don't —" I begin, but she's already coming down, legs through the chute, and I call, "Hold on!" but she doesn't hear me. She bends, and she looks my way, and she sees the first thing I did, and she screams.

It's a horror-movie scream. As soon as I hear it, I know there's trauma in Petra's background, something terrible. I grab her shoulders and turn her away and talk to her, calming her down as she presses her hand to her mouth and squeezes her eyes shut.

"Butler!" Dalton shouts, his voice echoing through the cavern. "Casey!"

"We're fine!" I yell back, but he just shouts again, obviously not hearing me, having only caught that terrible scream. I gently move Petra aside, crawl into the chute, stand, and yell again, but there's no response.

I duck down and look at Petra, crouching and breathing deeply. Then I look up the chute, and I curse. I've got a freaked-out boss and a freaked-out friend, and there's a cavern and two passages between them. I can't leave Petra. Can't leave the crime scene.

Rocks scrabble overhead as if someone is trying to make it through that narrow chute.

"We're fine!" I shout. "Just hold on!"

"Go," Petra whispers. "It's Eric. Stop him

before he gets stuck."

I try yelling again. It does no good. He's coming down, and Petra's right: he's going to get his damned self stuck. I tell her I'll be right back, and I scramble up the chute, making it into the other cavern at the same time Dalton comes through the first passage. His jeans are ripped. He's stripped off his jacket and is wearing only a T-shirt, his arms scraped and bloody.

"Goddamn it," I say, but I mutter it under my breath. The guy heard a scream and came running, slicing himself up in the process. I can't really fault him for that, can I?

"It's okay," I say. "I tried to tell you —"

"You're all right?" he says, his breath coming hard, adrenaline setting his blood racing so hard I can see it pulsing in his neck. "Someone screamed."

"Petra. She's fine. She's down there. I was, too, but came back up. We . . ." I hesitate. Shit, how do I say this? I can't just blurt —

"Butler?" he says. Then, when I don't answer, he steps toward me, his hand going to my elbow to steady me. "Casey? What's wrong?"

"There's . . . We found . . . It's a body part. Scavenged. An arm."

He exhales hard. "Okay." He peers into the drop, following the light from Petra's helmet. He grunts, seeing it's an easy passage, and starts getting in place to go down.

I touch his arm. "Eric?"

"Hmm?"

"I think . . ." I take a deep breath. "It's a young woman's arm. She's wearing nail polish. Purple."

His eyes close. That's all he does. Closes his eyes, his expression emptying as he crouches there.

"I'm sorry," I say. "I'm so sorry."

He opens his eyes. "Thank you. For warning me." He takes a deep breath and heads down the chute.

THIRTY-NINE

It's Abbygail. Dalton confirms she wore that nail polish for her party. Isabel gave it to her.

Dalton goes back up first. He wants to be the one to tell Mick. The second passage is probably even harder getting out than it was getting in, but he seems too numb to notice.

I hear Mick's reaction. It's a terrible sound. Worse than Petra's scream. It's animal pain, cut short quickly, and by the time I get up there, he's gone; one of the other guys went with him to make sure he gets to Rockton safely.

I bring up the arm. I've looked for other parts, but this is all I find. We'll have to conduct a more thorough search with proper lights tomorrow.

Anders examines the arm. His older sister is a doctor, and he'd had a year of medic training before the army realized his skills were better suited to policing. He knows enough to confirm what I'd feared — that this is not a part separated from the body by scavengers. Yes, a scavenger did bring it into the cave, but the separation is due to amputation. Dismemberment.

When Powys and Hastings died, people mourned. There were services. I had nothing to do with them, and the mourners weren't in my circle of new acquaintances, so the events passed with little notice on my part.

This is different. This is hell.

We aren't telling anyone that we suspect Abbygail was murdered. We can't panic them like that. As far as they know, she wandered into the forest, died, and her body was scavenged. That doesn't matter. Abbygail Kemp is still dead.

Dalton said that most everyone in Rockton joined the search when she vanished. I see that now. When we return with the news, it is as if Mick's howl of animal pain reverberates through the entire town. There's crying in the streets. There are questions now, so many questions. Anders and I try to leave Dalton out of it, but of course he won't stay out of it, because however much he's grieving, this is his town in crisis.

Petra recruits Diana and others to organize a candlelight memorial in the square. It gives people a focus for their grief. I'm still stopped at every step through town, people asking how and where and, mostly, the unanswerable why. But they are kind, too, and thoughtful. The cooks bring dinner to the station. Isabel drops off a bottle of her best Scotch. The guys at the bakery run the ovens late to make cookies for the memorial, and they bring by a dozen with a thermos of coffee. People ask what they can do to help, anything, anything at all — that's what I hear, even more than "what happened out there?"

I'm at Beth's clinic when she examines the arm. That is true hell, because she's examining the partial remains of a girl she loved. Her pain is palpable and almost too much to bear, but she insists on doing it. Anders helps until she snaps at him, so uncharacteristic for her that even Dalton jumps.

The arm was cut off at the elbow. Chopped with an ax, she guesses, like Powys's legs. She believes it was done postmortem. I don't know that's possible to tell, given the condition of the arm, but I don't question. This small mercy is all they have — to hope Abbygail's passing was painless.

I write the report for Beth as she dictates. Then I'm back at the station, compiling a full report. It's late now. I have no idea how late. I don't check because it doesn't matter. I will work until the work is done.

When the door opens, I get to my feet, expecting townspeople and ready with my script. *Yes, we found Abbygail's remains. No, we don't know anything more. Yes, there will be a memorial service. Yes, you can help with that.*

Dalton walks in.

I hover there, over my seat, and say, "Hey."

"Saw the light on," he says. "Figured it was you."

He comes in and, for once, he doesn't head straight to the back deck. He just stands inside the doorway.

"I'm sorry," I say. Then I grimace. "I've said that already, haven't I? Said it and said it and . . ." I inhale. "And now I'm rambling. Can I get you anything?"

He shakes his head, walks to the coffee station, and I see there's a bottle in his hand. Tequila. He pours rough shots into two mugs.

"If there's anything I can . . . ," I begin. "I mean, whatever you . . ." I slump back into the chair. "I'm just making it worse, aren't I?"

"You're fine."

"No, I'm not. I suck at this. At least, I do with people I know. I'm actually good at it with strangers. On the job, I was usually the one to break the news and stay with the families. Surprisingly."

He brings over his mug but leaves mine on the counter. "Why surprisingly?"

I shrug. "I'm not exactly warm and cuddly, as you may have noticed."

"Doesn't mean you don't care."

My cheeks heat at that, and I rise to retrieve the tequila shot he left me.

"Hold up," he says. "Need to ask you to do something before you drink that."

I sink back into the chair. "Sure."

"You sew?" he asks.

"What?" I'm sure I've misheard.

"Sew. Needle. Thread." He takes both out of his pocket and sets them on the desk. Then he peels off his jacket to reveal a gaping wound on his upper arm.

"Holy shit," I breathe.

"I nicked it coming out of that tight passage."

"*Nicked* it? You ripped your arm open, Eric."

He'd pulled his jacket on as soon as he came out of the passage, hiding the wound because it wasn't the time. Now, five hours later, it is finally the time.

"You need to get that fixed," I say. "There's a limited window for stitching before the wound starts to heal and it's too late to pull it together . . ."

Stitching. Sewing.

I look down at the needle and thread. "You're asking me to sew your arm."

"Yeah. Can't ask Beth right now. Will is busy. It's only a few stitches. If you'd rather not, though . . ."

I examine the wound. It's a couple of inches long and doesn't go very deep. Still nasty. Still in need of stitching.

"I'll run to the clinic and grab proper

equipment," I say. "Give me five minutes."

I really do run. Beth is gone, thankfully, because Dalton is right — we don't want to bother her with this. There are two emergency kits, which include sutures. Anders had carried one caving. Dalton just hadn't asked to use it because, well, that's Dalton.

I grab a kit, lock the door, and get back to him. As I walk in, he downs his shot of tequila.

"Smart man," I say. "This won't tickle."

He grunts.

"If it's any consolation, I actually have done this before," I say. "When I was a kid and my stuffed animals would rip, I'd use sutures. Does that make you feel better?"

I smile as I look up, but he only nods.

I clean the wound. "I'm kidding. Well, not about stitching up my toys. I did that. There actually *was* a time when I wanted to become a doctor. Of a sort. A veterinarian."

"Why didn't you?"

I laugh softly as I finish cleaning. "My parents freaked. Operate on *animals*? To them that's a waste of good medical supplies. You only become a vet if you aren't good enough to be a 'real' doctor. They took away my toys so I couldn't play animal hospital anymore."

I prepare the suture thread, still talking, mostly to keep him distracted. "But I have sewn people. Myself, actually. When I was fourteen, I went white-water rafting without telling my parents. Sliced up my leg. Stitched up my leg."

"You stitched your own leg?"

I shrug. "They were teaching me a lesson."

"Your parents *made* you stitch your leg?"

I slide the suture needle in. "It was fine. They supervised and gave me topical anesthetic, probably better than the one I just used on you. And it was a spot I could reach easily enough."

He's quiet, and I figure he's gritting his teeth against the pain. When I finish the stitches, though, he says, his voice low, "That's fucked up, Casey."

"Hmm?"

"Your parents made you stitch your own leg to teach you a lesson? That's fucked up."

"Which is why I don't usually share those stories. People get the wrong idea."

"Wrong idea?" he says as I clean the stitched wound. "They took away your toys because you wanted to be a vet. They made you stitch up your own goddamned leg. You do realize that's not normal, don't you?"

"My parents had their ways. Their ways were harsh. They thought they were preparing me for a world that was equally harsh." I pause in my cleaning. "Do I realize some of what they did was 'fucked up'?" I meet his gaze. "I do. But they're dead."

He nods, as if understanding. There's no

one left to confront about it. No one to hate. So I don't. I can't.

I put aside the suture needle to clean and then get my shot of tequila. I lift the bottle, asking if he wants another, but he shakes his head.

"I need to get back to Beth. She shouldn't be alone tonight."

I nod. He gets his jacket on, wincing slightly, but makes no move to leave, just looks around the station.

"Anything you need from me?" he says. "Before I take off?"

When I say no, he looks almost disappointed.

"Okay. Guess I'll go, then." He eyes the door without moving, and I can tell he isn't eager to get back to grieving, but he's right — Beth needs someone there, and there's really no one else who can do it.

"I know you're the boss," I say. "So I can't tell you to take time off. But if that will help —"

"Hell, no. Working helps. I'll be in tomorrow. Tonight, I just . . . Yeah, I should go." He walks to the door, and as he leaves, he says, quietly, "I suck at this part, too, Detective," and before I can reply, he's gone.

Day two of mourning. It is only now, when something goes wrong, that I realize exactly how efficiently this town usually works. Every day, I join the same neighbors walking to work. We pass the lumberyard, and it's already abuzz with activity. At morning break, I will walk to the bakery and get my cookie. The varieties may change, but it will always be warm from the oven at 10 A.M. I can grab a coffee, too, fresh brewed, and I'll linger a few minutes and chat with Devon and Brian, the couple who run the bakery. They're my equivalent of the morning paper. No gossip for those guys — just the news. After I get back to the station, Kenny will pop by to check on our wood supply for the stove. And so it goes.

We don't ever run out of wood because Kenny got busy or the local supply is low. I don't ever miss out on my cookie because one of the guys stayed home sick or just didn't feel like baking that morning. Everything runs perfectly and predictably.

When you think about it, that's amazing, given all the moving parts required. Something as simple as getting a sandwich at lunch means that the greenhouse workers must bring the produce to the shop that morning and Brian must bake the bread and the butcher must fillet the salmon . . . the list goes on. In the city, those parts are interchangeable. No tomatoes at the usual supplier? Grab replacements from elsewhere. Employee phones in sick? Call someone else. Salmon went bad? Substitute corned beef.

That isn't possible here. Yet the town runs like clockwork.

Today, the clock is broken.

I don't see my usual neighbors on the way to work. Kenny doesn't come by. The bakery has cookies, but they're peanut butter because those were Abbygail's favorite, and I would feel like a fraud eating them. I already feel like one.

I mourn the girl in that photo. The girl who kept that dingy stuffed animal and cheap tin necklace. The girl who had a crush on the sheriff. The girl who encouraged her boyfriend to go after someone he wanted more than he wanted her. The girl who survived hell down south, came up here, and made a new life for herself.

That's what people do in Rockton. Make new lives. But for Abbygail, it wasn't about having fun with a new persona. It was about putting a shattered world back together. About becoming the person she should have been. To do that at such a young age takes incredible strength. She clawed back her birthright — the right to be a capable, independent young woman — and she should have left this town, gone back down south, and lived the kind of life that, in a just world, she would always have had. But someone took that away from her. The place that gave back her life also stole it away.

I'm furious for her. Outraged for her. And I

mourn her. But I don't really have that right, do I? I'm surrounded by people who knew her and are in genuine pain at her passing. All I have is a photo and a stuffed toy and a tin necklace and secondhand memories. So I have no right to mourn. But I still do. Quietly and on my own, because that's how I spend my day. *Being* the clock. Being that one functioning piece of Rockton that keeps the rhythm and does her job. My job is solving this crime. Avenging Abbygail.

So I work. All day. Into the night.

It's dark out now. I'm standing looking at notes I've tacked up — easy enough to do when the station walls are made of wood. I'm brainstorming connections when Anders comes in. He grabs a beer from the icebox, walks up behind me, and says, "You need a whiteboard."

"I can't imagine that'd be easy to get on the plane."

"Ask Eric. He'll get you one."

I shake my head and continue mulling over the pages.

"Speaking of getting stuff from the boss, do you need anything?"

"Unless it's urgent, I'm leaving him alone."

"Let me rephrase that. Can you *find* something you need from him?"

I turn to Anders.

"He's kinda stuck with Beth," he says. "She needs the support, but . . ." He shrugs and eases back onto the desk. "Beth can be a bit . . . hovery, if that's a word. She's worried about Eric, how he's dealing with this, and for him, that's a little . . ."

"Suffocating?"

"Exactly. He's there because it's the right thing to do, and he knows she's in pain . . ."

"But he could use a break?"

He nods. "I could take him something — minor trouble in town — but Beth won't appreciate me bugging him with the trivial shit. You're the detective on Abbygail's case. She can't argue with that."

"I'll see what I can do."

FORTY

The moment I set foot in Beth's house, I know we should have rescued Dalton sooner. It's not Beth herself. She's grieving, and as a friend, Dalton wants to help. But there's an oppressive air in the house that would indeed suffocate him. An air of inactivity, of pressure to stay in one place. Dalton might spend hours on the back deck, but his brain is busy. Here, he's stagnant in every way, sitting in a chair, gripping the arms, like a boy at an elderly aunt's, counting down the minutes to his escape.

When I walk in, he's on his feet so fast I cringe with guilt. Last night, he'd tried to linger at the station. Hinted he'd appreciate a reason to stay. I should have paid more attention.

"You need something, Detective?" he says, with such eagerness that it drives the guilt wedge deeper.

"I'm sure it can wait," Beth says.

"I was just —" I begin.

"It's late," she says firmly. "Eric deserves time off, and whatever your question, there's nothing he can do about it until morning."

"Right, I . . . How about a drink? Both of you. Come out to the Lion and we'll —"

"Thank you, but no."

"I could use one," Dalton says. "You could, too, Beth. Casey? Run back and tell Will to join us after his shift. *After.* No cutting out early."

"Sure thing, boss," I say, and I'm out the door before Beth can argue.

A week ago, if Dalton had told me to make Anders finish his shift, I'd have thought he was being a jerk. Now I understand it's strategy. If Anders can't head straight to the Lion with me, then Dalton has an excuse for leaving Beth's — me drinking by myself at the Lion would be asking for trouble.

By the time I get there, he already has a table.

He's alone, and when I say, "Beth didn't come?" the flash of guilt in his eyes makes me regret commenting. I quickly add, "She's probably in need of a little alone time herself."

"Yeah. I didn't want to leave her last night. But another night on the couch? Hell, no." He stops and pulls a face. "That's inconsiderate, isn't it."

I slide into the seat across from him. "I

don't think you're ever inconsiderate, Eric."

"You been drinking already, Detective? I'm the designated local asshole, remember?"

"Someone has to do it. You recognize when you're being an asshole, which means it's not like you're too inconsiderate to know better."

"But if I recognize I'm being an asshole, and I still do it, doesn't that only make me more of one?" He rubs his face. "Fuck, I'm in a mood. You might *not* want to have a drink with me."

"Too late." I set two beers on the table, and open one as I sit.

"You got something to ask me? About the case?"

I take a long draft of my beer and then say, "Nope."

He chuckles. "All right. Yeah, I needed the break, so thanks. I'm just not good at the condolences shit. I want to be, but . . . you know."

"I do."

We share a look. He nods and then says, "I'm going to Dawson City tomorrow. Get away. Clear my head. I'll be doing research, of course. You want to come with me?"

I arch my brows. "Pretty sure that's not allowed, boss."

"Fuck that."

I laugh.

"No, really, fuck that," he says, putting down his beer with a clack. "You're my detective. We have a serial killer. You need access to the Internet to do a proper job. Fuck 'em if they don't like it."

"You don't really mean that," I say, my voice low.

He shifts in his seat. Like a chained beast, rattling its shackles. "I'll tell Val. *Tell* her. Not ask. If she argues . . . we'll see. But if you want to go . . . No, fuck that, too, because if I give you the option, you'll worry that it'll get me in trouble. You're coming. It'll be an overnight trip. Back for the memorial. We'll leave at noon. We'll spend the morning at the station, let Will sleep, make sure nothing new comes in before we go."

"Yes, sir."

Dalton looks up. I see Anders walking over. When he's close enough, Dalton says, "Thought I told you not to cut out early on your shift."

"Fuck that," Anders says as he sits.

I glance at Dalton, and we laugh, leaving Anders looking from one to the other of us, saying, "What?"

"Go get another round," Dalton says.

Dalton tells Val I'm going with him to Dawson City. She doesn't argue. It's only when we're in the plane that I notice there's something different about Dalton today. He's shaved. To be honest, the beard scruff suits him better. Without it, he looks younger, softer, not quite himself. Hopefully, it's a temporary going-to-town change.

When we arrive in Dawson City, the car is waiting. Apparently, there's a local guy who stores it, and the council calls and says, "Have it at the airport at two P.M." or "Pick it up from the airport at noon." He does, no questions asked, because the Yukon is not a place where people ask questions.

Dalton doesn't drive directly into town. He goes down several side roads and stops along one. Then he's out of the car, grunting, "Wait here." Ten minutes later, he's back, saying, "I'm going to drop you off at the inn. You get settled. I've got things to do."

"Like call your dad on that cell phone you just picked up?"

"What?"

"I'm a detective, remember? You didn't drive way out here to take a piss. You were getting something you keep hidden. The only thing you wouldn't want to keep in Rockton is a secret method of communicating with the outside world. It could be a laptop, but then you wouldn't have considered buying a tablet for online research. It's also hard to hide a laptop. So it must be a phone. A cheap one, presumably without Internet access. Something that just lets you place calls. But who would you call? Not a former resident — that would be unsafe for both of you. It must be your parents. And you'd only call from a secret phone if you're saying more than 'Hey, Mom and Dad, how are you doing?' What might you need from someone down south? A partner to help you dig through the stories in your journal. Someone you trust. Someone with detecting skills. Like the former Rockton sheriff who happens to be your father."

Dalton shakes his head, reaches into his pocket, and tosses a cheap flip phone onto the dashboard.

"Ding-ding," I say with a grin. "What do I win? There is a prize, right?"

He grumbles something about *rewarding* me by not bringing me to Dawson City with him anymore.

"You just need to get better at subterfuge," I say. "The correct way to do it would have been to drop me off at the inn first. Then I'd have suspected you were going to talk to a local source. It was the random ten-minute walk into the forest that gave it away."

More grumbling. Then he turns back onto the main road and says, "You got a pen and paper?"

"I'd be a lousy cop if I didn't."

"Write a list. Research questions you want answered. Ones we can't cover with an Internet search."

I pull out my pad and paper. I'm jotting down questions when he says, "That guy . . . the one who gave you the necklace and left that message on your phone . . ."

I tense. "Kurt."

Dalton adjusts his grip on the wheel. "I couldn't let you return his text."

"I understood."

"I can do it now. Through my father. Pass along a message to let this guy know you're okay. You want that?"

"I would appreciate it. Yes."

"Write it down, then. With his contact info. Include something so he'll know it's really you."

"Thank you," I say.

He nods and turns his attention back to the road.

The first thing I do is buy a tablet for Dalton. It's not easy because, well, let's just say you aren't going to find an Apple Store or Best Buy in Dawson City. Instead, I get one at a pawnshop, which is actually just a regular store that sells secondhand goods on the side.

When Dalton takes me to a place to use the tablet, it's the polar opposite of what I'd expect from him. Or from Dawson City. It's a coffeehouse. The type that offers organic, fair-trade coffee and a menu to cover gluten-free, vegetarian, vegan diets, and so on.

Dalton seems as at home there as he would in a country and western bar. The guy who can morph between the rough-mannered law-man and the conservationist outdoorsman and the coffee-shop intellectual in a blink, because he is all those things, bound together in one very complicated package.

He's already spoken to his father. He doesn't say much about that. It must be a decent relationship, or he'd never trust him to do sensitive research. When I ask if his dad knew about people being smuggled in, Dalton's answer is a vague mumble and shrug. I suspect he did . . . and turned a blind eye. Yet obviously he still does this research for Dalton. In other words, the relationship seems complicated, like Dalton himself.

What his father found throws a serious wrench into my investigation. Namely, Hastings's true identity — one that suggests he's *not* the guy Dalton suspected he was.

Dalton hasn't had contact with his father since Hastings disappeared, but he'd already had him investigating — because of the rydex issue — and he's just found the first hint of who Hastings might really be. He hasn't had time to dig deeper on his own. So we do now.

I research the name Dalton's father found.

"Fuck," Dalton says, leaning back in his seat.

"Agreed."

There on the tablet screen is a photo of one Jerome — Jerry — MacDonald. A pharmaceutical company chemist. Forty-three. Divorced. No kids. Worked at the same company since he graduated from university.

It's Jerry Hastings. Beyond any doubt.

According to Dalton, Hastings's entry story was that he'd been selling information on a new drug to a rival company. He'd been on the verge of getting caught when he agreed to pay a half million to hang out in Rockton until he could sneak back down south and enjoy the remainder of his ill-gotten gains. In other words, he's one of those white-collar guys whose misdeeds keep the town running. And judging by what I've found here, his story is true. He's a traitorous little weasel. But not a killer.

I spend the next two hours glued to that tablet, going through two cappuccinos, a muffin, and a bowl of homemade granola. At one point, Dalton wanders off. This is too much indoor time for him. When he returns, I'm on the front patio. It's chilly, but I'll survive.

I'm researching Irene Prosser now. I've compiled a list of clues to her real identity. I'm rather proud of the detective work on this one. After those X-rays suggested that her battered-woman story was bullshit, I started adding questions about her into my interviews. Subtle and casual queries that yielded someone who said Irene had mentioned two stepkids and someone else who commented that Irene's accent suggested northern Alberta.

With these tidbits, I come up with Irene

Peterson. Thirty-six. From Grande Prairie, Alberta. Attended Bow Valley College in Calgary. Formerly married to a man who has two kids. There's only a stub of a Facebook page, but I dig up a five-year-old photo. Dalton agrees it's a match.

From what I find, Irene Peterson divorced four years ago and cleared her Facebook page shortly after that. She returned to Grande Prairie, but after a few months, she moved to Edmonton. A string of addresses followed. The clues suggest a familiar story. Separate from abusive husband. Try to take refuge back home, and when that fails, flee to the city, hoping for anonymity.

I could be completely wrong. Maybe she committed a crime post-divorce that set her on the run. But I find nothing that refutes her entry story. I must accept the possibility that — like Hastings — she is exactly what she claimed to be.

"Which fucks up the theory that someone is hunting criminals who've been smuggled in," Dalton says.

Yes, that had been the next logical leap. If three murderers smuggled into Rockton wound up dead, there would be a strong case for vigilante justice.

"Except Abbygail didn't fit," I say. "Which means, while this does throw a wrench in the works, her death already did that."

At the mention of Abbygail, a shadow

passes behind his eyes, but it's gone in a blink as he refocuses.

"We need to find a new connection," he says.

"Or accept that there isn't one. Accept that you've got the worst kind of serial killer in Rockton. One who kills for no reason other than that he likes it."

FORTY-ONE

Before dinner, I buy gifts. Fancy pencils and a sketch pad for Petra, who'd commented that Dalton's idea of "art pencils and paper" came from a dollar store. Rose's Lime Juice for Beth, who shares my love of tequila but prefers hers in a margarita, and the dry mix they serve at the Lion doesn't cut it. Wool socks for Anders, who comes in from evening patrol and sticks his feet on the woodstove. I get pink hair color for Diana. I'm not sure if I'll give it to her, but I feel as if leaving her out of the gift-buying process would be a statement I'm not ready to make. I also buy two pounds of coffee, which Dalton spots when he picks me up after his own errands.

"For the station," I say.

It's the kind he was drinking in the café. He looks from it to the bag of presents. "You pay attention."

"That's kinda my job, boss. What's on the agenda now?"

"Dinner. Then a side trip."

The side trip takes us up a mountain outside Dawson City. When we reach the top . . .

"Wow," I say, my nose practically pressed to the window. Dalton puts the window down, and it seems "practically" might be an understatement. My head falls forward as the glass disappears, and he chuckles under his breath.

The view is unbelievable. The sun has just started to drop, and there's a sliver of pink to the west, over Dawson City, which sits like a toy town nestled along the winding river. To the east . . . well, there's nothing to the east except forest. Endless forest. Somewhere in the middle of it is Rockton, our invisible town, lost among the trees and the hills and the mountains and the lakes and the rivers.

With wilderness as far as the eye can see, it should be like the view from the plane, but it isn't. That was a spectacular painting. This is real. I know this forest now. I know what's out there — the awe-inspiring and the terrifying.

Dalton parks, and I'm out of the car almost before it stops. There are a few lookout spots up here at the top, and I try all of them, even fighting through the bushes and brambles when I see another I want to check out. Dalton walks to the highest point and watches me from a bench there.

When I'm finally done exploring, I hop up and stand on the back of the bench to get an even better look.

"Okay," I say. "Time to get to work, right?"

"No work."

"Hmm?"

"There's no work here. Just this." He waves at the lookout. "Thought you might like to see it."

I grin so wide I can feel the stretch of it.

Here, in the middle of this wilderness, I am something I've never been in my life. Free. Free not only of the guilt and the fear over Blaine, but free of expectations, too. I've lived my life in the shadow of expectations, and the certainty I will fail, as I did with my parents. Now those are lifted, and I'm happy. Unabashedly happy.

I look down, and Dalton's staring at me. I flash another grin for him, and he looks away quickly, his hands shoved into his jacket pockets.

"This is okay, then?" he says.

"No, it's awful. This is my bored face. Can't you tell?"

I'm teasing, but he drops his gaze and mumbles something I don't quite catch. I hop down and walk to a campfire ring.

"You want one of those?" he asks.

I look over.

"Bonfire," he says. "I brought stuff if you

do. Wood, tequila, bag of marshmallows."

My grin returns. I'm sure I look like an idiot by now, but I can't help it. "Yes. Please and thank you."

He pushes to his feet. "Like I said, we needed a break. I come up here most nights when I have to fly to Dawson. I've even fallen asleep on that bench. Unless it's a weekend, you don't usually get anyone else up here this time of year."

Which is kind of unbelievable. It is truly a once-in-a-lifetime view. But like Dalton said when I first arrived, there's plenty of scenery here for those who want to see it. This is their normal. *My* normal now.

"So you come up and have a bonfire?" I say.

"By myself?" He snorts and shakes his head.

"Ah, that's the real reason you invited me. Someone to roast marshmallows with."

Again, I'm teasing, but again he looks away and mumbles something.

I watch him build the fire. Soon we're settled in beside the flames, enjoying tequila in plastic cups and marshmallows on sticks. Darkness falls, and I barely notice. We're too busy talking. I remember the studies I mentioned, on lethal violence with chimpanzees, that subject I've been keeping in my back pocket for a moment just like this, when I have his attention and want to keep it.

It's not exactly light and cheerful conversation, but it works for us, and by the time we finish, I'm stretched out on my back, staring up at the stars. Impossibly endless stars.

"I really wish I had my phone right now," I say.

"Huh?"

"I have an app that identifies the constellations. You just point it, and it knows what section of the sky you're looking at and tells you what you're seeing. It's very cool."

He shakes his head. "Which one are you looking for?"

I smile over at him. "All of them."

He squints up into the sky. "First you need to find the North Star. You see it up there?"

I point.

"That's a planet," he says.

I try again.

"That'd be the space station." He directs me until I have the North Star and then he says, "Polaris doesn't move — it's a fixed point, so you can use it to find your way. It's not the brightest star, despite what people think. The easiest way to find it is to locate the Big Dipper — Ursa Major, or the Great Bear — and then track it to the Little Dipper — Ursa Minor, or the Little Bear . . ."

FORTY-TWO

I may have fallen asleep on that overlook, buzzing from tequila and sugar and blissfully at peace, staring into the sky and listening as Dalton pointed out every constellation we could see. He may have carried me to the car. I may have not woken until morning. Of course, all I remember is his voice, that baritone rumble, talking about Orion, and then it was morning. The rest I'll have to infer. He doesn't mention it the next day.

We're back in Rockton before noon. The day passes smoothly as the clock mends itself. The service for Abbygail comes in the evening. That's difficult, and when I see Diana walking alone, I go and sit with her on my front porch, the only two who didn't know Abbygail leaving the others to their grief. While we don't say much, it's more comfortable than it's been since that night at the bar. When she leaves, I consider giving her the hair dye, but I'm afraid she'll take it as a peace offering and, for once, I admit to myself that I'm not the one who needs to make amends, and so I resist the urge to try.

Come morning, the Rockton clock is ticking again. I see the same neighbors on my way into work. I get my midmorning coffee, with Dalton joining me, sitting quietly as Devon gives me all the local news and I munch a rare chocolate chip cookie. Apparently, *someone* brought chips from Dawson City, having recalled an off hand comment that they were my favorite. I'm not the only one who pays attention. Back at the station, Kenny drops by to check the wood and hangs out for a while, giving me tips that aren't exactly earth-shattering.

Yes, the town is back to itself, and we're back to work. I'm looking for a connection between the victims, while understanding that there may not be one. By day three, I'm entirely focused on Abbygail. She is where it started. The first one lured into the forest. The youngest and, as I see now from that memorial, the most popular. The girl everyone cared about. Or almost everyone. That's an easy place to start looking. Who had trouble with her? It's a short list. At the top of it is Pierre Lang, the pedophile who got into it with her shortly before she disappeared.

I question Lang more thoroughly now. I haven't spoken to him since Mick told me he suspected Lang of being Abbygail's secret

admirer. I hadn't been ignoring the lead —
I'd been gathering more information so I
could hit Lang hard. So far, I've managed to
find two people who confirmed Abbygail
received the gift of raspberries from an
admirer, but no one can tie that back to
Lang. Beth vaguely remembers something
about berries, but she says it's not unusual
for locals to leave little gifts at her door, in
thanks for treatment, so they could have been
for her.

So I have nothing on Lang, but I need to
take another run at him, because he's my best
suspect, and I don't foresee getting more
leverage soon. The problem is that Lang
avoided serious charges for years. He knows
I'm fishing, and I don't manage to do anything except scare and intimidate him. Which
is a start, at least.

I leave Lang's and pick up an admirer of
my own. It's Jen. She follows me for three
houses before yelling a racial epithet, because
that's just the kind of girl she is. Apparently,
this particular insult is supposed to get my
attention, and when it doesn't, she jogs up
alongside me and says, "I was talking to you."

"Oh?" I look at everyone else on the street.
"Right. You were. How can I help you today,
Jen?"

"It's how I can help you, *Detective.*" Jen
says it the way street thugs say *cop.*

"Okay," I say, as if I don't notice her tone.

"Do you want to go back to the station and talk?"

"Considering what my tip is? Not a chance." She steps too close for comfort, but I stand my ground. "I heard you talking to Pierre."

She means she heard Lang yelling at me. My side of the conversation was a little more discreet.

"You want to find Abbygail's secret admirer?" she says. "He's sitting in your cop shop." When I hesitate, she says, "Um, your boss?" She backs up and eyes me. "Unless the rumors are true and Dalton's *more* than your boss, in which case this tip sure as hell won't go anywhere."

I resist the urge to deny the rumors — she wouldn't listen. "If you have reason to believe Sheriff Dalton was interested in Abbygail —"

"I have more than 'reason to believe.' After Abbygail's birthday party, Petra and I saw them getting hot and heavy behind the community hall." My shock must show, because she sneers. "Sweet on the sheriff, are you, Detective? How predictable. All you so-called *educated* women — you, the doctor — think you're so smart, and yet you all fall for that hick. And who did he have his eye on? The teen hooker who thought he shit solid gold. That's what men want. Not a woman they can talk to. A dumb little girl who'll worship the ground they walk on."

"You say Petra —"

"Yes, your new pal Petra saw it. Go talk to her, since you obviously won't believe me."

"Can you tell me exactly what you saw?" I ask as calmly as I can.

"After the party broke up, Dalton and Abbygail were *k-i-s-s-i-n-g* behind the community hall. Which apparently was more his idea than hers, because after we walked away, I heard arguing. Abbygail was pissed off, and the good sheriff was in full-on defense mode. If she'd been in trouble, I would have interfered, no matter what you might think of me. The situation was under control, though. She was giving him a dressing-down, and he'd backed off, so I left them to it."

Petra works part-time in the general store. It's exactly what it sounds like — the place to buy pretty much everything you need. *Need* being the operative word. This isn't the place for luxury items. At least half the store is secondhand goods. Everything in Rockton is valuable for as long as it can be recycled. I find Petra sorting a stack of clothing into what can go immediately on the shelves and what Diana needs to repair first. When she sees my expression, she sticks on the BACK IN FIVE sign and ushers me into the back room.

"I need to ask you something," I say as she shuts the door.

385

"I can see that. What's up?"

"It's about Dalton and Abbygail."

She goes still, and I know it's true. I suspected it was — Jen wouldn't dare invoke Petra's name in a lie. But I had hoped that maybe Jen presumed I'd never actually investigate, and she just wanted to stir up shit. Now I see the truth in Petra's face. And it hurts. On so many levels, it hurts.

"Jen told me," I say.

Petra lowers herself onto a crate.

"Abbygail's party," I say. "Behind the community hall. Jen says you two saw them kissing."

She squeezes her eyes shut for a moment. "I'm sorry. I'd decided it wasn't worth mentioning. But after her death . . . I was trying to figure out how to tell you."

"Not worth mentioning? That the local sheriff was seen making out with a girl who went missing a few days later?"

"Making out? No, it was a kiss behind the community hall. Probably a drunken one. Between a young sheriff and a girl who was deeply infatuated with him. A momentary lapse in judgment for Eric."

"Did you hear the argument?"

"What argument?"

I tell her and she says, "I didn't hear anything. Yes, I left the party with Jen that evening. We aren't good buddies, but I understand there's more to her than the stone-cold bitch you see. She has issues. Lots of them. That doesn't mean she *isn't* a bitch. Or an addict. Or a part-time prostitute. It also means she lies."

"You think she's lying about the fight?"

"Maybe not outright, but I'd strongly consider the possibility that her hatred of Eric colors her interpretation. Think about it. If Abbygail had a crush on Eric, is she really going to tell him off for kissing her? Isn't it more likely that Eric realized it was a mistake, backed off, and she got angry? Embarrassed?"

"Just because she had a crush doesn't necessarily mean she'd welcome an advance."

I want her to argue my point. She only goes quiet and then says, "I guess so," and I'm left with this stark truth: something happened between Abbygail and Dalton, and he hid it, and now she's dead.

After I talk to Petra, I run home, if not physically, then mentally. I pretend I don't hear the hellos or see the waves and the smiles, and I get my ass home as fast as I can without actually breaking into a run. I stumble inside, close the door, and collapse against it.

Dalton and Abbygail.

I want to say that Petra is right, that the fight was because they kissed, and he backed off. But even that doesn't fit my image of him. Kissing Abbygail — drunk or not —

steps over a line. He was her mentor, her big brother, the guy determined to set her on the right track and keep her there. To kiss her was a violation of that trust.

I want better from him. There, it's out. The sad truth. That Abbygail isn't the only girl with a crush. Perhaps this is why I identify with Abbygail — because I'm not a grown woman seeing a man and saying, "I want that." It's my inner teen who looks at Dalton with just a touch of that starry-eyed gaze. Like Abbygail, I missed that stage in my teen years. If I liked a guy, I let him know. If he wasn't interested, I moved on without a backward glance. I was as efficient in my love life as I was in everything else.

I've polished over Dalton's rough edges, put him on a pedestal, and said, "This is a good man." A man with a strong and true inner compass. A man who would not kiss a damaged, infatuated, twenty-one-year-old girl. And if he did while drunk, he'd admit it to his new detective because it played into her investigation, and if he'd done nothing wrong, then there was no reason *not* to admit it.

Once night comes, I cycle through nightmares of Dalton and Abbygail. He kisses her, and that kiss is more than she wants, so she pushes him away. He asks her to meet him in the forest — he has something to show her, an apology for his bad behavior. She goes.

He kisses her again. She fights him off. Things get out of control and Abbygail dies. Then the accidental killing of Abbygail unleashes something in him, a twisted perversion of his need to protect his town. He'll cover up Abbygail's death by killing those he suspects of being smuggled in.

The next nightmare scene is right out of a movie — the female detective who is so enamored of her new boss that she never realizes he's the killer, even when the audience is shouting at her and groaning at her stupidity. Dalton lures me into the forest, and I run along after him like an eager puppy. Run to my doom. Deservedly so.

In a movie, he *would* be the killer. The last guy you'd suspect. The sheriff devoted to keeping his town's people safe is actually the guy murdering them? Ah, the irony. Afterward, viewers can look back and spot the clues that point to him.

Dalton didn't want Anders and me wandering off in that cave. He'd been the one who overreacted to Petra's scream. The brave and dedicated shepherd worried about his flock? Or the killer who knew what we must have found?

Dalton asked for a detective, but he also discouraged me from coming here. Maybe he only wanted to *look* as if he wanted a detective. Then, when he was forced to take me, he decided to build a relationship where I would trust him enough to share all aspects of my investigation.

And about Abbygail and Dalton . . . Am I so sure there *wasn't* a secret relationship? It's not as if he's dating anyone else in town. Or even sleeping with anyone as far as I can tell. Something is off there.

There's a *lot* off when it comes to Eric Dalton. Maybe those eccentricities and complications are a sign of deeper damage. Of a deeper schism. Of a truly dark side to his nature.

Those are the thoughts that keep me tossing all night. Then I wake — on the folding mattress he gave me, beside a stack of his books — and I look up at the fading stars and hear him telling me the constellations, and I can't see absolute darkness. Not in Dalton.

Or maybe I just don't want to.

FORTY-THREE

I need to talk to someone who isn't a fan of Dalton. Perhaps "fan" is the wrong word. He definitely has them. But there are plenty of people in Rockton who support him, and even most who are divided on the issue will grudgingly admit he's a good sheriff. The only people I've heard openly say otherwise are Hastings, Diana, Jen, and Val.

I only have to say nine words before Val cracks open her door: *I need to speak to you about Sheriff Dalton.* She ushers me in with, "Five minutes, Detective. I have things to do."

Her home . . . No, again that's the wrong word. This is not a home. The living room looks exactly like mine did when I moved in. While decor isn't a priority in Rockton, people still need to feather their nests. Petra's secondary source of income is sketching and selling wall art. Others knit blankets, quilt pillows, and make crafts from whatever else they find on the forest's edge.

The only thing Val has added to her room is a shelf of writing journals. One book is open upside down on the end table, with a pen beside it.

She doesn't offer me a drink. Doesn't even offer me a seat. I still lower myself to the sofa. She seems inclined to stay standing but then, with obvious reluctance, perches on the arm-chair.

"You don't have a high opinion of Sheriff Dalton," I say.

"I have an adequate opinion of his ability to function in his position."

"Nothing more."

A twist of her lips, as if she's holding back a sneer. "No, nothing more."

"May I ask why that is?" I say, then quickly add, "I'm not here to challenge your opinion. But as I investigate, I need to consider all possibilities, and you seem to be one of the few people who might balance the prevailing view of Sheriff Dalton."

"One of the few willing to badmouth him, you mean. If you're considering him for these crimes, Detective, I'm inclined to say don't bother. Not because he isn't capable of murder. He is. But he *isn't* capable of such careful crimes. Dalton is a blunt instrument. He's unsophisticated. He's uneducated. He's barely literate."

"Based on his written reports?" I hold back a note of incredulity.

"His reports are verbal. I doubt he's capable of writing them down."

"Besides feeling as if Dalton is undereducated —"

"Ignorant, Detective Butler. He is ignorant. A lack of education combined with an innate lack of intelligence. Have you heard his language? I'm sure you know that profanity and ignorance rise in direct proportion, and I've rarely heard it rise as high as Sheriff Dalton's. I don't think he even knows a word over two syllables."

I bite my tongue.

"Eric Dalton is a walking stereotype," she continues, "and he's too ignorant to even realize it. You've seen him sauntering down the street like the tin star in a spaghetti western. He has no desire to change, to better his life. He reminds me of the boys who used to ride past my grandparents' farm. Hooting and hollering at me from their rusted pickups, throwing beer cans out the window."

I open my mouth, but she's on a roll, her face animated.

"I told my grandparents those boys made me nervous, and do you know what they said? Come down off my high horse and get to know them better. I decided maybe they were right. So the next time the boys catcalled and offered me a ride home, I said yes. They drove me to the woods for a 'party' instead. Laughed when I insisted they take me home.

Mocked my diction and told me to stop being so stuck-up and have some fun. I calmed down and pretended to go along with it. Then, the first chance I got, I ran. I told my grandparents, and they said I'd misinterpreted. Because, apparently, kidnapping me was just those boys' way of being neighborly. That taught me all I need to know about men like Eric Dalton. And about how other people admire them and make allowances for them."

"Has Er— Dalton ever done anything like that?"

"To me?" She laughs. "I'm not exactly a teenager anymore."

"So that's his preference? Young women?"

She stops. "Do you mean Abbygail?"

I nod.

Val goes still. She cups her hands in her lap, and her voice lowers, that strident note vanishing as she says, "God, I hope not. You think he — ?"

"No." I'll give her nothing she can take back to the council. Dalton must have the full benefit of my doubt until I find irrefutable proof.

I continue. "I'm investigating all possible romantic links with the victims. There aren't many younger men in town, and Dalton was close to Abbygail, so I can't ignore that avenue."

"She was a good girl," she says, in that same soft voice. "I didn't think that when she first came. This isn't a place for girls like that. Runaways. Addicts. Whores."

I stiffen at the last word. I know she only means prostitutes, but it is a horrible word to use, especially for a teenage girl who turned tricks to survive on the street. What Val means is that Abbygail was not the kind of girl *she'd* been, and therefore she found her lifestyle distasteful — a sign of ignorance and low intelligence. Which I suspect, to Val, is the worst possible failing.

"Abbygail overcame that, though," she says. "Elizabeth set her on the right track. She promised me she would, and she delivered, and I give her full credit for that. Abbygail was a true success story, entirely due to the mentorship of strong women like Elizabeth and Isabel."

"You don't have a problem with Isabel, then? Her line of work?"

"If women are willing to debase themselves in that way, then it only means other women don't need to worry about men acting on their urges."

There are so many things I could say to that. Not about Isabel or her occupation, but about the idea of championing strong women while tearing down those you view as less strong. Less morally upright, too. I suspect that's a big deal to Valerie. Women are either good girls or bad. Men are animals at the mercy of their "urges." As for the role Dalton and Mick and other men in Rockton played in Abbygail's recovery? Irrelevant.

I say none of that, just nod and plaster on a thoughtful look.

"Abbygail had a bright future ahead of her," Val says. "To take that away . . ." She sucks in a breath and leans back, and I might not like this woman, but there is genuine grief in her face.

She continues. "If Sheriff Dalton was taking advantage of that poor girl, I certainly hope someone would have told me. But even Elizabeth is charmed by his swagger. She wants him to be a good person, and so she sees a good person. But he's not good, Detective Butler. There's something savage in him. He hides it, but . . ." She leans forward. "You know about his fascination with the forest, I presume."

I nod.

"Do you know what's in that forest, Casey?" She's switched to my given name, relaxing with a sympathetic audience.

"Settlers," I say. "People who left Rockton to live on their own. And what the locals call hostiles. The dangerous ones."

"They're *all* dangerous. They live in the forest with the animals because they *are* animals. The first month I was here, I went on a group outing. I wanted to experience this life fully. I got separated from the others and ran into two men deep in the forest. They made those

396

redneck boys back home look like civilized gentlemen. What little language these two knew, they used to tell me they were going to teach me a lesson about trespassing on their land. They took me to their camp and . . ." She straightens. "Like those boys, they were of such low intelligence that I was able to escape the next morning."

"But you spent the night in their camp."

"Yes, I could not effect my escape sooner. However, the point —"

"Were you . . . assaulted?"

Her face goes hard. "Of course not. I'd have died fighting if they'd tried. That was certainly their eventual goal, but they did not touch me that night."

"All right. So —"

"They did not touch me," she repeats, growing agitated. "I wouldn't have allowed that."

Which is a lie. The hostiles did rape her, their way of teaching a woman a lesson, and then either they dumped her or she escaped. She'd told no one about the assault. Perhaps she even convinced herself it had never happened. But as she sits there desperate for me to believe her, I finally begin to understand Valerie Zapata. What happened to me in that alley twelve years ago is not something that ever goes away. The shame of the beating, of feeling like I should have been able to avoid it, been stronger, been *smarter.* That is what

Val feels.

"I called Rockton a hellhole," she continues. "That's not exactly true. Hell is out there, all around us. Hell and unspeakable savagery, and Sheriff Dalton embraces it. He lets people go on excursions. He refuses to hunt down and exterminate those savages. The council listens to him. We could have a paradise here, Casey. An unspoiled Eden. But he will not allow it."

She leans forward. "He embraces that forest because it is a reflection of his own soul. Dark and twisted and savage. If you want to know who murdered Abbygail and the others, I say look to that forest, to the monsters out there. If you honestly believe it was someone inside this town, then yes, perhaps you should look at the savage in our own midst: Eric Dalton."

As I leave Val's, I try to weigh the information she gave me against her own experiences and prejudices. I know she's wrong about Dalton. Wrong in many ways. But there are kernels of truth in what she says, and I need to pick them from the raw and ugly mass of her own hate and fear.

"Casey?"

Mick is jogging toward me. It's the first time I've seen him more than in passing since I found Abbygail's remains. When I ask how he's doing, he shrugs and says, "Managing.

Like I said, I was certain Abby was dead. I guess there was still hope, though . . ." He shifts his weight and then straightens. "Isabel insists on going rock climbing with me this afternoon. She absolutely hates it, and I'm trying to talk her out of it, but she's determined to cheer me up. At the very least, I'll admit it's amusing seeing her try to scale a rock face."

"I'd ask for photos if we had cameras."

His smile grows more genuine. "There is a Polaroid for special occasions. Maybe I'll take it along. Anyway, I came to find you because I have something. Remember how I said someone left raspberries for Abby? Someone I suspected had also followed her?"

"Pierre Lang."

He shakes his head. "Not Lang. I liked him for it, because the way he looked at Abby made my gut burn. As if he was attracted to her but didn't want to be. You know what I mean?"

Given Lang's history, I know exactly what he means.

He continues. "But I could never connect him to the damned berries. Now I have a better suspect. Someone who should have gone on that list but, well, he was gone by the time I gave it to you, so I didn't see the point. Which probably explains why, on the job, I was never going to make detective. My brain doesn't work that way."

"Is it Powys?"

"Hastings. He made a few moves in Abby's direction. Sleazy-uncle stuff. You know: *Here, little girl, let me help you with that, huh-huh.* Abby just thought he was a creep. She said she could handle it, and he never made an actual pass at her, so I let it slide. But after we found her . . . well, I started thinking I should have given you Hastings's name. He *was* alive when she disappeared. So I did a little detective work of my own. He went on a raspberry-picking excursion and bribed Rodrigues — the guy in charge — to let him keep a pint. You can ask Rodrigues."

"I will. Thank you. Oh, and while I have you here, can I ask something completely unrelated?"

He manages a smile. "I would be very happy to talk about anything unrelated."

"I know. Thanks. It's about Eric. It's kind of personal, but, well, you worked with him, and you know him, and . . . It's about his, uh, dating habits."

Mick had tensed when I said "personal." But now he relaxes with a chuckle.

"If you're asking if he's seeing anyone, the answer is no."

"But he does . . . date, right?"

"You mean one-nighters? Not in Rockton. Too many complications now that he's sheriff."

"When you say 'not in Rockton' . . ."

"I don't pry into his personal business, but obviously I don't want you to get the idea he doesn't date or doesn't date women, because I think you should go for it. You'd be good for him. So from what I understand, he has one-nighters when he's down south. Here, though? According to Isabel, it's been years since he had a relationship."

"His last one went bad?"

"You mean did he get his heart broken? Nah. It was just a casual thing that was *less* casual to the woman he was seeing. She wanted him to go down south when her term was up. He refused. Iz says it got kind of ugly and kind of public. I don't blame him for taking a break and getting whatever he needs off campus, if you know what I mean."

"I do. Thanks."

FORTY-FOUR

I avoid Dalton for the rest of the day. I need to process everything I've heard and continue investigating and draw conclusions, and I cannot do that with the man himself in front of me, because if he is, I'll dismiss it all.

Steering clear of him is tougher when I'm back at the station, and every time I duck his notice, I can see his radar homing in on me. As soon as my shift ends, I take off. *Bad headache. See you in the morning.*

On the way home, Diana hails me, and I don't brush her off. This business with Dalton has me off balance, feeling uncomfortable in a place I'd embraced only days ago. Diana is my link to my other life, and right now I need that. She's thrilled to see me and seems to sense I need her, because she insists on me staying for dinner.

I agree, planning to use the opportunity to talk to her about Dalton. She's another of his nonsupporters, and I want to get her take on him.

Except, as it turns out, she didn't insist on dinner because she could tell I needed a friend. *She* needs one. She's having trouble at work, and her boss is threatening to fire her. That's no light matter here. Job disputes go before a committee to see if the issue can be resolved. If it can't and the worker is at fault, she'll end up on shit jobs for the duration of her stay.

According to Diana, this issue is entirely her boss's fault. Diana slept with the woman's ex, and her boss claimed that was fine, but obviously she's jealous, and now the bitch is out to get her. I cringe just listening to Diana, because I know there's more to it. Her boss wouldn't risk losing her own job over an ex-lover.

I remember what Dalton said about Diana inventing issues to get my attention. I'm uncomfortable with that because, in a weird way, it feels vain — thinking our friendship is that important. In my gut, I suspect the answer is far less flattering to me. I have been her rock, the one who is always there for her. The guaranteed friend. The one who has to stick by, because Diana knows what I did to Blaine. She's never threatened to tell anyone, but . . .

Oh, hell, I don't know what I'm thinking. Maybe Dalton's low opinion of her is coloring my own. And considering what I'm currently wondering about him, he should be the last person whose opinion I consider.

We never get around to talking about Dalton. I give Diana support and commiseration and then, after dinner, I go home to bed.

I wake to a pebble ricocheting off my cheek, scramble up, and peer down to see Dalton in the moonlight.

"Hey!" I call, my voice tight with anger. "Can't you knock?"

"You wouldn't hear me. And I didn't want to yell up to you and disturb the neighbors."

"So you threw rocks at me?"

"Pebbles." He pauses and tilts his head, as if realizing this may not have been the best move. "I need to talk to you."

"Tomorrow."

"No, tonight. I was going to wait, but I know you're mad at me, and I've had a few beers, and I've decided I need answers tonight."

"And if what I want is sleep, that's too bad?"

That head tilt, working this out, his brain fuzzy — a guy not accustomed to more than a beer or two at a sitting.

"I'd really like to talk," he says. "Just five minutes, and you can come in to work an hour late."

"That doesn't help when I'm too busy to come in late."

He pauses, thinking hard, and I know I

sound pissy. I'm not pissy. I'm scared. Terrified of going down there and buying whatever he sells, because I look at him in the moonlight, that confusion and worry on his face, his usual swagger gone, as he tries to figure out how to placate me, seeming a little bit lost. I want to tell him it's okay. Brush aside my fears and go with my gut.

"Five minutes?" he says. "Please? I know you're angry, and I can't figure out what I've done, and I need you to tell me so I can fix it."

Damn it, Eric, don't do this.

"I'm not angry," I say.

His voice firms. "Don't pull that shit with me, Casey. You've been distant since yesterday, and by this afternoon you could barely stand the sight of me. I need to know what I've done wrong."

I hesitate and then say, "Hold on. I'm coming down."

He's still on my back porch. The cross fox is out, prowling, and Dalton's gaze flicks to it and then back at me, like a schoolboy trying hard not to be distracted when he knows he's in trouble.

"It's about the case," I say.

"Yeah, I figured that."

"About Abbygail."

He nods, his expression neutral but his

shoulders tightening as if he's bracing himself.

"The night of her birthday party, you were seen behind the community hall with her."

Silence. Then, "Fuck," and he closes his eyes, swaying slightly, and I want to grab him and shake him and say, *No.*

Do not do this, Eric. Do not tell me it's true. Or if it is true, give me an excuse. Don't stand there with your eyes closed, looking like you're about to throw up, because that tells a very different story. One I do not want to hear.

"Eric?" I say.

"I —" His eyes open, and in them I see panic. Panic and guilt. Such incredible guilt. "We — It —"

He looks off to the side. At the fox and then away again.

"I need you to tell me what happened," I say.

"I know." His voice is barely above a whisper. "I will. I just . . . It's . . ."

He swallows and looks around for an escape hatch. He spots the back door and heads for it, throwing it open and walking inside, and I want to yell, *Hey! That's my house!* but I know there's no subtext in the intrusion. He wants to take this conversation inside, and so he does.

When I walk in, though, I see he wants something very different. He has my tequila bottle in hand, and he's pulling a mug off the shelf.

"I don't think you need that," I say.

"Yeah, I do. I really do."

He pours the shot and downs it so fast he gasps, grabbing the back of a chair as he doubles over, coughing. When he straightens, his eyes are watering. He closes them for a second and then looks at me and says, "I fucked up, Casey. I fucked up so bad."

I wave to a seat, but he shakes his head and stays standing, still gripping that chair.

"I was blind and I was stupid and I hurt her," he says. "I didn't mean to, but I did."

I struggle to stay calm. To *look* calm. "Tell me what happened."

"We left the party together. She'd had too much to drink, and someone had to walk her home. We were passing behind the hall, and she said she saw an animal dart under it. I followed, and . . . and she kissed me. I didn't see it coming. Absolutely did not see it coming. She'd pecked my cheek a couple of times, when I did something for her, and maybe that was a sign, but I thought those were just friendly kisses. This wasn't. I couldn't even process what was happening. When I did, I backed away. Fast. I told her she'd had too much to drink. She said she'd had just enough to do what she didn't dare when she was sober. She said . . . things. About me. How she felt. I panicked. I just

407

panicked. I said hell no. That wasn't happening. Ever."

He swallows and white-knuckles the chair. "I rejected her. Rejected her hard. I didn't mean to, but like I said, I panicked. She got mad. Said I treated her like a child. Said she felt like the only way she'd get my attention was if she walked into the forest and made me come after her. But she was drunk. Drunk and talking nonsense, and that's what I thought until . . ." The chair chatters against the wood floor, and I see his hands are shaking.

"Until she disappeared," I say. "By walking into the forest."

An abrupt nod. "That night, I stayed out until dawn patrolling, and then I put extra militia on during the day. But she came by the station and apologized. She said she'd been drunk and made a stupid mistake with the kiss, and she didn't really mean all those things she said. She apologized for threatening to go into the forest. She was angry with herself for saying I treat her like a child and then acting like one. Two nights later, she walked into the forest, and I wasn't paying attention anymore, and someone else must have been. Someone followed her and . . ." His voice breaks. "I fucked up."

This is the Eric Dalton I know. This is the story that makes sense, and the anguish in his face tells me it's true. All except one part.

That Abbygail went into the forest to spite him. There is nothing in the girl I've come to know that suggests she'd do that. Lash out and threaten to in drunken anger and humiliation? Yes. But she was mature enough to regret that the next day and apologize. She wouldn't do that and then take off.

Why did Abbygail go into the forest the night she disappeared? Only now do I realize that my sleeping brain really did figure it out, in a way. I dreamed that Dalton lured her in. What if someone else did, in his name? A note perhaps. And Abbygail, still smarting from his rejection, couldn't help but hope he'd reconsidered. That he'd taken time and realized he *did* have deeper feelings for her.

Come to the forest at midnight, Abby. Meet me by the big birch tree. I need to talk to you.

Streetwise Abbygail would only walk into those woods for one person. The guy she hoped would, one day, invite her there.

I don't tell Dalton what I think. I can't, because he'll still take responsibility. Instead, I say, "I don't think she'd do that."

He doesn't answer. Just reaches for the bottle.

"That won't help," I say.

"Sure as hell feels like it will."

He lets me take it from him, though, and slumps into a chair.

"So there's my drunken confession," he says. "Proof of exactly how incompetent your boss is."

"Bullshit, Eric. You're not incompetent. You just don't trust me to investigate."

"What?" He looks over, eyes struggling to focus.

"Why didn't you tell me?"

He closes his eyes and slouches. "Fuck."

"That's not an answer."

He reaches up and scratches his cheek, and opens his eyes, as if startled when he doesn't feel the familiar beard shadow. He's still shaving. For the trip, and then the memorial service, and now . . . well, I don't know why.

He straightens. "I felt guilty, and I didn't want to tell anyone what happened, and I thought there was no reason to. Not unless I worried you'd find out and think I —" He looks over at me sharply. "Unless you'd think I killed her."

"I have to consider it," I say. "For anyone."

He goes still. Then he says, "Right. Of course." He runs his hand through his hair. "I knew you'd have to include me in the suspects, but I didn't put that together with Abbygail and that night, because, well, I didn't kill her, so I never made the connection and . . ."

"You thought you didn't count."

He nods and slumps in his chair. "I told myself it didn't matter. I just didn't want . . . I knew how it looked. . . . I figured I blame myself enough that it's not like I need anyone else to point out that I fucked up."

"You only fucked up in not telling me, Eric."

We fade into silence. Finally he looks toward the steps. "I've kept you longer than five minutes."

I could say yes, and he'll go, but there's that look in his eyes, the same one he had the night I stitched him up, when he was hoping I'd give him an excuse to avoid going back to that oppressive house with Beth. Now he faces an equally oppressive one in his own empty house. Alone with his thoughts, like me in that cavern. Alone in the darkness.

"I have homemade herbal tea," I say. "A gift from the greenhouse folks, for solving the tomato case. I haven't actually worked up the nerve to try it. But if you're willing to be my guinea pig . . ."

The faintest tweak of his lips, not nearly a smile. "I am."

"Then you start the fire and the kettle. I'll grab a sweater and blankets, and we'll sit on the deck."

FORTY-FIVE

We've been out there for about twenty minutes, silently watching the fox hunt mice.

"You do have to consider me," he says, breaking the silence. "As a suspect. Anyone could be a killer if you push the right triggers."

I hug my legs closer and say nothing.

"You don't believe that," he says.

"I've heard the theory. It's been used in serial killer defenses."

"Yeah, I know." He catches my look and says, "I read up on serial killers in case we ever get one smuggled in. But the idea that anyone *could* kill is not an excuse. It's sure as hell not a defense. It just means you can't underestimate people. If pushed to the wall, we're capable of the otherwise unthinkable. It's the instinct to survive and to protect."

"And wreak vengeance?" I murmur.

"An instinct for vengeance? Nah. A drive maybe, stronger in some than others."

"Stronger if that protective instinct is

thwarted."

He peers at me. "What are you thinking?"

"Just . . . considering."

Once the clouds clear, it's a perfect night for the northern lights, the sky lit up with the most amazing show I've seen yet. I'm in no rush to sleep — I swear that tea still had caffeine in it. Dalton and I have moved from the deck to my bedroom balcony.

My fox has returned from its prowling, and Dalton's telling me a Cree story about a fox who outwitted a trickster god. Someone knocks at my front door, the sound echoing in the quiet. I call, "Back here!" and a moment later Anders appears in the yard.

He looks up to where I'm leaning on the balcony railing. He grins, and he's about to speak when Dalton moves up beside me. Anders's smile falters, but he finds a softer version of it, with a quiet, "Hey," and then, "I need to talk to you, Casey. Actually, both of you."

I look over the railing, measuring the distance to the ground.

"No," Dalton says.

"You don't think I can jump it?"

He snorts. "Do you think I'm stupid enough to say that, so you can prove me wrong? Get your ass down the stairs."

I climb onto the railing.

"Did I just give you an order?" he says.

"I'm off duty."

I jump. He mutters, "Fuck," as I drop. I hit the ground. As I straighten, Anders smiles and shakes his head. Then his gaze lifts to my balcony.

"You're still sleeping up there, right?"

I say yes, and there's a pause, and it's not until I hear a door close inside, as Dalton walks through the house, that I make the connection. I wave at myself. "Fully dressed."

"Which doesn't mean that wasn't about to change," he says. "I don't mean to pry . . ."

"Nothing to pry at. My balcony is the best place to see the northern lights. It was talk and tea. Not exactly scandalous." I lower my voice. "And please don't say anything to him that would suggest otherwise, or it'll be the last time I'll get company to watch the lights."

He smiles. "I'll volunteer."

"And you'd just watch the lights with me and expect nothing to come of it?"

"Uh . . . not expect, but hope? Hell, yeah. Eric's probably the only guy I know who could sit on your bed, stargaze, and *not* hope there was more coming." He leans in and mock-whispers, "You may have heard, he's a little weird."

"What's that?" Dalton asks as he steps onto the deck.

"Will says I'm a little weird," I say.

He snorts. "I'm not disagreeing after that stunt."

414

I shake my head and say to Anders, "What's up?"

"Just a situation that could require a woman's touch. Mick didn't go home after work tonight. He was tired, so Isabel said she'd close up. She sent him home at eleven. He wasn't there when she got back, and she's concerned. Considering we've had three murders, I don't feel right dismissing it."

"Is anyone else not where they should be?" I ask, as casually as I can.

"Hmm?" Anders says.

Dalton gives me his dissection-table look. Then he says for me, "Have we had any other reports of trouble? Anyone seen heading for the woods?"

Anders frowns. "No."

I nod, and Dalton and I head out for Isabel's while Anders goes to do a walkabout and see if he can spot Mick.

As Dalton and I walk over to Isabel's, I say, "About Mick, I heard you fired him."

He snorts. "Someone's spreading stories. Mick quit. He didn't much like being a cop. I think he only agreed to be one up here because it helped him get into Rockton. When the council brought Will in, they were willing to keep Mick on, but he jumped at the chance to quit. He did militia duty for a while. Then he hooked up with Isabel, and the only enforcement he's done since is kicking drunks out of the Roc."

"What's his story before that? Why's he here? If I can ask."

"He was on a task force taking down some drug guys, and he was the only one they couldn't pay off. They decided to get rid of him. He decided he'd rather not be gotten rid of. And hc wasn't all that keen on a law-enforcement career after that."

"Can't blame him."

"Nope, really can't. Either it's your thing or it's not. I need people on my team who want to be there. You do. Will does. Mick didn't."

A few more steps in silence. Then he says, "Earlier, you talked about vengeance and protection. You think someone took revenge for Abbygail's death. You meant Mick, didn't you?"

I nod. "Yesterday, Mick came to me about the raspberry thing with Abbygail. You remember that?"

"Her secret admirer?"

"At first, Mick had said he suspected Lang. Then, yesterday, he changed his mind. He said it was Hastings."

"Fuck. He framed Hastings for it?"

"No, I checked a few things afterward, and I'm ninety percent sure it *was* Hastings who left those berries."

"Which means Mick handed him over after Abbygail's body was found. And after he'd

416

sent you sniffing in another direction. Shit." Dalton rolls his shoulders. "If Mick thought Hastings murdered Abbygail and he executed him for it . . ."

"But would he kill Hastings like *that*? I know, I can't underestimate someone's capacity for violence. Still . . ."

Mick is no longer just Isabel's beefcake boy toy. He's a real guy. A likeable guy. Can I imagine him murdering Abbygail's killer? Yes. Murdering him in such a horrible way? No, I cannot.

"And then there's Irene and Powys," I say. "I haven't found any connection between them and Abbygail."

"They barely knew her. They moved in different circles."

"Then what's the answer? That Mick somehow thought Irene killed Abbygail and then whoops, my bad? Maybe Powys? Nope, wrong there, too. Ah, Hastings. That's it." I shake my head. "Makes no sense."

Silence falls.

"You're thinking maybe it wasn't revenge," Dalton says finally. "That Mick killed Abbygail, too."

"I have to consider it."

"Okay."

"Do you think it's possible?" I ask.

"I think I need to keep my mouth shut unless I can say something helpful."

FORTY-SIX

Isabel's place is hard to miss, given that it qualifies as positively palatial in Rockton. A two-story home, twice the size of mine, right in the downtown core. It's a rooming house, but since the extra beds aren't currently required, Isabel is allowed to rent the whole building.

She's sitting by the fireplace when Dalton and I walk in. She rises with, "About time. I was starting to think Will headed off to bed."

I take the seat beside Isabel's. "All right. Walk me through it."

"So that's how you're going to play this, Eric? Let your detective ask a few questions, so I feel you're taking me seriously? All right. First, let's clear the elephant from the room. Mick is not in anyone else's bed. I give him no reason to stray."

"Which —" I look at Dalton. "Maybe you should step outside."

"Why?"

"Because we'll be discussing my sex life,"

Isabel says. "Which would be less awkward if you'd step out, but I know you won't, so ignore him, Casey. If he gets uncomfortable, he'll leave, but I don't think Eric knows the meaning of the word."

"Okay, well, I was going to say that, given what you do here, you know as well as anyone that cheating isn't always about sex. Sometimes — hell, most times, I suspect — it's about filling other needs, including novelty."

"Having been a psychologist, I know that very well. It doesn't apply here. Mick is a simple man with simple tastes. And whatever you might think of our relationship, we care about each other. Deeply. But I'll set aside sentimentality and put it in words you'll better understand. Mick knows if I ever catch him stepping out, it's over. My ego's too healthy to take back a cheating bastard."

"Okay." I take out my notebook. "Give me your story."

We've been searching the town for two hours. We haven't mobilized the militia yet. It's just the three of us, going door to door. I'm with Dalton. I knock on a door and nicely ask if the occupant has seen Mick. Most times I get a sleepy "No, I haven't. Is something wrong?" If they complain about the hour, Dalton shoulders past and tramps through their house, throwing open every door with a look that dares them to utter the phrase "private property."

We do step into a few of the houses even when the occupant was polite — if said occupant is female and looks as if she could have enticed Mick into her bed. I do it with a few of the guys, too, because that's an even better answer — if Mick has needs that Isabel *can't* fill.

Am I hoping to find Mick cheating on Isabel? Yes. Because otherwise, I have to consider him for the role of killer. That's another reason for going door-to-door. Making sure everyone is accounted for. So far so good, but not finding Mick in another bed — *and* not finding anyone missing from theirs — raises another possibility. That Mick is actually victim number five.

We're two-thirds done when we reach Val's place.

"Hiding, Val?" Dalton says as she opens the door.

"No, of course not."

"Huh. Not even going to ask why I'd knock on your door at three A.M.?"

She fumbles through some excuse, but Dalton's right. By this point, most people are opening their doors before we even get there, having caught voices in the quiet night and cracked open a window to listen.

"You should get dressed," Dalton says. "Come out and get ready with a statement, in case folks get antsy."

"I think you can handle that, Eric."

"Sure, I could, but it would take me away from, you know, actually searching for our missing resident. I'm kinda thinking public statements ought to be your domain from now on, Val. Fuck knows, it's not like you're doing anything else."

The door closes.

"All right," he calls through the door. "You go get dressed. I'll tell anyone who asks that you'll make a statement in twenty minutes. They can gather right here and wait."

"Casey?" a voice murmurs behind me. It's Kenny. "I, uh, have something for you," he says. "A tip."

I lead him into a pocket of shadow. "What's up?"

"Nothing," Dalton says as he strides over. "As usual, he's just trying to get your attention. That right, Kenny?"

"No, sir. I've got a real tip for her."

"Yeah? You seem to have a lot of tips for Detective Butler. You never did that for me. I'm kinda hurt." He steps closer. "Stop hitting on her."

"What? No. I know you and her . . ." He clears his throat. "I know you wouldn't like that."

"Damn right I wouldn't. I don't appreciate you wasting my detective's time."

Which is not what Kenny meant at all. When two people of the opposite sex spend

421

enough time together, people jump to conclusions. The only reason they aren't outright saying anything is that I'm spending a lot of time with *two* guys, and no one wants to guess which I'm sleeping with and risk pissing off the other. Anders thinks it's hilarious. I find it amusing. Dalton has no idea it's even happening.

"Give Casey the tip," Dalton says. "And if it's bullshit, you're on chopping duty next week."

"You're looking for Mick, right? Well, I saw him around eleven. I was leaving the shop after working on a piece Isabel wants. When I spotted Mick heading my way, I thought he was coming to give me shit because it's late. So I say hi. He says hi and keeps going, heading around the lumber shed."

"Lumber shed?" I say.

"It's where we store the lumber."

"She means why would he be going that way?" Dalton says. Then he turns to me. "No reason."

"Could he have been heading into the woods?"

"He wasn't," Kenny says. "I heard the back door open. He went in."

"Inside the lumber shed? What's in there besides wood?"

"Nothing," Kenny says. "Not even much wood. The guys are just starting to bring in logs for winter, so it's mostly empty space right now. But, uh, very private."

"Private . . . ? Oh."

Kenny clears his throat. "I don't want to cause trouble. If I tell you that a woman went in there after Mick, and Isabel finds out I said it . . ."

"Then you didn't tell us," I say.

Confusion creases his features. Then he lets out a short laugh. "Oh, right. Ha. Okay. I didn't tell you."

"But if you did, who would you tell us it was?"

"I don't know. Female. Average height. Skinny. That's all I saw. Oh, and she was wearing dark clothes. Jacket to shoes. But I don't know if that's significant because, well, it's not unusual."

True, Dalton and I are both wearing dark boots, jeans, and a dark jacket. There isn't a lot of room to be fashion conscious in Rockton.

I thank Kenny for his time. Dalton says, "Come by the station after nine tomorrow. If the tip panned out, I've got some credits for you. If it doesn't?"

"Chopping duty awaits?"

"You got it."

"I can't guarantee they're still there," Kenny says. "It's been four hours, and if they're still there, then I know why Isabel keeps Mick around." He laughs, a *heh-heh* chuckle, and then says to me, "Sorry."

I smile. "Agreed. I suspect they're only there if they fell asleep, which would explain why he didn't get his ass back home before Isabel returned."

Another chuckle. "Right, yeah, okay. See you guys later, then. Hope you find him."

FORTY-SEVEN

We go straight to the shed, but we don't run. This isn't the killer's MO, so what we have here is almost certainly the scenario we hoped for: Mick is getting some on the side. While I struggle to think of him cheating on Isabel, I struggle a lot more to think of him as the guy who'd cut open a man, take out part of his intestine, and hang him in a tree to die.

Behind the shed is the chopping yard. There are a couple of sawhorses, but the equipment is all kept in the carpentry shop, which is better secured. The woodshed isn't locked. Most of the resource buildings aren't secured. You're welcome to help yourself to firewood or water or food if you suddenly find yourself needing it in the middle of the night. Of course, if you take it, Dalton presumes you plan to pay in the morning. If you don't, there's a 100-percent interest charge for each day you delay.

I go through the shed door first, Dalton

covering. As soon as we're in, we both stop short.

I inhale. "Do you smell — ?"

Dalton barrels past me. What we smell isn't blood.

It's smoke.

I can see the source: a smoldering pile of wood, flames just starting to lick up from the base. That's when I catch another scent, an even worse one.

"Eric!" I lunge to shove him out of the way, but he's already wheeling, and he grabs me and throws me aside, and we both hit the floor just as the fire catches the kerosene-soaked wood and whooshes up in a pyre of heat and flame. He keeps me pinned until we're certain that's all it is — fire, with nothing about to explode. Still, the wood stack is going up so fast, the heat is like a solid wall, smoke already filling the room.

Dalton yanks me to my feet and shoves me toward the door with, "Go!" I don't. I can't, no more than he can, because I see the remains of a broken lantern, and I know it didn't just fall over and accidentally start a fire.

Someone has deliberately set a kerosene-fueled fire. In the same place where a missing man was last seen.

"There!" I shout, as I see a foot behind the woodpile.

Dalton turns, and his face screws up like

he's about to snarl at me to get out, but I push past him and grab the foot. There's a split second when I remember Harry Powys's body, and I imagine yanking this foot only to realize that's all I have. It's not. There's a body attached, and before I can pull again, Dalton's there, helping.

It's Mick. His shirt is kerosene soaked, sparks already lighting it up. I let go of his foot, and I'm out of my jacket and slapping it on his now-flaming shirt as Dalton drags him from behind the burning pyre.

Dalton doesn't wait to be sure the fire on his shirt is out. Doesn't check for a pulse, either. There's no time. We're in a building filled with dry wood and doused in accelerant. He hoists Mick over his shoulder, and that's when I see the blood. The back of Mick's shirt is soaked with it, the fabric shredded. He's been stabbed in the back. Repeatedly.

Mick. Oh God, Mick.

Any thoughts of him as a psychotic killer vanish, and all I see is the guy I knew. The sweet, quiet guy. Devoted to his friend Abbygail. Devoted to his lover, Isabel. A guy I'd liked. Really liked.

We're moving fast for the exit. The fire is roaring now. Whoever lit it didn't stick around to be sure it caught properly, and when we first opened the door, the rush of wind must have caught the smoldering flame, finally bringing it into contact with the kerosene. Not that the *how* matters. It's just my brain processing, trying to keep calm and centered and temporarily forget the fact that there's a massive fire in a building filled with wood, in a town *built* of wood.

Dalton slaps the radio into my hand as we move. The smoke swirls so thick I don't even realize what he's given me until my hand wraps around it. I fumble for the Call button, but my eyes are streaming and I'm coughing too hard to speak. Dalton shoulders me forward. Get the hell out first.

We reach the door. I push him through, and I'm about to follow when I see something move in the smoke. Someone's still in here.

Shit! The woman who followed Mick.

The smoke has already forced me into a crouch, and even with my shirt pulled up over my nose and mouth, I'm hacking convulsively. I shove the radio in my pocket, get down on all fours, and start toward her. For a moment, I can make her out — a pale face and light hair — but then she's lost behind the smoke and the tears streaming from my eyes. I continue forward, feeling my way.

"Butler!"

I barely hear Dalton's shout over the roar of the fire. I move faster. I have to get to her before he comes back into this burning building.

"Casey!"

The door opens with a whoosh, the wind and the change in pressure making the smoke clear long enough for me to see the woman. She's sitting propped against a stack of wood, her hand resting on something red.

Resting on a gas can.

Shit, oh shit.

I just risked my life to save a goddamned killer.

"Casey!" Dalton shouts.

I try to answer but can barely whisper. I cover the last few feet to the woman. I'm here now — I can't turn around and leave her.

Under her dark coat, she wears a pale blouse. It's covered in blood. One hand clutches the knife, the other rests on the gas can. I grab the wrist holding the knife, and she makes no move to resist. Her fist opens. The knife falls. I take it. Then, as I reach to grab her shirt, I see it again. Pale pink blouse. Peter Pan collar. Embroidering down the front.

I know this shirt.

Blinking hard, I rise up on my knees until my face is inches from hers. Only then do I see more than a pale blur. I see Diana's face.

Her eyes are open, and she's staring right at me, but she doesn't seem to see me. She hacks, doubling over, and her coughing ignites mine, and it's a beacon for Dalton. His hands grab my shoulders and yank me back.

"No!" I croak. "Di—"

I can't even get the rest out. I'm coughing too hard, and he's picking me up, running for the exit, and I can't fight, don't dare. There's no way to communicate, and every second lost is a second we don't have.

He kicks the door open and we're through. Then he throws me to the ground. Literally throws me, like a sack of flour. I hit the grass, knife falling from my hand as I'm hacking and groaning, half blinded by the smoke. I twist around and say, "Di—"

But he's gone back for her, and I shout, "No!" and push to my feet. *I'll get her. I'll do it. I'll take that risk.* I don't want him taking it for her. I don't want anyone else taking it for her after what she's done.

It's too late. He's inside, and I'm left stumbling toward the shed, hacking so hard I can barely move. I reach the door, and I pull it open, and I'm about to go in when I hear running footfalls. Anders appears, others following, brought by the smoke seeping through the cracks.

They see the smoke billowing from the open door. Anders is on me, scooping me up to get me away from the fire.

"No," I croak. "Eric."

"Eric's — ? Fuck!" He sets me down as fast as he can, shouting, "Get Beth! Now!" but I'm right behind him.

He vanishes into the smoke before I make

it. Then I see him again, a stumbling figure. I leap to grab him, to direct him, but I realize it's not Anders. It's Dalton, with Diana over his shoulder. He manages one last step and collapses. Then Anders is there, thank God, and he's grabbing Diana as she falls, and I have both hands wrapped in Dalton's shirt, dragging him farther from the door. Anders shouts, and someone's there to help me. I don't even look up to see who it is.

We manage to get Dalton out of the smoke and away from the inferno pouring through that open doorway. I put out the fire on his shirt and jeans. That's when I realize he still isn't moving.

He's not breathing.

I start CPR. I don't even think whether I remember it well enough. I start and then Anders is there, saying, "I can do that," and I say, between breaths, "Am I doing it wrong?" and he gives a strained chuckle and says, "No."

"Chest," I say. "Take over —"

"Chest compressions. Okay. But if you need me to —"

"Got it."

"You've swallowed a lot of —"

"Got it."

I might have barely been breathing a minute ago, but all that evaporates as I focus on my task. Breath-one-two. Nothing.

Goddamn it, Dalton!

Anders's chest compressions are hard enough to crack a rib, but I say nothing. The look in his eyes tells me he's freaking out. Hell, we both are. I let him continue his compressions and tell myself a cracked rib is nothing.

My turn. Breath-one-two.

Goddamn — !

Dalton coughs.

We flip him over fast, and Dalton coughs up smoke-blackened mucus. He's on all fours, supporting himself, waving Anders away when he tries to help.

"Oh, my God," a voice says. Footsteps run over, and I look up to see Beth, her eyes wide with panic. "Eric!"

"Mick's dead," he says, his hand going up when she tries to kneel beside him. "Check Diana. Then Casey. I'm fine."

"You are not —"

"Diana first," he says with enough snap that I wince as Beth flinches. "Then Casey. I'm fine."

She backs up, looking confused and hurt, until Anders leads her to Diana.

"You okay?" Dalton asks me as he sits.

"I'm not the one who passed out."

"I'm not the one who caught on fire," he says, and reaches out to catch a lock of my hair, rubbing it between his fingers, the singed pieces raining down.

"It'll grow." I cough. "Shouldn't have gone

back in."

"Yeah, you shouldn't have."

"I mean you. She —" I hack again, hard enough that I feel like I'm going to cough up lung tissue. He thumps my back and looks toward Beth, but she's busy with Diana, so I say I'm fine, then, "She killed Mick. Diana. I —" I look over at the knife, the blade covered in blood. "She was holding that, and she had her hand on a gas can. The blood on her shirt . . . I don't think it's hers. I tried to tell you."

"Would *you* have stayed out?" He doesn't wait for a response. "Hell, no, you wouldn't. So I'd have gone in anyway. We have no idea what happened in there, Casey. An hour ago, we were considering Mick a suspect."

I stop. Blink. I just jumped to the conclusion that Diana murdered a man when I have no idea if that's what happened. Mick could be the killer and Diana saved herself from becoming his next victim, and all I thought was, *She's guilty.* My best friend. The woman I've known half my life.

Dalton leans toward me, voice lowered. "You okay?"

I nod. "Some smoke inhalation and —"

"Not what I mean. And a fucking stupid question anyway, isn't it? You're not going to be okay, either way this plays out."

"Boss?" It's Anders.

Dalton pulls back fast. He'd been leaning

in to be heard over the chaos. It wasn't as if everyone was standing around watching the lumber shed burn. A dozen men and women were fighting the fire with buckets of water and blankets.

"Eric?" Anders says, and we both push to our feet. "Mick's gone, like you thought. Someone should tell Isabel before she —"

At that very second, Isabel comes running around the building.

"Shit," Anders says, then, "I'll handle this."

He takes off to intercept her. Someone shouts for Dalton, and he looks over, squinting through the haze. His gaze follows the man's finger up to the roof, where flame has broken through . . . a scant few feet from the next building.

"Goddamn it!" Dalton starts running toward the others. "Sam! Kenny! Get everyone you can find. Tell them to bring all the water they can carry."

I jog up behind him. "Give me a job."

He looks me up and down, assessing damage, and then nods. "The building two doors down has more fire blankets. Grab two guys and bring all of them."

I nod and take off.

FORTY-EIGHT

As soon as the fire is under control, Dalton tries to send me to check on Diana. I pretend not to hear and keep hauling water. When the blaze is finally out, he says, "Get your ass over to the infirmary, Butler. If you don't want to admit you're worried about her, then I'm your boss ordering you to make sure a suspect is secured."

We're alone when he says that. No one else knows we found Diana with the murder weapon and accelerant.

"Sure as fuck don't need that," he said earlier. "Got enough problems without worrying someone'll try to lynch her."

I could say he was being colorful, but Rockton has taught me that you can't underestimate the speed with which we humans can undo a thousand years of civilization. We aren't nearly at *Lord of the Flies* level inside the town limits, but if you walk a mile into the wilderness, you'll find Golding's world come to life.

The changes that come with living this way are not all a *re*gression, though, and I see proof of that tonight. Everyone pitches in, whether it's helping with the fire or bringing washbasins and cold drinks and fresh clothes for those fighting the fire.

As for Diana, she's been taken home and sedated. I pop my head in, but she's unconscious. Beth's busy at the clinic treating burns and smoke inhalation, and I'm not going to interrupt her to ask about Diana's condition. So I head out to find Dalton. When I hear that Val has summoned him, I pick up my pace.

A lantern glows in Val's house. Voices drift from a partly open window.

". . . one resident dead, another half dead," Val is saying.

"His name was Mick. Hers is Diana."

"Don't correct me."

"I'm reminding you. I know how hard it is for you to remember people. Well, I'd say that you just don't give a shit, but it's been a fucking horrible night, Val. Otherwise, I'd also complain about how you didn't even leave your goddamn house, and that's a conversation best left for a more respectable hour."

"Five people are dead, Sheriff, and —"

"Here, let me save us both some time. Five people are dead, and I'm a fucking lousy sheriff because I haven't stopped a killer."

"We hired you a detective, and I don't see

436

that it's made any difference."

"Butler is doing just fine. Without her, you'd have had another body in that fire. I'm also not convinced tonight's crime is connected to the others."

"So your lack of progress is emboldening others —"

"It's been two fucking weeks, Val. Do you know how often we catch killers faster than that? Only when they're standing beside the damned body, sobbing a confession. That's pretty much the only sort of murders we get. This is different. Let us do our job —"

"The council is not pleased."

"Fucking shock of the century. Tell them I don't give a shit. Those exact words, please."

Footsteps as he heads for the door.

Val calls after him. "One building destroyed. Another damaged. Our entire stockpile of wood gone. Half our supply of water depleted."

"Yeah, it's called a fire. Which is why I've been telling the council for years that we need to be better prepared for one. If Casey and I hadn't been there in time, we could have lost half the fucking town. I'll pass on the council's thanks."

More footfalls. He is heading to the rear door. I back up past the corner.

"Murder, drugs, fire — this town is a mess, Eric. If you can't do the job —"

"The council will boot my ass out the front

gate. Heard it. Not concerned. I'm the best damned sheriff you've had since this place opened. And yeah, that includes my father. Otherwise, the council would have hauled him back to deal with these murders. Good night, Valerie."

He saunters out, his head high. The door slaps shut behind him, and he thumps down the porch steps. In a few long strides, he's beside the house. Then he stops, out of sight, and that steel melts from his spine and there's a moment there, of turmoil and fear, so unguarded and raw that my gut twists in shame for watching. I'm backing away when he notices the movement.

"I'm sorry," I say as I walk to him. "I heard voices and —"

"It's fine."

He starts walking and motions for me to keep up. At the road, he pauses to look at the still-smoldering lumber shed, at the smoke creeping over the town, at people with scorched jackets and soot-streaked faces on porches catching their breath, no one talking, everyone realizing how bad it could have been. He falters, that unguarded look returning for a moment before he blinks it back. Down the road, someone sees him and steps off a porch to wait. Someone else follows.

"Fuck," he says.

"I'm sure they just have questions, but you don't need to deal with that right now."

He exhales again, that slow stream of exhaustion. "Nah, I should . . ." He trails off, as if he can't even summon the energy to finish his sentence.

"We need to check the forest," I say.

"Hmm?" He looks over, eyes unfocused.

"We should check the forest, in case sparks spread to fire there."

"It couldn't have . . ." He catches my look and nods. "Right. Yeah. Should make sure."

"You head on in. I'll run over and tell them you'll make a statement later."

It's dawn now, which would make a lovely sunrise as we head east . . . if we weren't surrounded by towering evergreens. As it is, it's a peaceful walk, the early morning light seeping through. I think we're wandering aimlessly. Of course, we aren't. Dalton leads me to a fallen tree, one so big I need to jump up to perch on top of it.

I unhook the backpack I brought and take out two beers, wrapped in a towel.

"I snagged these from the station," I say. "We haven't slept, so technically it's not morning for us yet."

He takes one with a grunted thanks. We drink, staring out at the forest.

"Do you know Val was attacked out here?" I say. "Shortly after she arrived?"

"What?"

"She got separated —"

"Yeah, I remember. I wasn't part of the patrol party, but I helped search. She wandered off, got lost, and showed up in the morning."

"After being attacked by two men. Hostiles, I suspect, given her description. She said they threatened to teach her a lesson about trespassing and then fell asleep, letting her escape."

He looks over, frowning.

"They didn't fall asleep after threatening her. Not right away, at least."

He exhales. "Fuck."

"Yes, but she denies it, and we need to let her keep that delusion for now. But it explains why she hates this place and why she stays in the house. And partially why she doesn't trust you. You're connected to this forest. To the place that hurt her. To the men who hurt her. It isn't logical, but I get the impression that Val likes her compartments. Everyone fits neatly into one."

"Yeah." He stretches his legs. "I've always known she doesn't like me much. It's worse than that, isn't it?"

"Val's a bitch," I say. "What happened to her is horrible, but it doesn't make her less of a bitch."

"Nah. She doesn't have the spine to be a bitch. I wish she did, because that would be something I could fight. This?" He shakes his head. "Makes me feel like a dog barking at a dishcloth snapping in the wind. It might annoy the hell out of me, but barking at it doesn't do any good."

A few minutes of silence, and then I say, "It's bullshit, threatening to kick you out. They never would. They need you."

He shrugs.

"Seriously," I say. "No one would want to lose you."

"Locals, you mean. They're the ones who have to live here, and as much shit as I give them, they know this place needs hard-core law and order. But the council doesn't have to live in Rockton."

"While I still don't think they'd ever kick you out, it might help to have a plan B. To imagine what you'd do in the worst scenario. So you feel you have some control."

"I already know what I'd do."

"And it doesn't help?"

"Nope. Because I don't want to do it. It's just the only option. For me."

That's all he says. I'm curious, of course, but I know to keep my distance, too. We sit there, drinking, until he points his bottle at the forest and says, "I'd go there."

"Live in the forest?"

He tenses, as if he's assessing my tone. After a moment, he relaxes. "Yeah. There's nothing for me down south."

"If it's because there'd be a learning curve . . . ," I say slowly.

"No, it's because I'm not interested."

Maybe that's partly true, but it's partly bullshit, too. Dalton has too much ego to deal with the constant sense that he doesn't fit in. And I'm not sure there *is* a satisfying life for him down there. He's thirty years old and runs an entire town. People snap to attention when he enters a room. They respect him and they fear him and they admire him. Down south? He'd be a dictator in exile.

"You could start a new Rockton," I say.

He snorts a laugh.

"I'm serious," I say.

He looks over, lips still twitching, that smile extending to his eyes, warming them to a soft blue-gray. "You gonna help me start a new town, Casey?"

"I don't know. It would take time, and *someone's* only letting me stay six months."

He laughs at that, and it's a good sound to hear, a damned good sound, and when he looks at me again, his eyes are sparkling, and I feel . . . I feel things I don't want to feel, because I know there's no room in Eric Dalton's life for that, but I don't care. I'm not going to do anything about it, so there's no harm in feeling it.

"Build a new town, huh?" he says. "Sure. No big deal."

"Are you saying you couldn't handle it?"

He catches the challenge in my voice, and that smile ignites into a grin.

"You'd need to start small," I say. "Just take whoever would join you from Rockton and not worry about admitting new people for a few years. It would take at least that long to grow from a camp to a town. That's how you'd have to begin — as a camp. Preferably in spring, so you have until fall to get the first houses up."

"You're fucking serious."

"I am absolutely fucking serious, Sheriff Dalton. At least fifty people from town would follow you. That includes Will, Beth, and pretty much everyone in essential services. Hell, even I'd go, if someone decided I could stay more than six months."

He chuckles and shakes his head again.

I twist and lean toward him. "I'm not saying you should do it, Eric. I'm saying you should *plan* to do it. Work through all the details. Talk to Anders and Beth. They both know the shit the council puts you through. Make a plan. A solid plan. And the council will lose their hold on you because you have a backup, ready to launch."

He finishes his beer and sets it aside. Then he sits there, rubbing his chin, and I'm certain he's thinking of how to tell me I'm crazy without kiboshing my enthusiasm.

"Couldn't be too close to here," he says. "Fifty, a hundred kilometers away would work. There's plenty of land. . . ."

FORTY-NINE

Dalton never says he's going to follow my advice and devise a solid backup plan. But we do spend the next hour hashing it over, so I know he'll give it serious consideration.

He also never says anything about extending my six-month stay in Rockton. Was I hinting there? Yes, I was. I hate feeling that if I don't find a killer, I'll get my ass booted out before spring thaw. It also makes me feel like Dalton still doesn't consider me more than a casual acquaintance, someone whose company he enjoys well enough, but if she disappeared tomorrow he wouldn't miss her all that much. No insult intended, Butler. That's just how it is.

I don't dwell on that. There's plenty more to occupy my mind, starting as soon as we get back to town and see Kenny running for my house. He catches sight of us and jogs over, panting. "Casey? We need you at Diana's place. Now."

I take off at a run. Dalton is at my side. He

twists to talk to Kenny, only to see the man running five paces behind. An angry wave lights a fire under Kenny, and he catches up.

"Is she okay?" I ask Kenny. "Did something happen?"

"Diana woke up. Now she's freaking out. I sent Paul for the doc, and then I had to call two guys in to restrain her, and she clocked one of them and . . ."

I don't hear the rest. I kick it into high gear, leaving Kenny and Dalton behind.

As I climb the stairs to Diana's apartment, Jen blocks my path with "You'd better shut her up. Or I will." I refrain from hitting her. I may push her aside. She may stagger down a couple of steps. But any injuries sustained are due to Dalton's "get out of my fucking way," which startles her enough that she tumbles down the rest of the stairs. He steps over her. I'm already running into Diana's apartment, where she's struggling against two of the militia, shouting, "I want Casey! Where's Casey?"

As soon as she sees me, she stops. Then she launches from the bed and into my arms, sobbing, "What's going on? I wake up and my shirt's soaked in blood and all I can smell is smoke and they drugged me, Casey. Someone drugged me, and when I woke up and tried to ask for you, they threw me on the bed —"

"We restrained her, Casey," one of the guys

says. "I swear, that's all we did, and only because she was going to hurt herself."

I'm not sure Diana even hears him. She's sobbing against my shirt. Dalton tells the guys to leave, and they do. He takes a seat across the bedroom.

"Wh-What's going on?" Diana says after a minute.

I guide her back to bed. As I do, she sees Dalton.

"Why's he here?" she says.

"There's been a crime," I say. "The fire you can smell. I have to talk to you about what you remember, and he needs to be here."

"Why?"

"Because I'm your friend, and if I speak to you in an official capacity, there should be a witness."

"Then ask Will."

"Eric is my boss. Just talk to me. What do you remember?"

"Nothing. Not a fire. Not this blood. Not why someone pumped me full of —"

"What *do* you remember? The last thing?"

It takes her a couple of minutes. I wait as patiently as I can.

"I . . . I went out . . . No, that was . . ."

"Let's go back farther. Dinner."

She smiles in relief. "That's easy. I had dinner with you, here."

I prod: "And I left at eight. . . ."

Just after I left, Diana decided to go out

and had an encounter with Jen.

"I swear, she lies in wait just to give me crap," Diana says. "Once, she actually complained that I brush my teeth too loudly. I really need to get another place, or I'll be taking a stall in the stables just to get away from her."

She smiles, and all I can do is pray she's innocent . . . or she'll be sleeping someplace worse than a stable stall.

After escaping Jen, Diana hung out with a few others, playing cards. At eleven, she headed home.

"And . . . that's it. That's all I remember." She tugs at her earring as she thinks. "No, wait — I heard something. I was walking along the road near the forest, and . . . That is the last thing I remember. Someone must have come up behind me and knocked me out."

Beth appears at the door. I go outside with her where Diana can't overhear.

"Diana thinks she was knocked unconscious," I say. "Were there any signs of that?"

She frames her response with care. "Knocking someone out isn't as easy as it seems in movies. There would be evidence on the skull."

"And there's not. Also, Kenny saw her walking into the shed."

She nods. "Which lends credence to another explanation for why she can't remember anything. One . . . better supported by my examination."

"Which is?"

She pops her head back into the room and says, "I'm going to speak to Casey outside."

"No," Diana says. "If this is about me, say it here."

We walk back into the bedroom, and Beth says, "Diana was heavily under the influence of rydex. The dosage —"

"What?" Diana swings her legs out of bed. "No, I've never —"

Dalton clears his throat. She looks over at him, and hate blazes from her eyes. "I explained that." She turns to me. "I was at a party the night before last. I got drunk, and someone gave me dex. I was walking home afterward, and your sheriff waylaid me."

"I heard a woman stumbling around at three in the morning," Dalton says. "I wouldn't be a very good sheriff if I ignored that. I helped her home and —"

"You *dragged* me home," she squawks. "Chewing me out the whole way. Telling me how I was making things tough for Casey — poor Casey — and you weren't going to tell her about the dex because she 'doesn't need that shit,' and this was my second strike, if you ever caught me using again, you'd . . ." She trails off and swallows.

"I said I'd give her a week on shit duty," Dalton says.

"Was there rydex at the get-together last night?" I ask.

"No, there —" She catches my look and glances toward Dalton.

"Getting your friends in trouble is the least of your concerns right now, Diana," he says. "Mick's dead."

"What?"

"Mick is dead. You were found ten feet from his body. In a burning woodshed. With a bloody knife in your hand and an empty gas can beside you."

Diana reels back onto the bed, saying, "No, that can't be — Casey, tell him — that's not —" As she spins on me, the horror in her eyes hardens to anger. "Someone's framing me. The killer knocked me out —"

"There's no evidence of that," Dalton says.

"According to who? A doctor who was sued for malpractice and is arrogant enough to admit it?"

"Diana!" I say.

"If you got knocked out, there'd be a lump," Dalton says. "Show me that, and we'll have a very different conversation."

She rubs her hands over her head, scowling at him, and saying, "It must be here. And if it's not, then it was knockout gas or . . . or I was roofied at the party."

"Roofied?" Dalton says.

"Rohypnol," Beth says. "It's a sedative that can induce anterograde amnesia. But I don't have it in the pharmacy, and there was no evidence of anything except rydex in her bloodstream."

"Then it's the drugs," Diana says.

"Rydex doesn't render you unconscious," Beth says. "But it can cause blackouts and memory loss. Which doesn't mean that you aren't responsible for your actions. Only that you honestly don't remember —"

Diana flies at her, catching us all off guard. I recover first, just as she grabs Beth, and I pull her away.

"Did you hear her?" Diana says. "Telling me I might have killed Mick and forgotten it. She's a cold, sanctimonious bitch. I didn't kill anyone. You know that, Casey." Before I can open my mouth, she spins to me. "I did not kill —"

"I never said you did, Di. You need to let me investigate, and for that, I must be as dispassionate as possible."

"God, no wonder you two get along so well. You're like robots. I'm accused of murder and —"

"Stop." That's Dalton. He gets to his feet.

"You stay out —"

"No, you shut your damn mouth, Diana. Because if you're accusing Casey of not caring about you, I'll ask you to remember why she's here in Rockton."

"You asshole —"

"Diana," I say. "Don't."

"Don't what? I'm accused of murder, Casey. *Murder.* I'm not going to be framed by some fucked-up psycho sheriff. Ouch!" She jumps and turns to see Beth there, holding a syringe. A drop of blood soaks through the sleeve of Diana's shirt.

"You bitch!" she says.

"You're overwrought," Beth says. "A result of the lingering rydex, I suspect. You should get some sleep."

Diana makes a move to go after her, but it must have been a hefty dose; she's already weaving. I help her back into bed, and she seems to have forgotten what she was doing and lets me. As I pull up the sheets, she clasps my hand and slurs, "I didn't kill Mick, Casey. I swear I didn't." Then she drops off to sleep.

We get a full update from Beth back at the clinic. She hasn't had time to autopsy Mick, but the manner of his death seems clear. Six stab wounds to the back, most of them shallow but a few shoved in with enough force to do the fatal damage. She'll run a tox screen. His eyes and mouth odor, though, suggest he hadn't been drinking or using last night. She suspects he was attacked from behind, possibly as he was sleeping. By the time he woke up, his attacker would have done enough damage that he'd have been unable to escape or adequately defend himself.

Stabs to the back. Attacked while asleep. Any theory that Diana acted in self-defense is disintegrating fast.

"Sleeping in the shed would suggest sex in the shed," I say. "Were there signs of that?"

She nods. "Signs of protected sex — seminal fluid but not vaginal. I'll be examining Diana to see if there are signs with her. Presuming Mick used a condom, it'll be tougher to tell. I'll mainly be looking for any suggestion of nonconsensual sex, as Eric asked."

I glance at Dalton, but he's busy across the room on his radio. Rape is one possible reason why Diana might have attacked Mick in his sleep. Dalton is giving her the benefit of the doubt. Which is more than she's ever given him.

Beth talks a bit more about her findings. Mick's clothing had definitely been soaked in kerosene, as our noses told us. There are no signs of restraint. He'd almost certainly been dead from his wounds before he was placed by that woodpile. His body and clothing did show signs he'd been dragged. Probably not far, but with the fire, we'd have no way to confirm that.

"In other words, there's nothing to suggest that a woman Diana's size couldn't have committed this crime," I say.

"No. Also . . ." She looks toward Dalton, who's still talking to Anders.

"Go on," I say.

"There are cuts on Diana's fingers."

"Defensive wounds?"

"No. They're on the side of her palms."

She doesn't elaborate. She doesn't have to.

"Consistent with her pushing in a knife and having her hand slip and nick the blade."

"Yes. I'm sorry, Casey. I wish I could give you something to suggest she was framed."

"But you can't."

She shakes her head.

FIFTY

Dalton is walking me home when someone calls, "Detective Butler!" and I tense, recognizing the voice.

Dalton turns, saying, "No, Isabel."

"I'd like to speak to —"

"Casey has not slept. She needs —"

"It's okay," I say. I turn to face Isabel. "I'm sorry for your loss."

I mean it even more when I get a good look at her. She's not wearing makeup and she's still dressed from yesterday, her clothing disheveled and stained as if she's spilled coffee or a drink. I remember how Mick talked about her. Not a guy looking for a sugar mama. A guy in love. In Isabel's face, I see proof that the love went both ways.

"I'm sorry," I say again. "I can assure you we're putting everything we can into finding his killer —"

"You already have."

My head jerks up.

"It's Diana, isn't it? You found her with

him, in that fire."

"Which does not mean —"

"Of course it does. She lured him there. Mick said you were asking about her turning tricks. I wanted to speak to you about that directly and" — a flash of grief — "I didn't get to it nearly as quickly as I should have. It was no misunderstanding, Casey. She was acting out, in so many ways, and that was just one of them."

"You think that's why she'd lure Mick?" I ask.

"I know if she said she wanted to talk to him about it, he'd have met with her. Is that a motive for murder? I barely dare hazard a guess. Something's come loose in that girl's head. I suspect it was always only a little wobbly before, because otherwise you wouldn't have been friends with her. But since Diana's arrived here, it's broken, and you know it. That's why you backed off."

I open my mouth to answer, but Isabel continues. "Diana lured Mick there and killed him."

"They had sex," Dalton says.

"Bullshit. Mick would never —"

"There were signs he'd had sex shortly before his death."

"With *me,* Eric. In the back room about an hour before he left."

"While the Roc was still open?"

"Is that a crime?"

Dalton crosses his arms. "You left the bar unattended and had sex in the back room with your boyfriend, who wasn't feeling well."

"He was feeling fine then."

"Then I'd suggest you get your ass to the doc's to confirm that for our report."

"Confirm it how? He wore a condom."

"Produce the condom." Dalton nudges me. "We'll talk to you later, Isabel."

"It's about Diana." She steps between us to face me. "Information I've been debating telling you, because you already don't like me very much, and this won't help. But it's something you need to know."

"It can wait," Dalton says. "Casey's so tired she can barely stay upright."

"No, I . . ." I want to say I'll handle it, but I can't. "I'm sorry. Eric's right. Whatever it is, right now I'd probably only hear half of it."

"Then I'll talk to *you,* Eric," she says.

He exhales. "I'm just as tired, and I want to get Casey home before we both fall over."

"Will!" Isabel calls.

I see Anders down the road. He looks as if he'd been heading our way but was stopped by a citizen. He says a few quick words to the woman and then hurries to us.

"Will, could you please walk Casey home?" Isabel says. "She's exhausted, and I need to speak to Eric."

Dalton hesitates and then says, "Yeah, okay,

walk her home. Make sure she gets in bed."

"Alone," Isabel calls as we start to go.

Anders flips her the finger.

"You get some rest, too, Will," Dalton says.

"I'm fine. You guys need —"

"We *all* need sleep. I'm going home after this, and I'm not coming into the station before two. If either of you sticks your head out before then, people are going to demand a statement. You'll need to wake me up early to give it. I'll be pissed."

Anders smiles. "All right. See you at two, then."

Once we're back at my place, Anders comes in, and I get halfway across my living room and it's like my battery cuts out. I just stop. Then I start to shake. Anders is there in a blink, his arms going around me, and I try to brush him off, to say I'm fine, but he says, "Bullshit," and hugs me tighter, until I give up and let myself fall against him.

I don't cry. I want to, for the first time since those months in the hospital. But tears don't come. Instead, I just shake harder, as much as I try to stop. After a couple of minutes, Anders leans down and whispers, "It's about Diana, right?"

I nod, and I don't elaborate, and he just keeps hugging me, and as the shaking stops, I become keenly aware of him, the smell of him and the feel of him, that rock-solid presence and the beat of his heart, and I think of more than a hug.

I think of complete distraction, of sex with a great guy who'd give it and understand it was just the moment and expect nothing more. All I need to do is give a sign. Touch his hip. Press against him. Some small signal that he can choose to act on or not, and if he chooses no, then the moment passes without awkwardness.

I don't make that move. I know why I don't, and I choose not to pursue that reason, not to analyze it, because if I think about it too much, I'll decide it's a damned stupid excuse and, really, if that's the reason I'm holding back, then it's also the reason I should push forward, because *that's* not happening, that shouldn't happen, and this is the better choice. No, that's not true. This is the safer choice. This is the one that won't break my heart.

Anders kisses the top of my head. Then my forehead. Just light, fraternal kisses, but that's *his* move, his sign. All I have to do is lift my face from his chest, tilt it up, and let him put those kisses on my lips. I don't, and he gives my forehead one last kiss. Then I step away.

"I should get to bed," I say. "Let you go."

"Yes," he says. "You should get to bed. As for letting me go?" He takes my face between his hands. "I'm always here for you, Casey. If you need me, I'm here. If you don't? I'll still be here."

He kisses my forehead again, and I know he's telling me, whether I want more or not, he'll still be there. Which is, I think, the sweetest thing a guy has ever said to me, and I wish . . .

But there's no sense wishing, because it's only going to make me feel guilty and stupid — too stupid to take the damned good thing that's right in front of me, stupid enough to hold out for something I'm not going to get. That's the way it is, though, and one thing I won't be stupid enough to do? Tell myself I'm wrong and hurt Anders when it turns out I'm not.

"I'm going to crash here," he says, and waves to the couch. "Okay?"

I nod and smile. "Okay," I say, then I hug him and tell him thanks, a deep and genuine thanks, before I head upstairs.

I'm too exhausted to think about Diana. That does not, however, mean that I have a long and restful slumber. I set my alarm for one thirty, but I'm up an hour sooner, waking from a nightmare.

I'm sure Diana would not commit cold-blooded murder. She wouldn't even do what I had — kill someone in the heat of the moment. Could a combination of booze and rydex have sent her into a murderous rage? I want to say no — that someone framed her. But I find that nearly as impossible to believe as Beth does. Which leaves only one conclusion. That something has snapped in Diana, and I saw it snap, and I backed off, like Isabel said. Which makes whatever happened partly my fault.

In that distracted state of mind, I make my way downstairs. I'm walking through the living room when I see a figure sitting on my couch, and I jump back fast before I realize it's Anders. He's sitting on my sofa and staring at me . . . dressed only in my panties.

I know it's not my almost-naked body that has his attention. It's the scars.

I mumble an apology and hightail it back up the stairs. Anders follows, rapping on my door and saying, "Shit, I'm sorry, Casey, that was —"

"One hundred percent my fault," I say as I yank on some clothes. "I forgot you were down there."

"Still, I wasn't exactly being a gentleman and looking away, which is why I'm apologizing."

"There are a lot of scars."

It takes him a moment to reply. "No, I never noticed — I mean, you were naked, so I was —"

I crack open the door, hiding behind it as I smile for him. "It's okay. I know what I look like."

"You're beautiful. Hell, I have scars. Yours surprised me, sure, but it doesn't make you any less —"

"And we'll stop there," I say, my smile turning genuine. "I appreciate the flattery, but let's not make this any more awkward."

"It's not flattery. I . . ." He takes a deep breath. "And *that's* not making this any less awkward. Can I fix you a late breakfast?"

I nod and withdraw.

I come down as Anders is finishing the coffee.

"It happened in college," I say, standing in the doorway. "My boyfriend was dealing drugs on someone else's turf. We got jumped by a few guys. My boyfriend took off. I spent six weeks in the hospital. I went to confront him afterward and made the mistake of bringing a gun."

It's the first time I've said that to anyone outside therapy, and my heart is thumping so hard I can barely breathe.

"Shitty boyfriend," he says as he brings me a coffee.

I sputter a laugh. "Yes, but not really the point of that confession."

He shrugs. "Close enough."

"You don't seem surprised. You knew?"

He takes eggs from the counter. "No, but if someone had asked me why you were here, I'd have said you did something to someone who damned well deserved it. Which doesn't make it any easier." He looks at the eggs in

461

his hand. "Scrambled?"

"Sure."

"Good, 'cause that's all I can make." He takes out a pan, puts it on the blazing wood-stove. "Mine was in the military. I killed someone who *didn't* deserve to die. At all. I screwed up. Big-time."

"I've heard it happens over there."

He nods and turns away as he cracks the eggs.

"Which doesn't make it any easier," I say.

"Nope, it doesn't." He tosses the shells into the compost box. "Does being *here* make it easier for you?"

I nod. "It does. Like I said, it happened in college, so it's old news. But . . ."

"It never goes away."

"It still hasn't, and maybe this is just me hiding and pretending things are better —"

"Don't analyze. Eric does enough of that for both of us."

I laugh and sip my coffee.

"Which helps," Anders says. "Though I'd never admit it to him. He can be a pain in the ass, telling you exactly what your problem is, but some of us need that more than a therapist's couch. Someone who won't let us hide. When I came here . . ." He shakes his head. "I was a fucking mess. I didn't want to be here. Same as you — yeah, Diana told me you came to Rockton for her. I came because the one person who thought I was worth saving — my sister — put my ass on the plane, and I'd already let her down too much to ever do it again. Then I got here and . . ."

He sits across the table from me. "I know it's a cliché, but Eric saved me. When my term's up, I only hope that I'll have made myself useful enough that I can stay and keep repaying that debt. And, yeah, that's partly because I don't want to go back. I'm happy here. But I do owe him. I owe him big, and anything he wants from me? It's his."

He fingers his mug, and it seems as if he expects a response, so I say, "All Eric wants from you is exactly what he's getting: a damned fine deputy."

One corner of his mouth lifts. "Thanks. What I mean, though, is . . . I get the feeling . . . but I don't want to step aside if there's no reason to, but if . . ."

I wait for him to go on, but he only fusses with his mug. Then his head lifts. "Shit! The eggs."

He's hurrying back to the stove when a rap comes at the door. It's a familiar knock. One hard rap, pause, then a second, almost reluctant one, as if the caller would really rather just knock once for efficiency but then it would be mistaken for a bang and he'd have to start over again.

I call, "Come in," but I swear I hear the knob turning before I even say it. Dalton's booted footfalls cross the living room, and he sticks his head into the kitchen.

"Knew you'd be up already. Thought I —" He sees Anders and stops.

"I crashed on the couch," Anders says. "Now I'm making breakfast."

"Doing a shitty job of it, smells like. How the hell do you burn scrambled eggs?"

"It's a special talent."

Dalton walks to the stove. "No, it's having the damned fire too hot. Get out of the way." He looks at me. "You want scrambled eggs?"

"That's fine. I —"

"Do you *want* scrambled eggs?"

"Over easy would be better."

He looks at Anders. "Sunnyside up?"

"Yes, please."

"You know what would help, Will? If the one kind of eggs you can make is the kind you actually like to eat. Get out the bacon or sausage or whatever Casey has in the icebox, and then pour me a coffee while I make breakfast."

"Yes, boss."

FIFTY-ONE

We eat. We head to town. We make a public statement. Or I do. Once again, Dalton stands beside me, arms crossed, so when the time comes for questions, no one opens their mouth. This time, though, Dalton says, "If you've got any, you have sixty seconds to ask. After that, if you come by the station or stop us in the street, I'll charge you with obstruction of justice."

"And what's the penalty for that?" someone asks.

"I haven't decided. Forty-five seconds left."

He does let it go a little longer than that — allowing two questions. The first is about whether there will be water restrictions until our stock is replenished.

"No restrictions," Dalton says. "But the price of water and wood just doubled. However, we'll be looking for people to join a logging expedition and folks to haul water from the springs. Double pay for that."

The next question is from Kenny, who

wants to know if there will be a moratorium on carpentry. He's not really asking so much as getting Dalton to announce it, so no one comes to him wanting work done. He'll be busy rebuilding the lumber shed with others.

Val shows up then. Not to the actual statement — God forbid, because someone might ask her a question — but immediately after, to tell Dalton that the council wants to speak to him.

"Come on," he says to me.

"The council only wants —" Val begins.

"Too bad. Butler is in charge of the case, and presuming that's what they want to talk about, this will be a hell of a lot faster than passing on questions through me. Now, run ahead and get them on the line. We're a little busy here."

The council is one faceless guy on a static-stuffed radio frequency. The others are apparently listening, probably by teleconference, but we only hear from that one guy — Phil.

"We've received a case update from Valerie," Phil says after she introduces us, cutting off my hello.

"And there's nothing more *we* can add," Dalton says. "Detective Butler just issued a statement. There were no questions other than housekeeping shit. Now, the longer we're on this call, the longer we're not investigating the crime."

"Crimes," Phil says, emphasizing the plural. "You seem to have a lot of them, Eric."

"Yeah, we do. Weird, isn't it?" Dalton muses. "The few people here who've committed crimes had justification. Otherwise, we wouldn't let them in, right?" He continues before Phil can answer. "Mick's death was probably unconnected to the other murders —"

"Which is worse, isn't it? Two killers working in Rockton suggests an outbreak."

Dalton snorts. "Yeah. A contagious homicide rash. What happened last night was about those damned drugs you aren't interested in helping me clean up."

"Because, relatively speaking, rydex is no more dangerous than alcohol. Even less so, given that you average an alcohol-related death every eighteen months. It's the price you pay for isolation."

I clear my throat. "If you have questions on last night's events — or on the other case —"

"No, Detective Butler, we do not. We trust you have the other matter in hand. We also agree with Sheriff Dalton that last night was the very unfortunate result of recreational drug use. We've decided on a verdict."

"Verdict?" I say. "I've barely begun investigating."

"And if there is any sign that our decision is wrong, you may continue your investigation. For now, we declare Diana Berry guilty —"

"Whoa! Wait! You can't —"

"We can. We have. Our sentence is simple and fair, and if we are mistaken in our verdict, there is little harm done. Your friend will simply be removed from the community. Returned home."

"Returned . . ." I struggle to my feet, feeling like the floor has turned to rubber under them. "No, you can't. . . . Her ex . . . If she leaves, then I have to go to protect her." *Which I failed to do here.*

Dalton rubs his mouth and then says, "There's no reason . . ."

I wait two seconds for him to go on. Then I finish it for him. "No reason for me to stay."

His eyes widen. "What? No. I . . ." He rises. "Detective Butler and I have to discuss this. We'll step out —"

"No need," Phil says. "What Eric is trying to say is that there's no reason for you to accompany Diana home because she's not in any danger. Diana Berry did not come here because her ex-husband was stalking and beating her. She's here because she conspired with him to steal a million dollars from her employers."

I stare at the radio. Just stare.

Phil continues. "They engineered the situation to persuade you to come here. Graham convinced Diana that her employers had

468

discovered the theft, which appears to be false. He simply wanted her out of the way."

"That's — that's not —"

"Ask Eric."

"I never said —" Dalton begins.

"You contacted your father and asked him to look into it. Did you really think those calls were private, Eric? Nothing you do is private. We suspected you were checking residents, and we tapped his line to confirm it."

Dalton looks ill. His gaze flicks to me and then away. "I'll explain it all to Casey. Just let —"

"That isn't our concern. Diana is here under false pretenses, and therefore, under the provisions of her agreement, we may evict her. We were already considering whether to do so. The fact she is suspected — strongly suspected — of both murder and arson has settled the matter. Sheriff Dalton will escort her out tomorrow morning."

We've left Val's house. I'm heading for Diana's to . . . break it to her? Confront her?

I remember the night Diana was attacked, when Graham looked right into that camera and spoke to me. Made me feel helpless and impotent, unable to help her.

He played me.

No, *they* played me.

I'm halfway to Diana's before I realize Dalton is following. He's a half step back and hasn't said a word since we left Val's. When I turn on him, he starts, as if expecting a right hook to the jaw.

"Is it true?" I say.

"About Diana?" He hesitates. "Yeah. She —"

"I mean all of it. That you got your father to investigate, and you've known the truth for a while and never mentioned it to me."

His mouth opens and from the way he shifts forward, I think I'm about to get a long-winded excuse. But then he pulls back and says only, "Yeah."

"That's what Diana meant earlier. You'd threatened, if she ever used rydex again, you'd tell me she'd lied about the reason she's here. You were blackmailing her."

Anyone else would at least try to wriggle out of it. Dalton says, "Yeah."

"Why?"

"Because you didn't need to know that you came here to help her and it was all a lie. You'd already cooled your friendship, so I didn't see the point of hurting you, and if I was wrong, then . . ." He shoves his hands into his pockets and rocks back, and when the next words come, they look painful. "Then I'm sorry, Casey. I'm sorry if I fucked up."

He didn't fuck up. I've been finally crawling out of the hole I dropped into a decade ago. I want out of that hole, and I needed the cushion of lies for a little while longer, because this hurts. Hell and damn, this hurts.

"You suspected from the start, didn't you?" I say.

"Yeah."

"You suspected *both* of us of lying."

"It was too coincidental. For twelve years, no one bothers you, and then all of a sudden, you're *both* in trouble? Yours was the story I was more concerned about, though."

"Because I'm the one you had to work with."

"I thought you and the bartender staged the attack. So the council's people investigated, and I double-checked all their work, and I had my father do the same."

"Wouldn't it make more sense to have *Kurt* attack *me* and blame the Saratori family?"

He shrugs. "Maybe he offered to take the bullet for you. Maybe you knew it'd be tougher to get in up here if you were injured. But, yeah, that was one thing that suggested it wasn't faked. Anyway, no one found any evidence you'd staged it. And the fact you tried to get Diana in without you? Made no sense if your story was false. I wasn't completely happy, but then I saw that you honestly didn't want to be here. Didn't want to be anywhere, really, but you weren't relieved or happy or whatever I'd expect if you'd pulled one over on us."

"Diana was, though. When did you start

seriously investigating her?"

"I asked my father to look into it when I went to pick you up. By the time we went back to Dawson City, he'd found out about the missing money and the ex who had just paid off some serious debts. He also got proof they'd reunited — overnight trips and stuff."

Got another training seminar this weekend. At least the company is investing in me, huh?

He continues. "The Saratori thing really was a coincidence — one she took advantage of. And it did help you. I gave her that much. Bringing you along. Getting you out of danger. So I wasn't completely ready to write her off. I thought maybe there was another explanation for the money thing. And if she was back with her ex, why be screwing everything in pants here? Then I heard a rumor that she'd gotten wasted and talked about what she and Graham did, how she doesn't think he'll be waiting with the money when she gets back."

"Really? What a shock. So sleeping around was revenge." I take a deep breath. "Is this what Isabel was talking about last night? She heard the same rumor about why Diana is here?"

He nods. Then he looks to one side, and I notice Beth there. She's stopped, as if she was about to retreat.

"Sorry," she says. "I saw you two and wanted to give you the full autopsy report.

But I . . . I guess that can wait."

"How much did you hear?" Dalton asks, and she blanches, though there's no accusation in his voice.

"Not much, but . . . I already knew. I was going to speak to you about it today, Eric."

"Fuck," he says. "Did everyone hear that damned rumor?"

"Rumor? No. Diana told me. When I got her back home after the fire, she was in shock and, possibly, in pain. I gave her something and she, well, it must have reacted with the rydex. She got confused. She thought I was Casey and confessed what she did to her."

"She confessed," I say.

She nods, but I didn't phrase it as a question. It is no longer a question.

"If you like, I can be the one to tell Diana she has to go home," Dalton says, in a tone that says he already knows my answer but he'll offer anyway.

I shake my head and continue to Diana's apartment.

FIFTY-TWO

I want to do this alone. Beth won't let me.

"She's unstable, Casey, and last night and the drugs have pushed her over the edge. I'd really rather not sedate her again. Eric can restrain her, if need be, while you calm her down and make it clear she has no choice."

So they come with me but stay outside the bedroom. Dalton positions himself at the door, where Diana — resting in bed — can't see him.

Diana and I talk for a few minutes. That's not me avoiding the conversation. It's me unable to roar in, guns blasting, and demand answers. That will never be me, no matter how much I'm hurting.

I have no idea what we talk about. I answer her questions on auto-reply and ask some of my own without processing her answers. Finally, when she's calm, I say, "You have to leave, Di," as gently as I can.

"Leave?" She's still foggy from the drugs, and her face screws up. "You mean move?

Because of Jen? She complained about my screaming?"

"No, Di. You have to leave Rockton."

"Wh-What? No." She sits up abruptly. "I didn't kill Mick. I swear to God, I didn't. Just think about it, Casey. Why would I? Even if I was drunk enough to hit on him, Mick doesn't mess around on Isabel. Girls have tried. They all fail."

"They're kicking you out because you violated the terms of your agreement."

She stares at me and then says, "How? By having sex? Getting drunk? Using dex a couple times? Hell, by those standards, you and that fucked-up sheriff are the only people who still belong here."

"You came here under a pretense."

She stops. Her mouth opens. Shuts. Then, tentatively, "A what?" as if she's hoping she's wrong about the meaning of the word.

"A false reason. You and Graham staged your attack to make it seem your life was in danger."

"What? No. How can you even — You honestly think —"

She can't get the rest out, and I should seize on her horrified sputtering as proof that everyone else is wrong. But it's exactly that sputtering that tells me they aren't.

"You've seen how he treats me," she says. "To even suggest I'm lying about that . . . ?"

"Oh, I know Graham treated you like shit.

475

I also know that you can't quit him. You reunited again, and he convinced you to solve both your financial situations by stealing from your employer."

Her mouth works again. "S-Steal?"

"We have proof."

"You mean *he* has proof."

I don't need to ask who *he* is. I shake my head. "Di, don't do this. It isn't Eric —"

"So it's him over me?" She gives a harsh laugh. "Typical. The new boyfriend doesn't like your girlfriends? Dump them. God, women can be such bitches to each other."

I struggle for calm. "First, Eric is my boss, not my boyfriend. Second, I have never, ever, *ever* thrown you over for a guy. Which is more than I can say —" I stop myself. Won't play the blame game. "I'm sorry you feel that way, but —"

"God, you're such a cold *bitch*. You don't give a shit about anyone but yourself."

Dalton strides through the doorway, but Beth barrels past him, her face taut with rage.

"Bitch? You're calling *her* a —"

I grasp Beth's arm. "I've got this."

"No, Casey. I'm sorry. I know you think you deserve to be treated like crap, but you don't." She turns to Diana. "It wasn't enough to lie to get yourself in here. You had to bring a friend, so you wouldn't be alone. Casey doesn't like to complain, even when she has damned good reason, so I'm going to do it

476

for her. The real issue isn't that you lied to get into Rockton. It's what you did to get her in."

"I don't know —"

"You hired some Italian thug to make Casey think the Saratoris were after her."

"Wh-What? How would I —"

"Your ex set it up. That's what you told me when you were under the rydex and the pain meds. You confessed."

I stand there, behind Beth, my knees feeling like they're about to give way. I look at Dalton, but he's staring at Beth, as stunned as I am. Then he catches a glimpse of my expression, and he moves up behind me, his hand going against my back as if to steady me, and I need that hand, God I need it. I sway slightly, and the hand moves around my waist, holding me still.

"You're a lying bitch," Diana says to Beth.

"We have proof," Dalton says. "The council found the guy Graham hired, and he talked."

He's bluffing, but Diana buys it, saying, "He was only supposed to scare them. That's what Graham told me. The guy would wave his gun and maybe fire it off and then run after he delivered his message."

"And you actually believed that?" Dalton snorts.

The look Diana turns on him isn't disbelief. It's hate. She glowers as if he's responsible for all this. Dalton's responsible. Beth's responsible. Graham's responsible. I'm responsible. Everyone except Diana herself is responsible.

"Well, then, I guess I'm not the only one leaving, am I?" Diana says. "We're both here under false pretenses. So we're both getting kicked out."

Beth slaps her. The sound comes so suddenly, both Dalton and I jump.

"You accuse Casey of being a stone bitch?" Beth says. "You screwed up your life. Made bad choices and had to come here. Except you didn't want to come alone. So you dragged your best friend —"

"She *needed* this!" Diana says. "For twelve years, she's barely even had a pulse." She turns to me. "It's not just guilt over Blaine and looking over your shoulder for Saratori's men. You want to believe you bounced back after what happened in that alley, but no one bounces back from something like that. You needed to get away more than I did."

"Who are you to decide that?" Beth says. "Casey was doing just fine. Homicide detective before her thirtieth birthday? That's a hell of an achievement, and she loved her job. She'd also met a man she cared about very much."

"The bartender?" Diana snorts. "The only thing she cared about was that he was good in bed and he looked good *in* one."

478

"Then why is she still wearing his necklace?"

"Can we not do this?" I say. "Please?"

"The point I'm making, Casey," Beth says, "is that you were doing fine when Diana upended your life. I know you've been making the best of it, but —" She exhales. "If there's anything good to come out of this mess, it's this: you can go home. The council will fix the issue with your job, and I'm sure your boyfriend will be happy you're back."

I stare at her. I haven't even considered the fact I can go back now, because there is nothing to consider. Beth's wrong. I wasn't on the road to happiness down south. Hell, I hadn't even found the map yet.

I'm also damned sure Dalton isn't going to let me walk out on his investigation. But he hasn't said a word.

"Casey?" he says finally.

He's waiting for an answer. Because it's up to me. Totally my call. He doesn't care one way or the other, and after the sucker punch of Beth's revelation, this feels like someone grinding his fist in the same spot.

"Butler?"

"I . . . I need to think about it."

Silence. Then, "You need to think about it," each word enunciated so slowly and so coldly, it snaps like an icicle.

I turn to Dalton, and I see that same ice in his gray eyes. Cold anger and hurt, and I realize he *wasn't* saying he didn't care if I went. He was wondering why I hadn't jumped in to say I'm not leaving. Now he looks at me, the chill increasing with every passing second. Then he turns and walks out.

"Eric!" I stride after him, but Beth grabs my arm.

"He's fine, Casey. He's not going to be thrilled about you leaving midcase, but this isn't about him."

"No," I say. "It's about me, and I have no intention of leaving."

A look crosses her face. Confusion, it seems. Then she manages a tentative smile. "Good." She hugs me, and it's awkward, because neither of us is the hugging type, but she whispers, "I'm glad to hear it," and I realize she wasn't saying she didn't care if I left, only that she'd understand if I did.

"I should talk to Eric," I say, turning away.

"Let him go," Beth says. "He's stressed out and exhausted. Better he walks it off in the woods. Take some time and think about this before you tell him you aren't leaving. Be one hundred percent sure."

I nod and say I'm going to go think about it and maybe speak to Anders, and she smiles at that and says, "Yes, go talk to Will. I'll look after Diana." She mouths, "With sedatives," and offers me a smile, which I force myself to return before I take off . . . after Dalton.

FIFTY-THREE

Of course I'm going after Dalton. There's no doubt in my mind that I'm staying in Rockton, and I need to tell him that. He did not, however, head out for a quiet walk in the woods. I'm halfway across town when I hear the roar of an ATV and look to see him on one, ripping into the forest.

I don't have time to get an ATV. I know the path he's on, and the next one over will let me cut him off if I run. So I run as fast as I can, ignoring the stares and the calls of "Casey?" and "Detective?"

One of the militia guys tries to come after me, alarmed, but I yell back, "I just need to talk to Eric. He didn't take his radio," and he nods and waves away the concerns of anyone else who finds it troubling that their detective is running like a madwoman for the woods.

The paths converge about a half mile in, so it's no short sprint. But I manage to make it to the convergence point just in time to see him ripping around a bend. When he spots me, he's off the ATV almost before it comes to a stop.

"Get the hell back to town," he shouts to be heard over the engine.

I shake my head. "I want to talk —"

"No. You know the rules. Get your ass back to town. Now."

I loop past him and shut off the ATV. "I want to talk."

"And I don't."

I walk over to him and look up. "You're overreacting, Eric."

I expect a flash of rage and a hot denial. Instead, he says, teeth clenched, "Yes, which is why I'm out here. By myself. And why I don't want to talk."

I back up to the ATV and perch on it. He looks down the side path, the one he's just come from, and I know he's ready to walk away, leaving me with the ATV, so I can get safely back to town.

I take the keys from the ignition and pitch them into the forest.

"What the hell?" he says.

"If you walk away, so will I. In the other direction. Which leaves me out in the forest alone."

His eyes narrow. "That's not very mature."

"Just following your lead, Sheriff."

I get a glower for that.

"I admitted I was overreacting," he says. "It's been a fucking long day. I'm exhausted, and I'm on edge. This morning you said if I got kicked out of Rockton, you'd come with me, and then, a few hours later, you're thinking about leaving? What the hell was that this morning, Casey? Why would you say you'd come with me —" He breaks off, shaking his head sharply as he steps back, putting distance between us. "I'm tired, and I'm overreacting, and I'm going to ask you, again —"

"You never said I could stay."

"What?"

I slide off the ATV. "Twice last night, I said I *would* leave with you . . . if you weren't going to kick me out after six months. You never said you'd changed your mind."

"We were joking around. Fuck, how could you even think I still planned to send you back?"

"Because you've never said you changed your mind. Because you don't threaten unless you mean it, and until you say I'm allowed to stay, I'm going to presume I'm still on probation. I just found out that my best friend betrayed me. Completely and utterly betrayed me. Then Beth — whom I consider a new friend — tells me I have no reason to stay, and that stung. But you know what hurt a whole helluva lot more, Eric? When you let Beth go on about me leaving and said nothing."

"I was waiting for you —"

"To say I wasn't leaving. And I was waiting

for you to say I can stay. So it was a misunderstanding, and I'm here to clear it up. There's nothing for me to think about. I don't want to leave. I have work to do —"

"Work to do . . ."

"Yes, and I'd never leave you in the lurch like that."

"It's not about leaving me in the lurch, Casey. Goddamn it. This is about . . ." He looks away and lowers his voice. "Maybe you *should* go home."

"What?"

He groans and runs his hands through his hair. "I don't mean that. Fuck, of course I don't. If you're happy here, you can stay as long as you want. I just —" He turns away. "We need to get back to town."

I get in front of him. "No, we need to talk. If you don't want me in Rockton —"

"Of course I want you here," he says. "That's the fucking —"

He bites it off and turns again, ready to leave the other way, but I block him again.

"Don't do this, Casey," he says, his voice low. "Just let me go."

"And leave me here? In the forest?" It's a low blow, and the turmoil in his eyes almost makes me regret it, but I'm determined to hash this out.

I step closer to him.

"Back up," he says, barely unclenching his jaw.

484

"So you can run away?" I say. "No. If you don't want me here, Eric, you're damned well going to tell me now, not leave me dangling —"

I don't see it coming. One second I'm telling him off, and the next I'm against a tree, his hands on my hips, his mouth coming down to mine. There's one split second of *What the hell?* followed by another second of *Shit, this is a bad idea,* but by then he's kissing me, and I don't really give a damn where it came from or how lousy an idea it is.

He's kissing me, and that's all I think about, all I *can* think about, because it's no tentative *Is this all right?* kiss. Nor does it go from zero to sixty in five seconds flat. It starts at sixty and stomps down on the accelerator. I'm against the tree, and he's kissing me like I'm the first woman he's seen in ten years and he's not wasting one moment getting this kiss to its ultimate destination.

His hands are under my shirt, running up my bare sides and around my back, pulling me against him. Once, when he has to stop for breath, he gives a ragged, "I don't want to do this," but before I can even decipher the words, he's kissing me again, as if the sentiment didn't pass from his lips to his brain.

He says it again, as he breaks the kiss when my belt doesn't unfasten quite as fast as he'd like, but this time it's only, "Don't want to," before he continues wanting to and doing so, yanking out my belt and pulling at the button on my jeans, and kissing me so hard my lip catches in his teeth, and there's a jolt of pain, just enough to zap the top layer of lust from my brain, enough for me to hear his words again.

I don't want to do this.

Don't want to.

I could ignore that. He's leading, so I can just let him take this where he so obviously intends to take it, where he so obviously *wants* to take it, despite his words.

I'm squelching my doubts as hard as he is. I want this. Hell and damn, I want this. My whole body ignites at his kiss, at his touch, at the feel of him against me, and I want more. More, more, more, and *now.*

I don't want to do this.

Don't want to.

I shudder, and he takes that for passion and stops tugging my jeans over my hips and lifts me up onto him instead, straddling him as he pushes against me, his hands going to my face, holding it between them as he kisses me. A two-second break in the momentum for a sweet, deep kiss, and that's all I need. One moment's delay and a sweet kiss to remind me that this isn't a stranger I met in a bar, quick sex in the back hall, never to see each other again.

This is a guy I care about, and some part of him doesn't want to do this, and if I let him, it'll be guilt and shame and *That was a mistake* and *It won't happen again* and awkwardly avoiding each other. And it'll be more than that. It'll be heartbreak, because I care about him, more than I really want to care about any guy, and when it's over, I'll have sacrificed something good for five minutes of passion.

His hands drop to my waist again, pushing my jeans down, the lust reigniting, the kiss deepening, his breath coming harsh as he sees the end in sight and —

I pull back. "No, Eric."

He doesn't seem to notice, just pulls me to him again, pushing between my legs as he flips open the button on his —

"No, Eric." I put my hand on his chest and push him. "Stop."

He blinks. Then he pulls back, sucking in breath, and before I can even catch a glimpse of his expression, he steps away, letting me drop, and then turns and strides off.

FIFTY-FOUR

Dalton storms off and leaves me struggling to get my jeans on, and I feel like I'm back in tenth grade, kissing Matthew McCormack behind the school. When his hands slid under my shirt and I pushed them out, and he took off in a snit, never to speak to me again. Which is understandable at sixteen. It is not understandable at thirty, and as I watch Dalton walk away without a backward glance, I slam my fist into the tree, which is absolutely the stupidest thing I could have done, and I bite my lip to keep from yowling.

I cradle my hand, eyes closed, rage and frustration whipping through me so hard the pain almost feels good.

Damn him. God fucking damn him. And damn me, too, for not stopping him the moment he pushed me against that tree.

If you didn't want it, asshole, why did you start it? Start it and then tell me twice you didn't want to, like I'm a witch who cast a spell over you? Sweetest damn thing a guy has ever said to me.

I'm going to fuck you, but I really, really don't want to.

I almost slam my fist into the tree again. I settle for stomping the ground, and not caring if I look like a five-year-old throwing a tantrum. I *should* throw a tantrum. My life needs more of them. More? Hell, I can't even remember the last time I lost my temper, and God knows I have good reason.

Everything that brought me here was a lie. When Diana refused to go to the hospital, I felt so bad, so fucking bad for her. She was so beaten down and yet so strong. Strength? Bullshit. It was lies. Lies so she could be with that sadistic bastard.

She brought me here for the same damned reason as always. I was her rock. The dependable friend who would be there for her, no matter what. Time to go to college? Find one near Casey, so you don't need to be alone. Can't shake your ex? Convince Casey to move to a new city with you. Need to escape after stealing a million dollars? Run far, far away . . . but don't forget to take Casey. Diana's security blanket. Diana's guard dog.

I take a deep breath and look at the path. I don't want to go back to Rockton. Not yet. I want to do exactly what Dalton is doing. Walk it off out here, in the stillness and the silence, where no one can interrupt and say, "Hey, what's wrong?" and force me to put on a happy face. I'm hurt and I'm angry and I want to indulge that. For once, I want to indulge that.

I consider searching for the ATV keys, but I'm not even sure where I threw them. I still can't believe I did that. Completely ir-responsible. And I don't regret it for a second. Fuck all this. I'm going to start being a little irresponsible and immature. I've earned it.

That does not mean I stalk off the path. Nor do I head *away* from town. I'm being reckless, not stupid. Yet I get barely twenty steps along the trail before I see Dalton in the distance, just standing there with his back to me.

I'm cutting across to avoid him, and I know exactly where I'm heading — I'm on the proper angle — when I hear a twig crack behind me. I turn and see a distant figure. It goes still, mostly hidden behind a tree, but I recognize the build and the height and the glimpse of dark blond hair. Dalton.

Asshole.

Yes, following me when I've wandered from the trail does not make him an asshole. Under any other circumstances, it'd be a considerate thing to do. But in this mood, I resent the implication that I can't handle this on my own and change direction, planning to stay off-path a little longer.

Am I hoping to provoke him? Bring him

over here, snarling and snapping? Yep, because I'm in the mood to snarl and snap back. When I do immature, I don't do it by halves.

Except there is a reason I don't do immature and irresponsible. Because eventually it does cross the line into reckless and stupid. I'm so focused on goading Dalton by staying off-path that I'm not paying nearly enough attention to where I'm going. Then I stop catching those distant glimpses of him, and I'm sure he's sneaking up — I even hear twigs and needles crackle nearby — so I pick up my pace, weaving through the forest, hell-bent on annoying the shit out of him.

That's when the noises stop, and they stay stopped, and I walk for a few minutes more before I realize Dalton's not there. I lean against a tree, waiting for him to catch up. Only he doesn't, and the woods are silent, and I'm alone.

I head off in the direction that I'm sure will take me toward town. After about ten minutes, the terrain changes, growing rockier, which means I'm nowhere near Rockton. That's when I realize I'm lost.

I mentally call myself a whole lot of nasty names, but I don't panic. I retrace my steps. Just get back on the path. The problem? I'd been so intent on luring Dalton out that I'd paid little attention to my surroundings, and

I have no idea if I'm actually retracing my steps.

Still, I try to be smart about it. I use the tricks Dalton taught me for tracking — broken twigs, impressions in the soft earth, scuff marks in the rocky dirt. I find deer tracks and tufts of fur and that's it, and I have no idea —

I spot Dalton. He's twenty feet away, in the shade, and all I can see is the dark jacket and the color of his hair. Then he pulls back a little, as if realizing I'm watching, and I see his profile — the set of his jaw, the shape of his nose.

I take a deep breath. Then I abandon my pride and call, "Eric?"

No answer.

I start toward him. "Okay, maybe you provoked me, but yes, taking off was stupid. I've gotten turned around, and I have no idea where I am."

Silence.

I keep walking. "You can chew me out later. I deserve it. For now, let's just get back to town. We've had a shitty day, and we're both out of sorts and making stupid choices. So let's just —"

I round the two trees . . . and he's not there.

"Eric?"

I hear a twig crack one second too late. Hands grab me from behind, one around my waist, the other gripping my chin, as if ready to snap my neck. A body presses against my back and . . . the smell. God, the smell.

The hands wrench me around, shoving me back against a tree. The cold of a blade presses against my throat, and when I look up at my captor, I see . . .

Dalton. I see Dalton. His steel-gray eyes. His nose. His jawline. But the dark blond hair falls to his shoulders. A beard covers his cheeks and chin. Yet it still looks like Dalton, and with that, I have my answer. I know what's going on, what's been going on since last night, when we were on my balcony, watching the northern lights as Dalton told me a story about a fox.

I'm sleeping. I fell asleep on that balcony, and everything that's happened since — Mick's death, the fire, Diana's betrayal, Dalton's kiss — it's dream and nightmare woven into one, and this is proof of it.

But this man is not Dalton. I see that now, beyond the hair and beard. His eyes are set deeper. Shaped differently. His cheekbones aren't as high or as prominent.

This man looks like him; this man is not him. That's all that matters.

Yet it isn't all that matters. There's a knife to my throat and my hands are free and the gun is right there, under my open jacket, and I know, beyond a shadow of a doubt, that I could shoot this man before he slits my throat. But I don't, because the man with the knife to my throat may not be Dalton, but he's related to him.

That's when I see his jacket. A dark military-style coat.

"Jacob," I whisper.

"You know who I am? Good." His voice is rough, the words slightly off, with an odd accent. "I know who you are. Eric's girl."

"I work with Eric. In Rockton. I'm not his —"

The knife presses in. I struggle to control my breathing.

"I saw you kissing him," he says. "I've seen you before. Together. You're Eric's girl. I owe my brother. Now I can repay him."

Brother? Oh, shit. Shit, shit, shit.

I can hear Dalton's voice talking about Jacob. Telling me he's harmless. Absolutely harmless, he emphasized.

Dalton wouldn't lie about that. Nor would he leave his brother wandering out here in this condition.

I'm dreaming. I must be.

Jacob pulls back the knife, and I don't process the move. Don't wonder what he's doing. My gut foresees the strike, and the moment he moves, my fist hits his stomach and my other hand grabs my gun.

He falls back, and I kick him away, and I don't shoot. My brain assesses the threat, and I do not see the need to fire. There's a moment of relief, as if I've passed some test I was certain I'd fail. It only lasts a moment, because my kick isn't enough to knock him to the ground, and he's coming back up, knife slashing for my arm as I swing the gun at him.

Footsteps thunder behind me, and I instinctively twist, expecting attack from the rear.

"Jacob, no!"

It's Dalton, running for us. The distraction slows my strike, just for that heartbeat, and the knife slashes my arm. My gun still makes contact, but his attack has knocked mine into a glancing blow, and he only staggers back.

Jacob lunges at me, and I can't fire — the angle is wrong. I kick instead, and my foot connects. So does his knife, slashing my leg. We both go down. I bounce back, gun swinging up, but he's already in flight, stabbing me in the chest. Then he jerks back, the knife coming free as Dalton throws him aside.

"Stop," Dalton says, gun up, as Jacob tries to rise.

Jacob sees the gun. "You gonna shoot me, big brother?" He pulls his jacket open. "Go ahead. Can't be any worse than what you've done. Have you told her about that? Your girl there?"

"She isn't my —"

"She already tried that. I saw you kiss her. And now I know how to pay you back, brother."

"Pay me back? What the hell is going on, Jacob?"

"I've finally figured out exactly what you did to me." He starts walking backward. "I'm going to repay you, and if you want to stop me, you'd better pull that trigger."

Dalton's fingers flex, and I know he's thinking fast, thinking of what else he can do to stop Jacob, because he can't shoot him, not his brother. But if he lets him walk away and he attacks someone else?

I stumble backward and fall, gasping, hand clapped over my chest wound. Jacob takes off as Dalton runs to my side. Yes, I faked the fall, but when I try to rise again, blood gushes between my fingers and pain rips through me. Dalton yanks off his jacket and pushes it against the wound, saying, "I'm sorry, I'm so fucking sorry. It'll be okay. Everything will be —"

"Radio," I manage, and he curses at needing the reminder. He *did* bring it. He calls Anders. When there's no answer, his eyes widen, as he frantically pushes the Call button. Then we hear the hum of an ATV.

"I can . . . I can walk," I say, but he picks me up, pressing my hand against the jacket to hold it to my chest wound, and I feel blood rushing from my arm and my leg, but I say nothing, because he's already panicked enough, apologies rushing out on an endless loop of "I'm sorry, fuck, I'm sorry."

He runs, carrying me, as fast as he can manage. When he stumbles and I gasp, he slows, but that only makes the apologies come faster, and I tell him I'm okay, even though I know I'm not, the blood streaming, consciousness fading, my body shaking. I tell him anyway — *I'm fine, just fine* — and he keeps running until he staggers right in front of the ATV. Anders shouts, "Shit!" and brakes so fast he nearly vaults over the front.

As soon as the ATV stops, Dalton races over and lays me in the backseat.

"Holy shit," Anders says. "What —"

"Gotta get her back. Now."

"She's bleeding, Eric."

"I know!" Dalton snaps, and tries to shove Anders into the passenger seat, but the deputy pushes back, saying, "I mean that we need to stanch the bleeding first," and from the look on Dalton's face, you'd think I'd already bled out and it was all his fault. Curses and more apologies as he helps Anders get me out onto the ground.

"I've got this," Anders says.

"No, I —"

Anders holds him back, saying, "I've got it. You want to help? Give me your belt, your shirt . . ."

Dalton strips them off as Anders's gaze runs over me, assessing.

"Left thigh, right arm, upper right chest," I say.

"You're still with us," he says.

I nod. "Conserving energy. Chest worst. Didn't go in deep. Just . . ." I hiss in pain as I inhale.

"Relax and let me look."

I lie back. Dalton's tearing his shirt into strips as Anders pushes mine up over my ribs.

"There's water in the back," he says. "Eric —"

"Got it."

"Can I ask what the hell happened?"

Dalton hesitates. "It's my fault. I —"

"We got separated," I say. "I was attacked by a hostile."

"This close to town? Shit. We need to do something about them," Anders says grimly. "And we might need to reconsider the possibility our killer isn't from Rockton after all."

Dalton falters, the guilt and fear so strong it seems to paralyze him, as if he's back in that moment, facing his brother.

Facing his *brother.*

I haven't had time to make sense of that. I still don't. I only know that something is wrong with Jacob. Whatever Jacob says, Dalton's sin against him cannot warrant this level of vengeance. It just can't.

"Eric?" I say, and he snaps out of it, mumbling more apologies as he hurries over with the water.

Anders cleans and binds my wounds as best he can. With every light-headed dip toward darkness, I shake myself back, and I manage to stay conscious until they load me into the ATV. Then I lose the battle.

FIFTY-FIVE

I wake in bed. My bed. Beth is checking one of my dressings. Dalton's sitting on a chair he's carried up from downstairs. He's lost in thought, and startles when I croak, "How bad is it?"

"Could have been worse," Beth says.

I chuckle, which sends pain stabbing through me. "Damage report?"

She rattles it off matter-of-factly. Diana can call that cold, but it's how some of us process and deliver data best.

The leg and arm were both shallow cuts. They hadn't required stitches and shouldn't scar, but hell, it's not like I'd notice a few more anyway.

The chest wound isn't as shallow, but Dalton pulled Jacob off before the blade penetrated far. It scraped my rib, which kept it from nicking my lung. I'm not going to bounce off to work in the morning, but I'll be fine. In the meantime, the fact that I am relatively unconcerned about my injuries suggests I got a nice dose of opiates while I was unconscious. Beth confirms that.

"I also did a transfusion," Beth says. "I have blood in the clinic, but since you're a universal recipient and someone was very eager to make amends for getting separated in the woods, I did a direct transfusion."

It takes a moment for me to realize whom she meant. Yep, they are good drugs. I glance at Dalton, and realize the slightly dazed look on his face is more than guilt and exhaustion.

"You didn't need to do that," I say.

He says nothing.

"You should go home," I say. "Rest."

"Casey's right," Beth says. "I'll call Will to help you home."

"I'm fine."

"Eric . . . ," I say, and I start to insist, but I fade, slumping back onto the pillow. Beth tucks me in with, "Get some sleep. I'll send Eric home."

I wake to find Dalton still in the chair. Beth's gone, and he's alert enough now that when I open my eyes, he's at my bedside.

"Didn't obey the doctor's orders, I see."

"I understand if you don't want me here —"

"No," I say. "I do. But you look ready to drop."

"I'm staying."

"Okay." I shift so he can sit on the bed. After some prodding, he does.

I say, "No one else knows about Jacob, do they?"

He shakes his head.

"Was it a long time ago?" I ask. "The separation?"

He nods and then blurts, "If I'd had any idea he'd *ever* —"

"You have a brother in the forest, Eric. One of the hostiles is your *brother.*"

"He's not a —" He swallows the rest.

"Did it happen when you were kids?" I ask. He nods.

"I'm going to guess he was either taken from the town or he wandered off, got lost out there, and was taken in by settlers."

He pauses so long I don't think I'm going to get an answer. Then he says, "Something like that."

"And he blames you. Maybe you were with him when he got lost or he just blames you for not coming after him."

"Something like —" He runs his hands through his hair, head dropping as he lets out a noise between a growl and a groan. "Jacob's *not* a hostile. He's never been — What you saw out there — I don't know what's happening, but *that* is not my brother."

"Okay."

He waits for me to argue. When I don't, he shifts on the bed and faces me. "It happened when we were kids, like you said. By the time I saw him again, we were teenagers, and I tried to bring him to Rockton, but he wasn't interested, and maybe I should have dragged his ass in here and —"

He stops, breathing so fast he can't continue. He grips the bedspread, closes his eyes, and then continues, a little calmer. "The point is that he's always been welcome here, but he's not interested, and I respect that. As for what he blames me for . . . Yeah, I was a kid, and I made a mistake, and I thought I was doing the right thing, and . . ." He shakes it off. "Doesn't matter. He does blame me for the separation. But it's not like what you saw out there. *He's* not like that. Even the smell . . ."

"He might not have access to hot showers, but he usually takes better care of himself."

"*Much* better. Sure, we argue sometimes. About him being out there and me being here. But it's *arguing* — not swearing vengeance and threatening to kill —"

That fast breathing again. Anxiety and panic, and though I've never seen him like this, I recognize the signs. This is territory he avoids, like I avoid the subject of my past. It's the trigger that flips the switch from the hard-ass sheriff to the boy who lost his younger brother to the forest and hasn't ever gotten over it.

"We argue," he says. "That's it, and not

503

even much of that."

"You have contact with him. Like you said before."

He nods. "Plenty of contact. Social and otherwise. He trades meat and furs for things he can't get easily, like clothing and weapons. Maybe it's not exactly a normal relationship for brothers, but . . . fuck if I know what is." He makes a face, frustration mingled with embarrassment. He's right, of course. Anything he knows about sibling relationships comes from books. There's none of that in Rockton. Another reminder of how different his life is, and how very aware he is of that difference.

"It is what it is," he says. "And it's *not* like what you saw today. At all."

"When's the last time you talked to him?"

"Two days before you got here. He seemed fine. After we found Powys, I went out to speak to him, see if he knew anything, but he wasn't around. You heard Brent. That worried me, but then you spotted him when we went caving, so . . . I figured he was fine."

"He seemed okay the last time you talked with him?"

"Fuck, yeah."

"Taking care of himself?"

"Of course."

"How old is he?"

"Three years younger than me. Why?"

I tell him what I'm thinking. Schizophrenia.

Early adulthood onset, the sudden paranoia, the lack of interest in personal grooming. Dalton's well read enough to know what it is.

"I don't know if it can come on that fast," I say. "But it might have been a more gradual deterioration than it seems. I mean, he kept himself clean enough, but . . ."

"Yeah, living out there, the standards are different."

"And the fact that he *chooses* to live out there . . ."

"No," he says abruptly. "It may seem crazy to you, but it's a choice, and not a sign —" A sharp shake of his head, and he loses a little of his usual confidence, faltering as he says, "If I'd had any idea . . . I would have warned you . . ." He gets to his feet. "I'll take care of this. You're safe here, and you should get some sleep."

"I don't want —"

"Sleep," he says, and lowers himself into the chair. "I'm not going anywhere. We can talk later."

I stir from sleep, but not for long enough even to roll over and see if it's light out. I hear Dalton arguing with someone and think *situation normal.*

Then I remember it's far from normal as the last day floods back. Mick's death and the arson and the fact my best friend may have done both and she betrayed me and now

505

she has to leave, but then there was the forest and that kiss and then Jacob and a glimpse of another Eric Dalton, a side of him that I need to understand if I ever want to get closer to him, and that kiss, and dear God, am I actually even thinking about that, in light of everything that happened?

It's not as if a kiss somehow cancels out the horror and the pain, but it's easier to focus on, and I keep thinking of a poem I memorized in school, and I don't even remember why, but it wasn't an assignment. I think it just spoke to me, somehow.

Jenny kissed me when we met,
Jumping from the chair she sat in;
Time, you thief, who love to get
Sweets into your list, put that in!
Say I'm weary, say I'm sad,
Say that health and wealth have missed
  me;
Say I'm growing old, but add,
Jenny kissed me!

And I don't know why I'm thinking about that damned poem, except that I'm half asleep and still high from the morphine, and I'm listening to Dalton arguing with someone, and I'm glad he's feeling more himself, but I'm sad, too, because more himself means the rest has passed, and yet that's good, isn't it? Forget the kiss. It's silly. Inconsequential.

I have important things to occupy my mind and no time for that.

Say I'm weary, say I'm sad,
Say that my best friend betrayed me;
Say that I've been stabbed, but add,
Eric kissed me!

Seriously? Screw this. No matter how much pain I'm in, I'm not taking any more drugs. Good night.

FIFTY-SIX

I'm done with this shit. That's the thought filling my brain when I wake again. I went to sleep thinking about Dalton and that kiss, and I wake thinking about the exact same thing, but in a very different way.

He kissed me. It was 100 percent him, even as he was saying he didn't want it, and when I did the right thing and put a halt to it, how did he react? Stalked off in a snit after repeatedly lecturing me about being alone in the forest. He *left* me alone in the forest.

I'm pissed, and I'm going to let myself be pissed.

So when I wake and notice someone in the chair, I almost close my eyes again. Then I see it's Anders.

I rise and look around.

"Do you want me to get Eric?" he says.

"No," I say, perhaps a bit too vehemently. His brows shoot up, and I hurry on with, "It's fine. He needs a break."

"Sure as hell didn't want it, though. The

only reason he left was to tell the council they can go fuck themselves."

My brows lift.

Anders moves to sit on the bed. "They want him to take Diana tomorrow."

"I heard him arguing with someone downstairs. Was that the same thing?"

"Nah, that was Beth. She can . . ." He made a face. "You know what she's like with Eric. Trying to take care of him, mothering or whatever. She'd been pestering him to leave you alone and go rest, and he was already cranky about that. Then she tried telling him he shouldn't fight the council. That set him off. I feel a little sorry for her, but . . ." He shrugs. "She means well, but he *really* doesn't like her hovering and fretting over him, and she never takes the hint."

"Hmm." I shift in the bed, and I must wince, because Anders reaches for a bottle at my bedside.

"If that's morphine, the answer is no," I say. "I have work to do."

"Which you can't do if you're sweating with pain."

I wipe my forehead. It is indeed beaded with perspiration.

"Take a half dose," he says. "Then water and food."

"Speaking of hovering —"

"No, I'm *advising.* If you tell me to go to hell, I'll shut up."

"Okay, give me a half dose. What time is it?"

"Seven."

I look at the window and see twilight, which doesn't help. Before I can ask, Anders says, "It's morning."

"I'll take the drugs and any food you can scrounge up. Then I've got a list of people I want to interview."

"Um, you're not going to be leaving that bed for a few days, Casey."

"You can bring them to me."

He smiles, says, "Yes, ma'am," and pours my medicine.

I conduct two interviews before Dalton finds out. I hear his footsteps on the stairs, and I tense, waiting for the *What the hell are you doing?* Then he walks in, and I can tell by his expression the lecture is not forthcoming; I almost wish it was. He has that kicked-dog look from after Jacob's attack, when he'd been stumbling over himself to apologize.

He slips into the room and looks around, making sure we're alone before saying, "I, uh, hear you're conducting interviews from bed. Which is fine if you're up to it, but before your next one, we should talk."

"I'm busy, Eric, and I'd like you to go."

He rubs his chin. "That's a *fuck off,* isn't it?"

"No, it's a *please go away because I don't*

really want you here."

"Okay." He sits down.

"That's not —" I begin.

"You're angry, and you have every right to be. I will leave. Right after I tell you how sorry I am for what happened."

"You already did. Many times."

"I don't mean the stabbing. Of course, I'm sorry about that. I couldn't be *more* sorry. I mean what happened before that, which I didn't apologize for yesterday, because after Jacob, all I could think about was what he did. But what I did was inexcusable."

He waits a moment and then looks up at me.

"If you're expecting an argument, you're not going to get it," I say.

Dalton nods. "Yeah, okay. Understood. I just want to say that's not me, that I hope you know I'm not like that, and I don't know what the hell came over me."

"Yes, I know it wasn't how you normally behave, but you still did it. You said to hell with what's right, to hell with me, and did whatever you pleased."

His gaze is on the bedspread now as he shakes his head. "Yeah, no excuse. So . . ." He lifts his head and runs a hand through his hair. "How do we get past this, Casey? Maybe that's a stupid question. Maybe I should know the answer and not be asking you, but I don't, so I am, because all I can think to

511

say is that I'm so fucking sorry, and if I could undo it, I would. It will never happen again."

"You're right it won't happen again. Because I'm never going in the forest alone with you ever again. Not after that."

He nods, gaze lowered. "I know. But it won't happen here, either. I won't . . ." He clears his throat. "Whatever's going on with us . . . I mean, for me . . . It just . . . won't happen again. I promise."

Silence, as I try to make sense of that.

"You *are* apologizing for taking off on me in the forest, right?" I say.

His head shoots up. "What?"

"For stomping off in a huff and leaving me alone out there."

His eyes widen. "Hell, no. I didn't — I walked away, sure, but not far. I figured you could still see me. I was just . . . I was getting some distance. Cooling off. Not because I was angry. Just . . . cooling down. When I turned around, you were gone, and I didn't blame you, considering what I did."

"*What* did you do?"

He looks at me, part confusion and part wariness, as if I'm asking such a silly question that it must be a trick. Then he shifts his weight, looking uncomfortable, and says, "Forcing myself . . . you know. The kiss and . . . pushing. I didn't mean to, and I thought you were reciprocating, but clearly I misinterpreted, and when you told me to

512

stop, I didn't."

"You *did* stop."

"Only after you said it twice and pushed me away. I heard you the first time, and I don't know why I didn't stop." He shakes his head. "Fuck, yeah, I know. I was pretending I didn't hear in case you didn't mean it, and if you did mean it, then you'd say it again, only you shouldn't *need* to say it again and . . ." He exhales. "I fucked up, Casey. I really fucked up, and all I can say is that I'm sorry, and it'll never happen again."

I'm quiet for a moment, considering my words, then say, carefully, "I *did* reciprocate, Eric. You're the one who didn't want it."

"I —"

"Twice you said — very clearly — that you didn't want it. I'm not going to have sex with a guy who'll regret it ten minutes later. I'm especially not going to have sex with my boss if he'll regret it ten minutes later."

He frowns, and I can see he's honestly working through why that would be a bigger problem.

"Oh," he says after a moment. "Yeah, I guess . . . I hadn't thought — Fuck, I wasn't thinking *at all.*"

"You were stressed, and that was the outlet. I understand."

"I . . . No, it wasn't . . ." He's working this through, too, furiously. I'm suddenly exhausted, and I want to say, *Go, Eric. Just go.*

"Regardless of why you kissed me," I say, "I didn't have a problem with it. I didn't have a problem with it taking a second no to stop you. At that speed, it's harder to throw on the brakes. I did have a problem with you walking off, because I thought you just got pissy at me saying no. If that isn't the case —"

"It's not. *At all.* I was angry with myself —"

"Then I accept that, and I'd like to move on. My next interview should be here any second."

"I wanted to kiss you," he blurts. "When I said I didn't, I . . ." More hands through hair. Then hands shoved in pockets. "What I meant is that as much as I wanted what we were doing, I know we shouldn't. It's just a really bad idea for you and me to start something, and yeah, maybe that wasn't starting something for you, maybe it was just sex, but it was different for me, and —" He exhales hard. "Shit. Stop babbling. Okay. The point is that even if you were interested, there's a lot of crap in my life, and you don't need to share that."

Silence ticks past as I mentally vacillate between saying what I want to say and keeping my mouth shut.

Mentally vacillate? Hell, no. That makes it sound so calm and reasoned. My brain swirls, half of it screaming at me to do it, just do it, stop being such a wimp and take the leap, and the other half screaming at me to keep my mouth shut, don't go there, don't open myself up.

I raise my gaze to his. "And what if I want to share that?"

A one-second pause. A split second of surprise and something I can't quite catch. Then he looks away, and I feel that break like a punch. *See? See? I told you to keep your damned mouth shut, Casey.*

"You tell me I need to go after what I want," I say. "But this isn't about what I want, is it? It's not about whether I'm willing to share your shit. You don't want to share it."

"It isn't —"

"My next interview will be here any moment. Please go down and let him in."

"I —"

"Go, Eric. Now."

FIFTY-SEVEN

Back to the case. Because there is, you know, despite all the personal drama, still a killer to be found. Possibly two.

I already know Kenny had seen both Mick and a woman matching Diana's description heading into the woodshed. I question him thoroughly, but there's little more to get than that. One other person saw Mick heading toward that side of town. Another saw Diana. Again, not terribly useful, though I do glean a few more details. First, Mick and Diana were not seen together. Second, the witness who saw Diana definitely spotted her alone, meaning no one forced her there.

I continue interviewing people all day, but I don't get much farther. I confirm that Diana had been with the people she'd claimed to be with. She'd left at the time she'd claimed to leave. She'd been alone. She'd been seen heading in the direction she'd indicated, also alone. As for Mick, those at the Roc that night had seen it play out as Isabel claimed

— Mick left at eleven, about an hour after they disappeared into the back room together.

Dalton stays downstairs during my interviews. Whenever he has to leave, Anders stops by, and I suspect that's no accident. Dalton isn't taking chances. There's a killer in town and so his injured detective is under full-time guard.

It's Dalton who's down there when Petra comes by partway through my interviews. I hear them talking, and I sit upright. One thing I haven't had so far is actual visitors, so while it's possible Petra just needed to talk to Dalton, I'm hoping . . .

Light footsteps sound on the stairs and then a head peeks through the half-open door. "Hey, heard you're playing hooky, faking a knife attack."

"It's the only way to get out of work around here."

"No kidding, huh?" She sits on the edge of the bed and puts a rolled-up sheet of paper on the nightstand. When I glance at it, she says, "Look later. I hate being around when people see my work. There's that really awkward moment when they have to look excited no matter how much they hate it."

"Doesn't that go for any gift?"

She laughs. "If you're a nice person, I guess it does. So, how are you doing?"

"Healing. As knife attacks go, it wasn't too bad."

She shakes her head. "And otherwise? How are you doing?"

"You mean . . ."

"Diana."

I sigh and lean back against the pillows. "Besides feeling like a complete idiot? My best friend gets back together with her abusive ex, and I don't realize it? They steal a million bucks, and I don't know it? They have my lover shot, and I never suspect a thing? Some detective I am, huh?"

"I think you're wearing that whip out."

"Yeah, I know. I just feel so stupid. It's like reading a detective novel and you hit the end and the killer is a complete surprise, but when you reread, you realize all the clues were right there. Given what I do for a living, I should have seen them."

"You did. I know you did."

I shift position. "And doesn't that make it worse?"

"No, it makes you human. She was your friend. You wanted to think the best of her. You saw flaws, but we all have flaws. It's not as if she befriended you a few months ago to put this all in motion. You *were* friends. It just may have not been the healthiest friendship."

"To put it mildly . . ."

Petra continues. "I've had toxic friends. I've even been the toxic friend, when things were bad, really bad, and I needed so much and

I . . ." She stops and swallows. "And this is about you."

I look at her. "It doesn't have to be."

She manages a smile. "It will be, for now. I know Isabel would say confession is good for the soul . . . though I suspect she means so she can use your secrets against you, rather than because it's therapeutic."

I laugh softly. "Probably."

"But sometimes confessing trauma just feels like reliving it, you know?"

I think of all those times in a therapist's chair, retelling my story. It wasn't just about confessing. It wasn't just about that magical thinking, testing fate to see if I deserved to be caught. It was about flagellating myself, exactly like Petra said a few minutes ago. Reliving it so I could torment myself with every excruciating moment.

She continues, "I think my ten minutes are up, which means Eric will come tromping up those stairs at any moment. You need to mourn Diana, Casey. Let yourself mourn her. She *was* your friend. No matter what."

We hear Dalton's footsteps then and Petra leaves, and while she's talking to him downstairs, I open the sketch. It's me on Cricket, racing Anders back to the stable. I'm grinning, and I look so damned happy, hunched down in the saddle with my hair blowing back. There are others in the picture. Dalton on Blaze, following at a normal pace, and even if it's a still shot, I swear I can see him shaking his head at us. Petra's there too, cheering us on with others from our bar group, who'd been walking by at the time. Diana's with them. She has her arms raised, pumping the air and shouting as I take the lead. I see her face lit up, and I know that isn't fake. There'd been no reason to pretend anymore — we were in Rockton, and she'd gotten what she wanted from me, and yet she'd still wanted to be friends, still cheered me on in that race.

"Ready for the next interview?" Dalton calls up, and I wipe away a tear, quickly reroll the sketch, and yell back, "Send her up!"

When my interviews are done, I nap. I have to — I'm still exhausted. I dream of the forest and of Jacob, and even asleep, my mind works the case. It's possible that paranoid delusions drove Jacob to kill Abbygail, Powys, and Hastings in the forest. Irene could be a separate case, like Mick. But Abbygail died two months ago, and Dalton says Jacob was fine a few weeks ago.

I'm thinking of that and then dreaming I'm back in the forest, Jacob with the knife at my throat, and I feel his hand on my shoulder, and my eyes open, and I see his gray eyes right above mine, and I lash out, right hook catching him in the jaw, the left in the gut, and he falls onto me . . . onto the bed with me, and I realize it's not Jacob I've hit. It's Dalton.

He backs up fast, wincing.

"And you wonder why I don't keep a gun under my pillow."

"Yeah." He rubs his jaw. "My mistake. I thought you saw me." A strained half smile. "Well, unless you *did*. I probably deserve that." The smile lingers another second. Then it falters. "Or did you think I was — ?"

"I was just reacting to someone looming over me as I slept."

"You were having a bad dream," he says, and he waits, as if for me to explain.

I sit up and look around, blinking hard.

"I brought dinner," he says.

He takes a tray from the chair and brings it over and points out what he's gotten for me. Soup, because it's easy to eat if I'm not up to solid food. A sandwich if I am — peanut butter and jam, but he can get something different if he's chosen wrong. And pie. Brian at the bakery asked what he could make for me, and Dalton remembered we'd talked about apple pie. The rest of it is downstairs for later.

I don't want him to try this hard.

I want him to throw it off. *So, yeah, it's been a shitty forty-eight hours, Butler, but what's past is past, so let's move on, and I sure as hell hope you aren't planning to lounge in this bed tomorrow.*

I want Dalton's snap and his growl and his swagger. Instead, I get apple pie and "Are you sure PB&J is okay? They were making shredded venison for tomorrow's sandwiches. I could get you some of that if you want."

"What I want is for you to stop apologizing."

"I'm not —"

"Yeah, Eric. You are."

He nods, settles onto the chair, and watches me eat. Then he stands abruptly and leaves without a word.

"Well, that's more like it," I mutter under my breath, as I dig into the pie.

Thirty seconds later, he's back with the tequila and a shot glass.

"I don't want —" I begin.

"Good, 'cause you can't have it with the drugs. This is for me."

He starts to open the bottle. Then he stops, sets it aside, and walks out again. I hear the distant click of the front door lock. Then the tramp of his boots as he goes to check the back door. He comes up and closes the bedroom one, too.

I say nothing. He pours a shot. Gulps it. Winces and shakes his head sharply, his eyes tearing at the corners.

"Fuck," he says.

"Yep, you really should stick to beer."

He shakes his head and pulls the chair over to the bed. Then he pours another shot.

"Umm," I say. "That's probably not a good —"

He downs it, and he's hacking after that, his eyes watering. His hand, still clutching the shot glass, trembles. He notices and puts it down fast.

"We need to talk," he says.

"That's usually best done sober."

"Not for this." He wipes his mouth and straightens. "Diana said I'm fucked up. She may be a bitch, but she's right. Everyone knows it. They think it's because I grew up here. That's only part of it."

He rubs the back of his neck. "You said I don't want to share my problems with you. You're right. I don't share this with anyone. *Anyone.* Because if they already treat me like a freak, this isn't going to help." He looks at the shot glass, his fingers still around it. "So I could just keep refusing to talk about it. Be the guy with the deep, dark secret."

He smacks the shot glass down. "Fuck it. I'm not that guy. I don't want to be that guy. Not with you. So this is your last chance. If you'd rather not hear it . . ."

"I want to."

"Fine, but if you ever treat me differently because of this —"

"I'd like to think you know me better than that."

He eases back, his voice lowering. "Yeah. Okay. So, Jacob . . . I was ten. He was seven.

We'd wander in the woods for hours. Our parents taught us how to find our way, and we were always home by dark. Then one day we see these people. I'm curious. I make Jacob stay back while I check them out. It's a group, camping and hunting. For three days, I come back to watch them. Jacob's freaked out. He wants to tell our parents. I say no fucking way. I threaten to leave him at home next time. On the third day, he's still whining, so I tell him to get out of my damned face, and I stomp off, exactly like you thought I did yesterday. And that's when it happens."

"They take him."

"No." He inhales and straightens and meets my gaze. "Not him. They take me."

"And then what? You escape and . . ." I trail off. I mentally retrace his story, and I realize there's more than one way of looking at it.

"Your parents . . . ," I say. "The Daltons aren't your parents. They took you. From the forest. From . . ."

"Yeah."

I blink, and I'm trying so hard not to react, to act like this is no big deal. *Huh, guess I got that backwards. Interesting.*

But it is a big deal. A huge deal, because losing a little brother would be tough, but to be the one lost himself, to be taken from his family . . .

"So, yeah," he says. "That's where I come from. Out there. I was one of them. Still am, in a lot of ways. It's not as if the Daltons rescued me from parents who beat and starved me. At first, I fought like a wolverine. I kept thinking my parents would come. But if they tried, I never knew it, so I figured they'd given up on me. I was pissed about that, and then, well . . . life *was* easier in Rockton. The Daltons were good people. I didn't . . . I didn't have the experience or the self-awareness to really understand that what they'd done was wrong. Everyone said they did a good thing, rescuing me from the savages, and how lucky I was, and by the time I was old enough to know that wasn't true?" He shrugs. "The Daltons *were* my parents by then. There was no point going back, because I didn't belong there anymore. I didn't quite belong here, either. I'm just . . . somewhere in between."

I think of all the times I've been with him in the forest, seen how different he is there. All the times he's sat out on the back deck at the station, and we joke that he is an outside cat. But it isn't really a joke. He *is* that feral cat who's been brought indoors, and maybe life is easier inside, but he'll never stop feeling the pull of the wild. But he'll never quite be able to live out there again, either.

"That's why the council's threat is such a big deal, Casey. When I say I couldn't live down south, I'm not being difficult or stubborn or dramatic. I *could not* live there. I'd go back into the forest first. But it's not just the council. What if I meet someone here? Someone I want to be with? Someone from down south, who'll expect me to go with her after her term's up, but I can't, and if she wants me, she has to stay here and live a life that's as wrong for her as hers is for me."

"And that's happened," I say. "In the past."

"I met someone, fell madly in love, and then she left and broke my heart?" He snorts a genuine laugh. "Fuck no. Might make a better story. But no. When I was a kid, the women here . . ." He looks at me. "Maybe this is more than you want to hear?"

I tell him to go on, and then I shift back and motion for him to come sit on the bed with me, and that seems to surprise him, as if maybe I'd want him out of the room, across the town, somewhere far, far away. But he sits beside me and relaxes against the pile of pillows.

"When I was a kid — teenager, young adult — well, there are women here, obviously, and like you've seen, things are different, freer or whatever."

"Despite the overall lack of women, I suspect there were still some who were happy to teach a young man a few things about sex."

"Yeah. When you're eighteen, nineteen, that's pretty much heaven. Considering my age, the women never expected more than sex. But then I got older, and they started wanting to help me. Fix me. Like the poor guy who's never been off the farm, and they're gonna give him the confidence to get out there and make his way in the world."

"Which couldn't be further from what you wanted."

He nods. "I'd keep it casual, but they'd still start talking about how I could go down south with them, how they'd help me adjust. A few years back, I had a rough time with a woman who misunderstood, so I said fuck this shit. I've got more important things to do anyway, with being sheriff now and . . ." He scratches his chin. "And that's not what I'm trying to say at all. Where was I?"

"Thinking that the second tequila shot was a bad idea after all?"

A laugh. "No shit, huh? Okay, so . . . Right. I can't leave, and I'm not ever going to fit anyone's definition of normal, and that's what I meant when I kissed you."

"Uh-huh."

He squeezes his eyes shut and gives his head a sharp shake. "Let me untangle that. When I said I didn't want that kiss to turn into sex, I didn't mean I didn't want sex." He pauses. "That didn't untangle it at all, did it?"

"Not really." I sit up a little more. "You don't need to explain —"

"I'm going to. It just might take some time. Sex, yes. With you, yes. But not like that. Not

527

first-kiss-to-sex in sixty seconds flat, and then that's it and that was fun and let's get back to work. *That's* what I didn't want. The way it was going. Where it was leading. Not the sex part but the . . ." He struggles for a word.

"The *casual* part."

"Exactly. Right. Thank you. Yes. That's not what I wanted with you, and if I start there, how do I go back and say I want more? And, fuck, I can't want more, because I can't give more, and if I can't give more, then it's not fair to say I want more and . . ." He pinches the bridge of his nose. "And I really shouldn't have had that second shot."

I rise to my knees, ignoring the pain in my leg. Then I lean in and kiss him, just a quick press of the lips.

"Let's simplify this," I say when I pull back. "If you're ever forced to leave Rockton, you'll go into the forest or you'll build a new town up here. Not south. Never south. And anyone who wants to be with you has to understand that." I kiss him again. "I understand that."

He puts his hands to my cheeks and pulls me in for the sweetest kiss, slow and gentle and hungry, that hunger growing as his arms go around me, and he eases me back onto the bed and —

And I yelp in pain.

Dalton jumps back so fast he drops me, and I let out a hiss, my eyes shut, wincing as pain rips through me.

"Sorry, sorry, fuck —" he begins.

I open my eyes and stop him as he moves in to fuss with me.

"I'm fine," I say, through my teeth. "Just . . . I may need more painkillers before we try that again."

"Or we may need to not try that again until you *don't* need painkillers."

I purse my lips. "No, I'm okay with the painkillers."

He chuckles and adjusts my pillow, and I pull him down. He resists until he realizes I'm pulling him beside me, not on top, and he stretches out and I ease onto my side, my body against his, put my arms around him, and kiss him.

FIFTY-EIGHT

We're still kissing — very sweet, very careful kisses, keeping the temperature low — when footsteps pound up the stairs, and Dalton's on his feet, cursing and saying, "I locked the fucking door," when the bedroom one flies open and Anders stops short.

"Uh . . . ," he says. "The doors . . ."

"Were locked?" Dalton says. "Suggesting I was trying to let Casey have a quiet dinner?"

"Right. Sorry. I came by a few minutes ago, and I knocked. Then I tried the door, and when they were both locked, I kinda panicked and went back to the station for the master key."

I look at Dalton. "There's a master key?"

"Yeah, in the safe."

"Can someone explain why we even bother with locks in this town?"

"Fuck if I know. Makes folks feel better, I guess."

I shake my head and turn to Anders. "What's the emergency?"

"Uh . . ." He takes a deck of cards from his back pocket.

When I lift my brows, he says, "I thought you might be bored, so I was coming by to see if you wanted company and entertainment."

I pause, because I'm thinking that I had both, a few minutes ago, and I'd been very much enjoying them. However, given the fact I'm supposed to be recuperating . . . yes, I suspect there's a limit to how much longer we could have gone before we hit stitch-ripping territory.

I look over at Dalton. He sighs, ever so softly.

"Go make coffee," he says to Anders. "And grab the rest of the pie."

We play cards for a couple of hours, up on my bed. We talk about the case, too — about my interviews that day.

I can't mention Jacob with Anders there. I'm glad of that, because even thinking about him reminds me of what Dalton's told me about his past, and I'm trying not to dwell on that. He says he doesn't talk about it because he doesn't want to be treated like more of a freak than he already is. But I think there's more to it. He doesn't want anyone looking that deep.

I suppose hiding his past is easy enough. No one in Rockton was around when Dalton was brought in from the forest. People have cycled through many times since then. The Daltons must have made sure the story didn't circulate beyond those who'd been present. Dalton got to keep his secret and put forward the face he wants seen: born and bred in Rockton. The truth is so much more complicated. To even think of it — a boy ripped from his family, ripped from his life . . .

It was kidnapping, pure and simple. Yet not pure and simple, because the Daltons honestly thought they were doing the right thing, saving a wild boy from his savage family and giving him a better life. And it was, in some ways, a better life, and that's part of the complication. What was it like for Dalton? To realize now, as an adult, that he'd been kidnapped . . . and that he'd come to love his kidnappers and consider them his parents.

So, yes, complicated. For now, I'll stick with mindless card games. Of course, that has to come to an end — along with the pie and a pot of coffee. Anders leaves, and when he's gone, Dalton heads out of the bedroom, saying, "I'll lock the front door."

"After you leave, right?"

He turns slowly, looking at me as if he's really hoping I'm joking. When I say, "I think you should go," he stands there, not moving, then he runs one hand through his hair as he says, "Fuck, I thought we were . . ."

He tries to straighten, to pull his usual

don't-give-a-shit attitude back into place, but he doesn't quite manage it and finally shakes his head and says, "Took a few rounds of cards, huh? Okay. That's . . ." He exhales sharply, his eyes finding their steel. "Goddamn it, Casey, don't fuck with me. I don't know those games, and I sure as hell don't care to learn them. If you don't want me —"

"Oh, but I do, which is the problem." I stretch out on the bed. "Three problems, actually." I point to my injuries. "I'm ordering you out because I don't want to explain to Beth how I ripped my wounds open without getting out of bed."

It takes a moment to sink in. Then he grins. "Okay, then. I'll behave myself."

"It's not you I'm worried about."

He turns then, and his grin is something new, a little bit wicked and a whole lot pleased.

"I suppose my stitches can be resewn," I say.

"And add a few more days onto your recuperation? No. I'll stay in my chair. You stay in your bed."

"All right, then."

I start to peel off my shirt. I get it halfway over my head and he's there, tugging it back down.

"None of that," he says.

"You don't think I sleep in my clothes, do you?"

"Tonight you will. I'll keep mine on, too."

"Mmm, you don't have to do that." I reach over and slide my hands under his shirt. I have it off before he realizes he should probably stop me. Then I chuck it across the room, tug him onto the bed, and straddle him, my hands on his face, tilting it up.

"No . . . ," he says.

"What? I'm just getting a look at you." I run my fingers over his beard shadow. "You've stopped shaving."

"Yeah, got a little busy. I'll do it in the morning."

"That wasn't a complaint. I was really hoping clean-shaven wasn't a new look for you."

His brows crease and then he grunts and says, "Right."

"I'm guessing you did it for our trip."

There's this long, awkward pause, his gaze shifting from mine. "Yeah, I just . . . I wanted to look more . . ."

"Presentable for going to town."

He exhales, and nods quickly. "Right." And I realize that wasn't the reason at all, and I think of that trip, of the drive up to the lookout, with the bonfire, and I realize he sure as hell wouldn't have taken Anders up there.

"Well," I say, "if I have any say in the matter, I like you this way."

I bend and kiss him, and he kisses me back, a kiss that gets deeper by the second, until I accidentally wince as my chest wound stretches.

"Goddamn it," he says, backing up.

I start to slide out of my shirt again. He hesitates and then yanks it down, growling under his breath.

"Am I being difficult?" I say.

"Yes. Very." A mock scowl as he moves me off his lap.

"Huh. It's been a long time since I've been difficult. You're good for me, you know that?"

He shakes his head and retrieves his shirt. When he comes back, I whisk it out of his hands and sit on it.

"I like you better *that* way, too," I say.

He gives a growl of frustration.

I widen my eyes. "What? You're always telling me I should want more. Now I want something. Badly."

He picks me up. Carries me to the balcony and deposits me on the mattress.

"Mmm, even better," I say. "Fresh air and —"

"Your neighbors are out."

"Ask me if I care."

He tries to give me a stern look and then bursts into a snorting laugh, sits down beside me, and pulls me over to him.

"The answer, Casey Butler, is no. You know it is, and you're having some fun with me, which is . . ." He lowers his face until it's right in front of mine. "Fucking wonderful to see. Also, very hot. But the answer is still no. Now, do you want me to finish my story about the fox?"

"Um, no, I want you to —"

"After."

I lift my brows. "After as in 'after the story'? Or as in 'at some distant point in the future'?"

"After the story. Not sex, either, because once we start that, as gentle as I might plan to be, there are going to be stitches ripped. Guaranteed."

I grin. "Oh, I like the sound of —"

"No. But if you're still interested after the story, I'm sure I can find something less strenuous to help you sleep."

My grin grows.

"I take it that's a yes," he says. "Good. Now lie down and get comfortable. And not one word — or anything else — until the story is done."

FIFTY-NINE

I wake on my balcony with the birds singing, sunlight streaming down, a brisk breeze bringing the tang of evergreens and another smell, an unfamiliar one, the sharp smell of soap, from the arms wrapped around me and the bare chest against my cheek, and I stretch smiling, only to realize my sweatpants are still on, which means . . .

"Fuck," I whisper.

"Mmm?" Dalton says.

"I fell asleep."

A chuckle ripples through his chest. "Yep."

I lift my head to look up at him. "You knew I would."

He arches his brows.

"That damn story went on forever, and you knew I'd fall asleep."

"You needed your rest."

"Yeah? You know what I needed even more?"

I arch my brows, and he laughs.

"Oh, that's funny, is it?" I push up. "You

know what I call it? A tease. Offer a girl —"

"Still stands."

"What?"

He pulls me down again. "Offer still stands."

He tries to bring me into a kiss, but I resist, my eyes narrowing. "Let me guess. If I listen to another of your interminable stories —"

"I thought you liked my stories."

"Not as much as I like what you offered after it."

He chuckles. "I don't think I specified the nature of that offer."

"Anything will do."

He laughs then and pulls me up onto him as he rolls onto his back. "I like the sound of that. So you still want to take me up on the offer? No story required."

"Hell, yeah."

"Then tell me what you want, and it's yours."

I grin. "I like the sound of *that.*"

"Casey?" a voice calls. It's Beth, coming through my bedroom door. I scramble off Dalton so fast I nearly double over in pain.

"Goddamn it," he says, catching me and aiming a glare through the balcony glass.

"You forgot to lock the front door," I say.

"Doesn't do any fucking good."

The morning sun must be casting a glare on the glass, because Beth opens the balcony doors, squinting with a tentative, "Casey?"

Then she sees Dalton and recoils fast.

"Does anyone in this goddamn town know how to knock?" he says, brushing past her as he stalks inside to grab his shirt.

"I did," she says. "No one answered —"

"Then take the hint." He yanks on the shirt and heads for the door. "Check Casey out. I'll start the coffee."

He's gone, and she's staring after him. Then she turns to me, and I feel like I'm sixteen, caught with a boy in my room.

"Sorry," I say. "He was, uh, staying to make sure I was okay. We went outside to see the, uh, fox."

I shouldn't need to make excuses. But Beth's staring at me, and all I can think about is her warning me away from Dalton. I consider her a friend, and it feels wrong to get caught like this when I haven't breathed a word of it to her. Except there hasn't been a word to breathe. Whatever I felt, I've never been the sort to confide in friends that way. Let's be honest — I've never needed to, because I've never felt like this.

"The stitches seem fine," I say, as if that's an excuse. *See? We didn't actually have sex.*

I go inside and let her examine me. She doesn't say a word. When Dalton comes with coffee, I'm sitting on the bed in my bra and panties. He kicks open the door, his hands full, and Beth jumps to say, "Casey's —" but he notices my state of undress and walks in

539

anyway, and I guess that answers any lingering question.

This is the first time he's seen quite so much of me, and while it shouldn't be the circumstances I want, it actually is, because nothing can put a damper on a hot-and-heavy moment faster than pulling off a girl's clothing to see scar tissue.

He just walks over and hands me my coffee. Then he sits in his chair until Beth goes to wet a cloth for the dried blood. He waits until he hears her footsteps on the stairs, then he's there, leaning over to kiss me, his hands running up my sides, and normally, when guys do that, they make some effort to avoid the scars. Dalton runs his hands over me, everywhere, as we kiss. Then Beth's footsteps sound on the stairs again and he's back in his chair before she comes in.

When she finishes her checkup, Dalton asks before I do, "How long until I get my detective back on her feet?" and Beth hesitates, as if she suspects this isn't really what he's asking.

"I should be up and around today," I say. "Everything's healing. I'd like some non-opiate painkillers, but otherwise I'm good to go."

"I'd rather you wait another day, Casey," Beth says.

"I feel fine." Which is a lie, but I have a high pain threshold and low sitting-on-my-ass threshold.

"Stay in bed this morning," Dalton says. "Get up after lunch. See how it goes."

"Nothing too strenuous, though," Beth says.

"Sure," I say. Dalton sneaks me a quirk of a smile behind Beth's back. I cross my fingers, and he chuckles. She turns at the sound, but he's stone-faced again, sipping his coffee.

"Casey has something she wants to talk to you about," he says. "I'm going to let her do that while I make a few stops. I'll bring back breakfast for the patient."

He walks over and brushes his lips across my forehead, and I guess that means we definitely aren't hiding. Dalton isn't the sneaking-in-shadows type, and I understand that better now — he has so much he conceals that the rest is on the table, take it or leave it, no excuses.

He leaves. I get dressed, and I'm sliding into bed when Beth says, "I don't mean to pry, Casey . . ."

Then don't is what I want to say. But I know she means well.

"Yes, you warned me," I say. "And I had no intention of anything happening with Eric. It just . . . did."

"It shouldn't have." Her voice is sharper than I expect, and when I look over, her face is drawn with worry. "I'm sorry, Casey. I hate to interfere, but this is a bad idea."

I prop up on my pillows. "You're concerned

for him. I get that. But I would never do anything to hurt Eric."

"It's not Eric I'm worried about."

That surprises me, and I look over to see those worry lines etched deeper.

"Eric is a friend," she says. "And as a friend, I only want the best for him. But I consider you a friend, too, Casey, and there are things about Eric . . . It's not as simple as it seems. *He's* not as simple as he seems."

"I know."

Her look sharpens to impatience then. "You can say that, but you really don't. I have his medical file. There are aspects to his past . . ." She straightens. "There are things in his past that he does not talk about. Absolutely does not. I attempted to broach it once, and he shut me down so fast I nearly got whiplash."

His medical files. Of course. He may have had health issues when he arrived in Rockton. If there is one record of Dalton's past, that's where it would be.

"If you mean how he got to Rockton . . . ," I say carefully.

"That he's lived here all his life?" She shakes her head. "He hasn't, Casey, and I can't tell you any more than that, except that what happened to him before that means he's a deeply damaged man, and —"

"I know."

"You don't. I'm sorry. I don't mean to be harsh, but —"

"His files show that he wasn't born in Rockton," I say. "They tell where he *was* born. How he lived as a child. How he ended up here."

She has her mouth open as if she was ready to argue before I got a word out. Now she stares at me, openmouthed, and says, "He told you," and I see her expression, and I wish to God I'd just kept my damned mouth shut. She's been his friend for years, and he refused to acknowledge what happened, and now he's spilling his guts to someone he met a few weeks ago.

She straightens. "Yes, of course. That's Eric. If he's going to . . . get involved with you, he's going to make sure you know what you're getting into. He's a good man, Casey. But he's also dealing with some serious psychological issues. I think the damage can be fixed. It takes years, though, and as hard as I've been trying, I'm not sure I've made any inroads."

"Do they need to be made?" I say, as gently as I can. "I know there's damage. Hell, I know all about damage. But Eric's is a different kind. I'm not convinced it's something that needs to be *fixed.* I think it just needs to be understood."

"He can't live this way forever, Casey, stuck up in this town, a thousand miles from everything. It's not natural."

"It is for him. He's happy —"

"No, he's convinced himself he's happy. He could do so much more. *Be* so much more."

I bite my tongue because I can see I'm not going to change her mind. I remember Dalton talking about women from his past trying to "fix" him, and while he's never been romantically involved with Beth, the dynamics are the same, and that saddens me, because I expect better of her.

No, that's not fair. She's a doctor, and it's her job to fix people. She just doesn't see that this problem doesn't need mending, and I can't tell her so because that would be incredibly egotistical of me — the newcomer who claims to better understand a man Beth has known for years.

So I say, "Maybe. I don't know. Right now, though, there's something else I'd like to speak to you about."

I ask her about schizophrenia. I stick to my hypotheticals. Beth might know about Dalton's past, but there'd be no reason to mention Jacob in those files.

Unfortunately, Beth doesn't know much about the condition. Less than I do, it seems. She's a medical doctor, not a psychiatrist. I make a note that I'll need to bite the bullet and speak to Isabel instead.

"Do you know anything about ergot poisoning?" I ask next.

She frowns. "I believe it's connected to a fungus that can infect rye."

"Right. It's one of the possible explanations for the hysteria surrounding the Salem witch trials."

I somehow manage to say this as if I know exactly what I'm talking about. Because, you know, in my old life, I devoted myself to expanding my knowledge of the world, chasing any esoteric tidbit that interested me. Sadly, no. . . . That would be Dalton, the guy who reads about ancient Mongols in his spare time.

Dalton had suggested this theory. Not ergot poisoning specifically, because there's no rye growing here. But he'd wondered if some environmental poison could be responsible for Jacob's sudden and violent personality shift.

Dalton had listed off a half dozen things in the forest that could cause mental confusion and hallucinations. Beth knows nothing about any of them. I'll add this to the items for Dalton to research when he takes Diana to Dawson City.

We talk for a little longer. The subject of Dalton doesn't resurface, and I'm relieved. I value Beth as a friend, and by the time she leaves, I feel that's been put aside, at least for now.

Dalton brings breakfast. He can't stay long. We're sitting on the bed, propped up against the headboard.

"Fucking council wants me to get my ass to Dawson City."

"To escort Diana."

"Yeah." His tone softens as he looks at me. "About that . . . how are you doing?"

"Trying very hard not to think about it."

He nods, and I know what he's thinking, so I say it for him. "I need to talk to her, don't I? Try for some closure."

"Yeah."

"I'll do it before you leave."

"Before *we* leave. You're coming with me. I told the council you have more to research. They agreed to postpone the trip until this afternoon, and then we'll stay overnight in Dawson City. At the inn. Where no one can barge in the goddamn door."

"Ah, so that's your real plan. Not that you value my research skills. You just want sex."

"Damn straight."

He tugs me onto his lap. I turn to straddle him, and he smiles and says, "Even better," and pulls me into a kiss. It takes less than thirty seconds to get both of us shirtless, him fumbling with my bra before giving up and pushing it over my head, and then his hands are on my breasts and damn, that feels —

A distant knock sounds on the front door.

"Ignore it," Dalton says, still kissing me.

"Planning to."

I get the button open on his jeans and I'm pulling down the zipper when, "Detective

546

Butler?" It's my next interview.

Dalton whips my bedside book at the bedroom door and knocks it shut. I chuckle.

"Casey?" the voice calls from downstairs. "Are you okay?"

"God fucking damn —"

I cut Dalton's curse short with a kiss. I start to roll off him, and he tries to grab me back, but I whisper, "Dawson City. One private room. Eight uninterrupted hours," as footsteps sound on the stairs.

"Casey?"

"Just a sec!" I call.

Dalton grabs me and tugs me back onto him. "He'll wait five minutes."

"Kinda want more than five minutes, Sheriff."

He gives an abashed "Yeah, sorry. Fuck."

He rolls off the bed, gives me a quick smack of a kiss, and then grabs his shirt and walks out, still pulling it on, to the sputtered apologies of whoever is in the hall. I wince and shake my head. Apparently we aren't keeping this a secret from *anyone.*

I put on my bra and shirt, then call, "Come in," and start my morning of interviews.

SIXTY

I have three interviews scheduled, and two additional people show up, not with anything significant to add, but trying to be helpful, and I don't want to discourage that. When Dalton brings lunch, I'm talking to someone who recalls seeing Mick the night of his death. She spotted him walking toward the woodshed. Yeah, like I said, not useful, but I listen and thank her for her time as Dalton waits impatiently outside the door.

We go downstairs and dine on the back deck. I'm telling Dalton a story about the chase of a seventy-year-old wannabe graffiti artist when Isabel walks around my house.

"Ah," she says. "That's what that sound was. Eric laughing. I do believe I've never heard it before."

Dalton shoots her the finger.

She walks over and eyes us sitting hip to hip, Dalton's hand on my knee.

"Well, well," she says. "The rumors are true, then. Interesting."

"You want something?" he says.

"Good afternoon to you, too, Sheriff. No, I don't want anything from you. I came to speak to Casey about her investigation."

I tense, and Dalton gets to his feet.

"Down, boy," she says. "I'm not here to harass your detective." She lifts a folder she's carrying. "I found this in Mick's things, and I thought it might be important."

I check my watch.

"Yes, you have time for me, Casey," she says.

"I'm checking Eric's time." I turn to him. "It's almost one. You'd better go take that council call. I'll handle this."

He gives Isabel a look.

"I'll behave myself," she says.

"You better. Casey's been stabbed three times. Doesn't need your shit." He turns to me. "She gives you a hard time? Radio Will and have her locked in the cell."

"On what charges?" she asks.

"Pissing me off."

"Ah, the usual, then."

When he's gone, she says, "Well, he's in a very good mood. I'm glad to see it. I know Will was flitting around, but Eric's the one for you."

She steps onto the deck, and I expect her to take one of the chairs, but she gracefully lowers herself to sit beside me on the edge. "Does Beth know about you two?"

"Mmm, yeah. Eric isn't exactly making a secret of it."

"Hell, no. He landed the town's prize catch, and everyone's going to know it."

I give her a look.

She smiles. "All right, I'll give him the benefit of the doubt and say that's not the *entire* reason. So how did Beth take it?"

I shrug.

"Not well, but you don't know me enough — or like me enough — to confide. I'm sure you saw that one coming, though, given how she feels about Eric."

"She's very protective of him," I say.

"You noticed, huh?"

"Kind of hard to miss. He seems to bring out her maternal instincts."

Isabel chokes on a laugh. "Yes, Beth might be older than Eric, but that's not *maternal instincts* she's feeling."

I look at her. Then, "Shit. I had no idea. Are you sure?"

"Well, let's see. About eighteen months ago, she came and asked my 'professional' advice on seduction. She didn't tell me who she intended to seduce, but there was really only one option, so I told her I'd strongly advise against it. She ignored me and made her move. He shot her down. I believe she tries again every few months, to see if he's changed his mind. He hasn't. He wouldn't have even before you came along. She's been subtle enough about it that they can remain friends, but . . ."

"She's still interested."

"*Interested* implies she'd like a few hours of his time. Beth wants more. Much more."

"Damn him," I mutter. "Why the hell was he so insensitive this morning?"

"He is letting her know he's off the shelf. Bluntly, as he does everything, and yes, I feel bad for her. Beth and I don't always see eye to eye, but she deserves something good in her life. Unfortunately, that's not Eric, and it never was, so you can stop feeling guilty."

"I'm not —"

"Sure you are. I would, too, however much I'd know it wasn't my fault. You consider her a friend, hence you will feel bad. But she obviously didn't tell you she was interested. You did nothing wrong. Let it go. She's better off this way."

I shake my head.

Isabel looks at me. "You think she'd be happier chasing a guy who doesn't want her?"

She has a point, and I shrug.

"I know Beth and I aren't the only ones who don't see eye to eye, Casey, but I'm still hoping we can get past it. For now, how about you forget what I do for a living, and I'll forget you don't like what I do for a living. Yes, that's very generous of me, I know."

"I can't run interference for you with Eric."

Her eyes widen. "Are you suggesting I

would attempt to ingratiate myself with you to gain an ally in the sheriff's fight to shut down my establishment? I'm impressed. Yes, that's exactly what I hoped when I met you. But you treated me well with Mick, despite your personal feelings. You got stabbed by some madman in the woods, and you're already back on the case, conducting interviews from your bed. *Everyone's* impressed. So my overtures have gone from blatant self-interest to genuine interest. I would like to get to know you better."

"You can start by handing over that file."

She smiles. "Business first. I approve." She starts to pass it to me and then stops, her hand still on it. "The fact I'm bringing this to you is a sign of my trust in your abilities, Casey."

"No, it's a sign you want to find out who killed your lover."

"True, but this is . . ." She sets the folder on my lap. "Mick was hiding that. Which might suggest he was hiding other things, including an affair, and it's difficult for me to admit that. But if I thought there was a remote chance he was, I *would* admit it. As humiliating as it might be to have my young lover cheating on me, it'd be worse to protest and be proven wrong. Mick had faults. He had secrets. Screwing around wasn't one of them. But this was."

I open the folder. It's a sheaf of papers. On

the top one is a list of names. I've seen them before. In Dalton's journal. They're the real names of those he suspects are in Rockton under false pretenses.

I flip through the file to find notes on each name. It seems like exactly what I saw in Dalton's journal. Notes on the suspects and their crimes.

"You aren't asking me what those names are," she says.

I look up at her. "Do you know?"

"I've heard rumors that there are people here who shouldn't be. Secrets are profitable, and I may have been known to pay for them."

"Is that where Mick got these?" I ask.

"No. I've heard perhaps three stories. Not nearly in the detail of that file, and to be perfectly honest, I don't want those secrets, Casey. The only reason I'd care to know who those people are is so I can stay as far away from them as possible. When I want secrets, I want things like your friend getting here by lying about her ex. That's useful. What's in there is dangerous."

"So where did Mick get it?"

"All I can think is that he was keeping notes for Eric. That Eric was digging into people, and he didn't dare keep a record in his handwriting, let alone in his house. So he asked Mick to help. Which Mick would have. Given his own past."

"Which is?"

She taps the folder. "I added a page for him. If you have questions, you know where to find me."

Before Isabel leaves, I ask her about schizophrenia. We talk for a bit, but she doesn't add much to what I know. Some of it fits Jacob, and some of it clearly does not.

Afterward, I can't get to Mick's notes as quickly as I'd like. My next interview arrives early, and that's supposed to be my only interview for the afternoon, except Brian shows up, bearing information that is less than useful. However, he also comes bearing gifts: cookies and another apple pie.

I get the feeling those gifts were the point of his visits, rather than the uninformative information. He admits there's a good reason I haven't had any actual visitors other than Petra. Dalton has apparently been telling everyone else to leave me alone. Or, more accurately, leave me the fuck alone.

There's a moratorium on all social visits until tomorrow, by which time he's decided I'll be well enough to take them. I could argue with that, but he has a point. The interviews are taxing enough. It just would have been nice to be told why no one was coming to visit me.

I conduct the afternoon's meetings in my living room, getting myself prepared for the trip to Dawson City.

I'm packing when Anders comes by.

"Boss is tied up with council shit," he says. "They're going over plans for rebuilding the woodshed. To leave on schedule, he'll need to meet you at the hangar. I said I'd walk you over."

"Thanks."

He holds my duffel bag as I put in a change of clothing. "So, you and Eric, huh?"

I glance over.

"He told me. I think he figured he should be the one to do it, which I appreciate. We had a nice talk."

"Oh?"

"Yep. Let's see, how'd it go." He lowers his voice to Dalton's pitch. *"You hear about me and Casey?* No. So you and Casey . . . ? *Yeah.* Ah. You and Casey. *That okay?* Sure. I'm happy for you. *Yeah?* Yeah. *Okay. Good."* Anders looks at me. "It was a guy conversation."

I laugh. "I see."

"If it was anyone else, I'd be *less* okay with it, but Eric? He deserves you. You deserve him. I *am* happy for you both."

He gives me a one-armed hug, and I say thanks. Then I toss my toiletries in the bag, and he carries it downstairs. I need to grab my jacket from the back room, and when I come back, he's got Mick's folder. I'd left it on the front table when I went to pack, planning to take it for some in-flight reading. He's staring at the first page — the list of names. When I walk in, he slaps it shut.

"Sorry," he says. "I'm snooping."

"You're a cop. You're supposed to snoop."

He smiles, but it looks strained. He's had to pick up the slack while I recuperate and Dalton plays nurse. I catch a glimpse of the toll it's taking as he hands me the folder.

"You okay?" I ask.

He jumps, as if startled by the question. "Sure. Why?"

"You look seriously overworked."

"Always." He points at the folder. "Since I'm professionally allowed to be nosy, I'm guessing that's a list of real names?"

"Hmm?"

"Real names of locals."

"Something like that. Just a lead I'm chasing." I stuff the folder into my duffel, which he takes, then waves me to the door without another word.

SIXTY-ONE

We're heading through town when Dalton
joins us.

"All done with the council?" I ask.

He makes a noise under his breath, one I
interpret to mean he's annoyed at the inter-
ruption to his day but yeah, it's done.

"Meant to run the preflight check earlier,"
he says. "You okay with hanging out? Or do
you want to rest at the station?"

"I'd like to see how you do it. Not that I'm
going to be a pilot anytime soon, but I'm
interested."

That pleases him, and he nods. He talks to
Anders for a moment, before the deputy takes
off to run an errand. He'll bring Diana after
that, something I'm in no rush for.

We're on the edge of town when we spot
four of the militia, armed and on horseback,
heading for the woods.

"Hey, boss," Kenny calls with a wave.

Dalton eyes them and veers in that direction. "What's this? Don't need four guys for patrol."

"Hunting mission," Kenny says.

"Nothing on the schedule."

Kenny grins. "This is a different kind of hunt. We know you're busy, so we're going to find the bastard who cut up Casey."

Dalton tenses so fast I swear I hear vertebrae snapping.

"Whoa, no," I say. "We are nowhere near that point, guys. I haven't even been able to provide Eric with a description, it all happened so fast. I appreciate that you want to keep the town safe, but for now, we can best do that by staying out of the woods and posting a couple of extra guys on border patrol."

"It's not about safety, Casey," Kenny says. "You got cut up by some psycho out there. We're going to make him pay."

The other three nod. While it's sweet that they want to go after the guy who hurt me, I feel a bit like the wide-eyed maiden in a spaghetti western, the local gunslingers mounting up to go hunt down the villain who sullied my honor.

I look at Dalton, waiting for him to jump in with a loud and profane diatribe about exactly why this is a bad idea. But he's frozen in panic, and I know all he's thinking is that four armed men are hell-bent on riding into the woods and shooting his brother.

"No," I say, as firmly as I can. "I appreciate

558

the gesture, guys. I really do. But what we have out there isn't a killer who'll descend on us in our sleep. It's a guy with a problem, hopefully temporary, and —"

"So he's a psycho, like I said."

Okay, not the right tactic. "Eric and I will deal with this when we get back. We need to find this guy and see what happened to him or it could happen to others, and then we'd have a real problem."

Kenny's hands move on his rifle. "We're ready for it."

"*No.* The people in those woods have as much right to be there —"

"They're a threat. They've always been a threat. If we have the opportunity to wipe them out, for once and for all —"

"Do you actually hear what you're saying? We have a name for that, Kenny. It's called a massacre, and if that's what this town has come to, then some of us really need to get back south and get civilized fast."

His mouth works. One of the others says, "We didn't mean it like that."

"The answer is no," Dalton says, stepping forward, chin up, jaw set, the sheriff back. "Hell, no. Fuck, no. I-cannot-goddamn-believe-you're-suggesting-it, no. If you have a problem with the way I'm handling this situation —"

"Course not, Eric."

"If you have a problem with the way I'm

running this town —"

"No, we just . . . For Casey," Kenny says weakly. "We wanted to find him for Casey."

"And Casey doesn't want you to do it like this. So get your heads out of your asses, put those horses away, and find something useful to do, like cutting wood or hauling water. We need that. We don't need a bunch of yahoos in the forest, shooting anything that moves and hitting the folks cutting wood and hauling water."

"Okay. You're right. But . . ." Kenny lowers his voice. "We're not the only ones who want to find this guy. People are talking. Whispering about heading off while you're away."

"What? If anyone sets a foot outside this town while I'm gone —"

"They won't. We'll make sure of it. I'm just letting you know . . ." He looks down at Dalton. "Something has to be done, Eric. You know how people get."

"Then make sure they don't get that way. Not while I'm gone. Or I'll fire the whole fucking lot of you. Got it?"

They get it.

We continue to the hangar in silence. I want to tell Dalton it's okay, they won't dare go into the forest behind his back, but I know that doesn't matter, because all he's thinking about is Jacob, out there and messed up, with a whole town gunning for him. And the one

560

guy who gives a shit is leaving town.

Dalton starts his preflight check. When he notices me at his shoulder, he remembers I'd wanted to see, so despite the fact that instruction might be the farthest thing from his mind, he explains, because that's what he does.

He's checking some wires and telling me their purpose, and I ask what happens if they're loose or damaged.

"Then we don't get off the ground," he says.

"Important stuff, then."

He finds something like a smile for me. "Everything is important stuff up there."

"What about — ?" I lean over and then hiss in pain.

He grabs my elbow, steadying me. "You up to this?"

"If I'm not, can we postpone it and go look for Jacob?"

I'm instantly sorry I asked. Hope flickers across his face, followed by dismay and then anger, as his fingers tighten.

"That's a no," I say, gently pulling away.

He realizes how tight he's gripping me and apologizes as he rubs the spot. Then he straightens and says, "If you're not up to it, I need to go alone. The council is insisting and —"

"And while we're working on a backup plan, you aren't eager to push them, not over this. Okay, I'll be fine. But I should take my pills before we go. Where's my duffel?"

I look around, and he walks across the hangar to retrieve it. While he's gone, I slip my switchblade from my pocket. When he comes back, I'm tapping one of the wires.

"Did you check this one already?" I ask.

"Yep, I —"

I lift the cut ends. "Better check again."

He frowns. Then he sees the knife in my other hand, and he smiles, coming over to put his hand on the back of my head, tilting my face up for a kiss.

"Thank you," he says.

"I'm hoping it's not easily fixed."

"Yeah, it is, but no one else knows that. I'll get Val out here, show her the plane's not starting, and tell her I'll fix it before morning."

"And in the meantime, while it's still light out, you should comb the forest for the guy who attacked me."

"Yep, I should. You up to coming along?"

I hesitate. "Physically, yes, but . . ." I look up at him. "You don't want me out there, Eric. You know how I react to a threat. If Jacob came after you —"

"He won't."

"But if he did . . ."

"He *won't,* and if he did and you pulled your gun, then that's what happens. You can't worry about that, Casey. You almost got killed worrying about it. You should have had your gun out the moment we got separated in the forest."

"So shooting your brother would have been better?"

He puts his hand on my elbow, and I realize my arm's shaking. He tugs me over to him, his grip too firm to escape.

"You need to trust yourself more," he says.

I stare at him. "I'm sorry, but that is the stupidest damn thing you have ever said to me. Trust myself not to kill someone who presents a threat?"

"Blaine didn't present a threat."

I jerk back as if slapped. He moves forward, and I try to get out of his path, but he has me trapped between him and the plane.

"We're having this conversation, Casey. Yes, you react to threats instinctively. Yes, that's dangerous. But the only person you've actually killed *wasn't* a threat. He was a fucking coward who turned his back on you and let you get beaten in a way I don't even like to imagine, because it makes me want to hop in that plane and track down those bastards and do the same thing to them, and I don't care if they've cleaned up their act and become pillars of the fucking community, I'd beat them within an inch of their lives. And if Blaine was still alive? I'd beat him, and I *wouldn't* stop when he was within an inch of his life. You didn't go there thinking, *I'm going to kill the son of a bitch.* You lost control, and to you, that's worse. But you were reacting to what he'd already done to you. So unless you're telling me that you're afraid you'd shoot Jacob for what he's done to you —"

"Of course not. What he did to me isn't important."

He makes a face but seems to decide this isn't the time to lecture me on why it *should* be important. "Then you're not going to shoot him, are you? At least not lethally."

"If I fire a gun —"

"Then it's a good thing you also have that knife. Now we need to speak to Val."

Val takes our story at face value, without so much as a glance in the engine, and she accepts Dalton's decision to spend the rest of the day searching for my attacker, to avoid a lynch mob.

As we walk, I ask about his brother. Yes, I'm freaked out over the possibility I'll shoot Jacob, and I'm hoping that putting a face on him will stay my hand. It's a scattershot discussion at first, mostly me asking questions and him giving basic answers. I get the feeling I'm prying, but as we walk deeper into the forest, he begins to relax, and to talk — honestly talk — about his relationship with his brother.

Jacob blamed Dalton for leaving him. He went to Rockton and never came back. It was only after their parents died in a territory dispute with hostiles that Jacob found Rockton and his brother.

When they were reunited, Jacob had expected Dalton to return to the forest. Dalton had expected Jacob to come to Rockton. Each was furious that his own brother understood him so little.

"We were kids," Dalton says. "I was seventeen, Jacob fourteen. You can't see the other point of view then."

So their early relationship had been fractious. They'd go months without seeing one another. That changed as they got older.

"What you heard the other day?" he says. "He hasn't said those things in ten years. He hasn't acted like he *felt* them in ten years."

They came to accept each other's lifestyle, if not fully understand it. For Jacob, it seemed more selfish — he wanted his brother out there with him as a companion in his solitary life. With Dalton, well, it was exactly what I'd expect. He wanted to help his brother. Not bring him into Rockton — he got that now — but smooth out the rough edges of his life.

"He doesn't need to live in town," he says. "I just want . . . I want more for him. More options. Steady trading, a place to stay when the weather gets bad or the game dries up."

It reminds me of what Beth said about Dalton and her quest to get him to go south, lead what she considered a fuller life. The difference is that Dalton realizes it isn't fear or timidity holding Jacob back, so he has stopped asking and accepts that this is his brother's chosen life. He rechannels that frustrated urge toward those in Rockton who need and accept his help. Like Anders. Like me.

In those few hours in the forest, I'm not sure whom I get to know better: Jacob or Dalton. Once he starts talking about his brother, his fears and his frustrations pour out, and I don't think he's ever told anyone else this, and I appreciate it all the more for that.

We don't find Jacob, and after a couple of hours, I'm clearly flagging. We head back to town. Dalton will go back out with Anders after he's eaten and grabbed flashlights. Which means he'll have to tell Anders about Jacob, but he's decided he needs to take that step. For his brother's safety, he must bring someone else in on the secret, and the person he trusts most is his deputy. He'll just say Jacob is his brother and let Anders conclude that Jacob voluntarily left Rockton years ago.

Talking about his brother hasn't put Dalton in the lightest of moods. Not finding him makes it worse. So after we grab my bag from the hangar, I tell him I'll just head home, but he stops me with, "Can you come to my place?"

"In the morning?"

He shakes his head and shoves his hands in his pockets. "Now. I should get something to eat. Would you come back with me?"

"Of course."

I haven't been in Dalton's house. We hang out at my place, and he seems to spend relatively little time at his. I've seen it, of course. It looks exactly like mine, also on the edge of town. The first thing I notice are the books. It's hard not to. The only living room wall that isn't a bookcase is the one with the fireplace, and even it has shelves on either side. They're arranged by subject, and I swear there's something on every topic imaginable.

"I like to read," he says as he comes up behind me.

I look back at him and smile. "I know."

"You're welcome to borrow anything. There are more upstairs."

"I will. Thank you."

A moment of silence as I run my finger over a few titles. Then he says, "And thank you."

"For what?" I glance over my shoulder and he's standing there, hands in his pockets again, looking uncomfortable and a little bit lost.

"Everything," he says. "Understanding and just . . . everything."

I rise onto my tiptoes to kiss him. I just intend a quick kiss — I know this isn't the time — but it's like that's the sign he was waiting for.

His arms go around me, pulling me into a kiss that's careful at first, slow and cautious, his body held tight, waiting for any indication, that first signal that this isn't where I was heading. It wasn't, but it sure as hell can be, and I put my arms around his neck, my fingers in his hair, and that's all he needs to stomp that accelerator, and I swear it's not five seconds before we're on the floor and he's tugging off my shirt.

Then he stops. He blinks hard, breathing ragged, struggling to get it under control as he says, "Too fast?" and I want to laugh. I really do, because there's this note in his voice, the one that says he knows he's moving at the speed of light but he really, really wants me to say I see absolutely nothing wrong with disrobing five seconds after the kissing starts. So, yes, I want to laugh. Which would, of course, be the entirely wrong response. Instead, when he says, "Too fast?" I grin for him, reply, "Hell, no," and reach for his belt buckle, and he hits the gas again.

SIXTY-TWO

We're lying on the floor, naked. Or mostly naked, because given the speed, we didn't quite manage to get our clothing all the way off. My shirt is still hooked around one elbow and I'm pretty sure he only bothered getting one leg out of his jeans. But despite the practically nonexistent foreplay, he made up for it where it counted, and damn . . . I'm stretched out, happy and sated, and he's looking down at me, grinning, obviously very pleased with himself, and when I say so, he chuckles and says, "I just liked hearing you say my name."

"You mean saying your name while I'm coming."

"Uh-huh."

I laugh, and he tugs my shirt the rest of the way off and shoves it aside. Then he pulls me against him and says, "Didn't think I had a shot."

"With what?"

"You. Didn't like me very much."

"You didn't think much of me, either."

"Only because I didn't know you."

"Ditto." I shift, getting comfortable against his chest. "I think that's better, though. If it's at first sight, what does that mean? Other than that you appreciate what you see? Better to fall for someone once you get to know him."

"So you fell for me?"

His grin returns, and he looks so pleased with himself that I can't resist poking him a little with, "I'm speaking hypothetically. If you fall for someone, it's better if you get to know them first."

I'm teasing, and my tone should give it away, but there's this flash in his eyes, dismay and uncertainty, and he goes still, searching my gaze with that look I know so well, except there's more to it this time. There's worry and there's fear, as he hunts for something specific, not certain he'll find it.

"When I was in high school," I say, "girls always talked about falling for guys. I never understood that. I'd meet someone, and I'd like what I saw, and if he liked what he saw, then it was all good. If he didn't, no big deal — plenty of other guys out there."

"Uh-huh." He nods, but there's this new look in his eyes, one that wants me to stop talking, just please stop talking, because explaining only makes it worse.

"Then, when I got older, friends would talk

about more than just girlish crushes and infatuation. They'd talk about *really* falling for a guy. Meeting someone and it clicks and he's exactly what they want and if they don't win him — don't ever have a chance — they'll never quite get over it."

"Uh-huh."

"I never knew what they meant. I just didn't get it, you know?"

"Uh-huh."

I lean over, put my lips to his ear, whisper, "I get it now," and pull him into a kiss.

It's later. Significantly later. That zero-to-sixty first time seems to have been enthusiasm rather than preference, and I get a much slower second time around, one that makes me very grateful for those women who'd taken the time to tutor him.

Now we're lying on the floor, still in Dalton's living room. The evening chill has settled, and when I shiver against him, he rises, saying, "I'll get the fire going."

I shake my head. "I'll start it after you leave."

"I'm not leaving," he says, as he crouches naked in front of the fireplace, which is already prepped and ready to light.

I rise on my elbows. "Will's coming by —"

"And I'll tell him I changed my mind." He lights the fire and returns to lie down with me. "I want to stay here. With you. I can look in the morning, before we leave."

"As much as I'd love to say yes — please — you'll regret it if you don't look tonight."

He makes a face but doesn't argue. We lie there a little longer, but when the knock comes at the door, he says, "Yeah, okay." He starts to rise, then says, "You'll stay here?"

I nod. He passes me my clothes, and I dress. Then I send him into the kitchen to get something to eat while I answer the door.

When Anders comes in, he says, "How're you doing?"

"I'm fine." I glance over my shoulder at the kitchen and lower my voice. "Eric's a little distracted tonight."

Anders chuckles. "I bet he is."

"It's not that. He'll talk to you, and you'll understand more then, but just . . . just know that he's not himself. Not as focused as he usually is. I'd appreciate it if you'd . . ."

"Watch out for him?"

"Please."

"Always."

We talk for a few minutes. Then Dalton comes out with a sandwich in each hand. He holds one out to me. When I try to refuse, he pushes it into my hand with, "Take. Eat. That's an order."

"Yes, sir."

"Now, when you've done that, go upstairs, get in bed, and stay there until I'm back."

"Yes, sir."

Anders shakes his head. "Damn, that never works for me."

"It's all in how you say it," Dalton replies.

I laugh, tell them good-bye, and then take my duffel and my sandwich back into the living room to enjoy the fire while I eat.

As I eat, I take Mick's file and start reading the page Isabel added on him. Dalton said Mick got caught up in dirty cop business and tried to play it straight. That, it seems, is not the whole story. While it is true Mick had to get the hell out of Dodge — or, in this case, Vancouver — when he refused to play ball with guys on his task force, it seems the trouble went a few steps further. Mick's partner had also refused the payoffs. The drug guys had caught up with him and killed him. Then Mick tracked them down and killed *them*.

So Mick wasn't just a cop. He was a cop with a taste for vigilante justice. And two of our victims are in his files, as killers who escaped justice by buying their way into Rockton.

Isabel thought he'd been keeping notes for Dalton. She's partly right. These *are* Dalton's notes — the same ones I read in his journal. But there's no way Dalton let Mick in on his secret crusade, and he certainly wouldn't have allowed Mick to keep a copy of his notes.

Mick must have found out about the journal when he'd been working under Dalton and known where he kept it. They're a little out of date, and he's added extra notations, as if he'd been investigating on his own. Bartending is exactly the kind of job that makes it easy to learn other people's secrets.

I work methodically, reading each page. Dalton will be in the forest for hours. I'm in no rush, the fire is blazing, his couch is comfortable, and I've made a hot chocolate chaser for my sandwich.

The last page in Mick's file is for a guy named Calvin James. He's the only one Dalton didn't have in his book, which means this must be Mick's own detective work. James was a soldier who walked into his commanding officer's bedroom and shot him dead while he slept. Then he walked out . . . and shot and wounded two other men. He disappeared while being transferred to a military jail Stateside.

I read that page three times. Then I set it aside, and I stare at the fire, and I tell myself that I should be ashamed of the conclusions I'm drawing.

Mine was in the military. Killed someone who didn't deserve to die.

When the door flies open, I'm still staring into that fire. I keep staring as footsteps pound across the floor, even as I hear Anders say, "Casey?"

I turn, and I look at him, and that's all I

can do. I look, and I tell myself I'm wrong. I must be wrong, but I can't stop thinking it.

"Casey?"

It takes a moment to rise out of my thoughts, and when I do, I see Anders — really see him — sweat streaming down his face, his eyes round.

"It's Eric," he says. "I lost him. We were out there, and we were sticking together, and then — I don't even know how it happened. I stepped away for a second to take a piss, and I barely even turned my back and —"

"And he's gone," I say, and my voice is an odd monotone. "You lost him."

His brow furrows. "Right. Did . . . did you take something? For the pain?"

"Yes," I say, in that same hollow voice.

He exhales hard. "Okay, okay. So you're a little out of it. But I need you to come with me. Can you do that?"

"Go into the forest with you."

"Right."

"To look for Eric."

He swears under his breath. "Shit, you're really out of it."

"Just take me to him."

"I don't know where —"

"Take me to him."

He nods and grabs my coat. I put it on and follow him out.

SIXTY-THREE

It's dusk now, darkening into night. Normally, we'd take lanterns, but we don't bother with those, using the flashlights we keep in our jackets instead. As we walk into the forest, I still tell myself I'm wrong. I have to be, because if I'm not, what does that mean for . . .

Eric.

Oh, God, Eric.

I keep going back to that moment in my house, when I saw Anders reading Mick's list and the look on his face when I caught him.

Since I'm professionally allowed to be nosy, I'm guessing that's a list of real names?

Hmm?

Real names of locals.

Something like that.

Something like that.

As soon as I can take advantage of the narrowing path, I fall behind him. We're about a kilometer in. I go another hundred steps — yes, I count every damned one of them. Then

576

I say, "Calvin?"

I expect a "huh?" I *hope* for one. Desperately, desperately hope. But Anders jerks to a halt, his shoulders stiffening, and he stands there with his back to me.

"It is Calvin, isn't it?"

He turns then, and in his face I expect to see the final proof. Cold anger or maybe even a twisted smirk.

Yep, you got me, Casey.

But there's none of that. He turns, and all I see is Will Anders. Even when he notices the gun, pointing straight at him, he only closes his eyes and dips his chin, and says, "Okay," and it's not as if he's saying *Okay, you're right,* but *Okay, go ahead.*

Okay, pull the trigger.

"Where is he?" I say.

He opens his eyes. "What?"

"Where is Eric? What have you done with him?"

He blinks hard, as if trying to process what I've said. "Eric? You think — ? No. I didn't —" He starts toward me, but I raise the gun and he stops. "I would never do anything to Eric, Casey. Never."

"Because he *saved* you."

Emphatic nods. "Right. He did. He —"

"So he knows what you did."

Silence.

"He knows who you are and what you did? Yet he trusted that you'd never do anything

577

to him? You. The man who murdered his last commanding officer."

"That —" He stops. Swallows.

"That was different? The other guy deserved it, and Eric doesn't?"

At least five seconds of silence now. "The other guy didn't deserve it. Not at all."

"So Eric *doesn't* know what you are, and I'm sure he doesn't know that you've been playing stool pigeon for the council. That was your price of admission. You spy on Eric."

It's a shot in the dark, but he says, "It's not like that. It was at first, because, yes, that's the price of me being here, and now I only tell them things they can't go after him for."

"How thoughtful of you."

At a noise in the forest, he starts and looks over. "We need to find him, Casey."

"You killed all of them, didn't you? Were you trying to frame Eric? Take his job?"

"What? *No.* I have nothing to do with what's happening here. You're looking for a killer, and yes, I'm a killer. But I'm not the one who did this. *Any* of this. Please, Casey. We need to find him. I swear, if I'm responsible, you can shoot me. Hell, if I hurt Eric, I'll shoot myself."

"You realize that makes no sense, right?"

He pounds one fist against his thigh. "Because I'm completely freaking out here. Eric didn't just wander off. Someone else has him, probably his crazy brother. The one who, in case you've forgotten, vowed revenge on Eric. I'll walk in front of you. Keep the gun on me. Shoot if I try to run. But we *need to get moving.*"

"Turn around. Raise your hands. I'm going to pat you down and take your weapons. Then you'll show me where you lost him."

To say I don't trust Anders would be the understatement of the decade. He'd spent two years fooling Dalton, who is one of the best judges of character I know. I won't say the same for my character-judging skills — Diana is proof that I suck at it — but at least I'd known she had her faults. Being a cold-blooded killer is not a fault I'd ever have attributed to Will Anders, and there isn't a single person in Rockton who would. "The nicest person," "a real sweetheart," "just an all-around good guy" — those were the only ways I ever heard anyone describe him. Which must mean he is a helluva fine actor, and this panic is simply an extension of that act.

But is Anders the Rockton killer? It feels like the answer should be a huge "duh!" He could easily have lured his victims out — everyone trusts him. He proved he's strong enough to haul Hastings into that tree. And he has the medical know-how to have performed that horrific surgery. There is probably no one in Rockton who fits the killer's profile better than Will Anders.

The problem? Motive.

With Mick, I can hammer the pieces to fit the puzzle, even if my brain keeps rejecting the parts that don't fit, like why he'd mutilated his victims when, after his partner was horribly tortured, he'd executed the killers with a quick shot to the back of the skull. With Anders it's worse, and I feel as if I'm pounding those pieces in with a sledgehammer.

This doesn't add up for either of them. I'm missing something critical.

Yet I'm still certain Anders knows exactly where to find Dalton. Of course, he can't lead me there right away. He has to take me to the spot where he last saw him and pace, shining his flashlight around saying, "Shit, he tried to teach me how to track. Why didn't I pay more attention? Did he show you anything?"

"Yes."

"Well, then . . ." An exasperated wave at the forest.

"Sorry, let me start hunting for that trail, while turning my back to you . . ."

"Goddamn it! Fine. Let's make this easy. You have cable ties, don't you?"

He knows I do. I took two from him during the pat-down.

He puts his flashlight away, holds his hands

behind his back, and turns around. "Cuff me."

I do. Then I make him sit on the ground while I hunt. When I find signs, he says, "That's where we came in." Then, "That's where I left."

"All right." I walk to the first stop. "He's doubled back on this trail. Get up and walk ten paces behind me, whistling."

"Seriously?"

"Oh, I'm sorry. Is that an inconvenience?" I walk over as he rises and put my gun under his chin. "You know why I'm in Rockton. I hunted down my ex and shot him."

He shakes his head. "It wasn't like that. *You* aren't like that."

"Don't play that card, pretend we're buddies and you know me and I know you. However it went down, I murdered him, and I don't know if he deserved it, but *you* do. So do not think for one second that I won't shoot you. Now you will walk ten paces behind me and you will whistle."

We find Dalton. I only need to follow his trail for about ten minutes before I hear his voice. When I hear the second voice, I tell Anders to stop whistling and I break into a run.

I try to sneak up, but it's a choice between stealth and speed, and I finally give in, turn off my flashlight, and rely on the bright moon to guide me as I tear through the forest. I slow when I draw near enough to see Jacob's figure in a clearing, and I'm about to call a warning, but I see his arm rise and I don't think — I'm on the ground, a bullet whizzing past.

"Casey!" Dalton says. "Stay where you are!"

I lie there, heart pounding.

"I'm okay, Casey," Dalton says. "Just stay where you are. We're working this out."

I could almost laugh at that. His brother is holding him hostage. Bullets are whizzing past. *But don't worry, Casey, we're working it out.* So typically Dalton that I'm not sure if I want to smile or cry or scream at him.

"Jacob?" he says. "Focus on me, Jacob."

He speaks slowly, his voice low, like calming a wild beast, and when Jacob answers, it's only a grunt. Dalton keeps talking, in that same soothing voice. He tells his brother something's wrong, that Jacob knows something's wrong, that he can feel it, and they can get this fixed, that Dalton will do whatever it takes to get it fixed.

Dalton continues with variations on that and doesn't get more than a grunt or two from Jacob, which tells me the situation has gotten worse; his brother is unable even to articulate his rage. But Jacob does seem to be listening.

I can see Jacob through the trees. There's no sign of Dalton — I'm presuming he's sitting or lying down. When Dalton speaks,

Jacob turns toward him. He even lowers the gun. At any noise from the forest, he wheels my way. Twice he fires. Then his brother's voice lures him in again, and he forgets me.

I have two choices here. I can trust that Dalton will eventually calm Jacob enough for me to get his gun. Or I can provoke Jacob until he empties the clip. Except I can't control where he fires those bullets, not enough to be sure one won't be aimed at his brother. More than that, I trust Dalton in this. He's making progress.

I stay crouched and pick the clearest path from tree to tree. Jacob does hear noises and turns twice, but it's just animals in the forest. I'm finally close enough to see Dalton. He's sitting with his back against a tree, hands on his head. He doesn't spot me. I make sure of that. He's slowly talking Jacob down, and I'll do nothing to distract him.

Jacob paces the clearing. He wears the same clothing as when he attacked me. I can see my dried blood on them. He's filthy, his hair even more snarled, with bits of twigs and leaves caught in it, as if he's been sleeping on the ground.

"I know I left you," Dalton is saying. "I went away, and I didn't come back. I made a mistake. A stupid, selfish mistake. I left you, and I will never stop regretting that. But I haven't left you since, Jake. I've been here for you every time you've needed me. I will do anything you need. Just let me try. Something's wrong, and you know it, and I can help. Whatever it takes —"

A crash cuts him short. It's a sudden crackle of undergrowth, but it's not me. Jacob spins, gun up.

"Out!" he says in a guttural growl. "You! Girl! Out!"

When no answer comes, he fires, and Dalton lunges to his feet, and Jacob spins on him. Dalton puts his hands on his head again. I'm close enough that I can see sweat pouring off him. But I'm not close enough to get a clear shot if Jacob fires. I move into a better position as quickly and silently as I can.

"Out!" Jacob says. "Out or I shoot Eric."

A figure stumbles from the forest then. It's Anders, his bound hands hidden behind his back.

SIXTY-FOUR

"You?" Jacob says. "Where is the girl?"

"She's not here," Anders says. "That was me. It's just me."

"Liar!" Jacob spins, peering into the forest. I duck behind a tree.

"It's just Will," Dalton says. "My deputy. You've seen him in the forest with me. You saw him earlier. I thought it was Casey, but it must have been Will."

"Don't lie."

"I'm not, Jacob. It's Will."

"Eric's telling the truth," Anders says. "You're not feeling well, and you're confused and —"

"Shut up."

I peek around the tree to see Jacob with the gun trained on Dalton. My heart stops for a second. Then I force myself to move, to creep toward them, my own weapon raised.

"You want to aim that gun somewhere, Jacob? Point it at me." Anders tries for a smile. "You know your brother — he's going to do what you want a whole lot faster if that gun is pointed at one of his friends."

"Will?" Dalton says in a low voice. "Don't."

"He's your friend?" Jacob says.

Anders nods. "Deputy, friend, sure. So point that gun over —"

"Friend, girl, everyone but me," Jacob says to Dalton. "You stay away from me for them. For strangers."

"No, no, no," Anders says. "It's not like that. We work together. Eric and Casey and —"

"You stay with them." Jacob spits the words. "You left me. For them. For *strangers.*"

I see his finger move on the trigger. And I run. I don't shoot. I can't shoot. They're too close together, and there isn't enough light. So I run, making as much noise as I can, certain that Jacob will hear and stop. I see a blur of motion, and I'm moving too fast to realize what it is until I hear the shot, and then I see that Anders has launched himself — not at Jacob but in front of Dalton.

I hear the shot, and I see Anders, and in my head I hear myself screaming, but I don't say a word. I just keep running, toward Jacob now as he stands there, and I dimly see them both on the ground — Anders and Dalton — and I see blood blossoming on Anders's shirt, and I see Jacob and that gun, still pointed at them.

"Drop it!" I say as I burst into the clearing, my weapon trained on Jacob. "Lower that gun right now, or I swear I'll shoot."

He lowers it.

"Drop it, or —"

It falls from his hand, and he says, "Eric?" and totters there, and when I run over and take the gun, I see his face, the shock on it as he stares at his brother, on the ground, under Anders.

"Eric?" he says again.

I grab Jacob's hands and pull them behind his back and bind them with the cable tie. He doesn't resist, doesn't seem to notice. I bind him, and I shove him aside so hard he falls as I race over to Dalton. Anders is still on top of him.

Anders has been shot. And I don't care.

No, that's wrong. I do care. I just don't want to.

My impulse is to shove Anders off to get to Dalton, but I can't manage that. I don't need to. I can see Dalton's wound — it's a bullet to the top of his shoulder, and he says, "I'm okay, Casey. It's Will. Help Will."

He's been saying that for a while. I just haven't paid attention. He'd say that if he had a bullet through his heart.

Don't mind me. Help the other person.

Except the other person betrayed him. Isn't worthy of his attention. Yet that other person just saved his life. Threw himself in front of a bullet, and no matter how hard Anders might have protested his loyalty to Dalton, this proves it, and I cannot argue with that.

I cut Anders's cable tie and check his wound. It's a through-and-through shot to the chest bypassing his heart. He's fading into shock, and I pull him back by saying, "What can I do?"

"I've got it," Dalton says as he heaves himself up, face contorting with the pain.

"Sit down," I say. "You'll only hurt yourself more and —"

"It's my shoulder, Casey. Not my spine. I've got Will. You call Beth."

I stop. "Beth . . ."

He grips my shoulder, hard, peering down at me as if I'm the one going into shock.

I shake him off. "I'm fine. Where's the — ?"

He pulls the radio from Anders's jacket and slaps it into my hand and then kneels beside the wounded man.

"Will? It's Eric. I'm going to tell you where you've been shot, and you're going to tell me how to help you. Got it?"

I move away with the radio. I pass Jacob, who's blinking hard, as if trying to rouse himself from a trance. I keep walking, and Dalton says, "Casey?"

I wave that I'm just stepping away, but he starts to rise, to come after me, and I realize I'm going to need to do this in front of him.

I motion for him to return to Anders. Then I radio Beth. As I talk to her, Dalton glances over, his face screwed up as if he's misheard, and he's opening his mouth, but before I can silence him, he shuts it. He nods. Then he returns to Anders.

I finish the call, and I kneel beside Jacob.

"Something's wrong with me," he's mumbling. "Something's wrong."

"I know," I say. "But I need to ask you a few questions. Do you think you can answer them?"

He blinks harder and rubs his cheek against his shoulder, as if trying to wake from a deep sleep. Then he nods.

Beth arrives at a run, radio in one hand, lantern in the other as I give her directions until I can see her, and then I shout and jog to meet her.

"You *left* him?" she says.

"It's too late. I think he's gone."

"Wh-What?" Her eyes bug out as she runs to me. "Y-You mean — No, that's not —"

"Not possible?" I say. "Of course it is. What did you expect?"

She stops so fast she stumbles and grabs a tree for support. "Wh-What?"

"You drugged Jacob. I don't know what you gave him, but whatever it was, it was intended to cause delusions."

She stares at me. "What are you —"

"You gave Jacob drugged food, telling him you were a friend of Eric's. He'd seen you out here with Eric before — you made sure of that first. It solidified your story. Then, when he started getting sick from the food, you 'treated' him. While telling him about Eric's newest friend. A woman who wasn't any good for him, would hurt him, was keeping Eric away from his brother. It worked — Jacob did come after me. Only what you didn't anticipate is that little boy inside him, the one who still blames his big brother for leaving, the one who still wants to lash out at Eric, to hurt him."

Beth rocks there. Then she looks around wildly. "Take me to Eric. You're not a doctor."

"True," I say. "I could be wrong. But you were right about one thing, Beth. I am bad for Eric. I think he's a sweet guy, and a really sweet fuck. But that's it. What matters most to me is justice. So, if you want to treat Eric before he bleeds out, you're going to have to give me a confession."

She lunges at me. A well-placed kick in the shin sends her down, snarling, "You crazy bitch. You'd let him die —"

"He's an officer of the law. He knows the risks." I point my gun at her. "Now talk."

"Yes," she spits. "Jacob already told you what I did, and it was for Eric's own good, saving him from you —"

"Bullshit. You might be more than a bit delusional yourself, but you weren't trying to kill me because I was getting close to Eric. You wanted me gone because I'm dead set on solving these crimes. With Jacob, you got a two-in-one deal. An assassin to kill me and a scapegoat you could frame for the murders you committed."

"Wh-What?"

"It started with Abbygail's death. You suspected that Powys killed her and somehow Irene was involved. Maybe you were working on getting a confession out of Irene, and it went wrong. Then you and Mick went after Powys. That was the piece I was missing: Mick. I might have suspected you of that impromptu surgery on Hastings, as crudely as you did it to disguise your handiwork. I might have even linked you in via Abbygail. But you couldn't have hauled Hastings into that tree. You had a partner. Mick. The one person even more broken up about Abbygail than you. The one who'd have snapped when you made up a story about what happened to her. You had to convince him that story was true, because Mick was a decent guy and needed to be sure he had the right target. But then you realized you were wrong, and it was actually Hastings who'd killed Abbygail. You managed to talk Mick into killing him, too, but that's where you lost him."

"What?"

"You went overboard with Hastings. Mick was already uncomfortable with what you two did to Irene and Powys, but Hastings was pure sadism. Mick wanted out. He even pointed me squarely in Hastings's direction. And I made the mistake of telling you that he'd fingered Hastings as the guy who left the berries. Mick became a liability, so you killed him, conveniently framing Diana, in hopes that might get me out of Rockton."

"You can't prove —"

"Right. I can't." I waggle the gun. "But I'm holding your beloved Eric's life hostage, so you're going to give me what I want. Then I'll let you save Eric, because I don't *want* him to die — I'm just willing to let it happen."

"You're just as bad as them. A killer —"

"And I deserve to die, blah-blah-blah. Time's ticking, Doc."

Her face mottles. "They *did* deserve to die. I didn't need to fabricate a story to get Mick's cooperation. I told him the truth. How Irene came to me for dental surgery two weeks after Abbygail vanished. I dosed her up with diazepam, which made her very talkative. And there was something in particular she wanted to talk about. Confess, I think. Like your friend, Diana. Except in Irene's case, she confessed to Abbygail's murder."

"So Irene and Powys *did* kill — ?"

"Hastings had a thing for Abbygail. He'd

592

hit on her when they worked together in the clinic, but she'd have nothing to do with him. As for Powys, he didn't give a damn about a twenty-one-year-old girl. What mattered to him was the rydex. Hastings was getting cold feet, knowing Eric was onto him. So to secure his help with the drugs, Powys promised him Abbygail. Irene lured her out into the forest. Hastings raped her. It seems he expected her to 'come around' then — she'd see how wonderful it was and how wonderful he was. That didn't happen, shockingly. Powys knew it wouldn't. He wasn't securing Hastings's help with the rydex by giving him a girl. He secured it by making him a murderer. Abbygail vowed Eric and Mick would hunt Hastings to the ends of the earth for assaulting her, and Powys pushed Hastings until he lost it and strangled her. Then they chopped up her body and scattered it for predators."

I stand there, shocked into silence. It takes a moment for me to find my voice, and when I do, I say, "You switched out Irene's X-rays to make it seem like she was here under false pretenses, too. To help me draw the conclusion that I was chasing a vigilante eliminating killers."

"Which you were. So, Detective, do you agree they had it coming?"

"Irene? Powys? Hastings? Maybe. But Mick?" I look her in the eyes. "Absolutely not."

She blanches. Then her face hardens. "I'd made a mistake letting him in on it, and I had to correct that mistake."

"*Correct that mistake?* You made him a party to brutal, sadistic murders because he was grieving for a girl he loved. Then you murdered him when he regretted it."

"Mick was weak. That is where I made a mistake. He didn't like what we did to Powys. I knew he wouldn't help me with Hastings if he knew what I planned. So I did my surgery, knocked Hastings out, and put him in that bag before I called Mick in. Mick thought he was already dead when he hauled him up in that tree. When he found out otherwise, I had to admit I'd made a mistake letting him help me."

"So you killed him to protect yourself. Then you planned to frame Diana and let her die in that fire for no reason other than that it would give me a reason to leave town. When that failed, you remembered Irene's accidental confession and the rumors you'd heard about Diana. You doped her up and got her to confess to even more than you bargained for. But still I wouldn't leave. I ran into that forest . . . and into Jacob, the pistol you'd cocked to fire. Perfect timing . . . and yet I survived, and with Eric playing nurse-maid, you couldn't even make sure I died from unforeseen complications. Still, you could frame Jacob for the murders. Another innocent party whose guilt would doubly help you — blame him for the crimes *and* get him out of the way so Eric would be free to go south with you."

"You don't understand *anything,*" she snarls.

"Maybe," I say. "But I think we'll let the council decide." I turn and call, "You get that, Sheriff?"

Dalton walks out from a clump of trees. He's pale and pressing his blood-soaked shirt to his shoulder. But he's on his feet, walking toward Beth, and she falls back, blinking hard.

"Eric? You . . . you . . ."

"Yeah, he's fine," I say. "It's Will who's been shot."

"And you're going to fix him," Dalton says. "Or I'll shoot you before Casey can."

SIXTY-FIVE

And that's it. Well, no. It's not. When we talk to the council, Beth tries to retract her confession. That's when I bring up the trap left in the clearing with Hastings's body. I accuse her of trying to hurt Dalton, and she can't resist that bait, saying it must have already been there, defending herself and thereby convicting herself.

By morning, the council has sent a plane to pick her up. Apparently, they don't trust Dalton to get her out of Rockton alive. After that? Well, I don't give a shit what happens to her after that. I cannot forgive her for what she did to Mick, to Jacob, to Diana, and, however inadvertently, to Dalton. And there's hurt there, too, and I'll let myself acknowledge that. She'd become a friend, and I do not understand what she did. I do not.

As for Anders, he's fine. Physically, at least. The rest? That's a little more complicated. The next morning, I wake in Dalton's bed, and I lie there, trying to figure out how to tell him that the guy who saved his life is a killer who's been informing on him.

When Dalton wakes, he pulls me to him for a kiss, but then stops, wincing at his shoulder wound, and I take advantage of that to wriggle away and prop up on my elbow.

"I need to tell you something about Will," I say.

He shoots upright. "Did he get worse —"

"No, I'm sure he's fine. But . . . I found out something about him last night. That file Mick had on the people smuggled into Rockton . . . He'd stolen it from you but added an extra entry. On Will."

Dalton goes quiet and rubs his mouth.

"You knew," I say.

"Yeah."

"He's not in your book."

"I got rid of the page a while ago, in case anyone found it. I'd have told you if I thought there was any chance he'd killed Abbygail and the others. Or if you got involved with him."

"Okay." I hesitate and say slowly, "You knew his backstory, but there's more. In order to stay in Rockton, well, there was a price."

"Informing on me."

I blink at him. He shrugs. "That's obvious, isn't it? They let him in because they wanted leverage inside my department. Knowing who the spy is made it easier for me. I didn't tell

597

Will anything that I wouldn't want getting back to them. I did give him some stuff that could get me in a bit of trouble, just to monitor. After about six months, he stopped passing that along, and that's when I knew I could trust him. I still never gave him anything that could get me kicked out."

"Which is why you told me to keep even the murder investigation between us."

"Yep."

I lie back on the pillow. He stays there, on his side, watching me as I stare at the ceiling.

"How do you deal with what he did?" I say finally. "How do you reconcile that?"

"I don't."

I look over at him.

"Something happened over there," Dalton says. "In the war. All I know is that the guy who killed his commanding officer just sacrificed himself to save me. *That's* the person I need to focus on."

I expect any conversation with Anders will wait until he's recovered. It doesn't. He wants to talk to us, and Dalton realizes he's not going to truly rest until he does. Dalton wants to do this together. I refuse. He's the one Anders has worked with for two years. Been friends with for two years. Betrayed for two years. That's a conversation between them.

Dalton talks to him that afternoon. I go right after. I walk into Anders's room, and I sit on the chair by the window, and I stare out of it. He just waits until I'm ready.

"I want to know why," I ask.

"Why I shot my CO?" he asks, his voice low. "Or why I informed on Eric?"

The answer should be obvious. Why he murdered a man is far more important than how he wronged Dalton, but he knows which one I meant. And here is the truth of why this is so hard for me. Because it doesn't matter if I only met Anders a few weeks ago. I know him, and he knows me.

That's why nothing ever happened between us. I understood him, and so there wasn't that thrill of fascination and discovery that I had with Dalton. I understood Anders, and that's what twists in my gut now, because I want to say, in light of everything, that I obviously don't understand him at all. Like in the forest, when I kept waiting for him to turn into something else, someone else. But he didn't.

He did exactly what I expected of the man I'd come to know. He did exactly what I would have done.

"When you came to Rockton, you didn't know Eric," I say. "I'm sure the council told you stories that made him seem like a loose cannon. Informing on him was the price of admittance. Then you got to know him, and you realized you could help him by reporting things that didn't matter, making the council *think* he was being monitored."

Anders exhales. "Yes. Thank you."

"The shooting . . ." I prompt.

"Why did I do that?" He goes quiet long enough that I don't think I'm getting an answer. When he does speak, his voice is barely audible. "Anything I can say feels like an excuse. A good man is dead at my hand. Two good men were wounded. That can't be excused." He lifts his gaze to mine. "I think you understand that. Better than anyone."

"Give me a why, then."

"There is no why. Not like with you. They didn't . . ." He fidgets in his bed, wincing as he pulls against his bandages. "They did nothing to even remotely deserve it, Casey. It was me. All me. I was . . . I had problems. Coping. With the war. I saw something. Over there. A mission went bad, and things happened and something snapped. I blamed my CO, but not like that, not like I wanted to kill him for it. They put me on meds, and there were side effects. Rage, mental confusion. I wanted to stop taking them, and I just damned well should have, but I agreed to give it one more week."

He goes quiet, and I wonder if that's all I'm getting. Then he says, "I remember going to bed. The next thing I knew, I was standing by *his* bed, and then I'm suddenly outside his quarters looking down at two wounded men. I still do not know what happened. But that's no excuse, is it? I kept taking the meds when I knew better. No one else pulled that trigger. The army wasn't going to send me home with a dishonorable discharge. I was looking at life in a mental ward or a prison cell, which I deserve, because I *was* responsible."

I move to the bed, and I sit beside him, and that's it. We just sit there. In silence. Like we did in the cave. Lost in remorse and guilt that won't ever go away. Not for either of us. There are no excuses here. No easy answers, either. We'll spend the rest of our lives dealing with what we did. Period.

As for Jacob, Dalton's dealing with that, too. I'll help, as much as I can, but it's his brother, and I understand that. The fact that we no longer have a doctor in Rockton complicates matters — with both Jacob's withdrawal and Anders's recovery. We've called on anyone with any medical training to step up. Except that two of those three people are also on Dalton's watch list, having bought their way into Rockton. Complicated? Fuck, yes, as Dalton would say. But we'll deal. We have to.

Then there's Diana. We know she didn't kill Mick, but it doesn't matter. She's still being deported. I haven't talked to her since I learned the truth. I've been telling myself that I can have that talk in Dawson City, more privately. Except with Anders incapacitated, I need to stay behind as the only law enforcement in town.

Two days after Beth leaves, the council decides Dalton is well enough to take Diana out, and I promise to speak to her that morning. At eleven, Dalton finds me still at my desk.

"We leave in an hour, Casey."

I keep writing. "I just need to finish this report."

"I'll do it. You go see Diana."

When I don't answer, he shifts his weight and shoves his hands in his pockets. "I'm not pushing you because I'm a jerk, Casey. I just think if you don't . . ."

"I'll regret losing the opportunity for closure. Diana is about to walk out of my life forever, and there are things I need to say."

"Yeah."

I rise. "Let's go."

SIXTY-SIX

Kenny has Diana at the station. We're taking her out that way rather than marching her through town. We haven't let the others know what she's done, but news has traveled, along with the opinion that she shouldn't be allowed to get on that plane and sail off scot-free.

We go into the station, and Diana's there, with her back to us. Dalton takes Kenny out the back. I wait until the screen door shuts. Then I say, "I'd like to talk."

"Too late." Diana turns, and there's an ugly smile on her face. "You had time to talk to me, Casey. You didn't. You've lost your chance to apologize. I'm not giving you the chance to make amends now. I'm walking out of this shithole of a town, and I'm going south, to a real life, the kind I could never have while you were hanging around my neck."

I open my mouth, but she's going strong.

"I'm going to track down that asshole Graham and get my money. I have a plan all worked out. The perfect way to get him to do what I want." She gives that ugly smile again. "Because I've realized I'm kinda good at that, aren't I?"

She stands there, chin raised. After a moment she says, "Come on, Casey, hit me. You know you want to."

"No, I don't."

"How about you, Sheriff?" she calls. "I know you're listening. Making sure I don't damage your broken little girl. Come on in and tell me what a bitch I am."

"Nah," he says as he strolls in. "A bitch has spine. You're just pathetic."

She launches herself at him, and before I can intercede, he's blocked her. She spins on me and says, "I *saved* you. Look at you. A new boyfriend. New friends. An actual social life. And you're a goddamned local hero. Solved the mystery. Saved the town. All hail Casey Duncan — whoops, Butler. Casey Duncan is a murderer. Casey Butler is a hero."

"Are you finished?" I ask, and that really does stop her. Into the silence, I say, "Yes, I'm better off for coming up here. It was exactly what I needed. But you didn't bring me here to help me. You brought me here to help *you*. To be here for you."

"Um, no. I brought you to stop you from searching for me."

"That was probably part of it, but if you're going to pretend that we weren't friends? Bullshit. You don't hang out with someone for years because they're useful. But slant this your own way, if it makes you feel better." I turn to Dalton. "She's all yours."

I walk to the door as Val steps in and says, "Diana's still here? Good. There's been a change of plans."

We're at Val's listening to Phil on the satellite radio. I'm there with Dalton and Diana. Isabel is there, too — summoned by the council, though no one seems to know why.

"We've changed our mind," Phil says. "Diana is staying in Rockton."

I'm not sure who says "what?" first — or louder.

Phil continues, "It is the decision of this council that Diana is clearly unstable and poses a serious exposure threat. She will remain in Rockton until that risk assessment changes. Isabel will assist in Diana's rehabilitation."

Isabel opens her mouth. Diana cuts her off with, "You can't make me stay. That's kidnapping. Unlawful confinement."

"No, it's not," Phil says. "Eric? The council wishes to officially inform you that Ms. Berry is exempt from all laws restricting personal freedom of movement."

"What the hell does that mean?" she snaps.

"That you're allowed to leave," Isabel says. "If you want to walk into that forest and find your way home, Eric is not allowed to stop you. So this isn't unlawful confinement."

"No way," Diana says. "No fucking way." She spins to me. "Casey, say something. Tell them they can't do this."

Isabel bursts out laughing. "Really, sugar? You are indeed a piece of work."

I turn to the radio and say, "So how much is Graham paying you to keep her here?"

Phil doesn't respond, and that silence answers my question.

Diana wheels on Dalton. "It's all true. Everything you've accused me of. I had sex for money. I did dex more than twice. I can get witnesses to both. I wanted to have fun, and I broke the rules doing it, and you don't want me here. I'm going to be pissed off and only cause more trouble."

Before Dalton can answer, Phil interjects. "Any trouble you cause will be subject to double penalties, more if needed. This matter isn't open for discussion. You will be assigned a new job and new quarters, which will improve as your attitude does. Isabel will be in charge of making that determination. Now, good day."

He disconnects before anyone can respond. Even Val stands frozen for at least ten seconds before she says, "All right, then. The council has decreed —"

"Yeah, heard it," Dalton says. "Don't need the recap."

"Fuck, no," Diana says. "Fuck, *no*. I won't stay. You can't make me. You can't." She stomps her feet, and Isabel sputters a laugh. Diana flies at her.

Dalton hauls her back, and when she won't stop struggling, he strong-arms her toward the door. "Guess your first new residence will be the cell."

"You aren't allowed to restrict my movement. The council said —"

"Pretty sure that's not what they meant," he says, and as he passes me, he gives me a nod and mouths that he'll talk to me as soon as he can, and then he's gone, escorting a still-fighting Diana out the door.

"Well," Isabel says. "This should be entertaining."

I give her a look.

"Oh, I'm sure she'll leave you alone," she says. "She's stuck here, and the only person who'll listen to her badmouth you is Jen." Isabel's lips twitch. "This really could be entertaining. And you never know. Diana might see the error of her ways and become a vital member of the community." She looks toward the door as Diana starts shrieking outside. "Or not."

I don't even know how to process this. It's not what I want, by any means, but a small part of me says that I'm actually safer without

Diana wreaking revenge and informing on me down south.

"Ever had Rey Sol Añejo?" Isabel says before I can leave. When I turn, she says, "It's tequila."

"Oh, I know. Top, *top* shelf tequila."

"I have a bottle in my house. A gift from a past resident. I know you and Petra planned to get together after Eric and Diana flew out. He'll still be busy for a while, so I'm inviting you ladies to help me crack open that bottle."

I check my watch.

"It's never too early for Rey Sol Añejo," Isabel says. She looks at Val. "I'd invite you too, but I know socializing isn't your thing."

I catch a look on Val's face that says if we did invite her, she might actually come. I should extend the invitation . . . and the olive branch. Maybe another time.

"So?" Isabel says as we walk out. "Is that a yes, Detective Butler?"

I look down the road at a still-struggling Diana. Then I glance back at Isabel. "Yes. And please."

She laughs, hooks her arm in mine, and says, "Let's go find Petra. We'll send someone to invite the good sheriff to join us when he's done. We might even save some for him."